FLOWER OF ALASKA

'You cannot trust men! You cannot just go off sailing with any man who comes along!' snapped Thor.

'I don't,' said Laurel. 'But I'm here with you now! Can I trust you?'

'Well if you can't –' he began; then he looked at her. There was a demure smile on her lips. She was teasing him!

He grabbed her and pulled her to him, meaning to shake her. She fell against him, taken off guard. He put his hand around her face, bent down, and pressed his mouth hard to her half-opened pro-testing lips. The kiss burned all through him, the feel of her soft warm lips, her smooth cheek.

He went a little crazy. He had been anxious about her, scared to death when he thought of what might happen to her, angry with her. And now here she was, mocking him, teasing him, and they were alone, alone in the world, a wilderness around them, nobody for miles . . .

Forget-me-not

JANET LOUISE ROBERTS

SPHERE BOOKS LIMITED
London and Sydney

First published in Great Britain by
Sphere Books Ltd 1984
Copyright © 1982 by Janet Louise Roberts, Inc
First published in the United States of America by
Warner Books, Inc 1982

TRADE
MARK

Set in 9/10pt Compugraphic Garamond

Printed and bound in Great Britain by
Collins, Glasgow

Forget-me-not

Chapter 1

'Jade! Forget-me-nots! Come and see!' Laurel called softly. She knelt on the rough brown earth and gazed at the brave clump of pale blue starry flowers with tiny gold hearts.

The Tlingit Indian girl came over and knelt beside her. They gazed in silence at the miracle. The harsh winter had seemed to kill everything in the Alaska earth. Yet again the wonder had come, of flowers renewing themselves in the bleak land.

The two girls exchanged smiles. Sketch pads came out, then both carefully drew the little flowers, paying close attention to the weak, slender stems and the oblong, pale green leaves, in exact size, as Jim Winfield had taught them.

'Observe! Draw what you see!' he had told them over and over. 'Learn to see clearly. In botany that is absolutely necessary.'

Laurel's father had indeed taught them well. He was a fine nature artist himself. And Laurel's mother too had had a beautiful delicacy of touch, a talent which Laurel had inherited.

The sketches completed, the girls stood up and stuffed their sketchpads inside their parkas. From a distance they looked much alike. Both girls were fourteen, slim, sturdy, about five feet two. Close up, one saw the faces above their gray parkas, and saw the difference.

Laurel Winfield's clear, lightly tanned face showed her English and Welsh ancestry. Her cheeks were pink with the cold, her eyes dark brown, her hair a thick mass of brown curls now pulled back neatly into one thick braid. Her lips were young and tender pink, softly full.

Jade Nolan's features were distinctively Indian – the high cheek bones, swarthy skin, the broad face. Her black eyes could be warm

1

and laughing, or cold and distrustful. Her hair was straight and black, hers also in a long, single braid. Her eyes were not slanted, like the Eskimo eyes. They were much like Laurel's in shape. Her mouth was broader than Laurel's, with a large, straight lower lip and a bowed upper. There was a golden glow about her, of life lived in the sunshine.

'Now for a rabbit or two,' Jade said.

Laurel replied in the Tlingit tongue, which Jade had taught her when Laurel had come to Alaska four years ago, in 1897. This panhandle of Southeastern Alaska, a lonely place, had fostered that friendship between them. No other children lived within two dozen miles.

'Let's go near the river. I saw a burrow two days ago.'

Jade nodded. 'The Blue River attracts the rabbits. It is slow and gentle, and the wild animals enjoy the sand banks.'

They turned in that direction, rifles resting easily on their slim shoulders. The skinning knives Tom Nolan had made for them were in their identical belts. This life suited them both, some sixty miles southeast of Wrangell, south of the Stikine River, west of the whitecapped mountains. Even when the rainfall was heavy, the girls liked to go out and hunt together. And in weather like this, spring-like and sunny, it was sheer heaven.

A shot rang through the wilderness. In quick alarm Laurel looked to Jade.

'Father didn't come this way!' she cried, her face showing her shock, and she spoke in English.

'No, must be hunters.'

Another shot, another, then yells and fierce curses. Both girls broke into a run, rifles down in their right hands, moccasins skimming the broken earth. They came around a clump of Sitka spruces into the open area near the Blue River and saw a startling sight.

A brown bear was growling ferociously and clawing at a large body on the ground. The body lay limp, face down, arms about the head in vain protection. Blood had matted the blond hair; the thick parka had been ripped open at the back.

Nearer the river another man stood, trying in vain to load his rifle again. Blood flowed from his head and shoulder; he cursed as he fumbled for bullets.

Jade's rifle came up. She aimed and fired at the bear's head, but missed. Its head weaved around toward Jade, and Laurel yelled, shrilly, and waved her arm. The bear glared at her with angry, small red eyes, then started for her.

Laurel caught her breath and held it as she lifted the rifle to her shoulder. She aimed, at one shiny red eye, and fired. The bear came on; she thought she had missed, but it stumbled, then swayed and wavered. It went down heavily, and blood bloomed and filled its eyes and its nose. She waited.

Jade held her rifle ready to fire again, but it was not necessary. The bear rolled over and lay still, paws falling on its chest.

Laurel walked past the animal warily, still menacing by its bulk and reputation. A bear during the spring, right out of hibernation, seeking food for its ravenous appetite, could be the meanest animal she knew. But the bear lay still now.

The man face down was hurt badly and was unconscious. Just as well, she thought. She laid aside the rifle in the sand and bent down to him. She touched his head gently, and he did not move or moan. Was he dead? Her hand went inside the torn parka; she did not flinch from the sticky fluid. His heart beat strongly.

'He's alive, Jade,' she said.

Jade had gone to the other man, now stretched out on the sand, his rifle flung beside him. He had evidently fainted.

'This one's alive too,' she reported, her hand inside his parka. She took it out and wiped off the blood on the sand. 'No bandages, no medicine here. How do we get them back to your cabin?'

Laurel thought. The blood had stopped its greedy rush to the surface and was now drying in the cold wind.

'One of us must go back to the cabin, get two blankets and four poles; we must carry them back,' she said ruefully. 'If only Father were nearby. Your cabin's too far, and the cold is too much for these men. It's only May.'

'Hey!'

The girls turned about, startled from their absorption. Two people came from across the narrow river, now low. They splashed through the blue waters to the sand bank. Now Laurel could see one was a man, of medium height, with blond graying hair and small blue eyes. He was handsomely dressed in black knickers and a gray wool shirt, with a gray parka opened about him. The other was a girl, in the smartest hunting outfit Laurel had ever seen – of dark blue skirt and jacket, and a white blouse with a white stock about her long throat. And she had long blond hair tied up in a glorious chignon, with no hat to hide its glory.

The man ran up to Laurel and Jade and saw the two victims. 'My God!' he blurted. 'They're dead!'

The blond girl followed him more slowly, her look distasteful and shocked. She flinched at the sight and turned away.

'Father, we must get back to civilization!' she said sharply. 'I knew we should never have come on this stupid trip!'

Laurel cut through this quickly. 'Do you know these two? They're not dead, but must be treated.'

The man bent to the body at Laurel's feet. 'He must be dead,' he said flatly. 'He's not breathing!'

'He is alive,' she insisted, frowning slightly. 'I felt his heart. I'll go back to the cabin and get blankets and poles.'

The man gave her a disdainful look. 'What do you know, a kid like you?'

Laurel stiffened. 'I have lived in the wilderness,' she replied quietly. She hesitated. If she left Jade, an Indian girl, with these two greenhorns, they might go off and leave her. Indians were scorned hereabouts. She turned to her friend. 'Jade, please go back to my cabin. Fire your rifle twice; Father will come at once. Ask him to come with the blankets and poles. I'll wait here with these people; they can help us carry the men.'

She spoke slowly and distinctly so the two strangers would hear every word. If they tried to depart, she would really let them have it! And if words did no good, she would hold her rifle on them.

'It won't do no good,' the man said. 'They'll die out here without medical help quick.'

'No, they will not,' Laurel said firmly. She nodded to Jade, who said nothing and started off toward the cabin, running, 'We *can* help them. It's foolish to think it's of no use. Indian medicines are very good.'

The man peered more closely at her. 'Are you Indian? No, you

4

don't look it. Half-breed, then?'

She caught her breath at the insolence in his voice but said only, 'I'm Laurel Winfield. Your name?'

'Addison Leverett,' he said reluctantly. 'And my daughter, Miss Clarissa Leverett,' he added proudly, gesturing to the tall young woman, who gazed scornfully past Laurel's shoulder. She had pale blue eyes, like her father's but a little larger and certainly beautiful. She reminded Laurel of the haughty women on the boat coming to Alaska, wives who thought they were a sight higher on the social ladder than most other women, refusing to talk with even Laurel's sweet, loving, and well-educated mother! Laurel had resented it deeply; her mother had only laughed.

'Consider the source,' Mother had said with a twinkle in her dark brown eyes. 'I can't let anyone like that bother me! I hope you won't either, Laurel! They're not worth it.'

How sensible her mother truly was, even though her family had not thought her so to marry a poor artist and go off with him. But she had coolly forgotten her family to marry James Winfield. He had led her west, to places far from her home in Boston. They had lived in mining camps and Army posts on the frontier, where Jim had earned money sketching soldiers, their horses, and their Indian prisoners.

Laurel's mother and father had loved each other intensely. As artists, they had thought alike and had worked together – her mother with her delicate sketches of flowers and her nature studies, and her father with his strong drawings of people and the outdoors. They had meshed well, and their deep love had permeated Laurel from babyhood.

But her mother . . . That brutal first winter in Alaska killed her, she had never recovered from a cold that turned to pneumonia.

Jim Winfield became quiet, morose. Laurel turned to the Nolans to fill the gap in her heart. Since they were the only people for miles around, Laurel often thought how lucky it was the Nolans had a daughter her own age. Tom Nolan had taught Laurel and Jade to hunt and shoot, and live in the wilderness. Miriam had taught the girls how to cook the wild foods, to find berries and herbs, to sew, to cure animal skin. And Jade soon became her friend and constant companion. Yes, Laurel was very lucky.

She had bent down to wipe away the blood from the face of the blond man at her feet. A handkerchief soaked in river water went over his forehead gently. He was very tanned, she thought, very sturdy. She got up and went back to the stream to wring out the bloody cloth. Clarissa shuddered as Laurel went past her, and averted her face.

'God, I can't stand that!' She shivered in disgust.

'Watch your language,' her father snapped at her. Then, 'But I can't blame you, Clarissa. It's no sight for a delicate female.'

'You might see how bad the other man's injuries are,' was Laurel's mild suggestion. 'Who are they, anyway? Guides?'

'No, we have two Indian guides – for all the good those bastards are,' the man said, scowling. 'That one's Thor Koenig; the other over there is his brother Ewan. Their father is Olaf Koenig, the mining man from Sitka,' he added as though Laurel should know the names.

'What happened? Why were they hunting alone?' she asked.

'Oh, Ewan is hotheaded. He saw a bear and went after it. Alone. When Thor came back, one of the Indians told him, and he set out after his brother.'

Clarissa shuddered again and put her handkerchief to her face. 'Oh Father, it makes me sick to see all that blood,' she wailed. She did look sick.

'We'd better get back to the boat,' her father said.

'You'll have to help get these men to the cabin,' Laurel said in a calm voice, trying to hide her contempt.

'Well, don't expect me to hang around and bury them,' he said sharply. He glanced up at the dim sun low in the sky. 'We won't stay here till dark.'

'Jade should be back soon,' Laurel said, her voice cold. A man and his hunting partner should fight for each other, protect each other, get help if at all possible. A man alone in the wilderness often got into trouble. You had to trust your fellow men – but she could not, would not trust this man and his daughter.

Laurel continued bathing the blond man's forehead, and then went to his brother and did the same for him. Addison Leverett and his daughter drew away from her, but they were still there when Jade returned with Jim Winfield. When Laurel saw her father, she blinked back tears of relief and ran to meet him.

'Father, two men – injured bad by the bear, but they're alive,' she said breathlessly when she had come to a halt beside him. He nodded, saying nothing, then looked toward the two figures beside the stream bed. 'That's Mr. Leverett and his daughter,' Laurel explained. 'He keeps saying the men are dead. But they aren't.'

Addison Leverett came forward to greet Jim Winfield. 'Don't expect us to dig graves,' he said. 'I'll send my Indian guides over –'

Jim looked him over dispassionately, then knelt beside the first man, felt the pulse, and put his hand inside the jacket. Then he went over to the other man. He came back. 'Both alive,' he said briefly.

He set out the poles beside Thor Koenig, and Laurel knelt to wrap the first blanket about the poles. Soon they had a stretcher, and Jim, Laurel, and Jade gently lifted the injured man onto the blanket. The Leveretts stood about impatiently, watching as Laurel and Jade prepared a second stretcher.

'I'll take this one with my daughter,' Jim said. 'Jade, please help Mr. Leverett with the other man.'

It was an order, given in a calm tone. Leverett frowned, then handed his rifle to his daughter and went to pick up the back poles, leaving Jade to take the more difficult front handles. They moved slowly and followed Jim and Laurel silently across the rough spring earth to the cabin some two miles away.

It was a difficult journey; the two men were heavy. Laurel said nothing, saving her breath. Addison grumbled under his breath, swearing again and again.

When they arrived at the one-room cabin with the overhang roof, Clarissa exclaimed, 'But nobody lives here! It's fit only for animals!'

Laurel flushed. Her father had made it, with her help and that of the Nolans. They were proud of the cabin. They had cut and shaped the logs themselves. They had put on the roof with great care so that the overhang, where they tied meat in the springtime to dry, would shelter the front entrance during the heavy snowfalls of winter. It had been her home for four years. A vegetable garden lay at the side, neatly fenced in from small animals. And out beyond the garden in a patch of wildflowers was her mother's resting place.

To see it with their disparaging eyes was a shock. Laurel could say nothing. Jim did not seem to have heard them. He led the way into the cabin and set the stretcher down on the bunk that belonged to Laurel. They unwrapped the poles from the blanket, and Laurel went to the fire to make sure the water was hot.

Addison and Jade carried in the other man and set him down on Jim's bunk. Leverett straightened.

'Well, we have to be going now,' he said gruffly. He glanced about the small cabin and shrugged. 'Too bad you can't help them much here, but you can at least give them a decent burial.' He spotted Jim's panning equipment.. 'Hey! Gold hunting, eh?' He picked up the round pan and examined it curiously.

'Put it down,' Jim said, a bite in his tone.

Addison laughed. 'Touchy, ain't you? Must've struck pay dirt! Where is it, eh? I'd like to file a claim beside yours!'

It was the custom of gold country, when a strike was made, the discoverer could stake out two claims on the same creek, of 500 feet by 500 feet. Then gold-hungry men from miles away swarmed in to share in the luck, staking their claims as close as they could to the strike site.

Jim just shrugged. 'No luck yet. I make my living by hunting.'

'Sure, sure,' Addison jeered. He gave a last curious look around the dark cabin and moved to the door. Clarissa had not come inside, as though fearing contamination. 'Well, I've done all I can here,' he added. 'Goodbye!'

Jim followed Addison outside; Laurel went as far as the door and listened curiously. 'Where are your Indian guides?' her father asked.

'On the creek. We'll go back to Sitka and notify Thor's folks. Too bad. Nice fellows,' said Addison, moving away and taking his rifle from Clarissa.

'Safe journey,' Jim said with a brief, taut salute and remained to watch them soberly as they walked away toward the Blue River.

He lifted his hand to his eyes and peered toward the sun in the southern sky moving to the west. Laurel looked also and saw two forms black against the level earth. In the distance the snowcapped mountains of the Tongass formed the boundary between American land and Canada.

'Tom and Miriam are coming,' Laurel said with a sigh of relief. Miriam was a healer; she would know what to do.

Jim only nodded, standing with his hands on his hips as they approached. Laurel went back inside to make bandages and prepared to help Miriam.

'Your parents are here,' she said to Jade in Tlingit. The girl nodded, her face sad as she gazed down at Ewan, the younger of the two men.

'So handsome . . . and his face is much torn,' she murmured.

Outside came the sound of soft voices in Tlingit. Jim was explaining the situation to Tom and Miriam. As Laurel returned to caring for Thor, they came inside the cabin. Laurel gazed down at the face of the unconscious man whose wounds she was gently bathing. He looked older, more mature. She liked his strong jaw, so square and firm. His blond hair was clipped short; he must have shaved recently, she thought, for only a rasp of hair was on his cheeks. She hoped the gashes on his face would heal well. One near his left cheekbone was laid open wide; it would probably leave a scar.

Miriam observed the man Laurel was caring for. 'Bad infection if no care.' She muttered and shook her head. She went to the wooden shelf where Laurel kept the medicines, some she had made for Laurel, others from the States. She began to mix a concoction of herbs and hot water, and soon her efficient hands were bathing Thor's face and chest in the mixture. When she had finished, Laurel smeared on soothing salve and then bandaged him gently while Miriam was caring for Ewan.

They all worked in silence. Jim and Tom undressed the men and rolled them in warm blankets. They were still unconscious.

All looked to Miriam for her verdict. 'Need much care, two nights, three,' she said slowly.

'I'll stay up tonight,' Jim said.

'I'll help you, Father,' Laurel said quickly.

'You can take care in the daytime,' he said flatly.

'Me tonight,' Miriam put in. 'Tom tomorrow.'

So all five of them stayed in the cabin with the wounded men. They rolled up in blankets before the fire and slept deeply. During the night Laurel awakened to find Miriam bending over the older man, murmuring to him in reassuring tones. He lay still, gazing up at her curiously. The other man tossed in his bunk, and Jim rose to help him. 'Take it easy, young man. You'll be fine,' his calm voice soothed.

Laurel blinked in the firelight; her eyes felt so heavy. Tomorrow she must go over and get the bear. They could use the meat and the hide.

In the morning Laurel washed quickly and dressed in her warm clothes. Jade had gotten up with her, and they braided each other's hair.

'Best get the bear today before the animals do,' Laurel said to her father.

'Right. You shot it?'

'Yes, Father.' She could not help but be proud. 'Good shot, eh?'

'I'll have a look when you come back,' he said with a slight smile.

After breakfast Laurel and Tom Nolan set out on their journey. When they arrived at the creek, she looked around, puzzled. 'It was right about here – and nothing's big enough to drag it away. Where could it be, Tom?'

Tom was examining the signs, reading the marks in the sand and gravel. 'Nothing big,' he said. 'I think your white friends, they take away bear!'

'No! It wasn't theirs!' Laurel cried. But it was true. They had taken it, skin, meat – all of it was gone.

'Mean people,' said Tom. 'Well, maybe we get a couple rabbits.'

Rather sickened, Laurel agreed. She remembered the callous look of the man and his daughter. Yes, they could carry away her bear to sell the meat – and they'd keep the head as a trophy. She would not soon forget their deed.

She and Tom scared up some rabbits, and shot five before they returned to the cabin. Tom stayed outside to skin them and prepare them for the pot.

Laurel went inside to wash and to see how the wounded men were doing. Jade whispered, 'The older one stirred and woke up. But he went right back to sleep. The young one, poor soul, he still lies quiet. I think he's very sick.'

Laurel nodded, gazing down at the older one. She wondered

vaguely what color his eyes were. 'Those two people took our bear,' she whispered to Jade.

'No!' Jade replied. 'That is very bad.'

'They *are* bad,' Laurel said. 'I think they would've left the two men to die too!'

'Nobody is so mean,' Jade said, shaking her head. Miriam looked in silence at the two girls as they talked, her face thoughtful.

Chapter 2

After breakfast Jim rolled up in a blanket to sleep. Miriam lay down near the fire and closed her eyes too.

Outside, Tom finished skinning and preparing the rabbits, and brought two of them inside to Laurel who put them in the one pot of hot water and then added the vegetables. The soup would feed the injured men.

The older man stirred briefly. Laurel wrung out a cloth and went to him. Gently she wiped his face with the warm wet cloth. When she lifted the cloth, his eyes opened, and she felt the shock of those icy green eyes as he gazed up at her. He blinked and said, 'Who are you?'

'Laurel Winfield,' she said quietly. 'You were hurt by the bear. Please lie still. Would you like some water?'

He frowned slightly, as though trying to remember. He said, 'Yes . . . thank you.' And he seemed surprised by the weakness of his own voice.

Laurel went for a cup and dipped it into the water pot. She returned to him and held his head up slightly so that he could drink. She felt his shoulders shift in his effort to get up.

'Don't move,' she cautioned softly. 'Your back is injured. You might start bleeding again.'

He sipped at the water, and she took in the warmth and thickness of his golden blond hair as she cradled his head. How fair he was, in spite of the dark tan of his skin.

When she took the cup from his lips, he muttered, 'My . . . brother?'

'In the other bunk. He's not hurt as bad as you are,' she said. 'He sleeps now.'

'Good. Thank . . . you . . . kind . . .'

He went limp suddenly. She lowered his head cautiously onto the flat pillow filled with pine needles. She had made that pillow herself. She wondered if it felt comfortable for him, or crude. He's probably used to luxury and city life, Laurel thought.

His eyes were closed when she left him. She thought he slept or had slipped into unconsciousness. He was strong; perhaps he would not get fever or infection.

The other man stirred, and Laurel went to him with a cup of cool water.

He frowned up at her with blue-gray eyes. 'Where am I?' he asked crossly. 'I hurt all over!'

'You were injured by the bear,' she explained patiently. 'Here . . . drink. Do you feel feverish?'

'I feel like hell,' he complained but drank thirstily. When she took the cup away from his lips, he grinned at her. 'Hey, pretty girl, where did you spring from?'

'I live here,' she said calmly and moved away. His eyes made her feel odd. They slid over her like a hand caressing her, studying her form in the cotton shirt and long skirt.

Tom Nolan came inside then and looked down at the two men, surveying them. Then he nodded to the girls. 'You two go outside and do your work,' he said. 'I will watch here.'

The younger man, Ewan, was awake. 'Leave the pretty girls here,' he said fuzzily. 'I like to look at them.'

Jade looked at Laurel, who shrugged. They went outside silently, then to the vegetable garden where they began to dig holes for more seeds.

'I think that young one is spoiled by women,' Jade said and giggled, her cheeks flushed. 'He is very handsome!'

'Mr. Leverett said he was hotheaded,' recalled Laurel. 'Maybe he jumps into trouble and lets others get him out. I wouldn't care to go hunting with him.'

'Maybe not,' Jade said, 'but he says nice things!'

'Did he speak to you?'

'Last night. He said I was beautiful!' Jade tossed her dark head, and her black eyes sparkled.

*   *   *

Laurel was silent, troubled. Jade was beginning to talk about men and whom she would marry and where she would live. Laurel was not ready to think about such matters. And her future life troubled her. She did not want to worry about that yet. She did not feel keenly the need for anyone else in her life. Vaguely she knew she wanted to remain here always, in the wilderness, hunting, and fishing, and drawing. Yet – someday life must change for her.

From her many years of traveling across the wilderness and living in frontier camps and Army posts, Laurel had found a hunger for a settled life. She wanted to belong in one place to build a home and own land of her own – a piece of Alaska, which she loved. Yes. The wilderness called to something very deep within her.

In the States she had enjoyed the outdoor life, the mountains with their snowcaps, the wide plains, the thick forests, camping out. She loved to ride horseback when she could. She loved to walk for miles, seeing the wild animals, life in its rugged beauty, wild flowers, swift white streams of water, glaciers.

But when she had come to Alaska, all this had become more – more of everything. Mountains more beautiful, glaciers more stunning, vast rivers like the Stikine flowing between banks of thick green Sitka spruce and cedar and hemlock. The mountain ash with its brilliant red autumnal berries.

'Mine,' she would whisper as she gazed about the vast plains. But they were not hers, nor only hers for looking at. Her father squatted on the land, so did the Nolans. Someday, when my father finds gold, he will stake a claim, and maybe then we will truly belong to the land, she thought.

Someday she would own a piece of the land, this wildly beautiful Alaska. It would be her home, she would belong here, she would stay here forever. No moving on, no searching for anything more grand and satisfying. The land would be in her, and of her, and she would be of and in the land. Laurel had told no one, not even Jade, of this hunger in her. It was a secret, a precious secret she hugged to herself.

Longingly she had sketched out the piece of land she would like to have. It would be bordered by a lovely stream or river, like the Blue River. It would have sandbars, and wildlife, and lovely flowers. And in the center would be her house.

She had sketched out house plans, altering them from time to time as her knowledge grew. Now it contained two stories, with a porch all the way around, like the porches of where her mother had lived in Boston. Her mother had talked about porches. . . . 'They are what I miss – from that life,' Madeline Winfield had said with a light laugh. Her eyes had been deep brown and wistful.

In the summertime one sat on the porch or swung in the porch swing. And talked to one's beau. And watched the neighbors. And saw fireworks on the Fourth of July. Laurel could not imagine much of that, but it added to her dream, and now she had a porch all the way around her dream house.

She added a piano after a visiting hunter had told them about the piano in a honky-tonk, where someone played music and made everybody silent and wondering.

She added soft sofas, and chairs for everybody to sit in. She added real beds, four posters. She added delicate white curtains, not hunks of rough cotton to keep out the cold. And she kept the sketchbook hidden from even her father – he would be hurt by it. He set no store by houses, even cabins. He would as soon walk out the door and go somewhere else, she knew.

The day was bright and sunny; with a chill wind. It was nice enough to sit outside that afternoon. Jade and Laurel took their schoolbooks out and read aloud to each other. Jim Winfield wakened in mid-afternoon and came out stretching and yawning.

He carried his large drawing pad. As they read, he sat down on a wooden stool he had made and began to sketch them. They were accustomed to it. From time to time he corrected them in their reading and would stop to explain what it meant. They were reading from a book of English history.

'Now, in that time . . .' he would begin in his slow drawl. 'You need to understand what was going on in Europe. You see, the French general Napoleon was conquering other countries and grabbing everything in sight . . .'

The two girls listened eagerly as Jim made the dry history lines come alive. He had gone to college for two years before he quit to marry Madeline Rutherford and run off with her to be an artist. Although his parents had cut him off, it mattered little to him. He wanted to draw and paint, and that meant everything to him – that and Madeline. Sometimes Laurel thought that even she meant little to him. It had been his art and Madeline that was his whole life. But he was a good father to Laurel, and his slow smile and nod of approval were all it took to make her glow with pleasure.

'Did you write your essays?' he asked when the history was done. Laurel nodded as she opened the book of lined pages on which she wrote her current essays. Her father took the book and went over it slowly, correcting her English and spelling.

Jade was grimacing. She had not done her homework, Laurel knew and gave her friend a sympathetic smile. Jade's talent was for sketching and speaking, not writing. She had a vivid way of telling stories that had been handed down from generation to generation by the Tlingit Indians.

Miriam came outdoors as Jim finished correcting Laurel's essay. 'Men wake up now,' she said and went on out to the vegetable garden to pull some greens.

Jim got up and went inside. Laurel followed him. Thor was lying quietly, just stretching cautiously at his long length. Ewan was trying to sit up.

'Easy, young man,' Jim warned. 'You're not ready to get up yet.'

'Hell,' said the man. 'I'm sore from head to foot!'

'Watch your language,' the older man, Thor, said quietly but with an edge to his tone, 'Ladies present, and they've all been mighty good to us!'

Ewan grimaced, but winked at Laurel. She did not respond, feeling a dislike of him. He acted like a spoiled child, and he was older than she, maybe twenty.

Without being asked, Laurel went to the water pot and drew out a cup of fresh cool water. She went to Thor, propped up his head slightly, and helped him drink. She had seen him lick his dry lips, and when she held his head she felt the slight fever in him.

He drank deeply, then lay back. 'Thank you,' he said.

'Hey, don't I get some?' Ewan demanded.

She brought him a drink and thought how different the two brothers were. Thor never asked for anything, but thanked her. Ewan demanded attention, and never thanked. They look alike, but inside they're not alike, she thought. She liked to study people, and by silently watching she learned a great deal from the limited number of people she met.

Thor was speaking slowly to her father. 'I don't remember much . . . What happened about the bear?'

'You'll have to ask Laurel; *she* shot him,' her father said, then grinned his rare little quirk at the man's surprise.

Thor turned toward Laurel painfully, moving in the bunk. 'Lie still,' she warned quickly. She came over to him, bent, and put her hand lightly on his bare back. It was a shock, to feel him warm and muscular under her slim hand. 'I think you have a little fever. Father? Should I ask Miriam to make up a hot herb tea?'

Jim came over and touched Thor's forehead, and did the same for Ewan. He frowned slightly, then nodded. 'Yes, some hot herb tea, and whatever else Miriam thinks best.'

'You're not going to let that Injun woman doctor us!' Ewan said angrily. 'Listen, send someone to Wrangell and tell them to send back a doctor. Or better yet, carry us there. I don't want to die in this God-forsaken wilderness!'

There was a blank silence in the cabin. Laurel's face burned with shame. She hoped none of the Nolans were close enough to hear him.

Thor finally said, 'I don't think there is anybody to send so far, Ewan. And they are taking good care of us. And like I said, watch your language!'

The cool, forceful words shut up the younger brother. He scowled and pulled the blanket up over his shoulders in a petulant motion.

Laurel went out to Miriam. 'They are with fever.'

'I thought it would come,' Miriam said. She went inside then to prepare a brew of hot, strong bitter stuff, to judge by Ewan's grimace. He tried to spit out the first mouthful, but Miriam shook her head at him and held the cup to his lips. Laurel had no trouble with Thor; he drank his down in a few gulps and fell back on the pillow.

It was an anxious time. Fever gripped both men for several days and nights. It burned high, then low, then high again – infection had set in both of them from the rip of the bear's claws.

The men's natures came out in their sickness. Ewan took it as a personal insult, that he should be ill. He cursed, even in his

17

delirium, and demanded attention night and day. He tried to grab Jade and pull her down to him one day, and she had to wrestle with him to get free. Laurel finally slapped him sharply, to make him let go. Their parents were not in the cabin at the time.

Jade was flushed and excited, pulling away from him, her eyes wide and dark. 'He is a fool!' she panted. 'No strength in him, but he wants to wrestle!'

'You stay away from him,' Laurel said sharply.

Thor was far different. He was a big silent man – much like her father, she thought. Even with his fever he kept control of himself. He rarely called out, but she knew that he was suffering when he tossed in the bunk. She would bring a cool cloth to bathe his face and shoulders and back, or a cup of hot herb tea to soothe his fever. He would thank her faintly, the effort of drinking seeming to exhaust him. He was much worse off for a time than his brother; his cuts were deeper and more infected.

Ewan was sitting up in bed and trying to move his legs by the time Thor was rid of his fever and his cuts began to mend. Ewan would fuss, asking for this and that, taking their attentions for granted.

Thor lay quietly, sitting up painfully only when he began to regain his strength.

'We are a great deal of trouble to you, Mr. Winfield,' he said to Jim one day. 'I'm surprised my father has not yet come for us.'

'It's been only three weeks,' Jim said calmly.

Thor frowned. 'I had thought the Leveretts would go right back to Sitka.'

'Maybe it took them a long time,' Jim said. Thor leaned back and thought about that.

Later Laurel brought him some thick soup, and he took the plate and cup himself this time. 'Laurel,' he began, 'my brain was fuzzy for a time. Tell me what happened.'

At his indication she sat down beside the bunk on a three-legged stool her father had made. 'Jade and I were out hunting rabbits,' she began slowly. 'We heard the shots and yells, and came running. We saw the brown bear attacking you.'

'Attacking me? I was down then?' The cool green eyes surveyed her over the cup's rim. He tore off a piece of bread and put it to his mouth, chewing slowly.

'Yes, you were down. Ewan was trying to reload his rifle, out near the sandbar. The bear was wounded. So were you. Blood was all over.' She shuddered a little at the memory.

'Where was Leverett?'

'I don't know. Somewhere behind the trees, I guess. Anyway, Jade shot and missed. I shot the bear in the eye as Jade distracted him. He finally fell down. Then Leverett and his daughter came; we talked. Jade went for Father and blankets, and then we brought you back to the cabin.'

Ewan asked, 'What happened to the bear? I want the trophy head.'

'It isn't yours. Laurel shot the bear,' said Thor, with a twitch of humor in his generous mouth. His eyes twinkled at her.

'Your friend has it,' Laurel said flatly. That still stung, that they had walked away with her bear.

Thor lost his smile. 'Leverett took it?' he said sharply, a frown line between his thick blond eyebrows.

She nodded. 'It was gone the next morning. We could've used it,' she added angrily.

'Damn,' Ewan said, and laughed. 'If that isn't like Leverett! The greedy bastard.'

For once Thor did not bark at him. 'I'm sorry, Laurel,' he said with a brief shake of his head. 'That was wrong. I'll make him pay for it.'

'What good is money?' asked Laurel. 'In the wilderness one does not need money. We needed the meat!' At the look on his face, she recalled that he was a guest. 'But we have meat now,' she added quickly. 'Tom Nolan shot a deer last week, and we can always get rabbits.'

He was silent as he handed the plate and cup to her. She got up and went to rinse the dishes. For once Ewan was also silent.

Both men got up for a short time the next day, trying to walk, Thor leaning on Jim's shoulder, and Ewan on Jade's shorter frame. He laughed and teased Jade. Laurel watched them both soberly.

She took advantage of the fresh breeze and sunny June sky to do the laundry. Jade came back and helped her lift the heavy materials in and out of the hot suds, then down to the stream to rinse them.

Then they brought back the trousers, shirts, and blankets and pegged them on the line behind the cabin.

They blew in the breeze and dried by evening. The girls took them down and folded them in the cabin. Laurel felt hot and tired. It was a heavy task in the wilderness, but it was easier in the spring and summer than in the winter.

Jade and her parents returned to their home that night. The cabin seemed larger with three people gone. Jim and Laurel sketched before the campfire. Thor was sitting on a blanket nearby, watching them silently.

Ewan was sitting up in bed, unable to gain interest in one of Laurel's books. He tossed it aside impatiently. 'You got anything to drink?' he asked.

She got up at once. 'Water or tea?' she asked.

He burst out laughing. 'You innocent!' he teased. 'I'm asking for a real drink!'

She looked puzzled, glanced at her father. 'We do not have whiskey,' he said flatly, not looking up from his sketching.

'Oh, hell,' grumbled Ewan. 'I can't wait to get back to bright lights, women, and whiskey!'

Thor's mouth was compressed. Laurel sat down again and reached for her sketch pad.

'May I see?' Thor asked, and she handed it to him silently. He turned the pages slowly and thoughtfully. 'You have a fine talent,' he said as he handed it back to her.

'Thank you.'

'She needs studio training,' Jim said bluntly as he laid down the pencil. 'Someday she should go away to school in the States.'

'Oh, no, Dad!' cried Laurel, shocked. 'I never want to leave you!'

'You will one day,' he said. 'You should go to Boston maybe. Your mother's brother will welcome you.'

Laurel was too startled for speech. She stared at her father. After a pause he went on painfully.

'Your uncle, Arnold Rutherford, wrote after – I wrote to him about your mother's death. He offered to take you in. He has two daughters about your age. I said not yet. But one day you should go, Laurel. You should have a good education, meet girls your own age, young men. Have a great time, have fun, like other girls do.'

'I don't want to leave Alaska, Dad,' she said in a low tone, her head lowered. 'I love it here, the wilderness, the wild things of the earth –'

'I know,' he said. 'That's why I didn't send you.'

Thor was listening in silence. Laurel had the feeling he did not miss a thing. Ewan was humming in his bunk, tapping his fingers on the wooden sides, irritably.

Thor insisted on giving Laurel his bunk, and he rolled up on the floor beside her father. She slept indifferently that night, thinking of what her father had said. He would not send her away from Alaska, would he?

During the next week she talked some to Thor – and a little to Ewan but not much. Thor was kind, interested in her. Ewan was interested only in teasing her and trying to kiss her. She avoided him.

Their injuries were healing now. Ewan was up first, galloping about, getting tired, and having to rest again. Thor took it more slowly and deliberately.

Ewan was ready to go. 'We could borrow your boat,' he said one night to Jim Winfield. 'We could send it back –'

Jim's brown eyes gleamed with unusual humor. 'No boat,' he said.

'No boat!' Ewan yelled incredulously. 'How do you get out?'

'Walk,' Jim replied. 'But we don't go.'

'Hell! It's two hundred miles to Sitka by boat! And plenty of water in between. All islands!'

'I know.'

Thor was listening in quiet, dry amusement. He finally interposed. 'We can build a boat, Ewan,' he said. 'Plenty of wood.'

'Oh, my God,' groaned Ewan.

A few days later, when Thor was finally able to walk about and was taking longer walks each day, two people arrived. Jade and Laurel saw them first. They stared in awe as the beautiful large sailboat came into view on their flowing Blue River gleaming in the late afternoon sun. Neither girl had ever seen such a large fine boat. The sails were huge and white, the wood was shiny with lacquer. A man got off, not Leverett, a much bigger man.

21

He put his hands to his mouth and called, a big bellow of a yell. 'Hellooo there! Are my sons about?'

And Laurel knew. 'Yes!' she called back.

He laughed, a big happy laugh. Then he turned back to the boat. An Indian in a red head scarf helped a lady ashore, and the big man took her arm.

'Look at that lady!' Jade admired.

Laurel had been looking at the big blond graying man. He was as tall as Thor, a hulk of a man, heavier by forty pounds. He had laugh lines crinkling about his sharp green eyes, and his cheeks were tanned and ruddy. He looked nice.

Then she looked at the woman on the man's arm. Was this Thor's mother? Young, slim, sleek like a seal, with black shining hair and black eyes like sharp pins. She looked right through the two girls, and her sharp nose seemed to turn up to the blue sky. She was wearing red and black, with a high neck about her throat, and frills at her wrists. She was as out of place as a high-stepping horse on a farm.

'I'm Olaf Koenig,' the man said, reaching out his huge hand. Laurel put her hand in it, and it was briefly lost and crushed. He let it go and beamed down at her. 'I knew my boys would not give up to a bear!' he said with a laugh. 'That damn Leverett, he didn't get back to Sitka until four days ago! I would've come sooner. Are they chafing at the bit?'

Laurel did not know what that meant. She said politely, 'They are now both over the fever and beginning to walk well, Mr. Koenig.'

He lost his smile. 'Fever?' he asked sharply. 'Who nursed them?'

Laurel indicated her silent friend. 'Jade's mother and all of us,' she said. 'Mrs. Nolan knows herbs and medicines.'

'Well, well. It seems I owe you plenty,' he said.

'Well, pay them, Olaf, and let's collect the boys,' the woman said sharply, not bothering to lower her voice.

He gave her a hard look, but it did not seem to trouble her.

'If you will come with us,' Laurel said.

He walked beside her, Jade on her other side, the woman stumbling after them on high heeled boots. He asked her name, then told her they had become worried after the boys had not returned home for weeks.

At the cabin, Thor was outside. He stood up, grinning, and came toward them. He and his father went into each other's arms, and as his father started to pound his back, Thor winced. 'Hey, Dad, easy.'

Olaf Koenig stopped at once. His face seemed to pale. 'Tell me about it,' he said abruptly. His face was showing his pain as he looked at his oldest son.

The woman seemed to pay no attention to Thor. She was glancing about, her nose wrinkling in revulsion at the cabin. Ewan came out then and saw his mother.

'Mama!' He enveloped her in a great hug. Her aristocratic sharp face softened, and she hugged him back.

'Ewan! My boy. You truly are all right!'

He was laughing and kissing her. 'I'm starved for good food and drink! Not a glass of wine or whiskey to be found around here!'

'You poor boy!' She was laughing also. 'And living in this miserable cabin! Come along, we'll soon have you on the boat and into some clean clothes. And a feast as soon as we get back to Sitka!'

He turned, his arm still about her, and saw Jim Winfield. 'Hey, Jim,' he said with a familiarity he had not dared before. 'Meet the prettiest stepmother a man ever had! This is Sidonie.'

'Mrs. Koenig, darling,' she corrected him, frowning. She gave a brief, curt nod to the silent Jim. 'I suppose we have you to pay for taking care of the boys,' she said.

'It was our pleasure,' he said soberly, his hands still in the pockets of his trousers.

Sidonie Koenig had a fascinating little accent. Laurel wondered about her. So she was their stepmother then. She looked so sharp and all edges, Laurel knew she could not be any person's mother.

'I thank you.' Olaf Koenig seemed to disregard his wife's insolence. He spoke pleasantly to Jim. 'You have been most kind to my sons. I won't forget this.'

'No trouble,' Jim drawled, his eyes narrowed in the way Laurel knew. He was concealing his dislike of the situation.

'They saved our lives, Father,' said Thor. 'Laurel shot the bear, and she and the rest nursed us back to health. I am most grateful.'

'And so am I, so am I,' Olaf agreed warmly. 'I wish I could think how to reward you, but money won't do it.'

'No, it won't,' said Jim, with a narrow smile. 'We were glad for the company. Be on your way tonight, I expect?'

Thor looked at him, then at Laurel standing soberly beside her father. Jade had drifted into the background to watch quietly from afar, in the way she had.

'I guess it would be easier for you,' Thor said quietly. 'Now that the boat is here, we'll give you back your cabin. I thank you for your hospitality, as well as for saving us.'

He went over to Laurel, tipped up her face, and looked down at her with his thoughtful green eyes. 'Thank *you*, especially, Laurel. You're quite a girl,' he said. He bent and brushed her lips lightly with his own large generous mouth. She felt a shock go through her, like a touch of a burning fire.

Jade slipped inside the cabin and returned with the men's parkas, which she and Laurel had carefully mended. Silently she handed one to Thor, who smiled. 'Thank you, Jade. I appreciate all you did. Tell your folks thanks again. I hope to see you again soon.'

She nodded and approached Ewan silently, her eyes downcast. He took the parka from her and patted her cheek casually. 'Thanks, Jade. You're a honey. See you!'

He turned away to put his arm lightly around his stepmother. They started away, with no further words to the others.

Thor looked at his father and shook his head as though they had similar thoughts. Olaf thanked them all gravely once more. He shook Jim's hand, and bent and kissed Laurel's cheek.

'Thank you for my boys,' he said softly and smiled down at her like a big giant.

'You are most welcome,' she replied.

Jade came up and slipped her arm in Laurel's as they watched the two men stride away after the other two. The figures became smaller and smaller against the pinkening sky of sunset.

Jim went back inside the cabin. Jade said 'And tonight, they will be on the beautiful boat going back to Sitka. . . . and we will not see them again.'

'He said he hoped to see us again.'

'That means nothing,' Jade said bitterly. 'When he was alone with me, he said many pretty things. When his beautiful step-mother came, he did not even look at me!'

24

'It's better if he doesn't look at you, Jade,' Laurel said slowly. 'I wouldn't trust him much.'

'Oh, Laurel, you do not like men,' Jade said, giggling suddenly, with a sudden change of mood. 'Wait until you are older!'

Laurel shrugged and went into the darkening cabin. She and Jade started the dinner. Jade would stay overnight, as she often did when caught by dusk. Her parents did not want her to wander about in the dark.

She thought Jade was wrong. She did like some men – her father, Tom Nolan . . . and Thor Koenig and his father. She liked them very much. Especially Thor. The touch of his mouth still lingered on hers. She raised her hand to her lips stealthily.

He was so tall, so strong, so controlled and smart. He would be fine to lean on, if one needed to lean on someone. He's not one to let one down, she thought. He would be always sturdy, strong. It's there, in his steady eyes.

Chapter 3

Laurel glanced down from the high ridge into the plain and could see the green tundra and wildflowers, the distant blue of the waters that made up the Inland Passage. She and her father were wandering along the slopes of the mountain nearest their cabin, along the white sands.

Jim had decided to look for gold this summer. Laurel thought her father was trying to make up for Jade's absence. He knew his daughter was lonely without her friend. The Nolans had gone back to their home village, one hundred miles south, to spend the summer.

Thor and his brother had been gone for four weeks. It seemed a lifetime. But the Winfields had not been quite alone. Some gold seekers had strayed aside from the Inland Passage up to Skagway, and had come into their valley. Jim had told them the Stikine River passage was dangerous, and from there it would be difficult to get to the Klondike. But they were greedy for gold and didn't have the money to take the overcrowded river steamers north. So with their heavy packs, the gold pans dangling from their necks, they had paddled up the Stikine into the interior. Jim had shaken his head. 'Fools,' he said briefly.

Jim set the wooden rocker down beside the stream and with the length of pipe he had bought diverted the flow from a small waterfall into it. He was totally absorbed in his work, as he always was. Whatever he did, he did with his whole heart.

Laurel turned from the glorious view out over the plain to the rivers and lakes, back to her job. She bent to shake the rocker gently.

'Go upstream about twenty paces, honey,' said Jim. 'And try your luck with the gold pan. Don't get chilled.'

'All right, Dad,' she said obediently and went upstream from him. It was rather fun. They had found a few tiny little specks of gold, which she kept in a small bottle. Not worth much, but fun.

Maybe someday they would make a strike. Maybe someday she would have pretty clothes to wear, like Clarissa Leverett and Mrs. Koenig. Maybe someday she could build her big house with the porch and own her piece of Alaska.

She bent to the work and panned out some of the gravel, shaking it, then letting the water run out. What was left was gravel. She moved her fingers through it gently. No sparks today, no hints of yellow. The July sun was golden though, and so were the buttercups. She smiled and picked several of them, carefully laying them in a piece of cloth to take home and sketch.

They stopped in mid-afternoon to return home slowly. Laurel had the rifle over her shoulder, the gold pan in the other hand. Jim carried just his rifle. He had left the wooden rocker there to continue another day.

Jim was first to see the smoke drifting from their chimney. He paused, frowned, peered in the distance with his keen eyes. Laurel waited in silence. He finally nodded, and they went on without words. He was cautious, though, and had his rifle ready as they came closer. Laurel checked her rifle, and it was loaded and ready.

Then two big men came out of the cabin door and waved in big circles at them. She caught her breath. 'It's Thor and his father!'

Such rejoicing bubbled up in her, she felt like laughing and singing and dancing. Instead she walked on with her father, rifle down, waving in response to them.

'Hello, there! Hope you don't mind. We came to hunt with you!' Olaf Koenig called in his cheerful bellow. He was tanned and ruddy faced and beaming at them.

'Glad to have you,' Jim said in his calm way. But from his flush and smile, Laurel knew he liked the two. 'Your other son here?'

'No,' said Olaf flatly. 'Just Thor and me. You been gold panning?' He saw the pan in Laurel's hand.

'Looking around, no luck,' Jim said briefly. 'Come in and sit. Laurel, what do we have for dinner?'

'Rabbit,' she said with a small grin at Thor. He had got tired of rabbit, though he had been too polite to say so.

'Hah!' he said now. 'I fooled you. We brought our own deer along.'

'You've been hunting already,' said Jim, with a broader grin than usual.

'That's right. Saw the deer on the way and couldn't resist. Say, this is beautiful country,' Olaf said, looking about. The sun was drifting down to the horizon and painting the distant mountain peaks with crimson. The tundra was a tender green, and near the cabin the tall spikes of lupin, blue and rose, mauve and white, stood tall and bright.

'I like to watch the sunsets,' Laurel said shyly. They all stood and watched as the crimson, red, and scarlet streaks painted the sky, turned the earth red, shimmered on the waters, and made a golden red glory of the mountains to the east. When the bold sky show was finished, they went inside, talking slowly, like friends.

Laurel began to prepare the dinner. Thor and his father had made it easy – they had skinned the deer, cut a large piece and put it into a pot of hot water. All she had to do was add vegetables, let them cook, and serve the whole on tin plates. They had even cut the remainder of the deer in strips and hung them out to dry, high above the reach of wolves. After dinner they all sat to talk before the fire.

The two men told news of the outside world. 'Thousands of gold hunters are streaming through,' Olaf said ruefully. 'Some stay in Sitka for a time, then go on. Most just rush through, though, on the river steamers. They're charging God-awful amounts to let a fellow stand on the deck and ride along! Guess they all think they'll get rich.'

'How good are the gold fields? Big ones?' Jim asked casually.

'So they say. Huge nuggets and chunks being brought down. But I figure it's the bankers and the smart business men who'll end up with all the money,' Olaf said, shaking his head. 'The amounts they charge for food, clothes, pans, and such-like! It's criminal. But the fellows up there, stuck in the mud and snow, they'll pay anything.'

'I'm surprised you and Laurel haven't gone along to the gold fields,' Thor said quietly. His keen green eyes surveyed Jim and then Laurel.

Jim shook his head slowly. 'Not for me. No place for a girl like Laurel. Those folks have to be tough, or die.'

'You wanted to once, Dad,' said Laurel. 'I remember, you and Mother talked about it.'

'Yes, before your mother died I thought about going to the gold fields. Your mother . . . she'd go anywhere I wanted. She made an adventure out of it.' Jim half smiled, his eyes dreamy.

They were all silent then. Jim's life had changed when Madeline died. He had no ambition, no drive, no eagerness for life. Laurel, sighing, knew she was no substitute for her mother in her father's life. She could not give him the strong will for adventure, for a bright life. The light in Jim had burned out.

'You should think of Laurel,' Olaf said. Then, with a glance at his son: 'She'll be wanting to live in civilization one day and have pretty clothes.'

Jim looked vaguely surprised. 'Laurel? She's just – what, honey? Twelve?'

'Fourteen, Dad,' she said. 'This is 1901, remember?'

'Oh. Well, she has years yet,' he said, but he looked worried.

'Reminds me,' said Thor. 'I brought a few things from the stores for you and your pretty friend Jade.' He got up, went to the corner, and brought out some rustling packages. He looked at them, sorted them out, and handed two boxes to Laurel. 'Yours, Miss Laurel!'

'Me?' she asked weakly. 'For me? What are they?' She let the packages lay across her lap. They were so large, yet not heavy. She pressed the corner of one experimentally, and a flush came into her cheeks. Her brown eyes were wide.

'For you. I got Leverett to pay for the bear, and then I went to the stores and got a few things for you and Jade. Where is she, by the way?'

'She and her folks went back to the village,' Jim said. 'I think they want to make up with her kin and arrange a marriage in a couple years.'

'I wondered why they didn't live with their village people,' Thor said. 'Open the packages, Laurel! What happened to the Nolans? Fuss over kinship?'

He's shrewd, thought Laurel, and he knew the Tlingit Indians. She slowly unwrapped the first package, taking care with the paper. It was nice white butcher paper; she could use it for drawing.

'Tom and Miriam got married against the village's wishes,'

explained Jim. He was watching Laurel with her packages. 'They were cast out and have lived away from their people. Something about marrying too close, in their own clan. Anyway, they went back this summer to make it up, if they can. Jade needs someone to marry one day.'

'Ohhhh!' breathed Laurel, as she drew out first a lovely, red plaid dress, then a thick, blue wool skirt. Under that was a gray parka with fine white fur on it. 'Ohhhh how beautiful!'

'I got them a mite large,' explained Thor. 'Figured you might grow up a bit more in the next year or so.' He was flushed, but composed.

'Never figured to see him buying female clothes,' his father said with a big chuckle, then subsided at his son's glare. 'Well anyway, he did, and he got some for Jade too. I thought they was pretty. I like red,' he added with satisfaction, his hair ruffled by his fingers, his cheeks ruddy.

Laurel stood up and held the dress to her. 'I think it'll fit good,' she said. 'Thank you . . . very much . . . Thor. You are most kind.'

Thor urged her to open the other parcel, a smaller one. In it she found a pretty sewing basket, outfitted with all kinds of threads, needles, and pins. And two white blouses, so fine and delicate she would be afraid to wear them. And a long white garment – a night-dress! He had bought her a nightdress! She got deep red and felt hot as a summer night. She thanked him in a stifled voice and put away the clothes on pegs along the wall. She put Jade's packages in a corner away from mice.

The next day they all went hunting. It was a jolly expedition. Thor and Olaf did not keep silent the entire time. Jim was more talkative than usual too. He smiled and laughed so much that Laurel was surprised. He did seem to like the men very much.

They did not find much the first two days, but the men did not seem worried about it. Another day, they went up the hill to the rocker and helped pan for gold, working efficiently in their boots, up to their hips in ice-cold water from the mountain.

'The sand is white gravel,' Olaf said thoughtfully. 'Good sign. You say you got some few grains? Maybe the main stuff is up higher.'

'Could be. Or down lower,' Jim said. 'It might settle below.'

'It's all a gamble,' said Thor cheerfully. 'Laurel, did you bring your sketch pad? Look at this.' He was bent over a clump of tiny white flowers with five frail petals on each stem and a gold heart of fuzz. She sketched it while he watched in approval. 'You're a fine artist,' he praised her.

'Mother called this "water crowfoot," ' she said easily. 'She had a book about flowers and could name almost all of them. I still use it. But there are lots of flowers up here that aren't in the book. Some-day I'd like to write a book about flowers and put in all the Alaska ones – with my drawings and painted in the right colors too.'

'That's good. Say, there's something else I didn't give you. For-got!' He snapped his fingers and looked cross at himself. 'A box of paints. It's in my knapsack. All kinds of oils, and some brushes the fellow at the store said were right for that.'

'Oils!' she breathed. 'Oh, I would like that!'

They tried them out that night, she and her father. It was diffi-cult to use on the slick white paper, but she managed to draw one flower design. Thor watched Laurel, praised her, and even her father said she had a fine talent and was improving nicely. He was very particular.

Another night she sketched all of them, each in turn, and also the group of the men before the fire, talking and playing checkers. When the days were fine, they went hunting again and managed to bag an immense moose, about two years old and a huge specimen for his age.

That kept Laurel and Thor busy for several days cooking some of the meat, cutting and drying other strips. When they were finished, she had enough meat to last several months.

Thor went fishing with her, and they got some fine salmon and trout. They ate some for their dinners and dried the rest. Then Laurel went blueberry picking and showed Thor her favorite mead-ows. They picked many pails for eating – and for preserving for the winter too. She felt a housewifely pride in her small stores of goods ready for the winter. Thor teased her lightly; she only laughed.

'I like doing this,' she said. 'And it's a relief to have enough food on the shelves for when the rains are heavy or when we have thick snows. We have more rain than snow in the winter, but it can get very cold and disagreeable.'

'What do you do then?' Thor was shortening his stride to match hers as they strolled to the Blue River, fishing poles in hand, rifles on their shoulders.

'Oh . . . pile logs on the fire. Read. Sketch. Sometimes the Nolans come over and we spend the time together. Jade and I have our lessons to do. I've done all the arithmetic books, though, and most of the history. I wish we had more books,' she added wistfully. 'Oh well, we'll get some more someday.'

He scowled. 'Drat it. I should've thought. I could've brought you some books, easy as not.'

'Oh, I wasn't hinting!' she exclaimed, aghast.

He laughed softly. He had a deep melodious voice, with a hint of an accent and she loved to listen to him speak.

She asked him now, 'Are you English. I mean, British?'

He shook his head. 'No, we came over from Denmark when I was ten and Ewan was seven. We settled in Eastern Canada for a time, but Father was restless. We came further and further west and settled in the mountains for a time. Then Mother died. Father got very quiet. He was very unhappy . . . Her name was Brianna.' He said the name softly, as though it meant much to him. 'She was pretty and blond-haired, with beautiful blue eyes.'

Laurel thought of her own uninteresting dark brown hair and brown eyes. Clarissa was blond though. Was that why he liked her?

'And then you came to Alaska?' she asked.

'Yes, in 1896.'

'We came the next year, in 1897. Mother died in 1898.'

He listened to whatever she said with intense concentration. 'And you miss her a great deal?'

She nodded.

'So I feel about my mother.' His accent was stronger. 'She was very good, very strong, very sweet. A softening feeling. Then Father married Sidonie Valin.' He grimaced, and Laurel knew at once he did not like her much. 'She's French,' he added. 'She likes to dress up a lot,' and his tone was expressionless.

'And she has no children?'

'No,' he said abruptly.

She felt uncomfortable. She changed the subject. 'What does Koenig, your last name, mean? I know who Thor was.'

'The god of Thunder of the Norse. And Koenig is the word for king. Ruler, and so on. Like rex in Latin for king and czar in Russian.'

'Oh yes. I should've remembered about that,' she said with interest. 'Father told me once.'

'You have a good memory,' he complimented her.

Both heard the long whine and then the short bark. Laurel's eyes opened wide as she searched the long tundra plains, the rivers to the west and north.

'Did you hear that?' Thor asked sharply, pausing to listen.

The short barks came again, then a long low whine.

'There, across the stream!' Laurel's slim hand pointed in the direction. Across the thick grasses and wildflowers she could just make out a shape dragging itself along. It looked like a gray wolf, hiding in the brush. She stiffened, anxiously. 'Is it a wolf?'

'I don't know,' answered Thor. They approached the bank of the stream cautiously. The animal raised its head, and they saw the narrowed slant eyes, the deep gray fur. The animal kept dragging itself as though hurt, and Laurel and Thor could now see the deep dark patch on its shoulder.

'If that is a wolf, I'd better finish it off.' Thor's rifle went to his shoulder, but he hesitated.

'Oh wait. Please wait,' begged Laurel. 'It might be a husky dog. Some of the gold hunters have dogs with them.'

The animal had seen them and, with a long whine, made itself go into the deep cold waters toward them. Then it slipped on the slippery pebbles and fell over into the icy white waters. Laurel began to run, impulsively, toward the stream.

'I'll go! Stay back!' Thor ordered her, and she obeyed without thinking.

He waded into the stream cautiously, stopping below where the dog was struggling feebly against the flow of the current. Fortunately it was July and not March, or the depth of the flow from the mountain snows would have overwhelmed the animal.

Laurel waited, her heart pounding, as Thor bent over and caught the animal with his knees, and then with his arms. He examined it quickly, his hands running over the thick wet fur, then picked it up bodily and strode to land. Once he was on the gravel, he paused to get his breath. The animal was large and hung limply over his wet arms.

'Let's get back to the cabin,' Thor said curtly. 'His leg is broken, and I think there's a bullet hole in his shoulder.'

'Oh, the poor thing! Is it a dog?' she asked curiously.

'I think so, though sometimes you can't tell until you look at the teeth.' He grinned. 'If you wait too long to look inside their mouths, you're out of luck,' he teased.

Laurel could not smile. Ever so gently she patted the wet shaggy head, and the long fluffy tail wagged feebly. 'I think it's a dog,' she said. 'Wolves don't wag their tails, do they?'

'The ones I've met didn't,' Thor said. 'Do you have wood for splints?'

'Yes. I brought in some splinters yesterday for the fire and to light the candles. I'll wrap a couple in cloth so they won't hurt him.'

At the cabin Thor put the wounded animal on the blanket that Laurel had spread near the fire and examined its leg and shoulder wound.

'The bullet is in there, giving him hell,' he said with tight lips and a frown. 'I'll have to dig it out. You better go outside and shut the door, Laurel, in case he gives me trouble.'

His eyes were icy green. Laurel gave him a shocked look. 'Oh no, I will not!' she said positively. 'I'll stay right here. I'll hold his head and pat him. He won't be any trouble, will you, dog?'

Thor sighed, but he did not seem angry. 'I might've known you'd be stubborn. All right, hold his head, get acquainted. I'll sterilize a knife and have bandages ready. And some of that good ointment.'

Laurel sat beside the animal, drying it with a cloth, and crooning to him. The dog did not bark; he was silent and reserved, eyeing her with questioning slanted dark eyes. The fur was gray and thick, so thick she could dig deep and not find the muscular body beneath. It was a husky, all right, born and bred for the hard, harsh conditions of Alaska, part dog, part wolf.

'I wonder whose it was,' she murmured.

'Probably part of a dog team,' said Thor, returning. He held out a long sharp knife to the fire, and then right into the flames, turning it slowly. The dog watched him alertly, without a sound. 'He's been trained, and there are leather marks on his shoulders. I imagine he broke his leg, and the owner shot him, but he got away. He must've been running for miles, his feet are so torn by stones.'

He met Laurel's questioning look. 'I hate cruelty of all kinds,' he added more quietly. 'He's been beaten too, Laurel. There are scars all over him.'

'Ohhh,' she cried out, and bent her head to that of the dog and caressed the animal gently. 'And he's so quiet, so proud and quiet, after all that!'

'Yes. A proud dog, a good animal,' said Thor. 'Well, hold on to his head, Laurel. And keep talking to him quietly.'

She obeyed, but did not have a bad time of it. The dog whined only a little and pressed itself shudderingly to her body as Thor probed for the bullet. He made quick work of it, went in fast, dug it out of the festering flesh, and brought it out, a small smashed piece of lead. He examined it carefully, then laid it aside, and washed out the wound with disinfectant. The dog growled in his throat, but made no move to bite.

Thor pressed out some of the pus, then put on ointment, and bandaged the shoulder so the dog could not lick off the salve. 'Okay, fellow, you're a brave one,' he praised the animal and patted his nose and head.

Laurel laid him down and brought a bowl of fresh water. He licked it up thirstily and accepted a piece of dried moose. He was chewing at it when her father and Olaf returned. As they came near the cabin, the dog heard the noises, and he lifted his head and whined sharply.

Jim opened the cabin door. The dog gave a single short bark and remained alert until Laurel said, 'All right. Good dog!'

'Well trained,' said Thor.

'What's this?' Jim asked in amazement. He and Olaf went to examine the animal. After some minutes the dog allowed them to pet him and study him more closely. 'Fine animal. Someone may come for him, Laurel,' Jim warned.

'I doubt it,' said Olaf. 'Looks like, with that leg, the owner was getting rid of him, shooting him like that.'

Thor looked angry again, but said no more.

'What will you call him?' Olaf asked with interest.

'Rex,' Laurel answered. 'He looks proud, like a king, doesn't he?' she blushed as Thor looked at her and smiled.

'Yes, he does,' her father agreed.

Rex watched her intently through the evening as she moved about preparing dinner, washing the dishes, sitting down to sketch. When she went to bed in the bunk, the animal whined, and tried to get up.

Thor picked him up, blanket and all, and deposited him beside Laurel's bunk. 'There. He'll be a good guard dog for you, Laurel,' he said. The dog settled right down.

Laurel reached out of her blankets and stroked the thick hair. The animal made a short sound in his throat, that was all. It was remarkably quiet.

She went to sleep, with the sounds of the men's deep voices murmuring at the fire. They sounded very serious. She wondered what they were discussing.

Thor and Olaf stayed two more weeks. Laurel had never felt so happy. Olaf liked Jim, and her father was more open and even jolly. They hunted together, panned for gold, talked, laughed, played checkers, read, talked some more. Thor seemed content to listen, but he too seemed quite at home here. He spent much of his time with Laurel while she roamed about and sketched, with Rex limping three-legged after her. The wounds did not keep him down long. Thor said the leg would heal in about eight weeks or less.

All of them shared appreciation of the beauties of Alaska and of its dangers. They would stand and watch the sunrise, fish contentedly in the rushing streams, and gaze at the shimmering rivers in the afternoon sun. One time, when a female bear and her two cubs approached them, they were all silent, watching, and wary, ready to run. All refused to shoot a female with cubs. Laurel was glad of that.

Thor awoke them all softly one night, about two in the morning. They went out, sleepily, wrapped in blankets, and gazed up in awe at the ever-fascinating northern lights. The sky was alive with the gray-green shimmering display of wavering lines toward the North Pole. They came and went, disappeared to reappear in wonderful patterns. Finally they died down, and Laurel stumbled back into her bunk.

Next day Thor said, 'Sorry I woke you. I'm crazy about those lights. I love them in the winter, when they're all colors.'

'I do too, but I haven't seen them often. Dad won't let me stay up,' Laurel confessed.

He smiled and ruffled her hair, as though she were a child.

They were out walking to be alone together that last afternoon, when Thor cried out and pointed up. A raven and his mate were leaving a tree, flying off with widespread black wings.

'Good luck!' said Laurel quickly. 'That's the sign of Jade's clan.'

'Yes, the raven is good luck,' Thor agreed, yet Laurel wondered if he really believed in ravens and good luck. But he did not seem mocking.

Next morning the men made ready to depart. Laurel was sick to see them go. She had become accustomed to their grand company, and she silently worshipped Thor for his understanding and gentleness toward her.

Thor bent and patted Rex. 'Take good care of Laurel now,' he said in a commanding tone.

The dog whined softly, just as though he understood. His long plumy tail wagged; he kept his injured leg off the ground, but his handsome head was alert, his black eyes intelligent.

Olaf Koenig bent and kissed Laurel's cheek. 'Take care of yourself, little girl,' he said kindly. 'Come and visit us someday. I want you to come to Sitka and stay with us.'

'Thank you, Mr. Koenig,' she said politely, thinking she never would but that he was kind to welcome her.

Thor kissed her cheek also, and then turned her face so he could brush his lips lightly against hers. 'Goodbye, take care. Thank you for a wonderful summer, Laurel,' he said just for her, his deep melodious voice in her ear.

'I enjoyed it,' she said, and that was an understatement. She made herself smile and smile, and wave and wave, until they stopped turning about and their figures were small black dots beyond the streams.

'Well . . . that was very pleasant,' Jim said as he turned and went into the cabin.

Laurel stood outside with Rex until the chill finally drove her inside. She felt blank and empty. Thor had gone.

Chapter 4

The Nolans returned toward the end of August. They were troubled, and unhappy; Jade was angry, then depressed.

'They did not like us,' she confided in Laurel. 'They were stiff and formal. They did not want us to stay. They told my parents, "You made the choice years ago. It could not be undone." '

'Oh, Jade!' Laurel paused in her sketching to study her friend's troubled face. 'Will they hold a grudge all this time?'

'It is not the . . . the grudge,' Jade said carefully, tossing her black braid over her shoulder. She wore the long blue skirt which Thor had brought for her, and with it a blue-checked lumberjack's shirt. She looked so attractive with her golden tan and sparkling black eyes.

'What then?'

'They said my parents did wrong to marry in the clan. It is . . . too close. And they do not want me to marry any of them. The young men found me attractive,' – she tossed her head coquettishly – 'but their mothers scowled at me.'

Laurel was silent, troubled, not willing to ask awkward questions. Jade sketched for a time, the small careful lines that Jim had taught her.

Finally she said, 'But I guess I will marry someone from another clan. My parents will take me to visit another village next summer.'

Her eyebrows were drawn together, straight black and fine. Her full mouth pouted. She had been hurt, Laurel felt.

'Well, there's no hurry,' said Laurel. 'We are only fourteen.'

'There were girls in the village, promised, younger than I,' Jade said flatly.

Another time Jade said, as though she were thinking and thinking about it, 'Maybe I will not marry an Indian! Maybe I will marry a white man! White men find me attractive! And I do not have to marry an Indian and live in a village!'

Laurel did not know what to say. She felt that Jade was remembering Ewan Koenig, and she did not like that young man. She felt uneasy around him.

Autumn came, and the tundra turned gold and crimson before fading to brown. Jim shot a deer, and they dried the meat for winter and felt quite satisfied with their stores. He worked often on the rocker and stream, and although Laurel panned conscientiously, she did not really expect to find much.

The signs were that the winter would be a cold one. The animals developed a thick fur early, and the birds flew south early. Laurel looked up at the October sky to find great flocks of geese, starlings, and blackbirds flying about, finding their leaders and direction, then forming in great arrows of purposeful flight.

She stood and watched as the geese honked and flew south in their huge, black arrow shapes in the sky. And she listened too as the shrill cries of the blackbirds filled the air. The heavens turned almost black with them when their great groups formed, flew in circles, darted about, then headed south.

Rex barked at them, his ears and nose pointed up toward the sky. Although the splints were off his leg, he still limped a little, but he could run faster than Laurel. He was her devoted friend, and Jim confessed he felt easier about Laurel, now that she had the large dog.

She patted his head. 'It's going to be a cold one, Rex,' she said aloud. She liked to talk to him. He was company for her when Jade could not come over. And he reminded her constantly of Thor. She remembered Thor's big gentle hands ministering to the great gray animal, working with him, petting him, soothing him.

Rex whined in his throat, looking up at her with his narrowed black eyes. He looked like a wolf, but more gentle. And he adored being petted. She could dig into his fur and rub his chin, and he would arch with ecstasy.

The lupins faded and drooped. Laurel gathered the last of the berries and put them up. And one morning there was thick ice on the streams. A few days later they had the first blizzard, and the snow was thick.

They were not used to having so much snow on the western slopes of the Coast Mountains, south of Wrangell. Tom Nolan made new snowshoes for Laurel and Jade and taught them to walk on the snow. It was fun and much easier than trying to walk in just their high boots.

Jim and Laurel went up to the rocker until the waters froze. Laurel gave up then and stayed in the cabin much of the time, cooking, doing the laundry, sewing some new curtains from lengths of fabric the Nolans had brought back from their journey. Some days she and Jade could not meet at all, the snows and winds were so bad.

Jim had taken his pick with him often. And one afternoon he returned early, a strange excitement flaring in him. Laurel had been warned by Rex's low whine and had gone outside with the dog to greet her father. The low afternoon sun shone in red rays across the glistening snows, casting a long shadow behind Jim as he walked on snowshoes toward her.

He came close and waved his hand. He did not try to speak until they had gone inside, out of the bitter wind. Then he set the small leather poke down on the table.

Laurel opened the strings of the poke; the leather bag felt unusually heavy. She looked inside, then blinked in surprise at the glinting stones. She poured them out on the table, and gasped. Gold stones, all shapes, all sizes, some as large as walnuts!

'Oh, Dad!' she whispered. 'Is it . . . really gold?'

He nodded 'I think so,' he said. 'I've been finding more and more. Today I came across a long vein.'

She sat down on a stool limply. Her fingers touched the golden stones timidly. Some were covered with dirt, some had been cleaned and shone dark gold in the lamplight.

'But there's an awful lot here,' she whispered. 'And . . . there's more?'

'A lot more, Laurel. I guess we'll be rich one day, if the vein goes back as far as I think it does. It's in the side of the mountain, and it'll take a lot of work to do it. Probably have to wait till spring.'

He sighed, sat down, and watched her with a grin.

She was unable to take it all in. Gold. Her father had struck gold!

What would this mean? They could own a piece of Alaska land. They could built a house, a large house, a proper house!

Tom Nolan and his family came over a few days later, when the winds had died down. After the greetings Jim took the gold poke from its hiding place and spilled the nuggets out on the plank table.

'Whewww!' whistled Tom Nolan. 'You found gold, huh?'

'Sure did. I staked it out. And I want you to stake next to me, Tom.' Jim beamed.

Tom grinned, but shook his head slowly. 'Not me, Jim. I will help you, though . . . when the weather gets better. You are going out to file a claim? You better. Gold men all about.'

'Sure. When the ice breaks in the spring, I'll go out to Wrangell and file a claim. But I got the stakes up and all properly marked for two claims – discoverer's two claims. Why not file next to mine?'

Tom looked at Miriam, who looked down at her hands.

'My brother is dead,' Tom said slowly in the Tlingit tongue, his hands eloquent, his heavy face sad. 'I go to the village with my wife and daughter, and I ask, "Where is my brother?" They tell me he went up to Skagway, over the Pass into the snows. He work hard, and he found a little gold. Then he was gone. Men found him dead in the snow, his head bashed in. Men go crazy with gold fever. They killed my brother for his little piece gold. No, Jim. Gold makes men crazy. I don't want it.'

Laurel felt a cold chill go down her spine, and she shuddered. Jim listened, his brown eyes sad.

'Yes, I guess that can happen, but *I* don't mean to go crazy with this. I just want enough for Laurel, for her education maybe.'

'For me, Dad!' she exclaimed. 'No, it's for us!'

'I don't care about it,' he said simply. 'But what the Koenig folks said made me think. You should go to Sitka – for a high school education – and have nice clothes. Maybe I could build a house there, until you're grown up. Maybe work in town. Olaf said I could get a job in a shop there, doing carpentry work.'

'Oh, Dad, you'd hate it!' She was distressed, yet thrilled that Olaf had thought about her, and maybe Thor had too. 'No, this is where we belong, in the wilderness,' she tried to say firmly.

'Who will you marry?' he asked sadly. 'Tom, *you* know. You worry about Jade. I worry about Laurel. Who will the girls marry?

No, they need to live in town for a time, and the gold will help.' He ran his fingers through the golden pebbles absently. 'I don't know how much this is worth, but there's more up in the hills. Enough for Laurel, I figure.'

They talked of other matters then. The village, and Tom's relatives, who had not welcomed them. The old days. The lost days. How Alaska was changing with all the newcomers, the ones who wanted to take gold from Alaska and then go back home.

'They do not love Alaska as we love her,' said Tom, shaking his sleek black head. 'They do not see her beauty, the mountains, and the lakes, the animals and the birds, the flowers and the trees. No, that means nothing. It is gold, gold, and gold. How one can get rich quick.'

Laurel said in her low voice, 'That's not what I want. I want to own a piece of Alaska . . . to live here . . . to be part of the wilderness . . .'

She had said it and they smiled kindly, but they did not truly understand. Even Jade did not understand, so Laurel was silent. She kept it in her heart, her own dreams and wishes.

Nights, sometimes, she dreamed of Thor. She would dream of his strong face bending over hers, bending to her, and his lips brushing across hers. He was speaking, and then she would turn over and wake up. He would go away then into the mists of morning. But sometimes he came back, and she loved those dreams.

When the weather was not so bad, Jim went up to the gold works. He returned later that day with pokes full of large nuggets.

'There's a small fortune up there, Laurel,' he told her. 'Come spring, we'll work out a lot more and I'll go to Wrangell to file claim. Reckon we'll have a lot of company, with other men coming to file. I best send you off to Sitka then.'

'But why, Dad?' She was really puzzled. 'You'll need me to keep house for you and help on the claim.'

'I don't want you around the roughnecks. In fact, I'd like to send you to Boston so you'll meet some real gentlemen.'

'Oh, Dad!' She began to giggle, thinking he was teasing. But he frowned at her. 'You're *not* serious?'

'Very serious.' He was spreading out the nuggets on the wooden

43

table, sorting out the largest and finest of them. 'Olaf said you were a fine lady, and you shall be! You should have a good education, fine clothes . . .'

He had a length of copper wire and a tiny instrument. As she watched, curiously, he arranged the nuggets in order by size and then began to carefully file into the center of one of the nuggets.

'What're you doing, Dad?' she finally asked.

'Making you a necklace,' he said, then smiled his slow shy smile. 'You should have a necklace of our first gold, honey. To keep always.'

'Oh, Dad, you don't need to do that!'

'Don't need to. I want to.'

Jim Winfield worked for many evenings that winter on the necklace. He cleaned and polished the gold nuggets, choosing only the largest and finest ones for her necklace. Then he would drill holes through the center of each one and string it onto the copper wire, tying it on with a knot in the copper. Then he would string on the next one, until he had a long necklace of the finest gold nuggets for his daughter. It reached halfway to her waist, it was so long.

He gave it to her sometime around January. 'I don't remember when Christmas was,' he said apologetically. 'Never could keep days in mind.'

'It doesn't matter,' she reassured him. They never kept Christmas, not after her mother had died. The Nolans didn't know anything about Christmas, and there was no one to celebrate with. 'I like this awfully much, Dad. I'll keep it always. Thank you.'

She kissed his cheek shyly. They did not show much emotion to each other. She knew he loved her and worried about her. And she loved her silent artistic father.

She put it on over her thick red shirt and blue sweater. It shone in the firelight.

'Keep it under your coat when you go out,' he warned. 'Someone might want to snatch it.'

'I will, Dad.'

He put the other gold away in pokes. There were five pokes of gold now in a cigar box up on the shelf. The January days were so bitter cold that they mostly stayed in the cabin. Rex slept beside the fire, his nose on his paws, and snuffled now and then at his own

44

dreaming. Laurel sketched or read, or dreamed. Her father sketched or read, and they were silent, content in each other's company.

Jade came with her father those few times the weather cleared. The snows were deep, and they traveled on top of it in their snowshoes. They would stay all day, and the girls would laugh and talk, and sing the Indian songs Jade knew. Sometimes they played in the snow, throwing balls or making figures of packed snow. Rex would bark a little, though he was always very quiet, like a wolf, prancing around them, his thick tail wagging and sending snow in sprays.

Jim and Tom went up to the claim to pace it off again and adjust the stakes to make it 500 feet by 500 feet. Jim had made a long tape measure of cloth, marking it off carefully with the long ruler he had. Now they could measure the claim more exactly. Tom helped him figure out where it was in relation to the mountain and the streams, and they marked that off and wrote it down for the day when Jim would file his claim.

'Yep, I'll have company next summer,' Jim said rather distaste-fully. 'The gold prospectors will all come in to file next to me. Why don't you file for yourself, Tom?'

Tom would always shake his head. 'I told you, Jim, not for me.'

Jade looked as though she would say something but kept her tongue still. Later she said to Laurel, 'I would like some gold, for me and Mother. But Father is set against it. Says it brings evil.'

'Do *you* think it does, Jade?' Laurel asked worriedly. That cold chill went down her back again, and she fingered her gold necklace nervously.

'I don't know. Father says something makes him know that. And he is often right. Mother says he is always right.' She giggled. 'Oh well . . . one day I will have a husband, and he will be always right!'

'Oh, Jade, you silly!' laughed Laurel. 'Always thinking about a husband!'

'Well, we are growing up, Laurel!' Jade leaned down and formed a snowball and flung it at Laurel, hitting her on the chest. Laurel scooped up some snow and flung it back, and their laughter filled the cold air.

Rex barked and ran from one to the other, as though begging them to give him the ball. The balls were of snow and when he tried

45

to bite one, it went to nothing in his mouth. Laurel laughed and laughed at his silly expression, and he sat on his haunches and grinned up at her, his dark eyes sparkling.

She hugged him, and roughed up the fur of his head. 'You silly,' she said fondly. He woofed and put his head at the neck of her parka and sniffed her and licked her throat.

That night, after Jade and Tom had gone home, Jim asked, 'What would you do, Laurel, if you had all the money you wanted?'

'Do?' She bit the thread of the blue blouse she was making. She lifted the garment to study it. It was light blue and would go with the dark blue skirt Thor had brought her. 'Oh, I'd like a big house one day, with a porch. And furniture with silk cushions,' she said. 'What do you want?'

'Nothing, except for my girl to be happy,' he said seriously. 'I've neglected you, Laurel, and that hurts me. I should've sent you outside to school when . . . when your mother died. But I was selfish and kept you with me.'

'It was what I wanted, Dad,' she said steadily. 'I wouldn't have gone without you.'

He was silent. She lifted the length of cloth Tom Nolan had brought her and asked, 'Shall I make a blouse for Jade from this, Dad?'

'Why don't you make her one from the red? That's more her color,' he said absently.

'All right. Yes, she likes red.' Happily Laurel cut and measured and cut again, and started sewing the blouse for Jade that night. Tom had brought several lengths for her, and she did not need them for just herself. She had made two more heavy shirts for her father from the thick red-and-blue check lengths, and they had replaced his shabby ones.

The sewing and her sketching and reading and playing outdoors with Rex filled the winter days. Some of the late January days and early February were too bad to go outdoors for more than a few minutes. But Laurel was content, and her father seemed happy enough. She had work to do that kept her busy, and she was useful to him, cooking and cleaning and doing the laundry. They read in silence or sometimes aloud to each other. They sketched, and Jim helped her improve her perspective and line.

46

She used up the oil paints and regretfully put away the empty box. Thor had been kind to think of them for her. She thought often of Thor, in the long dark winter nights.

One night she and Jim went outdoors about three in the morning, to see the glorious array of the aurora borealis, the northern lights, and she wished Thor could see them with her. It was so beautiful, all crimson and green and streaks of gold – the most color she had ever seen in the night skies.

'You'll never forget these lights,' her father said. 'They're colors of the gods.'

'I know, Dad. I wish I could paint that.'

'Look at the colors, the shapes. Observe, observe.'

And she did, but they kept changing and swirling and misting into each other. They stared until they were about frozen, and then went inside as the lights finally dimmed. The next day she tried to put it down in watercolors. Her attempt seemed feeble next to the reality of the lights.

This is my land, she thought. I belong here. She dreamed often now of the house she would have someday. The big house on an island, and porches all around, and big rooms. She would furnish each room, and she planned it all out. She would put a big dining table in one room and have guests whenever she wanted. And they would serve the best food, and have candles on the table, real candles of wax, not smelly lamps.

There would be grand silk curtains at the windows. Maybe blue curtains with gold cords like her mother had described from a grand Boston house. And the outhouse would not be freezing cold; it would be warm and comfortable – though she could not imagine how that could be.

And Thor would come to visit, and say how grand it all was, and approve of all she did. His eyes would be a gentle green, and he would smile at her, and he would kiss her lips . . . lightly, just so, a quick brush of her lips. She would be wearing a beautiful dress, and he would think she was lovely. She would be so beautiful for him.

The house would be all secure, and belong to her, and she would never have to move again. It would sit on a big piece of land and she would have a garden with all the flowers she loved. Roses . . . yes, she would have roses. And pansies, as she vaguely remembered them, and lilacs. And forget-me-nots of pale blue and gold.

She would have a grand garden, and people would walk in it and on the green grass, and admire it. And she would have a little stream running through it, like the Blue River. And she and Rex would play in the garden.

The land would be hers, and she would belong to the land. It would be her house, and she would have friends to come and dine. She dreamed on, smiling, sewing and not seeing what she sewed.

From her windows she would be able to see out over the lakes and rivers to the snowcapped mountains. She would see the glacier too. Or if it was too far away to see, she would own a beautiful white sailboat and she would go sailing to the glacier and admire it. Yes, she would do that.

She could travel all over Alaska and see everything, all the wonders she had heard about. The volcanoes with their steam, the great ice bay of glaciers, the places where the whales were, and the brown seals, and the puffins, and the Eskimos.

She loved the land, and she would always belong here, and she would be always secure. That was her dream during the long winter nights, by the fire.

Chapter 5
1902

Laurel had spent the day with Jade. Now it's time to go home, she thought, glancing at the sky. The dusk still came early. She strapped on her snowshoes, and Jade came outdoors with her from the small smoky cabin.

'You come tomorrow,' urged Jade.

'Not tomorrow. I must do laundry.'

'Next day, then.'

'I'll see.'

'Or I will come over,' Jade added cheerfully. The days were flexible. They could do what they wanted, so long as the chores were accomplished.

'Fine. I will see you!'

The Nolans waved from the doorstep, and Laurel set off, Rex bounding by her side. The snow was hard and crusty, and she walked easily on it. In a few weeks it would get mushy and begin to melt; now it was like walking on gravel. Except that sometimes she would sink down, and Rex would bounce back and bark at her, reprovingly, as she foundered out of the snowbank.

It was some distance, but she made good time. The sun was just sinking toward the horizon and beginning to glow red on the snow as the cabin came in sight beyond a low clump of trees. Then she saw the figure in the distance, a bulky dark figure on snowshoes, hunched down as he walked along, away from her. She frowned slightly. Had a gold prospector gotten lost and stopped to ask the way? They had not had many visitors since the first snows had fallen.

The figure was outlined now in red against the snow and the setting sun, and it seemed aflame, almost eerie. She shrugged off the notion. The gold talk had made her jittery.

Rex growled in his throat as they approached the cabin. He drew closer to her protectively and slid against her skirts and feet.

'What is it, Rex?' she asked. He growled, low and long.

The cabin door hung open, not closed against the cold. And there across the threshold lay the body of a man. 'Ohhh no-o-o,' she cried in a hushed tone.

She gave one last look toward the distant figure disappearing now toward the river. It was hunched against the cold, and the legs moved on the snowshoes heavily, pushing. It moved oddly, lurching along in a distinct motion she would not forget.

Rex began to run away from the cabin, bounding through the snow. She called him sharply. 'Rex! Come back! Rex, come back here!'

He paused, reluctantly, and then obeyed, growling and snarling. His head kept turning toward that distant figure, which had now almost disappeared.

Laurel felt sick inside as she bent slowly to the figure. 'Dad?' she whispered. The figure did not move.

She knelt in the snow and touched his face. It was covered with blood. She touched his temple; the pulse did not move. His throat – there was no pulse. He was covered with blood, from his hair to his throat. His jacket was torn from his body and lay in the dirt. He must have put up a terrible fight, she thought with part of her mind.

She made herself put her hand inside his thick shirt, the red-check shirt she had made for him. She held her hand to his chest. There was no movement of breath or heart. He was dead.

'Oh . . . Dad –' she muttered. She could not cry out; she was too shocked. She was cold, shivering.

Rex whined beside her, looking at her anxiously, then at the figure.

Laurel got up and bent to wipe her hands in the snow; the sticky blood was drying on them. She licked her dry lips, glancing toward the north. The figure was gone. Would it return?

She pulled down her parka hood and clicked her fingers at the dog. He came with her obediently. Wearily she set out for the long journey to the Nolans.

It was dark when she arrived. The cabin was shut tight. She called to them and the door opened, sending a stream of dim light onto the snow.

'Laurel?' It was Tom Nolan, helping her inside. 'What is the trouble? You come back?'

'Father . . . he's . . . dead . . . killed . . .' She was shuddering . . . great long shivers of exhaustion and stress.

He caught his breath in a deep gasp. He brought her in and shut the door. Rex huddled close beside her.

'Tell me,' he said. Miriam came to her and drew her to the fire. 'Jim . . . is . . . dead?'

She nodded. 'I saw a man going away . . . toward the river. . . . Dad must've struggled. . . . blood all over him. . . . I felt his pulse and heart. No movement . . .' She caught her lower lip in her teeth to still the trembling.

'It is the gold,' Miriam said heavily, her dark face somber.

Jade came to Laurel, took her in her arms and hugged her. Silently, sympathizing, holding her close.

'I must go there,' said Tom Nolan. 'There are animals always about.'

Laurel nodded her head, sickened. The body could not remain there overnight.

'We will all come and remain together,' Miriam said decisively. Unspoken was the thought that the murderer might return. 'Then you will come and live with us.'

Laurel had not thought that far ahead. No, she could not live in the cabin alone. What would become of her? She thought of her fine dreams, her plans, her father's plans. All for naught. The blows of a murderer had struck at her future, and it was smashed to pieces.

Dad, Dad, she wept inside. She could not cry aloud. Not yet; she was too shocked and frozen.

They traveled in the dark, Tom carrying a torch to light their way. It was a silent grim procession. Laurel walked with Jade, Miriam behind them. Rex trotted alongside Laurel, as silent as they were.

At the cabin Tom knelt beside his friend to check for any sign of life. When he had convinced himself that Jim was gone, Tom carried his body inside. The cabin was in a mess. The chairs and stools had been flung about, evidently in the midst of a fight. Boxes had been opened and strewn around. Laurel searched the shelves for the cigar box of nuggets and gold dust; it lay on the floor now empty.

'He took the gold,' she announced.

Miriam muttered to herself. 'It is evil, evil.'

'The gold isn't evil,' Laurel said bitterly. 'It's men!'

Miriam and Tom tenderly washed Jim's face and head and removed the rags of his coat and shirt. 'In the morning I will dig a grave beside his woman,' Tom said.

The ground will be frozen hard; it will be too difficult, thought Laurel. She could not look at her father's body lying near the fireplace. Then, once she had looked, she could not look away.

They lay down and slept, somehow, that night. In the morning they got up and did what had to be done. Tom dug, and Laurel helped, then Miriam and Jade, then Tom again, until the frozen earth had been tossed aside and the hole was deep enough. They wrapped the body in a blanket and carefully set it into its grave. There were no flowers to add. Laurel said the prayers from their thin New Testament, and Tom tossed the earth back on the stiffened body.

'I will make a nice stake for the head,' said Tom. 'Like the one I made for his woman. I have a piece of cedar for it.'

'Thank you, Tom.' Laurel said.

Miriam turned away heavily from the grave. 'We will pack up what you want, Laurel, and you will come with us. It is not good to remain here.'

It took several trips to bring the supplies from that cabin back to Tom Nolan's. Tom brought his sled the second trip, and that made it easier to bring the jars of blueberries, the dried meats, the sacks of flour and sugar, the jars of sourdough starter and spices. Then they took the stools, the chairs, the crude table Jim had made, Laurel's sketches, and Jim's artwork, the few books.

By evening Laurel was settled in her new home. Her bunk was next to Jade's, and it was a tight squeeze, but they were used to that. The Nolan cabin was about the same size as hers, and all their supplies were kept in the same places, so it was not difficult to become accustomed to living there.

They were kind to her. She knew them, and they knew her. But it was not like living with her father, and this could only be temporary.

'I must plan what to do in the summer,' Laurel said after the first shock had died.

Tom brooded at the fire, his pipe in his mouth. 'What do you wish to do? Where do you want to go?'

'Go? I don't want to go anywhere. But I would like to file the claim on the gold,' she said. 'I have to have money to live on.'

Miriam frowned. 'The gold is evil,' she said again.

'Gold is not evil,' repeated Laurel patiently. 'And it buys much in the white men's stores. If I can work the claim, I can have enough money to buy food and clothes, and more tools.'

They were silent, thinking about that.

'Jim wanted you to go outside, go to school,' Tom said finally, knocking out his pipe against the side of the stone fireplace. 'Maybe you should go to Boston.'

'That takes lots of money,' said Laurel. 'We don't have money.'

Silence again. She fingered the gold-nugget necklace, which was all she had left. Maybe she could sell that. What would it bring? But somehow she could not think of that, not now. Her father had made it for her. He had wanted her to have the necklace of the first gold he had found. If he had not found gold would he be alive now? she wondered. She thought so.

For the first time, she began to think clearly. Who had done this horrible deed? A passing prospector who had seen the gold pokes? On impulse, wanting the gold? She could not believe it. The prospectors she had met were of all ages, and eager, with sparkling eyes, to find their own claims. They wanted adventure, the thrill of finding gold in the earth.

Then she saw it again, so clearly, as the artist saw details, was trained to see details. The hunched figure walking awkwardly, lurching on the snowshoes, the figure in red against the snow. The black, dark figure against the red of the setting sun. She shut her eyes, could see it all: the tiny figure of black, outlined in red, against the white snow and the setting sun. She would never forget that.

Who had he been? A passing man, never to be seen again? Someone who had wandered by?

It was very strange. The prospectors had all gone by, had asked the way, waved, and gone on, their faces eagerly turned to the North, to the pots at the end of the Alaska rainbow. They wanted adventure, the thrill of making their own discoveries.

'They love the hunt, honey,' Jim had told Laurel several times. 'They love the searching. When they do find gold, they whoop it up in the saloons, spend it all, get drunk, recover, and go back to hunt again. Few men hunt gold for the sake of going into business or using the money for some purpose. It's the search that draws them.'

She had listened, wondering. If she found gold, it was for the sake of having her piece of Alaska, her house with the porches, her settled future and security in a place of her own.

One day she would have her own house, a big one with many rooms. She would marry a fine young man, and somehow the dream man had a thatch of dark gold hair and brilliant green eyes, wide shoulders and a slow understanding smile.

They would marry, and she would have several babies, and hug them and love them, and never be alone again. She would keep a fine house for them all, and cook and sew and work hard for her family. And they would all be so happy, they would laugh and sing.

And she would walk in the wilderness and see the huge icy glaciers, and the snowcapped mountains and the proud moose on the hillsides. The rivers would flow blue-white with the milky glacier melts. The flowers would bloom in the spring and summer, and in the autumn the tundra would be scarlet and gold. It would be a wild place, with silent star-filled nights and skies with green trembling lights. Her land, her Alaska. It would be her home, forever. Never tamed, always fierce and free.

She came back from her dreams, to find Miriam studying her with worried black eyes. And she realized that to them she would be an additional burden. She must find her own way, figure out how to make her own living.

'I must earn some money,' she said. 'I must make my own way. Tom, will you show me how to file on the claim?'

His blunt uncomplicated face showed worry. He stared at the fire, then at his hands, ruminating.

'You are a girl,' he said finally. 'How can you file on the claim? How can you work the claim? Men take it from you. It is bad.'

Yes, she was but fourteen and only a girl. Laurel sighed deeply. 'But I could file on the claim, and I could try to work it,' she insisted. 'Dad said it looked rich, that there's a vein back deep into the mountain. He found some good nuggets . . .' She touched her nugget necklace.

'I would help you, as I would help your father,' Tom said slowly. 'Let me think about it for a time. When the ice goes, maybe we will know then.'

That was all Tom would say for now. She had to be content with that. But knowing his superstitious fears of the gold, she worried that he would not want to have anything to do with it. And she thought herself that the gold had brought evil. It had probably brought her father's death.

But how had anyone known that he had found gold? Had it been an accident, that someone murderous had come along, had searched the cabin for something, had found the pokes?

If a prospector had been searching around, and had seen Jim up at the rocker in the hills, had watched him sluicing for the gold, or digging with the pick, then the fight might have taken place up there. Or the prospector might have stolen back secretly to work the mine at night.

Yet the fight had taken place at the cabin. Jim had fought the man and been murdered on his own doorstep.

The first shock was beginning to wear off. Laurel would awaken in the night, not in her own cabin. She did not hear the steady even breathing of her father in the bunk across from hers.

Jade would be in her bunk next to Laurel. Across from her was the double bed with Miriam and Tom. The cabin smelled of herbs and smoke and grease from the skins Miriam worked.

Laurel would lie awake for a time, desolation rolling over her. Never again on this earth would she talk to her father, work with him, see him study her sketches and point out places to improve. Never again would they talk of the past or the future. And she was alone in the world, with nobody she knew to belong to.

She could not stay here forever. Tom Nolan and Miriam were good to her. They would not throw her out, but all must change. Jade would marry. . . . And what would become of Laurel?

So many troubles had descended on her shoulders. The future

loomed as something ominous and worrisome. How could she earn her own way? What would become of her? What should she do about the claim? Try to file on it? Worry about being killed for it?

Sometimes she would be sketching a scene from the doorstep of the Nolan cabin, and a wave of grief would wash over her. She had been thinking, she must show this to her father and get his advice on how to get that angle right. And then she would remember, all over again, she could not show it to him . . . he was gone. Never again could she turn to him.

She would not hear his voice, slow and methodical. She would not see his slow shy smile. She would not look up and see him working across the table from her, his hand moving in its slow sure way to draw what his mind had pictured.

Her mother was dead, so early, and Laurel missed her more than ever. Now her father was dead also, and youth had flown with him. How could she ever be young again, when life made its harsh demands on her. Father and mother both gone, and she was alone in the world.

She grieved for them, and for herself, in panic and desperation at times. She felt so alone.

March 1902

It was March, and the weeks were going by. The snows melted by the streams first; then the ice in the rivers of the hills melted. Snowshoes sank through the crust, and it was hard going when Jade and Laurel went out to shoot rabbits.

Jade and Laurel went twice to the stream in the hills, where Jim had prospected. The stakes were still there, falling over a little, and Laurel pounded them harder into the ground. They had Jim's name on them, 'J. Winfield,' and the date, and the approximate location. Someday I will file, she thought. She must file, her father had died for that gold; it belonged to them. And one day it would pay for a piece of Alaska land. She must own her bit of Alaska, so she would belong somewhere.

Rex was a comfort. When she sat on a log and sketched, or sat silent, the pencil still in her hand, he would come up and nuzzle and sniff at her, and encourage her to come and play. Or he would sit on his haunches next to her in the cabin and look up in her face, as though he could read her and understand her. She would put her hand on his head and rub his throat, and he would rumble a soft song for her. He missed Jim too. She knew that, when he would look around, then race to the old empty cabin only to come up short, and sniff around.

Laurel went into the old cabin a couple times, unbolting the latch that kept out the animals. She stepped inside, and heard the emptiness, and saw the blankness, and it was painful. Half the furniture had been moved out. The sketching blocks were gone, and Jim's easel. No coats hung on the pegs, no dresses or coats. There was no fire in the stone fireplace, no pots and pans of water, or steaming soup. She kept it straightened up, and the mice out, and swept over the floor with a broom. No dust gathered; there was little dust in Alaska.

Then she went out and latched the door again. Rex would whine and nuzzle her hand, as though to say, 'It's all right. I'm here.'

'Yes, Rex, let's run awhile,' she said, and they raced across the snows, she in her boots, and he with legs lifting high in the slushy snow. Their shadows were cast long across the snow, and in the sky the first few birds were returning, calling and circling over the spruce and cedar.

Spring would come before long.

Chapter 6

Thor Koenig had been feeling uneasy all winter, whenever he thought of Laurel Winfield and her father. Those two alone in the wilderness, with only Indians nearby, vulnerable. Jim was a smart man in some ways, but naive in others, too trusting. And Laurel was only a child.

He waited impatiently for breakup in the spring. When he saw the ice in the rivers and streams begin to break and the snows to melt, he went to his father.

He found him in the office of the mining company, in town. He went in and shut the door. His father looked up, his heavy, shaggy head alert.

'Ah, Thor. I was thinking about you. About this summer –'

'Not now, Dad. I must talk to you about something else.' He sat down in the chair opposite. Olaf looked at him keenly.

'Go ahead.'

'I'm worried about Jim Winfield and his daughter. I want to bring them back here.'

'It'll take about a month . . . but all right.'

Thor smiled. He and his father were much alike in their mental processes. 'No questions?'

Olaf shook his head. 'No. You just figure out how to persuade them to come,' he said, and a grin curled his big mouth. 'Jim's stubborn.'

'We'll have to figure out a job for Jim, one that he won't figure is charity.'

'He does good carpentry work. We can start there.'

'Okay,' said Thor, standing. 'I'd like to get started. May I borrow Fred and Joe?'

'Sure. And take the larger sailboat. You may want to bring back their gear. Thor?'

'Yes, Dad.'

'Do a good job of persuading them, son,' Olaf said seriously. 'That's too fine a girl to stay in the wilderness, with gold hunters all around. She's getting too pretty; it could be dangerous for her. Bring *her* back at least.'

'Right, Dad. About the copper mine in the North –'

'I'll send Ewan, get him out of my hair for the summer,' and Olaf grimaced. Ewan played around too much for their liking. 'He'll do a good job if there aren't too many distractions.'

'Fine.'

Thor saluted his father and went out, relieved that he could get on his way. He packed up and left early the next morning.

Within little over a week he and the Indians were tacking in to the small harbor where they had stayed before. He told them to stay with the boat, just do some fishing nearby; he did not know when he would return. He strapped on snowshoes, put his pack on his back, and started out, rifle in hand.

The snows of early April were melting fast, and that made hard going with the snowshoes. But he made it to the Winfield cabin by early afternoon. He frowned as he approached. No smoke from the chimney, and no sight of figures playing about. He had thought to see Laurel and Jade, with the dog Rex.

No barks in the air, no shouts of welcome. He came up to the cabin and knocked hard at the door. No answer. Then he saw that the door was bolted from the outside, and he lifted it and went inside.

He stopped short, shocked. The cabin was almost empty. Only a bunk was left, and the fireplace and shelves. The books were gone and the clothes from the pegs.

'God!' he muttered. Where had Laurel and Jim gone? Had they gone to Wrangell? He went outside, bolted the door again, and walked behind the cabin. Then he noticed the small fence and the two graves.

Blood thundered in his head, and he felt dizzy as he forced himself over to the graves. He bent over. The nearest one was of

MADELINE R. WINFIELD. The next one – he moved to that. A new headstone of wood and neatly carved letters: JAMES WINFIELD, DIED FEBRUARY 1902.

He straightened up, his mouth tight. Jim . . . Jim had died. How? Fever, probably. Poor poor Laurel, to face that alone. But where was she? She must have gone to the Nolans, unless she had somehow gotten to Wrangell.

He would try the Nolans first. Surely they would know what had happened. He left the cabin and headed toward the Nolans, three miles or so from there.

As he approached the cabin, Rex started barking and raced toward him. Thor felt immense relief, especially when he saw the two figures in parkas walking in his direction. He waved; they waved back.

He came up to them and grinned. They smiled back, but Laurel's face was white and strained, and he saw the blue shadows under her eyes. They did not try to speak outdoors, the wind was too keen.

He went into the small smoky cabin with them. Miriam was scraping furs at the table, and she gave him a big grin of welcome. Tom was not there.

'Tom?' he asked at once.

'Out hunting,' Laurel said. 'Please sit down. You are most welcome.'

He sat down on the three-legged stool and pushed back his parka. The room was warm and stifling in its smoke. It was either not so well made as the Winfield cabin or more crowded with people and furs.

They were silent, waiting for him to speak, to tell his news of the outside world. Miriam scraped busily with the flat-bladed knife to remove the last flesh from the fur.

'How did it happen?' he asked Laurel gently.

Her dark eyelashes flickered. 'He was murdered,' she said quietly.

He caught his breath. 'Murdered? You saw it?' What a horrible thing for her. He wondered at her composure, thought it was hard won.

She might live in the wilderness, but she was not a tough, hard-boiled woman. She was a girl, gently raised, for all her surroundings.

'I saw the man going away,' she said slowly. 'I was returning from Jade's cabin with Rex. We came to the cabin . . . saw the man going away on his snowshoes . . .' She told him carefully what she had seen, how the man looked, how Jim was. Her voice did not break, but there was tragedy in her face.

Thor listened quietly, his gaze on her. Poor poor child, to go through this. She had adored her father. They were much alike – sensitive, artistic, gentle people.

'And the man did not come back?'

'No, at least we have not seen him.'

She cannot remain here, he decided while he listened to her. More than ever, she must be taken from here. He waited until Tom came back, and he saw the relief in the Indian's stoic face. The man knew also, he could not take care of a white girl in this wilderness.

After their dinner of stew and sourdough bread, Thor announced, 'I'll take Laurel back to Sitka with me. Father and my stepmother will welcome her.' He had his doubts about his stepmother, but that could wait. 'She will live with my family until we decide what is to be done.'

'She has family in Boston,' Tom said quickly. 'Laurel is not alone in the world.'

Family is important to Tom, thought Thor. Family could take her in, family had duty. Well, maybe.

'Do you have letters from them?' Thor asked of Laurel.

She nodded, to his relief. 'I have a box of letters my father kept.'

'Well, we'll pack up everything you want to bring with you. Remember, you can buy more clothes in Sitka. Why don't you leave some of your things for Jade, you are the same size.'

'Yes, I'll do that.' Laurel seemed more cheerful, especially at the idea that she could give gifts. 'And Miriam, you'll have use for the pans and such.'

They went to bed, but Thor lay awake for a time, planning. Laurel should have an education, and he had a feeling she would

61

want to remain in Alaska. Well, they would see how matters worked out.

The next day they began to sort out Laurel's possessions. She found an opportunity to speak to Thor.

'You're not obligated to take care of me,' she said anxiously. 'I don't know what your family will say.'

'Father is anxious about you,' he said. 'He wanted me to see if you would return with me, you and your father. He had a job ready for your father. I'm sorry we didn't bring you back with us last summer.'

Her face shadowed, and she looked away toward the hills to regain her composure. 'He wouldn't have left. He loved the silence and the peace here.'

'Yes, but it's no life for a girl,' he told her bluntly.

'But I love it,' she said simply. 'The wilderness has been my home most of my life. It will be hard to live in a city. But I'm not ungrateful, and I wish to earn my living. What can I do for you and your family? Cook and clean?'

He smiled, slowly, his big broad smile. 'No, Laurel, you'll be our guest. I want you to relax and enjoy life. You'll go to school or have a governess to teach you as your father wished.'

'But I won't earn my way in that manner!' exclaimed Laurel, shaking her dark head, which caused her braid to flop down her back. She brushed it back impatiently. 'I must work, Thor!'

'Later on, when you're grown up.' He was definite about that.

'Maybe I can help your stepmother in the house.'

Thor thought of his mother's precision, her impatience with the maids, her anger when something went wrong. 'No, Laurel, I don't want that,' he said firmly. 'I want you to be our guest, to enjoy yourself. Don't worry about working now. You've worked hard all your life. Just relax and enjoy yourself, and do some painting. That should occupy you, and you may be able to sell your sketches,' he added with inspiration.

She looked dubious but was too polite to argue longer.

'Thank you. I'll find a way to repay you,' she said primly, seriously.

'Of course,' he said, patting her arm. 'Now, what more do you want to take with you?'

She has such a pitiful amount of goods, he thought. She left most of her clothes for Jade, on his suggestion. She would need all new clothes, hers were so worn, and his stepmother would be horrified if Laurel wore such garments in her home. She took a box of papers and Jim's sketches, and her notebooks. She left behind most of the books, taking only the Bible and the thin Testament and one history book she was fond of. The rest were left for Jade.

'What about Rex?' she asked wistfully, patting the dog's head, and it looked up intelligently, with its slanted eyes.

'He's your dog, so of course he must come,' Thor said. 'He won't be welcome inside the house, but we have a large kennel, and there shall be a place for him. I think he guards you well.'

Laurel looked immensely relieved. 'Thank you,' she said, as gratefully as for herself.

There was no more reason to remain. Laurel was packed, and Thor was impatient to be on his way. Early the next morning Laurel said her farewells and they started out. She found tears choking her throat as she hugged and kissed them all, Tom, Miriam, Jade, her dear friends and protectors.

'I don't know when I'll see you again,' she said, her voice closing up.

'When the gods will it,' said Miriam placidly. 'Be good, and work hard,' she added, folding her worn brown hands.

Jade's face crinkled up, but she suppressed tears, her mouth working a little as she began to wave. Laurel turned back again and again, waving, until the three figures were dim in the distance. Rex bounded alongside her, and Thor plowed his way before her. She was not alone, yet she felt as though she were leaving home to go to some distant unknown.

They came to her cabin, all closed up and desolate. Thor waited beside her as she said a last farewell to the graves of her parents. He did not say comforting things; he did not say he would bring her back. His face was solemn, and his eyes were icy green as he stared down at the long mounds and the wooden headpieces.

Then they went on, silently, to where the sailing vessel waited. The two Indians greeted them, and put her gear on board. There were two cabins, and a tiny bathroom, where she could wash in a pitcher of water. And there was a little kitchen, with a wee stove and kettle of hot water. She wandered about, learning her way, and came up on deck.

'We'll set sail early tomorrow,' said Thor. 'Looks like the weather will be good. That's hopeful,' he said, pointing to the sky. It looked clear, and the sun was reddish.

'Yes, we have had much snow and rain already,' Laurel said in a subdued voice.

Thor put his big arm about her, and hugged her shoulders, unexpectedly. 'Don't feel lost, Laurel,' he said gently. 'You're going to be fine. It will be strange for the first few days, but then you'll settle in.'

'Thank you,' she said. She felt warm and comforted when his arm was about her; when he took it away, she felt cold again.

It was odd, being on a sailing ship much of the time. She did not sleep well the first night. The ship kept rocking back and forth, though they had pulled up in a small harbor. Early next morning the ship set out for Sitka.

Thor pointed out things on the way, the small islands, the stands of Sitka spruce, a bear and its cubs paddling in the waters trying to catch fish. He was a good companion . . . at times silent, then talking to her, then silent again, standing next to her and leaning on the railing.

He did not try to jolly her up or make her forget her loss of her father. He was just there, calm, interested, willing to talk or be quiet as they chose. He's ten years older, much more mature than I, Laurel decided. He wore well and was as nice as she had remembered from last summer.

He talked a little about his work. He helped his father in the silver mine near Sitka, and they were exploring to find other mines, such as a copper one in the North. Ewan was up north this summer, he had said, and she was relieved that she would not have to meet Ewan just now; he disturbed her.

She worried a little about Thor's haughty stepmother, but maybe the woman was kinder than she had appeared at first. She quite evidently did not like the outdoor life, and she may have been uncomfortable at the cabin and the tundra.

Thor let Laurel help with the fishing. They caught some fine trout and salmon, and she helped cook it at the tiny stove if it was raining. If the weather was fine, they drew up at a harbor toward evening, and the Indians would start a fire. They would have fish, and she would make sourdough biscuits, and Thor would take out jars of cranberries or blueberries to add to the biscuits. Nothing tastes as good as the hot food on a cool evening as they sat beneath boughs of fragrant Sitka spruce, looking out over blue-purple waters while the sun slowly set.

Sometimes the Indians slept on the bank, but Thor always insisted that Laurel sleep in her bunk. She felt cozy and warm there, and protected. She would not have minded sleeping in the open, curled up in a blanket.

Sometimes she felt that Thor was overprotective toward her. Her father had not fussed when she got her hair wet, or got chilled in the evening. But Thor would scold her, make her go inside the cabin and rub her hair dry. Sometimes he would put a blanket around her and tell her to be careful.

'I'm fine,' she protested one evening. She looked at him with a small smile on her lips. 'You're not used to being a father, that's your trouble!' she said.

'What are you talking about?' he snapped, and his green eyes blazed fire at her.

She shrank. 'I just meant – I mean even my father didn't act this way,' she protested. 'He trusted me to take care of myself!'

His lips compressed, his eyes still glazed. 'I'm not your father,' he said shortly, and turned and left her. She gazed after him in bewilderment. Why was he so angry? Did he resent having to look after her?

But she could take care of herself, and she vowed to be more independent and not worry him. She would not be a burden to anybody; she refused to be that. Maybe she could find a job in Sitka.

She would be fifteen this month, in a few days, on April 10. Timidly she asked Thor what day it was.

'Gosh, I don't know,' he said naturally. 'About April five or ten or fifteen, I suppose.'

'Oh. Well, then I am fifteen,' she said. 'I could get a job in Sitka, maybe in the cannery, couldn't I?'

'No, you cannot,' he said bluntly. 'When are you fifteen?'

'On April 10, but I wasn't hinting,' she added quickly.

He grinned, and ruffled her hair, once more acting as though she were a child under his care. 'Well, we'll have a party for you and get you some presents to make your eyes shine,' he teased.

Laurel was almost sorry when they came into Sitka harbor. She watched with wide curious eyes as the ship was tacked in and the sails lowered. Willing hands at the dock helped tie up the sailing vessel.

She saw more buildings and people than she had seen in years, since she had gone to Alaska. Children ran along the docks, calling to each other. Rex was out of his mind with excitement, his dignity ruffled at being carried to shore.

The Indians, Fred and Joe, carried their gear up to the house. She and Thor walked along with Rex. She was trying to take in everything at once, her head swiveling from side to side. There was the Russian Church, St. Michael's, from the days of the Russian occupation and building of Sitka as a fur-trading post. There were the old cannery buildings, and the trading post buildings with their tall wooden posts.

And the houses! She gasped at seeing houses two, even three stories high. Some had porches in the front; one even had porches on three sides of the house. And there were stores, and lamp posts, and plank sidewalks to keep one out of the mud. Most of the buildings were of logs and planks, but a few were of sun-dried brick.

Thor turned and led her up a side street, a rather steep ascent out of the muddy main streets. There was a large house alone at the top of the street, a large, rambling two-storey house of white painted logs, with a huge front porch.

It was surrounded by flower gardens, just beginning to bloom after the long winter. There were bushes and vines, and a summer house in the side garden, and kennels in the back, and a large stable with horses and carriages. It was the biggest, finest house she had ever seen.

'Yours?' she gasped to Thor.

The Indians were dumping the gear on the porch. A woman stood in the doorway, a tall slim fashionably clad woman. Sidonie Koenig, she saw.

'My father's house,' he said briefly, and Laurel began to understand that he did not feel really at home there, but he smiled and led her forward.

The woman watched them come, a thin smile on her lips.

'Here you are at last. Your father has been watching for you,' she said politely. 'And here is little Laurel.'

Laurel was almost as tall as the woman, but she accepted that, with her schoolgirl braid down her back and her awkwardness. She shook hands politely and was shown inside the beautiful hallway, with its polished wood and wall rack for coats, and a bench for blankets.

'Clarissa Leverett has missed you sadly, Thor,' said Mrs. Koenig, smiling at Thor. 'I never see her but what she asks when you'll return. You didn't tell her you were going away!'

'You might ask her and her father over for dinner, to meet Laurel,' Thor said politely.

'Oh, I will; perhaps tomorrow night, if that's convenient. Come this way, my dear. I'll show you to your room. It is our best guest room. Your father insisted,' she said over her shoulder to Thor.

Laurel did not know how to take that. Did his father insist against Sidonie Koenig's wishes? Or was she showing Laurel she was very welcome?

'You are most kind,' she murmured, following her hostess up the steps. Thor came after them, carrying Laurel's first box of papers.

They came to the upstairs hallway, also polished and shining. Mrs. Koenig led the way along the hall to the back and right side. She opened a door, looked about sharply, as though to find fault. She indicated that Laurel should come in.

Laurel found herself in a large room with a huge four poster bed, darkly polished. The white counterpane was of chenille, very neat and clean. The room seemed huge, with a large, tall wardrobe for her clothes, a table with a lamp of roses flowered on glass, a pitcher and basin of porcelain. The windows were at the back of the house, overlooking the kennels, reminding her of Rex.

'Oh . . . Rex, my dog!' she said quickly, turning around.

Sidonie frowned. Thor said, 'Joe took him around to the kennels. Don't worry, he'll be well looked after. You can see him presently, and he'll want walks daily. I think he'll be good protection for you in Sitka.'

'Now why would a child need protection in Sitka?' Sidonie asked in exasperation, her thin lips twisted. 'I'm sure Laurel will do very well.'

'She's getting to be a young lady, and there are always drunks around,' said Thor, not smiling. 'I don't want her going out alone, without the dog. I'll set this box here, Laurel. We'll be bringing up your other gear in a minute.'

'Thank you, Thor.' She felt awkward being alone with Sidonie. The woman hesitated, then turned about to leave the room.

'I hope you'll be comfortable,' she said stiffly.

'Thank you, ma'am.'

Laurel drew a long breath when she was at last alone. She heard the voices of the Indians as they worked outside with the dogs. She pulled back the lace curtain, marveling at its whiteness and beauty. She looked out at the kennels, making out Rex being put into a kennel of his own, separated with wire fencing from the other dogs. Oh, how he would hate not running free. She must take him out often. It would be strange, living in a city.

After Thor brought her other gear, she hung up her few dresses, her long blue skirt and blouses. For dinner she put on her one good dress that she had made recently, of blue-check cotton. Over it she hung her nugget necklace; it was her only piece of jewelry.

Thor noticed it at once; so did his stepmother.

'My word,' said Sidonie Koenig. 'What a barbaric piece of jewelry. Did the Indians make it for you?'

Laurel flinched. 'No, my father made it, out of the first nuggets he mined from the claim.' Her hand went to the chain protectively. She had thought it so beautiful.

Thor said, oddly, 'From the claim? He found gold?'

Olaf was looking at her also. The maid had left the room to get the next course after the soup. She felt odd at the long rosewood table, with the white linen and gold-rimmed china. It was all so grand, with the oil lamp in the center of the table.

'Yes, last winter. These nuggets were the best. But he found more and put up stakes. He was going to file in the spring.'

Her voice choked. Sidonie frowned. 'Well, I suppose you can sell the gold and have something to live on,' she said practically.

68

'I don't want to sell it, not this one,' Laurel said. 'Father made it himself.'

'No, you must always keep it,' Olaf Koenig said. 'It is a fine memento of your father's work. By the way, my dear, did you bring some of your father's paintings and sketches? I should like to see them. We must get them framed.'

Sidonie looked cold and disapproving; it was her usual expression so far as Laurel was concerned, as Laurel discovered in the next weeks.

After dinner Sidonie left them to see to some household matter. Thor said quietly to Laurel, 'Where did your father find gold, Laurel? Up where he was working?'

'Further up in the hills,' she said. 'Up the stream. We could see for miles from the ledge. It was a sheer drop, and he dug back into the hills beside the stream. That's where he found the gold. He put in stakes and marked them.'

'But he didn't file the claim at Wrangell?'

'No, he was going to in the spring,' she said. 'When the ice broke up, and he could get out.'

'How much did he find?' asked Olaf. 'Did it look good?'

'He had five pokes and some smaller nuggets,' she said, her hand on the necklace. Olaf asked to see it. She took it off and handed it to him. Thor examined it also, but they said little.

'Well, keep it, child,' Olaf said, handing it back to her. 'It is a lovely piece of work, and it will grow more valuable with the years. Don't wear it on the streets, though; someone might be tempted to grab it from you.'

'Yes, I will be careful.' Laurel promised, then sighed, for now she was in civilization and there were other dangers about. She knew how to cope in the wilderness, among wild animals. But among men . . . it would be different. Yet, in the wilderness of Alaska there had been deadly danger as well, as her father had found.

'I suppose the murderer of your father took the other gold,' Thor said.

She nodded. 'All the pokes were gone. The necklace is all that's left, and that's because I was wearing it.'

Sidonie returned, and the maid followed with trays of coffee cups and a huge pot of coffee. They drank solemnly, and she enjoyed the strong coffee.

Sidonie was more animated and amusing when the men were there. When they were not, as Laurel found, she was cold and distant, and Laurel felt her disapproval.

That first week, Thor took Laurel out and helped her shop for clothes. She could not pay for anything, but he did not even tell her prices; he put it all on his account at the various stores.

She was soon supplied with more garments than she had thought existed in the world. Any day she wished she could wear a new blue full-length skirt, or a gray or a red one. And there were delicate cotton blouses trimmed in lace to go with them.

The store had lengths of silk and velvet, and Thor bought more than what was needed by her to make up five full dresses, with the help of a fashionable dressmaker of Sidonie's choosing. Sidonie reluctantly approved the fact that Laurel could sew well.

There were lengths of deep soft sapphire and silk of blue and shot silver. Thor picked out a rose moire silk with gold lines in it, and a white taffeta gown, already made up in what Laurel thought with pleasure was a most adult style.

He also bought her a beautiful gold locket on a gold chain . . . for her birthday, he had said when Sidonie protested his extravagance. 'You're spoiling the child,' Sidonie said coldly, but he only laughed and shook his head. He did not pay much attention to what his stepmother said, as Laurel had discovered. He went his own way.

Thor also bought her a fine cape of blue-and-red plaid wool, with a fur collar, and another coat of practical wool in a gray cloth. With boots and shoes, gloves and hats and scarves, he soon had her dressed up for Sitka.

Then he departed, suddenly, and without warning. He would be gone about three weeks, he explained and took off. Laurel felt desolate, and Sidonie was furious. 'I have asked people to dinner and dancing this Saturday!' she protested.

'We will all enjoy the occasion,' her husband said placidly, a gleam in his green eyes so like Thor's.

'But where did Thor go?' wailed Sidonie. 'And what will I tell

Clarissa? She was counting on Thor being here!'

'I sent him away on business,' Olaf said. 'He has much work to do and cannot be hanging on girls' coattails all the time!'

'But he adores Clarissa,' said Sidonie.

Laurel went back to the kennels and took Rex for a long walk in the hills, just the two of them. She too felt forlorn and deserted, but she had no right to. Thor was good to her, but he did not adore her.

Chapter 7

Laurel dressed early for the party Saturday evening. She was nervous, but the Indian girl who helped her praised her. 'You look much more beautiful than anybody else!' she said.

Laurel gazed at herself in the large mirror on her dresser, and hardly knew the girl who stared so seriously back at her. She wore the white taffeta gown; it had a demure heart-shaped neckline, and with it she wore the gold locket. She wished Thor could see her. The maid had dressed her dark curly hair high, and she looked almost grown up.

Her white slippers were the finest she had ever seen, and she wore stockings of such delicate silk she was afraid she would rip them. She looked like a lady. She wished her father could see her now.

She went downstairs, to see if she could help. But Sidonie frowned, and muttered something about how Laurel's dress was too adult.

'Nonsense,' said Olaf Koenig. 'She looks charming. And she is all of fifteen.'

She stayed close to Olaf that evening; he was so kind, and bluff and hearty. He introduced her to everyone, and saw to it that she met two prospectors and their wives. Two children came, about twelve; Sidonie said they were companions for Laurel.

Clarissa Leverett and her father came. He was dressed suavely in a black silk suit, with a white stock and a gold nugget chain for his huge turnip-shaped gold watch.

Clarissa was stunning in a violet gown which was so low cut that Laurel gazed at her in fascination. How did she keep the dress on her shoulders? The gown hung on her arms, showing the white sloping shoulders, and setting off the necklace of amethyst. She had a charming smile, which looked stiff when she discovered Thor and Ewan were not there.

'Neither of them?' she asked blankly.

'The naughty boys,' Sidonie said smilingly, as though they were children. 'They say it's business, but I shall scold them! I particularly wanted Thor to see you in that adorable gown!'

Clarissa preened, and some men complimented her on the gown and the high feathered headdress of gray. She was seated near the head of the table. Laurel was put at a side table with the two smaller children, a boy and a girl, who fussed at each other in low tones.

After an elaborate dinner of Russian caviar, salmon, bear steaks, and a huge cream cake, Sidonie led the way to the formal parlor. The rugs had been rolled back, and an ensemble of piano, violin, and flute played for dancing.

Laurel stood awkwardly in the doorway, uncertain whether to join the children or the adults. Sidonie came over to her.

'It's almost nine o'clock, child, you had best go to bed,' she said curtly.

Laurel stared at her, wide-eyed. 'To bed, ma'am?' she gasped. Nothing had been said about her retiring early. 'I'm not ill!'

The thin mouth compressed in a red line. 'Children go to bed early, and I will not have you contradicting me!'

Laurel stiffened; people were staring at them. 'Yes, ma'am,' she said in a low tone, her cheeks flushed with embarrassment. 'I'll just say good night –'

'No need,' said Sidonie hastily, but Laurel was already making her way to Olaf Koenig.

'Mr. Koenig? I'll just say good night, sir,' she said and held out her hand politely. 'Thank you for the lovely evening.'

'Good night?' He looked surprised, taking the cigar from his mouth. His green eyes narrowed as he looked over toward his wife. 'No, no, the evening is young! My dear, dance with me. I claim the first dance!'

And he laid aside his cigar and insisted on moving her around the room to the music. Then he turned her over to the next man he met. Sidonie looked enraged but could say nothing. Olaf politely foiled her at every turn. Laurel did not retire until the last guests had left.

This was the first prick, but not the last one, that Sidonie administered to her young guest. Laurel asked to help in the house. Sidonie said she could help with the dishes, but not the cooking. 'I will not have the chef upset,' she said.

Olaf found out and put a stop to it. 'No! She's our guest,' he said to them both sternly. 'Laurel, I want you to enjoy yourself until school starts next autumn. Why don't you paint or go to visit your friends?'

She spent many a day painting or drawing in her room. Olaf had given her permission to borrow any of the books in his study, and she kept herself supplied from among these riches. She would choose a few new books while he was away at his office, so she would not disturb him. Then she would remain in her room reading.

She walked with Rex at least once a day, fine weather or rain. He was as confined as she was and welcomed the long walks around Sitka, studying the store windows or roaming the docks and watching the ships unload their ketch. With Rex at her side, Laurel did not fear any of the rough men, no matter how they looked at her. Rex was too large and ferocious in appearance for them to bother her. Most of them were kind, but there were always a few exceptions, and some drunks also.

The maid came for her one afternoon as she was sketching. 'Madame wants you to come down for tea in the parlor,' she said.

'Like this?' asked Laurel dubiously, pointing to her navy skirt and white blouse.

'Think maybe you dress up,' grinned the friendly maid. Natasha had been with the Koenigs many years, she said, and she was now a quiet friend of Laurel. Her wise dark eyes saw much that went on.

Natasha pulled out a blue silk with a pretty lace collar, and Laurel hastily donned it. Natasha brushed out her hair and tied a blue silk ribbon around the thick mass to hold it back neatly.

When Laurel went downstairs, the tea party was in progress. She hesitated in the doorway.

'This is our young friend, Laurel Winfield,' Sidonie introduced her in a rather patronizing tone. 'She's staying with us for a time.'

She shook hands with several guests, nodded and smiled to others, and seated herself on the edge of a straight chair.

'Your tea, Laurel!' Sidonie reminded her in a strong whisper, and with an obvious frown.

Laurel got up, and went over to take her teacup and saucer.

'Laurel has been living in the wilderness in a log cabin,' said Sidonie. 'This is all so new to her!'

Clarissa laughed. She was sitting on the sofa near Sidonie, stunning in her violet satin gown. 'I should say it is! You should've seen that poor cabin! Like an Indian hut! And of course her only neighbors were dirty Indians!'

Laurel bit her lips, took a small cake, and went back to drink her tea in silence. One lady near her said, 'Was it terribly primitive? I refused to go with my husband up to the gold fields! I refused to live like a native!'

'It was comfortable,' Laurel said stiffly.

'Did you have to shoot your meat? The men seem to enjoy that, but I don't see how any lady can be expected to handle meats like that,' said another woman.

One woman looked rather amused at all that. Laurel noted her and went to talk with her. She confided she had lived in the wilderness with her husband, and had enjoyed it. Laurel exchanged recipes for sourdough bread and enjoyed herself for a time. The woman, Mrs. Jenkins, added a low tone, 'You must not mind some of these women, Laurel. They are not happy here. But most women come to Alaska because they enjoy the wilderness.'

She was wearing black and looked rather sad. Laurel wondered what her story was, but thought it might be impolite to ask. She was relieved when the tea was over and Clarissa and her followers had departed.

Thor returned after three weeks, looking satisfied with his journey. He refused, smilingly, to say where he had been, evading questions with the deftness that spoke of long practice. He soon saw how Laurel was being treated by Sidonie and Clarissa. It was very evident at the dinner party Sidonie gave on his return.

Thor paid attention to Clarissa, and he seemed to like her. But when she insulted Laurel's modest gown, he looked thoughtful.

The next day he spoke to Sidonie about Laurel. 'I think she should learn etiquette, Sidonie,' he said abruptly at dinner.

Sidonie raised her graceful hands in horror. 'My dear Thor, I am much too busy to undertake Laurel's education in the social graces! My schedule is full from morning to night!'.

Olaf looked at Thor; Thor looked steadily back at him. 'Laurel is a lady,' said Thor. 'She should have some assistance in learning things which her mother would have taught her had she lived.'

He waited. Sidonie's red mouth was a thin line, and her penciled black eyebrows were raised. 'Do not look at me, my dear boy,' she said briskly. 'You might hire a governess for her, if you want to put more money into the girl's education! I think it's a waste of time myself!'

'That will do, Sidonie,' snapped Olaf in an unusually gruff tone. 'Thor, I will see you in my study after dinner.'

They talked for a long time. Sidonie was impatient, but sipped her coffee and said nothing, waiting for them to return to the drawing room. Laurel felt somehow that her future was being weighed in that study, and her apprehension was high. What could they do with her? She longed for school to start, but that would be months yet. And how could she endure living here, so often alone with Sidonie? The smart Frenchwoman despised her and did not bother to hide it.

Sidonie and Olaf were such a strange match. Laurel could not imagine how they had come to marry. And though Sidonie seemed to admire Thor – she was always trying to get his attention – he did not seem to return that admiration.

About nine-thirty the men returned from the study. They said nothing about their conversation, to Sidonie's visible impatience.

Next morning, however, Thor remained at the breakfast table while Laurel finished her bacon and bread. 'I should like to show you the offices this morning, Laurel,' he said. 'You have not had a chance to see around.'

'I would like that,' she said soberly, feeling he had more in mind than a tour of the company offices. 'Shall we take Rex?'

'Yes, of course. How is he?'

'He's fine,' she said, although Rex was missing freedom as much as Laurel was.

They had scarcely started out, with an excited Rex at the fore, when Thor said, 'About your relatives in Boston, Laurel.'

'Yes, Thor. I have an uncle, Arnold Rutherford, my mother's brother.'

'And he has a family?'

76

'His wife, Aunt Gertrude. And two daughters, about my age, Delia and Hazel.'

Now she knew what direction his mind was taking. They were going to get rid of this encumbrance. Her heart was sinking down into her boots.

Thor was silent for a time as they strolled along the plank sidewalks. He kept lifting his beaver hat to acknowledge bows from men and curtsies from ladies. Laurel nodded automatically to them, smiled when they smiled, remained sober when they did. Everyone was curious about her. What place did she have in the lives of the important family, the Koenigs?

'Father and I have been discussing your future, Laurel,' he finally said. 'I had hoped you could remain in Alaska with us. But my stepmother is not as helpful as I had wished. And you deserve the education of the lady that you evidently are. Your mother and father would have wished it.'

She doubted that. Her mother and father had loved the wilderness and disdained social graces and civilization. However, she was silent. She knew she was an embarrassment to Thor now. She must be sent away. But to go all the way to Boston! And away from Alaska!

What choice did she have? None. She could not make a living, she could not live on charity. She could not be the Koenig's guest forever.

He went on slowly. 'I have been thinking about Boston, Laurel. It would be a good place for you to be educated. They have fine schools for girls there. And you should have further art training, better than you can have here. You have a grand talent, as good as your father's, I believe. I would be sorry if any lack of forethought on my part should stifle your talent.'

He was so polite and kind, she could not protest, not cry out that she would do *anything* – she would even take in laundry or wash dishes forever – if only she could remain in Alaska.

She made herself remain silent, clicking her fingers for Rex to return from his curious investigation of a grocery storefront. He came back to her, and nuzzled his nose in her hand. She stroked his thick fuzzy head mechanically.

'It won't be easy, Laurel, but you said your uncle had asked for you,' Thor continued. 'I'll take you south with me, on to Boston on the train. I'll see you settled at your uncle's. If they are not kind, I'll make other arrangements. There are good boarding schools for girls. What do you say?'

Laurel stole a fleeting look at Thor. He was so tall, so handsome in a rugged masculine fashion, with his rough thick blond hair, his tanned face with the square jaw, his icy green eyes like the waters of Alaska. He fit the land and is like the land, she thought. He and Alaska were somehow entwined in her mind; they were part of each other. And she must leave them both, perhaps forever!

What choice did she have? If she remained, she would be a burden to him. If she left, she might learn much, be able to make some sort of living, perhaps as a schoolteacher, and one day return to Alaska, and to Thor. At least to see him again.

'They sounded kind, Thor,' she said at last. 'I think my uncle was fond of my mother and would care for me for her sake.'

He looked immensely relieved. 'Good, Laurel,' he said heartily. 'We shall set out soon, then. It will take about a month for the journey, and another month for me to return. I'll buy some trunks for you and hatboxes.'

'What about Rex?' she asked timidly.

He looked at the dog, running before them, stopping to race back. 'I'm sorry, Laurel,' he said slowly. 'I don't think Rex would be happy on the journey, or in Boston. It is too much city for him. I'll take care of him for you though. I promise.'

It was as though he said 'until you return,' and her heart lifted a little. 'Thank you, Thor. He likes you very much,' she said quietly.

If she left her dog here in Alaska, she would have to return for him one day, wouldn't she? She felt a little better about it as she prepared to pack and make the long journey south. Thor made reservations for them both on the next packet.

Sidonie exclaimed when he told of his plans. 'You're taking the girl to Boston? You, Thor? You cannot spare the time! Send someone else! And besides, it's not proper! You cannot escort a girl about!'

He kept his face expressionless. 'Mrs. Jenkins desires to return home to New York with her two children, now that her husband is dead. She will accompany us,' he said calmly.

Sidonie could not contain her disgust. 'And you will take a laundress with you! Really, Thor, you go too far! There are limits to charity!'

Her husband rumbled. 'Mrs. Jenkins is a lady who happens to take in laundry to make a living for herself and her girls. I knew and admired her husband and would be glad to go myself, to assist her. I fully approve of Thor's undertaking, and I would advise you to say no more, Sidonie!'

When he spoke like that, Sidonie had to stop her sniping, and she finally gave up. But she grumbled to friends about Thor's wasting this summer on the journey.

Laurel finally spoke to Thor. 'Is there no one else you can send with us, Thor? It will take quite a bit of time for you.'

He smiled and pinched her cheek teasingly. 'I wouldn't trust anybody else with you, my girl! No, I'm glad to go with you and make sure the Rutherfords are suitable guardians for you. Besides, I have important business in Boston that should not be put off.'

He never said what the business was, making her believe he had made it up on the spur of the moment. Nevertheless, she was glad for his kindness, and for the opportunity to be with him longer, though she must leave Alaska.

The most painful parting for her was with Rex. The dog whined and could not understand why she was not taking him for his usual walk when she came around to pet him one more time. She had to blink back tears as she walked away rapidly, disregarding his short sharp imperative bark. She might never see him again. But she would return. She must return to Alaska. It was her land, her home, the land she loved.

Thor, Laurel, and the three Jenkinses set out on a bright day in June. Many had come down to the docks to see them depart, some friends, some sort of curiosity. Laurel waved and waved, until she could no longer make out any figures on the dock.

On the trip south to San Francisco, the ship was not crowded. It was nothing like the trip north to Alaska. When every bunk had been taken, children slept with a parent and men spent the days and nights on deck sleeping in blankets. The trip south was a much easier one, and most of the people were going on vacations or to see relatives, or to return home disappointed from the gold fields.

Most of the gold hunters had remained to scratch for the precious metals in the ice and rock of the frozen North. In this year of 1902, more were still streaming up from the States to seek their fortunes. Laurel wore her nugget necklace under her dress, rather uncomfortably. She did not feel safe wearing it in the open.

Thor divided his attentions equally between her and Mrs. Jenkins and the two young girls, and saw to it that they were as comfortable as possible. He was a handsome young man, and older girls and women made eyes at him, but he did not seem to see them. He talked some, and exchanged information with the men, discussing the future of Alaska, politics in the States, the state of the world. Laurel was proud that they seemed to listen to him with respect, young though he was.

In San Francisco she was bewildered by the whirl of traffic and the multitudes of people, white, Chinese, Spanish, black, Indians. They did not remain long though, only long enough for Thor to transact some business for a few days, then buy tickets for their journey east.

He drove the women and girls around town in a fine carriage, but would not let them go out without him. They remained in their plush red-velvet suite in the hotel when he was busy.

He took them to see the famous spots of San Francisco pointing out the docks, Telegraph Hill, the grand mansions, and elegant restaurants. And their last night in town, he wined and dined them in a restaurant called the Golden Nugget, where the floor show of dancing girls made them open their innocent eyes wide. Laurel liked the music best, especially the piano tunes, and she resolved more than ever to have a piano in her house one day, in Alaska! And perhaps she would learn to play it also!

Finally they took the train, with three compartments next to each other, and were on their way. Laurel kept the older Jenkins girl with her, her mother kept the younger. Thor had a compartment with an elderly man. They met for meals, and for conversation. Laurel spent much of the time at the wide windows, watching with wonder as the wide Western landscape unfurled before her. The mountains with their snowy peaks even in late June, the waterfalls, the flowers.

Then the desert and vast plains, mile after mile of spare grass. And finally the larger towns, the cities of the East.

And finally they arrived in New York City. Thor ordered Laurel to remain in her room with the door locked while he took the Jenkinses to their relatives. This was a wicked big city, and she must take care!

Laurel was so worried by everyone's warnings that she could hardly enjoy New York City. Still she felt secure with Thor. He took her out one evening to a theatre, and she saw her first play, which was affecting and made her weep.

Two days later they went to Boston on the train. The end of her journey! She was deeply moved, thinking it was the last she would see of Thor for a long long time.

'You will write to me, won't you, Laurel?' he asked as the train's wheels clanked on the rails.

'Oh, yes. I'll write.'

'And tell me how you're doing and if you're happy.'

She nodded, her brown eyes large beneath the new smart rose-colored bonnet. She twisted her gloves in her slim fingers.

'And will you write to me?' she asked timidly. 'And tell me how . . . how Rex is doing.'

He smiled with his green eyes, and they were kind and warm today. 'Yes, and what I'm doing, and how the land looks,' he said. 'You look like a lost child. Sit up straight, and look like a lady!'

She caught her breath, and straightened her back, and lifted her chin. 'Like this?'

'Like that. You'll do fine, Laurel. You have courage.'

Laurel was to recall Thor's words often in the months and years ahead.

They took a carriage from the station and drove to Maple Street, where they found the square white house in which the Rutherfords lived.

It was a fine three-storey house with a cellar and an attic. One thing that reconciled Laurel at once was the porch all the way around the house, a porch where later she often sat in the summers and talked with her cousins. It was a comfortable house, a lovable house, and the porch was like arms around it.

81

Thor escorted her up the path to the front porch and rang the doorbell. A maid answered, a fine tall Irish girl with a gray dress and a white starched apron and tall white cap.

'Good day to ye, sir!' she said.

'Good day,' said Thor. 'Thor Koenig's compliments, and may we see the master of the house, Mr. Rutherford!'

'Come in, sir. The master is not home, but the mistress is here.'

She showed them into a fine parlor of all black furniture, and ferns and stiff aspidistra in the corners, a parlor crammed with tables and chairs and books and china ornaments and portraits and thick red velvet draperies and white lace curtains. It was the finest parlor Laurel had ever seen, and she was afraid to move.

Presently a small plump lady was coming in from the hall, a lady with light brown hair and blue eyes, and a slow deliberate dignified movement. She looked at Thor, then she looked at Laurel, and she went quite white, and put her hand to her plump bosom and the long gold chain.

'Good heavens, Madeline!' she gasped.

Laurel blinked. 'That was my mother,' she whispered. Thor was standing, fine in his navy blue serge suit and stiff white collar.

'May I introduce to you, madam,' he said formally, 'Miss Laurel Winfield, who I believe is your niece, the daughter of Madeline and James Winfield.'

The woman held out her arms, and Laurel went into them. She hugged Laurel tightly, and there were tears in her blue eyes. 'Madeline's daughter, well I never, I never!' she kept exclaiming.

Thor introduced himself, then said, 'I brought Laurel to you from Alaska.'

'Bless you, my dear, bless you! How kind you are!' And she sent for the husband from the dry goods store.

Arnold Rutherford soon arrived. He was as plump and as kind as his wife, a little taller, and vaguely resembled his sister Madeline. He greeted Laurel kindly, welcomed Thor, and said, 'Of course she must live with us!'

Thor went to Mr. Rutherford's study with him, and they had a long and evidently satisfactory conversation. Thor stayed for dinner that evening. He had some business the next two days, returned for another dinner, then departed again for Alaska.

Thor left so fast, she thought afterwards, there was no time to cry. He squeezed her hand, gave her a smile, and brushed her cheek with his lips.

'Be sure to write!' he admonished. 'Father and I will want to hear from you regularly!'

'It will be good for her to learn to write correct letters,' Mrs. Rutherford said placidly.

Then he was gone! But Laurel had no time to grieve, no time to sit in the corner and mope.

Aunt Gertrude, as she must be called, believed that idle hands made work for the devil. She had a time for everything, and everything in its time. Furthermore, her three girls, as she included Laurel, must be proper housewives, and nobody should say she neglected a girl's proper education!

Laurel was at once absorbed into the Rutherford household. She had a room of her own next door to Hazel, and Delia was on Hazel's other side. Delia was the elder, seventeen now, with curly hair and a pretty face, and a practical manner. She was tall and slim, danced well, and helped in the store on Saturdays.

Hazel was a year younger than Laurel, fourteen, with a plump tomboy body, a mischief-making mind, fond of tennis and rowing on the river, and given to wild gossip. She promptly began to confide in Laurel, for Delia disapproved of gossip.

Aunt Gertrude divided the work of the household, so that all three girls would be trained properly. One week Laurel would be in charge of the menus, making sure the right groceries were on hand, the meals planned, served, and all went well in the kitchen.

The next week it would be Hazel's turn in the kitchen, and Laurel would be in charge of bed-making, linen-mending, and laundry. If sheets needed to be turned, she was to supervise the maids in that task. The ironing must be done properly, all Mr. Rutherford's shirts washed and starched properly. The lace collars were washed by hand, as were the undergarments, by a covey of Irish maids.

The third week Laurel would be in charge of the house cleaning. Everything must be dusted, all the ornaments in the parlor, all the stair railings and the carpets, all the rooms turned out once a week, and everything spick-and-span.

It was good experience, though wearing. Aunt Gertrude prided herself on her reputation as a housewife. Uncle Arnold was on his way to becoming a wealthy man, so they could afford servants and fine food and wines. They entertained, and everything must be spotless.

In the autumn Laurel was entered in the same school as her cousins, though they each had different lessons. She was tested, and began the long process of catching up in the subjects in which she was deficient. She took arithmetic and mathematics; history, both American and European; handwriting; prose writing; and health.

Uncle Arnold and Aunt Gertrude believed in a healthy mind in a healthy body. Food was nutritious, and all put on a plate must be eaten. One must eat breakfast, no matter how rushed for school. One must dress properly for cold weather, with boots, woolen dress, petticoats, stockings, scarf, hat and mittens. One must not go ice-skating on the pond, that was dangerous.

Hazel disregarded that latter, and stole out several times with Laurel to skate. It was a delicious secret, and they managed to do it several times per winter, in spite of scoldings when they were found out.

Delia was more concerned with convention. She was much like her mother; prim, precise, and earnest. But she was a nice girl, and good-hearted, and Laurel learned to like and admire Delia. Delia taught Laurel to dance and arranged for lessons with boys as partners at the local dancing academy. Delia taught Laurel to embroider, and to crochet and to knit, and to do the fine sewing that added to her ability as a seamstress. Both she and Aunt Gertrude approved of Laurel's sewing ability, and her fine talent in dressmaking.

All of them learned manners from a woman who came once a week to teach them French, the art of conversation, and social graces. The little faded lady was timid as a mouse, but she had been raised well, and she taught them how to hold a teacup, how to converse about nothing, how to curtsy, how to stand when one's elders entered the room.

Remembering Sidonie Koenig's scorn of Laurel, and Clarissa's taunting laughter, Laurel studied and learned well all these necessities of life. She did her homework carefully too. She wanted the Rutherfords to be proud of her, and not sorry they had taken her in.

She was grateful to Uncle Arnold. He had been very fond of his sister, and with an effort refrained from speaking ill of that artist with whom she had run off. He gave Laurel the same treatment as his daughters, listened to them, treated them with lengths of fabric from his store, saw to it that they never lacked for pin money.

Laurel was even given time to work on her sketches and painting. A school mistress had told the Rutherfords that she was uncommonly talented, and though they did not approve of this particular talent, they listened to her and made sure Laurel had lessons.

Laurel worked hard, and the days and weeks flowed past. But she never forgot, deep inside her, her resolve to return one day to Alaska, to her own land, to the great wilderness of green and gold and blue, the rough land that was her home. One day, she would go back and live there; she vowed it. She would own a piece of Alaska and build a house there of her own.

Chapter 8
1903

Jade missed Laurel terribly. With the Winfields gone there was nobody else around for many miles.

In the spring of 1903, Jade looked forward to a trip to Wrangell. They would need to trade furs for flour, bullets, a few other essentials. But once they had returned they might not see anybody else at all for another year, unless gold prospectors wandered by.

So when a hunter approached the cabin one day, she was delighted. Here was somebody to talk to, someone new to tell them the news of the world. The man came closer and pushed back his parka hood. Jade stared. It could not be . . . it could not . . . But it was!

The handsome young man with the big smile, the blond hair shining in the sunlight – it was Ewan Koenig!

'Hello, hello!' he called and waved his hand at them.

'Who is that?' muttered Tom Nolan, frowning. 'Oh. It is the young man who lost the fight with the bear!'

He had an unexpected sense of humor sometimes, belied by his grave face, 'Oh, shush, Papa,' Jade urged in an agony. 'He might hear you!'

Ewan came closer and paused to give them his greetings. 'You *are* still here!' he said, with evident pleasure. 'I was afraid you had moved on!'

'No, this is our home,' Tom Nolan said, and shook his hand ceremoniously. 'You recall my wife, Miriam, and my daughter, Jade?'

'Yes, yes, your beautiful daughter Jade,' teased Ewan. 'And now more beautiful than ever! It's been two years!'

'How is Laurel?' asked Jade eagerly. 'She is still in Sitka, yes?'

'Ah, no. I did not even see her,' he said with regret. They welcomed him into the cabin, he entered, and set down his rifle. 'When I returned from the North in the autumn, I heard that Laurel had been there. But Thor had taken her down to the States, to Boston, to live with her relatives.'

'No!' Jade exclaimed in disappointment. 'She has left Alaska! I may never see her again!'

Ewan shrugged. 'She may come back; she left her dog Rex. But who knows? I understand her uncle is rather wealthy. Well, well, how are all of you? You look well,' and his gaze on Jade was smiling.

'We are all well, thank you. No illness,' said Tom.

'You will take dinner with us?' invited Miriam. To their delight, he agreed heartily.

He complimented Miriam on her cooking and said the sourdough pancakes with blueberries were the best he had ever eaten. He was charm itself, and they were also glad to see and talk to someone new.

When he asked to stay the night, they agreed, and he rolled up in a blanket before the fire. At daylight he got up with Tom, went out to get firewood, and stoked the fire.

'What are your plans?' Tom asked pleasantly. 'Do you come to hunt?'

'You guessed it.' Ewan smiled. 'I have the summer off to go hunting as I've been a good boy!' He gave a comical grimace. 'I've worked in the mines for Father solidly for almost two years, and he gave me the summer off. What kind of game have you seen around?'

'Moose,' said Tom. 'Brown bear, deer, rabbits, of course. Ptarmigan. Mountain goat. What do you seek?'

'Oh, I'd like a bear head for a trophy,' said Ewan cheerfully. 'But I'd like to go fishing, get some trout, salmon. And just have a good time hunting. I expect you can use the meat to dry for winter.'

That suited Tom. Jade could tell by the look on his stolid face. He nodded at Miriam. 'Well, please stay with us, if you will, and we shall hunt with you. Or, consider us your friends and return to us during your hunting trips.'

To Jade's delight, Ewan chose to remain with them for much of the summer. He was not always a cheerful guest; he was moody and cross when he missed a shot. He was like a child in his tempers, and the Nolans were quietly amused at him.

'He has been spoiled much,' Miriam said when he was away. 'He thinks always to have his own way in the world! He has much to learn.'

But he was interesting. He had many stories to tell, some so exaggerated they had to laugh, others about the gold hunters, the miners, the society of Sitka, people in Juneau, and greenhorns who came north expecting to pick gold off the ground.

He enlivened their evenings with his stories, his games of cards and dice. He did not play for money; they had none. But they would invent payment, in another pancake or a dish of berries, or some wild plan of Ewan's.

If he won, which he often did, he would have the choice of where to go hunting the next day, or whether to go fishing. He took a childish delight in winning, and it did not matter to them.

He teased Jade that she did not go hunting alone with him. 'Why should I?' she asked puzzled. 'If we find bear, it is safer to be together with my parents.'

'But there is more to hunting than hunting,' he teased.

'Do you have a boyfriend?' he asked.

They were sitting outside the cabin, scraping deer skins for Miriam. Ewan did not like the task; he grimaced over it, but he worked along with Jade on the small table from Laurel's former cabin.

'Me? No.' She blushed and bent her head over the skins.

'You surprise me. I thought your parents would engage you to some young man from your village.'

She frowned, troubled. 'The village men do not want me,' she said in a low tone. 'There is coldness between my parents and the others in the village.'

'What happened?'

She told him. 'They married against the wishes of the elders; they are of the same clan. We are of the Raven, in the division of the Eagles and the Ravens. A Raven must always marry an Eagle. An Eagle marries a Raven. They were both Ravens.'

'So what?' he asked, puzzled.

She touched the jade emblem on the thong around her neck. It was the device of a Raven. 'I take the tribe of my mother. I am a Raven, and I must marry an Eagle. But all know I am the child of both Raven parents. So the mothers refuse the marriage of me to any of their sons. I do not know who I will marry now.'

He frowned over it. 'I expect it was to keep from intermarrying too much.'

'Yes, that is it,' she said, relieved that he understood.

'Well, you are a very pretty girl, Jade. You will marry someone handsome,' he said and grinned. She did not know if he joked or not.

When Ewan looked at her admiringly, from her head to her heels, she felt pretty. She was sixteen now, and she had black straight hair to her waist, when it was loosened from the braid. Her eyes were black and large. She had a nice face, her mother said briskly, and Jade would peer into the small mirror or into the still surface of a lake to see herself. She would see an oval, with a large red mouth, large black eyes, straight black eyebrows, high cheekbones with tawny gold color. And her figure was slim, yet rounded.

She always kept her clothes neat and clean, she bathed often, even in the wintertime when it was cold, and she shivered using the basin before the fire. She had noticed her breasts filling out and getting round and plump; she had had to let out some dresses and blouses. And when Ewan looked at her, his gaze was often on her round breasts, pushing out the fabric of her blouse.

It was June now, and she often did not bother to wear a coat during the afternoon hours. The sun beat down on her and felt warm and kind.

'There, that is the last of it,' she said as they finished scraping the deerskin.

'I'm glad of that! Let's go to the stream and wash up,' he said, rising from the ground and stretching. 'All right to leave the skins out here to dry?'

Miriam came over and examined the skins critically. She nodded her dark head. 'Yes, this is fine. I will take care of them now. Thank you.'

Ewan caught Jade's hand in his. 'Come on, then, bring a towel and we'll go wash. I smell of deer!'

She laughed. 'So do I.'

She got a towel and a rare piece of soap; she felt extravagant. They walked together to the stream. Ewan stripped off his woolen plaid shirt and bent over the stream to splash water over his shoulders and arms and chest. She stole shy glances at him as he did so.

Timidly she washed her hands, shoved up her sleeves, and washed her arms.

'Oh, come on, Jade, don't be bashful!' he said, laughing. 'Take off your shirt too! The water is cool and pleasant.'

She shook her head, turned away from his look. 'No, not with you here,' she said primly.

They were about a mile from the cabin; nobody was around. The waters of the stream were very blue, echoing the blue of the vivid sky. The grass was very green and lush, and clumps of wildflowers dotted the green, the yellow and the blue, and the white and red ones. She bent to pluck some of the fragrant yellow ones, then put them in her braid.

'Oh, come on!' he said again. He came over to her half naked and laughing, water dripping from his body. 'Take off your shirt, or I'll dump you in the water!'

She squealed and rolled away from him. He dived on her and wrestled with her, bellowing with laughter. Her body felt warm. She could scarcely breathe when he lay on top of her. She wriggled.

'Get off,' she said, gasping for breath.

He put his face down close to hers. He had let a beard grow this summer; it was straggly and blond with golden lights in it. His blue-gray eyes were very blue today, and brilliant.

'Kiss me first,' he said.

'No, I should not,' she said and turned her face away.

'One kiss!'

'No, please –'

He put his face down and held his cheek against hers; it was warm and scratchy, and felt thrilling to her soft skin. He moved his head slowly, forcing her head to be still, her other cheek against the grass. Then he put his full mouth on hers, the lips unexpectedly hard and wet. She was shocked at how much she liked the touch. He held her still and kissed her again.

He lifted his head; he was not smiling. 'Like it?' he asked softly.

'Ummm,' she said, her body getting more hot and limp.

'You're very beautiful, Jade. You have such a lovely body, all soft and rounded. I like your breasts.' He put his hand boldly on her shirt over her breasts and felt her.

'Oh, don't do that!' she said, horrified. She tossed her head back and forth. 'That is not right!'

'It feels right.' He grinned. 'I like to feel you.' And he unfastened the buttons of the woolen shirt and put his hand inside. She had not worn an undershirt today, it was too warm; and he touched her soft skin and fingered the nipple until it hardened.

She felt little hot thrills running down her body to her thighs. She wriggled uncomfortably under his body, lying half on top of her. She licked her lips, trying to find words to make him stop. Yet she did not want him to stop. Her awakened young body wanted more . . . and more . . .

'You're so pretty,' he was saying softly. 'You feel so soft and silky. God, I love to touch you. I've been looking at you and wanting to touch you all over like this . . .' And his hand went down to her waist, and inside her belt. He touched her rounded stomach, and she shivered.

'You must stop!'

'Why? You want it as much as I do. And you don't have any boyfriends, do you? Let me teach you how good it feels . . .'

'No . . . no . . . it is wrong.'

But it felt too good to be wrong. She lay limply while he played with her, his mouth touching her chin and cheeks, the scratchy skin of his chin rubbing over her and making her aware of his masculine feel.

Then he put his hand down to the hem of her skirt and brushed the cloth upward. He fondled her leg. She drew it up sharply, trying to pull it from him. It only made that easier for him to put his hand farther up her leg.

He put his head down on her chest and held her tightly under him. He was breathing more heavily. Jade lay still, her breath came in little pants of excitement. She liked his kisses; she liked the words he whispered, thrilling words she had not heard before.

'You're so lovely, so sweet . . . silky . . . fragrant . . . so young and lovely. I want you, Jade, I want you. You can make me happy. I'll make you very happy . . . want to make you happy . . .'

He came over her, fully, and put his hips to her bare thighs. He had pulled off his trousers, and he was naked to her. She felt the hard masculine flesh against her young silky thighs, and his fingers teased her to response. She flinched a moment, then opened up to him. She opened her eyes and saw the blazing blue sky above her and a few white clouds drifting, then all was blurring . . .

Her hands went to his hard bare shoulders and gripped him. Her fingers clenched on his muscular arms, slid down to his elbows, then up again, seeking the cool hard feel of him. He pressed himself to her, growling against her throat, and his mouth clamped hotly onto her.

He pressed harder, and with a sharp cry she fell back on the grassy softness of the tundra. 'Oh, no . . . no!' she cried.

'Shut up . . . be quiet,' he ordered, and put his wide lips on hers, forcing her open mouth to receive his tongue so that she half-choked and could no longer cry out. His hips pushed again and again at hers, until he broke through the maiden flesh.

He hurt her, but he soothed her with his voice and the slide of his hips on hers. 'It's all right, Jade . . . come on, you'll love it,' he muttered. And she began to enjoy it, the strange new feel of his hardness in her. It was exciting, nerve-wrenching, thrilling, to feel him inside her, pressing up into her. He moved faster and faster on her, sliding in and out, pressing on her, and then he groaned, and fell over on her.

A spurt of what felt like hot water came inside her. She was amazed again at the sensation. It felt good, and she lay still to feel it. He drew out slowly and smiled down at her, a look of intense satisfaction on his sulky handsome face.

'There . . . did you like that, Jade?'

'I . . . don't know . . .'

'Sure you did. I enjoyed it. You're a beautiful girl, Jade. A truly beautiful girl,' and his hand caressed her naked thigh. Then he sighed and lay back on the grass, stretched luxuriously.

Uneasily she lay beside him; one leg was across her naked legs. He seemed to sleep in the warm afternoon. The sky was bright blue, the earth was green, the waters were blue, all the world was green and blue, the color of summer and heat and new life. Flies buzzed in the grass, and flowers sprang up where only the snows had been. Her hand brushed the grass and released new fragrant odors. She felt new and different, a strange girl, someone odd and wild.

Emotion had released itself in her; she had known love and passion. She could never go back to what she had been; she did not want to return to that green girl. While he slept, she got up, slid off her blouse and skirt, and moved to the blue waters. It was not deep. She sat down in the water and slowly splashed the fresh coolness over her arms and breasts, over her shoulder and thighs.

She was absorbed in the sensation, the coolness where he had touched her and held her. She did not see him get up and move, lithe as a young panther, down to the water, until he splashed beside her and sank down into the two-foot stream. Then his laughing brown face appeared beside hers. He splashed her with his hands, sending water in sprays over her. He kept staring at her slim brown body, at the pointed pink breasts, the young thighs and downy silky hair.

In self-defense she splashed water on him and laughed as they played together. He caught her, and pulled her naked body to his, and put his mouth on hers. His hands slid over her silky wetness, intimately.

Then he took her again in the water. It still hurt, but he held her on his knees and caught her tightly against him. He bounced her on his knees, and in the pain she also felt keen pleasure, and moaned and leaned back against him.

He held her with her back against his body and rocked her back and forth, and sensation after sensation raced through her rounded slimness. His mouth bit softly at her wet shoulders as he held her more tightly and then came again in her.

'You really are lovely, you know it?' he said. 'You are really marvelous. I should've come last summer. Wow, what I missed!'

'I was lonely last summer,' she said huskily. His hands were cupping her breasts; she could not see his face as he was behind her.

'Were you? So was I? We should've got together,' he said, nibbling at her shoulder. His hands squeezed one breast, and he thumbed the pink nipple until it stood up taut and tight. He stroked her thighs gently, then rolled her off him with a laugh. 'Time to wash up and get dressed, or your folks will come after us,' he said.

His careless words were a shock. She burned with shame when she

93

realized what she had been doing. She had permitted him the liberties of a married man! And they were not married, nor had he spoken of marriage.

But of course he will, she thought uneasily as she dried herself and dressed hastily. She stole shy glances at his magnificent strong body, at the hard thighs that had pressed hers, at the hairy chest that had pressed to her breasts. How handsome he was, how strong, how fine! And he loved her . . . didn't he? He had said such fine words to her.

He was laughing and swinging her hand as they went back to the cabin. But he dropped her hand when they came in sight of their cabin . . . and her parents. When they came up to Miriam, still working with the furs, he said, 'Tomorrow we will go hunting again. I'll bring you a bear this time, eh?'

She was studying them anxiously. 'You were gone long time,' she said slowly. 'You swim in river?'

'Yes, we went swimming,' he said smiling, seeming unconcerned. Miriam looked at Jade; Jade could not look at her mother.

'I will begin supper,' Jade murmured and went into the cabin to put the water on to boil. Dreamily she put in a piece of deer meat and some onion and greens. She scarcely knew what she did, her body was still soft and melted.

She was crazy about Ewan, he was so loving and affectionate. In the next days and weeks he found opportunities to be with her alone. Not long, but long enough. At nights she lay awake and dreamed of him, lying there rolled in a blanket before the fire.

Ewan kept hunting with them, and Tom was happy because they got two bears. Ewan cleaned the heads and set one aside, the finer one, to take to Wrangell later to be mounted. He kept saying happily, 'Wow, what a hunt! I've never had such a head. Father will be envious of me! This head is better than the one Leverett took! Wait till he sees this!'

He seemed to think of nothing but hunting and fishing. He brought in loads of salmon and trout, and Miriam salted many for the winter. They had a fine stock in the small smoke house behind the cabin.

But he always found time to be alone for a bit with Jade. They would steal off – to her shame – to wash at the stream, to lie in the sunshine and make love, lazily. Or he would take her hunting with him alone, and while they lay in the tall grass, waiting for a moose to come closer, he would roll over on her and kiss her, until they were both crazy for the final ecstasy of the embrace.

She felt shame, and the shock of it when he took her roughly. But usually he was very slow and gentle, telling her how lovely she was. She knew it was wrong, but she kept thinking he would speak of marriage. A man and a woman loved, made love, got married, and made babies. That was the way of life; she knew it from her parents.

Except . . . Ewan never spoke of love or marriage. He wanted her, but he did not say love to her. She loved him, but she did not say love to him, she reasoned. May be the time of saying love had not yet come.

So she hugged him in the shadows of the spruce trees and the cedar trees, and rolled with him under the thick bushes, and laughed as he kissed her and mauled her teasingly. He pretended to be a bear, growling at her, and mauling the shirt from her, and teased at her breasts with his big mouth. He would pull at the nipples until they hardened with desire.

Then he would lift up her skirt, or pull it off completely and they would roll naked in the thick green grass. They would crush the grass and flowers and herbs under them as they rolled and laughed, and hugged and kissed.

He would put her arms about him and roll her over with him, until their bodies came closer and closer and they could no longer resist their young heated desires. Then he would pull her even closer and press down on her hotly.

When they were tightly together, he would roll over and over, and she would stare at the sky and the grass, until all was a blur behind her eyes. All the blues and the greens, together until they were jade, he said.

He pressed his lips on the jade raven at her breast, until the imprint of it was on her skin. He hurt her at times but she could not protest; she wanted him as hotly as he wanted her. 'Jade, Jade, Jade,' he would mutter at her. 'You are the land itself, all blue and green,' and he would kiss her passionately.

All blue and green, the blue waters of the summer streams, the blue of the summer sky, the green of the grasses and herbs and flower stems. And the pink nipples like the pink flowers, the wildflowers, here so briefly, gone tomorrow.

And the smell of the earth on their bodies, and under them, as they made love fiercely. It was the summer, and they were so young and full of desires.

Chapter 9

'Laurel, here's a letter for you . . . from Alaska!'

'Oh, thank you, Uncle Arnold!'

He beamed on her kindly as he handed her the large brown envelope. The envelope was heavy, but it was stained with watermarks, and the letter inside was also stained. It had traveled a long journey, that letter, from Sitka, Alaska, to California, to Boston, Massachusetts. But it had arrived!

'Dear Laurel,' read the letter from Thor. It was the third one he had written to her, but this was much longer than the others. All had been put carefully in the little carved wood jewelry box Aunt Gertrude and Uncle Arnold had given her that first Christmas in Boston.

'How are you? I hope you're studying hard; I expect that you are. All goes well here. I went to the copper mines this winter, and took Rex with me. He misses you. When I say your name to him, he stops and looks up in my face and says woof, woof, just as though he knew what I said. Rex is a good companion and guard dog. I have trained him to stay near me, and he protects me. Not that I need protecting, mind you, but he warns whenever anybody comes near.'

Laurel stopped reading, and went back up to the first words. She was frowning slightly. Thor had been at the copper mines, and Rex was protecting him. She wanted to read between the lines. Was Thor in danger? What danger? Did men try to steal copper from the mines, as they did from gold mines? She would ask Uncle Arnold casually about copper, to see if he might give her a clue.

She went on reading then.

'I've decided to build a house for myself, and for my future wife – should any girl decide she could put up with me.'

97

'Oh, my goodness,' gasped Laurel at this point. Was Thor really thinking of getting married? To whom? That horrible Clarissa? She was so pretty, and she put on an act when she was with men, to make them think she was kind and gentle. But she wasn't! She was mean and malicious, and Thor would be miserable with her. She bit her lips thinking of Thor with Clarissa. The image hurt her.

'You said one time you had been thinking about a house you would like to build one day. Would you mind sharing your ideas with me? I would want a house comfortable for a lady, with all the conveniences she wants. What kind of house would you build for yourself, if you built in Sitka? I have a plot of land overlooking the sea, up on a hill, about a mile from Father's house. It has about five acres, plenty of room for stables and kennels, and a garden.'

She set down the letter for a time, dreaming. A house for Thor! He loved the outdoors, and large windows to see out, just as she did. And a garden, with some of the lovely large and colorful flowers that grew only in Alaska.

'If you have time, I wish you would send me some house plans and give me some ideas. I'm sure you would think of ideas that I would not.

'All are well here. I haven't been back to your former cabin, nor seen the Nolans. I hope to get over that way, but work has been heavy. Father has bought a ship to take out our copper and other metals. The gold mine goes well, and so does the silver, he has hired about a dozen more men. The times are booming for Alaska. More men come all the time in the spring to autumn months, the ships are full of prospectors. I don't know how many will stay and become good Alaskans.

'Are you planning to remain in Boston? Have you settled down well? I hope you have, yet I hope also that you have good memories of Alaska and think of us often. Father sends his best regards. And so do I. As always, Thor.'

Laurel drew a deep sigh of pleasure. It was such a good letter, sounding like Thor, breathing of his spirit. She could almost see his smile as he wrote. That slow warm generous smile of his large lips.

'What do you hear from Thor?' asked Hazel, curiously. 'Papa said you had a letter from him? Do you mind telling me?'

'I don't mind, Hazel. He is well and building a house.'

'A house? Doesn't he live at home?'

'Yes. But he is getting older; he's about twenty-six now, just ten years older than I,' Laurel said slowly. 'I expect he wants a place of his own.'

'Is he getting married?'

'He might, though, he didn't say he was exactly.'

Hazel studied her cousin with curious eyes. She was sitting in Laurel's room, their homework was done. They had a half an hour before bedtime, and the girls liked to talk at the end of the day.

Delia knocked lightly at the open door. 'May I come in?'

'Come in, yes, Delia!' Laurel stood up politely as her elder cousin came in. Delia smiled at her and came to sit down in the other straight chair, straightening her full skirts precisely as she sat down.

'Father said you had a letter from Alaska. Was it a good letter, Laurel?'

Laurel could not refrain from beaming. 'Oh, yes, it was good, Delia. Nice and long. Would you like me to read it?' she asked, because she knew both were dying to hear it and she did not mind; it was not terribly personal, though privately thrilling to her.

She read it aloud, savoring the words. The girls listened with wide-eyed curiosity. Then began the questions.

'Do you have house plans, Laurel?' This was Delia.

'Oh, I have ideas. I have from the time I was very young,' said Laurel. 'I'll sketch out some plans for him. A nice large parlor, for entertaining. Windows with a view of the sea. And things like that,' she added hastily.

'Be sure to put in a sewing room,' Delia said practically. 'A man might not think of that. And a laundry room, where ironing can be done also. Sometimes houses have a skimpy space for ironing.'

Laurel scribbled that down on a sketch pad. 'That's a good idea, Delia.'

'I would put in lots of space in a garden, to play with dogs,' said Hazel. 'And a big porch for rainy days. Do they have rainy days in Sitka?'

'They sure do!' laughed Laurel. Her eyes grew dreamy. 'I can remember days when Dad and I didn't go outside the cabin for weeks at a time, it was such soaking rain. But when the sun came out, oh, such glorious flowers had sprung up! Big yellow marsh marigolds, yellow and purple flags, buttercups, fireweed, pitcher plants, hollyhocks, besides all kinds of small flowers, like violets and anemones.'

'I always think of Alaska as deep snow and ice and Eskimos eating whales,' remarked Hazel, with a laugh. 'You talk about it as full of flowers! And cute things like rabbits and seals.'

'Well . . . Alaska is many things; it is a varied land,' Laurel said with a reflective sigh. 'I remember the tall mountains, with the snow on sharp jagged peaks, and the glimpses of blue-white glaciers from the ice fields to the rivers below. The sky a vivid blue, the grass so bright green in the summertime, and the many streams winding down from the mountains. Sometimes waterfalls dropping sheer from a cliff, all white and sparkling in the sunshine.'

Hazel had her chin propped in her hand. 'But it's a harsh tough land, isn't it? Why would a woman like it, like you, Laurel? Your eyes always shine when you talk about Alaska.'

'It's hard to explain,' she said slowly. 'I love the land. We lived in many places that were beautiful in the West, some in wide stretches of dusty plains, with horses racing across the desert and sagebrush. And once on a mountain near a vivid blue lake, with cedar and pine . . . oh, that smelled so good, it was like living in a perfume of Nature. And nobody for miles; it was all our own, until the lumbermen moved in.'

'But your father always wanted to move on,' said gentle Delia, troubled. 'Could he not be satisfied when he found a perfect place?'

Laurel hesitated, then shook her head. 'As I think back, I believe Mother and Father both painted and sketched for a time. Then when they had put down their impressions, they wanted to move on. I remember Mother saying there were so many beautiful places in the world, she wanted to see them all! Of course, they never did, but they did see many of them, and so did I.'

'Would they have settled in Alaska if they had – I mean, if they – ' Delia hesitated delicately.

'If they had not died?' Laurel never evaded that word, die, or the word death. It was a blunt word, an honest word. No passing on, or going to the next world, or going up to heaven for her. Death, the end of the known life, a fact she recognized from meeting it early. 'I don't know. Father seemed happy in Alaska, but he was already talking of moving north, maybe up to the Klondike. He didn't care if the cabin was small; it was just a place to leave the rest of one's clothes, the food, and pots and pans. A place to hang one's hat, he would say.'

'But you don't feel that way? You want a house?' asked Hazel, thoughtfully. She had matured a little this winter, and Laurel felt that she too was growing up. It helped to be with the other two girls, to share their thoughts and dreams.

'Yes, I do want a house. I guess, from moving so much as a child, I wanted to belong somewhere,' confessed Laurel.

'I never told Dad, but I wanted one place to stay. A place to own, a piece of land that would be mine and no one could take away from me.'

'Why not in Boston?' Delia asked gently. 'This is a nice city, with many conveniences, and you love music. Father is going to take us to more concerts this next winter because you have expressed your appreciation so much.'

'Your parents are very good to me,' Laurel said passionately. 'Nobody could've been kinder! You have the best parents in the world.'

Hazel and Delia looked very gratified.

Delia said, generously, 'Mother says you are the easiest guest possible, and you work hard all the time. She says we have both settled down since you came!'

'But why not in Boston?' persisted Hazel. 'Don't you like Boston? We could all have houses close together, what about that?' And her pretty face sparkled with enthusiasm.

'I feel I don't belong here,' Laurel said slowly, puzzling over her own thoughts. 'I feel that Alaska is my home. The big sky, the feeling of freedom, the wide spaces, the land for the taking. The huge trees, and the very smell of the spruce and cedar – it's all so beautiful, so satisfying. I can breathe free!'

'Girls?' Aunt Gertrude was at the door. 'I'm sorry, dears, I know you're enjoying your conversation, but it's ten o'clock!'

Hazel and Delia got up at once and said good night. Laurel kissed her Aunt Gertrude's cheek, and her aunt smiled warmly at her. She was a perfectionist, and a housekeeper never satisfied, but she was a good woman, and immensely kind.

But when Laurel went to bed, she could not sleep for a time, thinking about Thor's letter, the house, and Alaska. Yes, she did long for Alaska. There was no place like it, the wide spaces, the white clean land in the winter, the wild animals, the excitement of the unknown, the icy breath of the glaciers, the beauty of the blue rivers and blue sky. My Alaska, she thought, and longed to see it again and to belong there.

Someday she would buy a piece of land and build a house. Until then she would be satisfied to help Thor with his house. And the very next day she began to sketch and plan for him.

Within weeks Laurel had an outline made, several pages of house drawings: one page for every floor of the house; another for the outdoor view and the gardens; another plan for the five acres, with stables and kennels all neatly set out.

Then she showed her new family how it looked, and they spent several pleasant evenings going over the plans with her, offering suggestions.

Uncle Arnold was practical, pointing out some difficulties in arranging the plumbing, and so she changed the kitchen and bathroom arrangements to suit his theories.

Aunt Gertrude studied the rooms carefully and pointed out a better way to set the bedrooms and the halls. Laurel changed some to agree with that, but kept the others, the ones with huge windows overlooking the sea. 'Yes, they will be colder, Aunt Gertrude, but the view is important. It will not do to set the house with its back to the sea!'

'Well, it will waste heat, but you know the area, best, my dear,' said Aunt Gertrude comfortably. 'Besides, Mr. Koenig will probably have his own ideas about that. It was kind of him to ask your advice and give you something to think about.'

Was that why Thor had asked? Laurel felt disappointed; she had wanted to believe he cared what she thought.

Delia suggested larger closets, for wardrobes might be difficult to ship to Alaska. And a large walk-in linen room. She wanted one of her own in a house of her own, she confessed with a blush.

Hazel kept a critical eye on the outdoors and suggested a good arrangement for the stables, especially if Thor kept several horses and two carriages.

They were all so enthusiastic and interested that Uncle Arnold suggested that all the girls work out house plans of their own, 'to give them time to think about their futures,' he said. Aunt Gertrude approved, and many an evening that winter was spent with drawings spread out on the parlor table as the girls worked out house plans.

Delia was sewing for her hope chest, and Hazel began hers also. Uncle Arnold gave them generously of his dry goods store, and they could pick and choose linens to work and towels to make up. With their encouragement Laurel also began a hope chest, only her secret wish for things she could use in Alaska.

So she began to fill her hope chest with thick practical towels and cloths, linen tablecloths with good firm seams, practical size napkins rather than tea size.

Aunt Gertrude praised her practical sense but suggested a few more frivolous items, some dainty tea aprons of silk and lace, guest towels that were about a foot long, lacy napkins. Laurel listened, but she did not make many of those; she wanted to return to Alaska with items she could use there.

And for her clothes, she had always sewn with an eye to returning to Alaska. She was not tempted with many items of velvet and lace and crystal beading. No *mousseline de soie* sleeves for her blouses; she used linens and cotton muslins. Her coats were of cloth, some trimmed with furs that wore well.

Laurel found one big restriction of her personal freedom in Boston – corsets! She could not believe the tight ugly garments that she must wear under her clothing. In Alaska she had sewn petticoats and bloomers, and wore those beneath her dresses, nothing tight and restricting. Hazel longed for that! 'I wish we didn't have to wear whalebones,' she said wistfully. 'They're so uncomfortable!'

But Aunt Gertrude insisted, though she did not want them to wear tight ones that restricted the waist and the breathing of her girls. Still, what Laurel did have to wear was enough to make her long for her freedom in Alaska.

Laurel worked out the house plans for Thor's house, copied them, and mailed them to him by November.

In January Uncle Arnold brought her another letter, 'from Alaska, my dear Laurel!' with his pleased smile.

She took the letter, but it did not look like Thor's handwriting exactly. She glanced at the return address.

'Oh, it's from Mr. Olaf Koenig!' she said in surprise.

'You may read it now,' Aunt Gertrude said. 'I'll finish the menus for you.'

'Thank you. You're most kind, Aunt Gertrude.' Eagerly she sat down to open the letter carefully and read its contents.

To her great surprise the letter enclosed a draft on the Wells Fargo Bank in the amount of $200, in her name. She stared at the paper in wonder.

Then she read the letter.

'My dear young friend Laurel,' it began pleasantly. 'I hope you are well and this finds you happy. We miss your young fresh presence here. However, Thor tells me you are doing well in school and enjoy your cousins immensely. Uncle and Aunt are good to you. I am glad of that. You are a fine young lady, and your father Jim would be proud of you.

'I am happy to say my affairs are proceeding excellently, thanks to my labors and those of my sons, especially Thor. He is a mature young man, and I am proud of him. Ewan is growing up, but more slowly. He still likes to play. He took last summer to go hunting and visited with your friends, the Nolans. They are well, he reported to me.

'We have a new large vessel for sending metals to the states, and it is well fitted out, with a worthy captain. We plan to ship more copper next summer and to add another vessel. The ships will return with passengers, then take more copper south.

'No more news for now. Your friends in Sitka send greetings. Your affectionate friend, Olaf Koenig.'

Laurel read the letter aloud to her relatives that evening and all commented on it exhaustively.

'He sounds prosperous,' said Uncle Arnold. 'Good, good. I like to see a man work hard and do well.'

'And your friends . . . You've been anxious about your friends, the Nolans,' Aunt Gertrude said, sewing on a petticoat and studying the effect on the crochet border.

'Yes, I'm so happy someone has seen the Nolans,' Laurel said, looking at that line in the letter. Secretly she was a bit worried. Ewan had gone to see the Nolans, and Jade. He was two years older now; had he matured at all? Or would he be mischievous and try to tease and kiss Jade?

Still, it was a month's wonder, that letter. The wealthy and busy Olaf Koenig had bothered to write to her, and pay the high cost of a letter. And he had sent her all that money!

Uncle Arnold and Aunt Gertrude talked with her about the money and finally decided for her that it should be saved. She had wanted them to take some of it against her board, but they were offended.

'No, no, my dear. You're the daughter of my sister,' Uncle Arnold said gently. 'And you pay your way, by working as my daughters do. And you've been sewing Hazel's clothes for her, and help in so many ways. No, no, keep the money against your future.'

And he put it into a savings account for her.

After that, no letters came for months. They were shut in by the ice probably, thought Laurel. A few ships would come and go, but Thor might be up north in the copper mine again, or even back further inland, searching for more mines. The Koenigs were very ambitious, and they had the money to invest.

Laurel worked hard in school, doing well in all her classes and catching up with subjects which had been neglected by her years of wandering with her parents. She especially enjoyed her painting lessons, and the teacher was an earnest young artist this year. She encouraged Laurel to experiment in painting.

Laurel used her advice to paint freely, and sometimes she came again and again to the theme which haunted her dreams. A scene of the Alaska wilderness in snow, and in the foreground a bloody figure lying half over the threshold of a log cabin. Off in the background to the right, a figure on snowshoes moved off into the darkness and redness of the setting sun. The teacher frowned over this.

'My dear Laurel, you're not usually so morbid!' she exclaimed. 'What is this scene?'

'My father's death,' Laurel answered in a low tone. 'He was . . . killed!'

'Oh, my dear!' said the teacher, her hand to her mouth. Seeing her shock, Laurel did not show her the next pictures like that.

Laurel did not want to paint such scenes, but now and then she felt she had to, to get it out of her system. But she put the water-colors away, and did not show the sketches to anyone again.

Most of the time she painted pretty scenes. She enjoyed painting Hazel; her lively face was a good subject. She painted Hazel playing tennis, her face red and her middy blouse coming loose from her wide belt. Hazel playing with the neighbor's fuzzy white poodle. Hazel shoveling snow, her breath puffing.

And she painted pretty Delia, who did not mind sitting still as she embroidered or tatted the border on a linen tablecloth. Delia was always smooth-haired, neat, a little smile on her lovely mouth, her hair now in a bouffant hairdo that set off her smooth cheeks and forehead.

She painted Uncle Arnold sitting with the evening newspaper, and Aunt Gertrude arranging flowers. She gave them the paintings, and they were pleased with them. When visitors complimented them on the likenesses, they were proud to say, 'Our niece Laurel did these, is she not talented?'

But best of all, Laurel liked to paint flowers. She had painted almost every rose in the garden, said Hazel. And she did flower studies of the pansies in spring, the lilies of the valley, the peonies and phlox bushes of summer, the blue iris and the daisies. In autumn nothing was safe from Laurel's happy paint brush, the crimson maple tree, the golden oaks, and the autumn flowers – the gladioli, marigolds, asters of purple and mauve and yellow.

Delia would arrange a vase of flowers, and when the rains were too damp to go outdoors, Laurel would sit before the vase and paint. She tried to make every flower and leaf and stem exact, and both the art teacher and the botany teacher praised her. It was the way Jim Winfield had taught her, but Laurel could rarely bring herself to speak of her father. There was still unspoken criticism of 'that artist fellow' in the Rutherford household, though they rarely said anything directly against him. He had carried off Arnold's beloved sister, who might be alive today but for him.

Laurel could not say fiercely, as she longed to say, 'But Mother loved the life. She would rather have lived a short life with Father, in the wilderness, than a long life apart from him.'

That was impractical, and irrational, to their view. They were

106

good people, though, and kind to her, so kind she could not say mean things to them at all.

Then in June, after school was out, and the girls were busy with their summer projects of linen-turning, pillowcase making, hope chest filling, a visitor came. It was a man named Bill Prentice. Laurel had met him briefly in Sitka.

Aunt Gertrude sent for Laurel, and she came down to the parlor and stared. 'Oh, it's Mr. Prentice!' she finally said.

His ruddy face beamed as he shook Laurel's hand shyly. He had worked for several years for the Koenigs. 'Pleased to see you, miss!'

She introduced him to Aunt Gertrude, and her aunt sent for Arnold. Mr. Prentice had returned to the East on the death of some relatives; there was an estate to be tied up. He had news of everybody in Alaska, and a letter and parcel from Thor.

Arnold came from the dry goods store and the girls came down from their work. Mr. Prentice was invited for lunch and to spend the afternoon.

The parcel was a large rectangular package, well bound in cardboard and brown paper. Laurel opened it on the parlor table, much puzzled. It was very light for its size.

'Thor said to open the letter first,' suggested Mr. Prentice. 'It explains what's in the package.'

So Laurel opened it and skimmed the long letter. 'Oh, he has pressed some flowers for me!' she exclaimed in delight.

Delia's and Hazel's faces fell. They had anticipated presents, furs or jade or ivory. But . . . pressed flowers!

Laurel opened the parcel then, carefully. She was delighted with the contents. Thor had worked through the summer and into much of the winter, gathering flowers, pressing and drying them, and stacking them ready for mailing.

What work he had gone to! She thought of him pausing to gather the flowers, dry them, press them, take care of them on his rough journeys about the country, through snows. And saving them all, just for her! She was thrilled at the idea he had taken all this trouble for her.

And the flowers had kept much of their color. She exclaimed over the delicate wildflowers, the anemones, the violets of deep purple, the white lobelia, the pale blue veronica, bluish purple gentians, shooting stars of mauve, rose-colored laurel, yellow willow herb from the mountains, delicate spirea, buttercups, and best of all a clump of her favorite pale blue forget-me-nots.

Not only had Thor taken care with the blooms, but he had labeled each page in a heavy black ink with the names of the flowers he knew. He must have asked people about them, she thought, for some were ones he had not known when she talked with him. Tears filled her eyes. He had been so thoughtful!

'Do you like it, miss?' Mr. Prentice beamed anxiously. 'I heard tell he worked a long time on this. He was asking me all the time to take good care of the parcel!'

'Oh, you couldn't have brought me anything I would like more!' she cried with such passion that he blinked, and eyed the parcel with more respect. To his view it was not the kind of present young ladies liked, but this lady must be different. 'I will be able to paint all of these, you see,' she tried to explain, her face glowing. 'I tried to paint them from memory, but I couldn't do them all. I had sketches of some of them, but not of many.'

'It was most thoughtful of Mr. Koenig,' said Aunt Gertrude, rather relieved that the present from the forceful Mr. Koenig was so innocuous. He did know how to treat a lady with respect, she felt. 'A considerate gift for a girl of Laurel's tender years. And she certainly has a talent for painting.'

'Oh, that's it, then,' said Mr. Prentice. 'Well, Mr. Koenig will be right pleased you're happy with it, and if you write, would you tell him I delivered it in good order?'

'I certainly will, and I thank you kindly,' said Laurel, gathering up the pages tenderly and anxiously, to carry them to the table in her bedroom. She saved the letter for later reading, returning at once to the parlor to hear Mr. Prentice's news. He was a good storyteller, as many of the lonely men of the Arctic were, and had a graphic way of describing events.

He really sang for his supper, as Uncle Arnold said later with a grin. The big man told them about his hunting, a fight with a huge trout that did not want to be caught. He described some of the new mine operations in the Arctic conditions of deep snow and ice. He told them all the news of Sitka, whether they knew the people or not. It was all one to him; if the story was interesting, it was worth telling.

They listened wide-eyed, those Boston people, yet feared it could not be completely true. Laurel also admitted some private doubts whenever he gave her a large friendly wink. But she believed the stories of his struggle over a grizzly bear, his near death from frostbite, the long trek through the snows, with Thor behind a dog sled, to get an injured man to a doctor.

He stayed for dinner that evening and told them more stories, then reluctantly took his departure. Uncle Arnold sent him home in his carriage, to the relatives, and cordially invited him to return again. Mr. Prentice came once more before his return to Alaska, and Laurel had a letter and a package of her sketches to send back with him to Thor.

She wrote a long newsy letter to Thor, about her studies, her relatives and how kind they were, the concerts she had attended, her sketching, her delight with the flowers he had sent.

She also went through her recent sketches, found a dozen she liked, and sent them to him – paintings of the Charles River, some autumn trees, Hazel and Delia reading by the lamp, her aunt and uncle working in the garden. She sent one done by memory of Rex. And she had sat in front of her mirror and carefully worked out one of herself dressed up in a blue silk gown and lace Bertha, with her hair done up in a coronet about her head, and her new earrings of gold from Uncle Arnold bobbing at her ears. She studied it anxiously. Did she look more mature, much older? She did not want to look like a child to him; after all she was seventeen, it was 1904, and she had celebrated her seventeenth birthday in April.

Laurel was finally as satisfied as she could manage to be with the sketch, and sent it also. 'I am so happy with the flowers you sent by Mr. Prentice,' she wrote. 'You were so kind and thoughtful to work on them, and save them for me. I've missed the flowers and my Alaska friends and hope to return one day before long. I have one more year of finishing school, and my studies are going well. Do give my best regards to your father; he was most kind to write to me, and I hope he received my letter last winter. And thank you for the good long letter. I am happy to have all your news. With very best regards from your friend, Laurel.'

Chapter 10

Ewan had decided to take his bear's head to Wrangell, to have it mounted. He was restless too, so suddenly one August morning he took off and was gone.

Jade stood silently watching him depart, in dismay. He had left! And with no more than a cheerful word of thanks for their hospitality! And she had said nothing of what she wanted to say.

He had spoken no parting words to her. Perhaps he would return this autumn, yet – . No, he was going back to Sitka, he had said.

The first days without him were dismal. She had become accustomed to his demanding presence, his plans for each day, his wants, his wishes. Now he was gone, and all seemed so very unbearably quiet.

She was so absorbed in her unhappy thoughts that for a time she did not pay attention to her body. Then abruptly she was aware, and terrified. Her blood had stopped flowing in the monthly cycle. She waited, it did not come. And the following month it did not come either. Her mind seemed paralyzed; she worked mechanically. She was pregnant! And Ewan did not return.

She could not force herself to tell her parents. They would be shocked, probably angry and accusing. Surely Ewan would return and marry her! He too would want the child. He would want a son like himself, so big and strong. Yet –

He did not know she was pregnant; she must tell him. But how? There was no way to get a letter to him, unless she went to Wrangell. And how could she tell him in a letter? No, she must tell him herself. She must go to Wrangell.

She finally thought of a way. She told her parents she did not want to remain in the wilderness that winter. 'I have been consider-ing I should get a job,' she said.

'A job? Why?' asked her father blankly.

'Because I cannot remain here forever. I must learn to work and earn my living. For you, it is different,' she said carefully. 'You can work with furs and Mother helps. But I am not married —'

'Ah,' said her mother significantly. They were all silent consider-ing. They were not able to arrange a marriage for their daughter with their friends and relatives. Therefore Jade must go out in the world and meet other men. That made sense.

They accompanied Jade to Wrangell, crossing the wide river, and paying the boatmen for their aid. In town they looked about uncer-tainly. They had often camped near this town when selling their furs. But now they had to find Jade a decent place to live and a job. Finally they saw one restaurant, where a woman worked alone and ran the boarding house upstairs too.

Mrs. Simpson was a widow in her thirties, and a busy bustling woman. Jade approached her timidly.

'May I talk to you? I need a job. I can cook,' she said. The woman brushed back her wispy hair and surveyed the dark-haired Indian girl.

'And you talk English too,' she said, unexpectedly. 'What cook-ing can you do, girl?'

'Meats, sourdough biscuits, preserves, greens. And I can wash up and clean house . . .'

'How old are you?'

'Sixteen, ma'am.'

'And your folks approve.'

'Yes, ma'am.' And Jade hurriedly brought in her parents to meet Mrs. Simpson.

The woman offered Jade a job, at five dollars a week, with her meals and a room upstairs for her to live in. It was sheer wealth for the girl, and such a relief to her parents. The Nolans left the next day to return to their cabin for the winter. They would come again in the spring, they said.

As soon as Jade had a spare hour, she hurried over to the man who mounted animal heads and asked him about Ewan. He told her that Ewan had said he might come back that winter, but more likely in the spring, to claim his head. The man had mounted the head for Ewan and had it in the back room.

So Jade waited and hoped, but Ewan did not come back. The town was small, and many men came to the restaurant; surely she would know when he came.

During the week, the townsmen would come in for their lunches, usually talking business. They looked Jade over, and some tried to chat her up or ask her to go out. She firmly refused, averting her eyes shyly from their bold stares. Mrs. Simpson watched, and approved.

On the weekends, the lumbermen came in from the forests up the Stikine River, where they had their camps. They came in sometimes to have good food but more often to drink. She avoided them. One man was pleasant to her, a grave dark man named Garth Fleming. He seemed to sense her shyness, and when any drunk came near her, Garth would speak sharply to the man and send him off. Garth was so big and tall he usually had his way with no fights.

He did not ask Jade out; he just sat and watched what went on, usually at the table near the window. He wore blue jeans and a red-check shirt, like the lumbermen, but he seemed more serious than the rest of them.

Mrs. Simpson told Jade. 'He's a nice fellow, has a cabin in town that he keeps up. His wife died a couple years ago; she was a nice little lady. Died in childbirth.'

'Oh, that's too bad,' said Jade, shocked. She put her hand to her stomach involuntarily. So people died often in childbirth? Her mother had said nothing of that to her when Jade had come to puberty and her mother had told her about sex and marriage and all that.

She felt a quiet sympathy for Garth Fleming then. He had a sad look about his dark eyes. He had black straight hair like an Indian's, but he was not Indian; she knew by his face. But he was big and powerful, with long arms. She thought he would be a man to protect one, if a girl needed it. And he never talked fresh to her.

By November her pregnancy was beginning to show. Mrs. Simpson drew her aside one evening after work. 'Jade, have you been messing around men?' she asked bluntly.

Jade had tears in her eyes. 'No, not really, Mrs. Simpson! I had one lover, but he will come back and marry me . . . really, as soon as he knows!

Mrs. Simpson sighed. 'Oh, Jade, I knew something was wrong. Well, mornings and afternoons, you best lie down for an hour. And tell me if you don't feel good. There's a pretty good doc in town, Dr. Byam. Have you told your folks?'

'No, ma'am. I wanted to wait . . . until I got married.'

Mrs. Simpson looked at the hopeful face and shook her head. 'Well, I'll try to do what I can,' she said wearily.

She was good to Jade that winter, not letting her work too hard. But Jade felt strong, and she worked sturdily through the days and evenings. It helped that she did not have to go outside in bad weather. Living upstairs, she could just wash and dress, and come down early to help with the breakfast. Mrs. Simpson had the next bedroom, and no men could bother her.

They tried to talk to her that winter, the bold-eyed men, noticing her condition. They asked her out, laughed and teased her, mocked her, some of them.

'Where's your man, Jade?'

'Did your man run out on you, Jade?'

'Come and live with me, Jade. I'll take good care of you!'

She would answer them firmly, 'My man is coming back to marry me,' and she would almost believe it. She had to believe it; she would die otherwise, she thought.

Garth Fleming sat and ate, his long legs sticking out from under the table, never mocking her. He would ask her quietly how she was doing. 'Fine, Mr. Fleming,' she would say. 'Would you like some hot apple pie tonight?'

'Did you make it, Jade?' he would say seriously.

'Yes, sir.'

'Then I'll have a piece. You're a good cook.'

'Thank you, sir.'

And she would cut him an extra big piece, and put a piece of cheese on top, just for him, because he was kind.

He worked hard through the week, she thought. He was big and tough, and quiet. Other lumbermen treated him with respect and avoided him if they got drunk. His boss sometimes came in and ate with him, and they talked trees and plots of land, and how much timber would go out in the spring.

He saved all his money, she found out when one man mocked

him for not drinking. Jade asked him why he saved it.

'Going to buy me a big piece of land one day, Jade,' he said seriously. 'Going to go into business for myself. Do the lumbering, hire some good men, make money. This is a big new land, and I want a piece of it.'

Men could do things like that, she thought. Not women.

'I wish you luck then. Reckon you'll get what you want,' she said shyly.

'Why do you say that?'

She thought about it, pausing at his table. 'Some men get what they want, because they work hard at it. Others don't, because they are all talk.'

His face relaxed, and a slow rare smile came to his large mouth, lightening his dark face. 'Reckon you're right about that, Jade. Hate to think I'm all talk.'

'No, you aren't all talk,' she said primly. She poured more coffee for him and moved on to another table. Talking with him made her feel good and warm; he was so pleasant, and he treated her like a white girl, a human being.

In Wrangell she was finding out the difference between being an Indian girl and being a white girl. The white girls got the raised hats and the bows and scrapes, and the nice words. The Indian girls got the bold stares and the nasty whispers and the suggestions no matter what kind of girl one was.

And now that she showed her pregnancy, it was all the worse. Some nights Jade cried in her pillow, from anger and loneliness. And anxiety. When would Ewan come and make everything all right?

Finally the cold bitter winter decided to leave, and some light southern winds came along and blew out the ice in the river. She watched the ice chunks melt and bump each other and pile up, then move out. Surely he would come soon.

Then one day she saw him in the street. Her breath caught; then she slammed down the coffee pot and ran out of the restaurant, without stopping for her coat and scarf. 'Ewan, Ewan,' she cried, wild with joy.

He turned around and saw her. Now all would be all right. The

114

long waiting was over; he would take care of her, he would marry her. The anxiety and doubting were over.

Then she saw his face as he stared at her taking in the bulk of her body. 'Jade,' he gasped. 'What in hell –'

She panted, coming up to him, almost overbalancing. She was eight months along, and it was hard to keep her footing in the muddy street. The mud was thick and gray and slick.

'Oh, Ewan, you came, you came!' she sobbed, catching hold of his arm.

He stared down at her, and the distaste on his face was sickening to her. 'My God, Jade, what have you done?'

She stiffened. 'I'm having your baby, Ewan,' she said in a low tone. This was not the way she had imagined the scene. She had thought she would meet him properly in the parlor at the boarding house, and he would take her in his arms and kiss her, and ask her to marry him.

'My baby?' he laughed shortly. 'Got any proof of that? You've been messing around men, Jade!' But his blue eyes were turning gray with anger, and he didn't look into her eyes.

'You know it's yours,' she said steadily. 'Last summer –'

He cut her off with: 'You should have been careful.' He tried to shake off her arm and started walking along the street. She clung to him and walked along hastily beside him, not regarding the stares of the passersby.

'You know it's your fault,' she said quickly. 'Ewan, you owe it to me. We got to get married. I'm due in another month, in May. We can get married in town, there's a preacher –'

From the side of her eye, she saw Garth Fleming going down the street on the other side. He saw them and paused. Embarrassed, she turned Ewan toward her.

'Now, listen, Jade, you got yourself in trouble. I don't owe you anything!' He jerked free of her and turned the corner of the street, walking down toward the river. Jade saw a large boat there. It must be his! she thought. And he would be going!

She gasped, in pain and pleading. 'Listen, Ewan, we must get married! You won't be ashamed of me. I can talk good English, and cook, and –'

'I'm not going to marry any Injun girl,' he said between his teeth, his blond face red with fury. 'I'm a Koenig; we're big people! What would my folks say? And you're Injun. Whites don't marry Injuns!'

'Yes, they do! Yes. . . they do!' She burned with the injustice. 'I'm a good girl, you know it! And plenty of men marry Indian girls! I know some –'

'Well, I don't, and I don't have to,' he said and shook off her arm once more. 'Don't follow me, Jade! I'll get mad!'

He kept striding along with his long legs, and she could scarcely catch up with him. 'Ewan, please stop! Please listen to me! You must marry me! I have been waiting for you all the winter. . . it is your baby. You'll be proud of him . . . and I'll work hard . . .'

Jade half sobbed, half pleaded. He kept his face averted from her, yanking away from her whenever she grabbed at him. She stumbled on the slippery ground and caught at him again to hold herself upright. He turned on her.

'You let me go, Jade! Damn it, stop following me! I don't owe a damn Injun anything! You're there for the taking; no one needs to marry you,' he hissed, his face close to hers, the eyes glazing in fury.

She fell back dismayed; then fury came to the fore. 'Oh, you damn – you damn man!' she gasped, her fists clenched. 'You said all those sweet words, and you didn't mean them. You tried to fool me.'

'It wasn't hard, Jade. You wanted me to,' he said roughly. 'Go on, Jade, face up. You asked for it. Go along and stop bothering me. Find yourself an Injun to marry.'

Anger possessed her, and rage at being so treated. She faced him on the waterfront, near his boat and the two curious Indians on board it, watching.

'You're no good!' she raged furiously, her hands on her hips. Tears of rage poured down her face. 'You're no damn good! You said words to me, and you owe me plenty! If my father was here, he would fight you, he would!'

'But he ain't here,' jeered Ewan. He turned his back and started toward his boat. In fury she ran after him and pounded on his shoulders and back.

'You listen to me!' she cried.

He flung his arm and struck her as he tried to push her away. 'You stay away from me!' he yelled.

She slipped, but caught at him to save herself once more. The thick gooey gray mud was slick, and on the river bank the mud was sliding down toward the cold icy waters of the Stikine River.

He flung his arm again, trying to push her away. With a cry of fear, she felt herself sliding, slipping toward the river. He shook himself, and she lost her balance, uncertain at best because of her late pregnancy. She fell and slid right into the river.

The cold shock of it caught her breath; then she began to scream. She choked, the river water in her mouth; she coughed, and got more water in her throat. She threshed about, unable to find bottom it was so deep.

She had hurt her side against the end of his boat when she fell, it was sticking out of the water near where they had fought. Now her side pained her and doubled her up. She fought, kicking, trying to scream a plea to Ewan.

Strong arms caught and grabbed at her. A firm voice said, 'Quit kicking!' and she stopped, relieved, as someone held her up. Had Ewan come for her? But no . . . it was not his voice, it was lower, deeper.

Choking, gasping for breath, she was drawn firmly out of the water, slipping and sliding up the muddy bank. One of the Indians on the boat held out a paddle, and Garth Fleming caught hold of it and hauled them out onto the mud again. Then he was pulling them both up further on the mud bank, and onto the wharf, where he could get a footing on the planks.

She was half unconscious, unable to breathe for the water in her nose and mouth. He picked her up, both dripping wet.

'What're you doing?' growled Ewan. 'She can manage herself!'

'Get away from me,' Garth hollered at Ewan. Jade could only half make out what they were saying. It didn't matter. All that mattered now was breathing, and resting; her side hurt her so much. Oh God, the baby, she thought. Oh God, had she hurt the baby?

'Haul off,' said Ewan, in a faraway voice. One of the Indians grunted. He was leaving, him and his boat, but she could not even cry out to him.

Garth was carrying her away, his clothes dripping wet, as hers were. He carried her down a side street, along the plank boardwalk, and still further, an alleyway.

He kicked open a door and brought her inside. He set her down carefully at the fireplace. 'Take off your clothes, Jade. I'll get you a blanket,' he said gruffly.

No time for modesty, and she was dazed by what had happened. She struggled out of her plaid shirt and thick long skirt, her brief underclothes and heavy wet shoes. Garth was there with a long blanket to wrap around her shivering heavy form.

Then he bent to the fire and lit it, neatly, quickly. Soon the fire was crackling up in the fireplace. She looked around, dazed, to see the cabin.

It was a big one, she thought. She was in a sort of parlor, and through one door was a room with a big bed. The kitchen was off the parlor, with a big black stove with pipes going up to the roof. Garth knelt before her, with a thick towel in his hands, and began to dry her hair, which streamed down over her face and shoulders.

'Was that your man?' he demanded as he sat back on his heels and stared at her.

She nodded, and tears dripped down her face.

'Not much of a man,' he grunted. 'You're well off without him!'

She gulped. 'But I love him, and he loves me!' she said, bewildered and lost. 'Last summer, he loved me. Why did he do that, if he did not love me? He would have married me.'

'You poor foolish child,' he said roughly.

He got up and went to the kitchen, and soon brought back some hot coffee with whisky in it. She gulped it, choked, and felt some better, but it made her sleepy. He picked her up and put her into the big bed in the other room.

When she woke up, Mrs. Simpson was there. They talked over her head about her, though she was awake.

'Big bruise on her back,' said Garth. 'I don't know if it will bring the baby sooner. Next days should see.'

'I can't take care of her,' said Mrs. Simpson slowly. 'It could take night and day, and I got my work to do. I'm sorry for her, but I can't do it.'

'I can . . . take care . . . of myself,' said Jade weakly, fighting the blanket that was wound around her. Her pride was hurt, and her feelings.

'Stay quiet, Jade,' Garth ordered. He tucked the blanket tightly

118

about her shoulders once more, so she felt like a baby in a cocoon. 'I'll take care of her. Won't hurt me to take off work for a time.'

'Well, I'll stop in,' Mrs. Simpson said, sounding relieved. 'I'll take her back when she's well. She's a good worker.'

'No, I'll take care of her. She needs someone to look after her,' said Garth, sounding more alive than he usually did, not so deep-down stolid. 'This child is about alone in the world; her folks are far off in the mountains.'

'You want to?' asked Mrs. Simpson slowly.

'Sure.' They went to the door and murmured some. Jade stirred restlessly.

The door shut. Garth had come back. He sat by the side of the wide bed. The bedroom looked nice, with chintz curtains at the windows and a nice chair with a pillow on it. She blinked at him.

'You can't take care of me,' she said weakly. She tried to sit up, but the blanket held her, and a hurt in her back made her cry out.

'You lie still. Back hurt much?'

She nodded, weak tears in her eyes. She blinked them back.

'Let me see.' He uncovered her gently and rolled her enough to see her back. He whistled softly. 'Huge bruise, Jade. You must've banged your spine. I'll get the doctor.'

He went out and came back with old Dr. Byam, thin, graying, stooped. The doctor examined her back and asked her questions.

'It's a wonder the baby didn't come with all that banging about,' he said bluntly. 'Well, she has a chance. We'll see how the spine is. I'll drop by tomorrow. Let me know if her birth pains start. She could have a bad time.'

'I'll call you.'

Garth paid him, and Jade wanted to protest. But what could she do? She tried to thank Garth. 'I got money in the bank from my earnings,' she said weakly.

'Shush now. I'll take care of that. Let me know if you start feeling pains.'

She remembered that his young wife had died in childbirth. What if she died also? Somehow, right now it did not matter. She turned her face to the wall and remembered the disdain on Ewan's handsome blond face. How could he have turned from her? He had loved her, he had! She remembered all the words he had said to her last summer in the thick fragrant grass.

Garth's hand touched her forehead, smoothed back the thick black loose hair. 'Want anything to eat?'

She sighed. 'Yes, I guess . . . thank you.'

She must eat for herself and the baby. He brought a thick vegetable soup with a deer meat flavor, and she drank all of it.

'Good girl,' he said briskly, and went away to let her sleep.

She lay still for several days, getting up only to use the outhouse near the back of the cabin. Garth helped her gently, impersonally, as though she were a child. One evening she asked him how old he was.

'Twenty-seven. Ten years older than you. Does that seem old?'

'Not really.' But it did seem old, and he was mature and grave, not smiling much any time. She guessed he had seen many seasons of sorrow. She was glad to sink back into bed. She felt older too, much older than last summer when she had laughed and wrestled with Ewan, and had known his lovemaking.

'Does it hurt much to have a baby?' she asked him, her fingers picking restlessly at the quilt coverlet.

'Sometimes, but I'll get the doctor and he'll ease you.' His hand stroked her forehead; she liked the gentle soothing touch. He pushed back her hair. 'Shall I brush your hair tonight?'

'Please, if you want to.'

He brought the pretty brush; it had belonged to his wife, she thought, and he half sat her against the pillows while he brushed gently at the tangles of her long, thick black hair. It came to her waist; she had been so proud of it, especially when Ewan caressed it and praised her beauty . . .

'Jade?'

'Umm,' she murmured, half asleep against the pillows.

'You need someone to look after you.'

She thought of her parents; they would be shocked and disappointed in her. Maybe they would cast her off.

'I can look after myself,' she said drearily.

'It'll be hard after the baby comes. Babies need a lot of care,' he said quietly. She looked rather fearfully into his hard, strong dark face, almost as dark as an Indian's from years of working under the sun and in the blinding snow. The sun reflecting off the snows could be hotter than where there was grass.

'But what can I do?' she pleaded, catching his wrist with her slim fingers. 'What man would marry me? I'll have to work for us both.'

'I would marry you, gladly,' he said.

She looked at him blankly. He had never made a move to her; he had never said fresh words; he had never tried to kiss her.

'Why would you?' she asked.

He had a half-smile for her. 'You're a good cook, a good housekeeper,' he said. He got up. 'Think about it, Jade. I'd be good to you. And you need a man to look after you and the young one,' and he said that tenderly, as though he welcomed the idea of the baby.

She did think about it, lying in enforced quiet on the wide bed, looking out the wide wooden shutters into the green trees as spring came on slowly in Wrangell. He was a good man, a tough man, but a kind one to her. And maybe he did want a wife, and she would try to be a good wife and cook and housekeeper for him.

It isn't the way I had thought it would be, she sighed to herself. She had dreamed of excitement, such as she had had with Ewan, giggling and laughing, and having a good time. But maybe that didn't last in marriage anyway. Maybe men get cross and tired of a woman, like Ewan did of her.

And Garth Fleming had offered her a marriage, and a ring.

She agreed to the marriage, tired and worried about the future, and her baby. Garth brought the preacher Reverend Jennings, and Mrs. Simpson and Dr. Byam came and were witnesses as Garth stood beside the bed and held her hand and married her. He put a gold ring on her left hand, and she lay and looked at it after they had all left.

For a marriage present, Mrs. Simpson brought her some baby clothes and two little baby blankets. It was kind of her, but Jade felt listless and lost. Garth just treated her as normal, and didn't even try to kiss her.

A few nights later Jade felt the pains starting. Garth got up and waited with her until they came closer together; then he went for Dr. Byam.

There was wrenching pain, but not bad; the baby came rather quickly as Jade pushed and breathed as they told her to. Mrs. Simpson came in the morning, and the baby arrived soon after.

Jade knew something was wrong when the baby didn't cry much.

He was too quiet, and his little face was a pasty white; he looked like a doll, and waxy and still. Garth took the baby away to feed him some milk, and all was quiet in the parlor.

The doctor stayed awhile, then left, saying he would come back later. She lay and slept weakly, glad it was all over. It had been painful, and she was worried, with what little strength she had.

Garth brought the baby to her, and he lay in her arm for a while, sleeping. His little face was so still, he didn't move much. 'He isn't all right, is he?' she said to Garth softly.

'Doc isn't sure, yet,' he said, and bent and gently touched the little face. 'He's a game little fella; he might make it.'

But he didn't make it. He lived about three days; then his little eyelids didn't open anymore, and he stopped breathing. His lungs, said the doctor. Jade had not even named him; she had felt somehow that God didn't mean for him to live.

The fall in the river had hurt her, and the baby. She tried to hate Ewan, but it took too much effort. She had loved him so. She loved him yet, yearning for him to come and say he was sorry, that he really loved her, that he wanted her.

But he didn't want her. And Garth had married her, all in vain. Garth took the poor little boy of the baby and buried him outside, with a small wooden headpiece that he carved for him. He put 'Baby Fleming' on it and set him beside his wife's grave and the other little baby grave.

'I guess some babies don't last here in Alaska,' said Jade.

'Afraid not.' His face was still and somber as he stared at the fire. She sat wrapped in a blanket, in the chair before the fireplace, and tried to make sense of it all.

'I should not have fought with . . . him,' she said painfully. 'I should have thought first about the baby. But I was so mad and so muddled in my mind.'

'I know, Jade. The doctor thinks he might not have lived anyway,' he said gently. 'His lungs were formed bad. He couldn't breathe much from the first. Don't think about it; don't worry.'

'But you married me,' she said softly. 'And I appreciate it. You are good to me. But you need not have married me.'

'I know, but we did get married, and we are staying married,' he said, his jaw very square and his black eyebrows frowning. 'You just think about getting well and strong, Jade. You won't have anything to worry about. I'll always look after you.'

She was silent, feeling guilty. He had married her because she needed him, but one day she would be well and would not have to lean on him. It was nice to lean on him; he was strong and tough; a body could lean on him and never worry at all anymore. But she should take care of herself. She had been wicked and had been with a man before marrying, and now she had to pay the price. The baby had also paid the price . . . poor little one. She thought of his little perfect waxen features and closed her eyes in pain. She could have loved him, her little boy.

'Maybe someday,' said Garth out of the silence, 'someday you might have another baby, with me, and he will live, and we will be happy, all of us. Do you think about that, ever?'

She had not thought about that. He had scarcely touched her except to take care of her in her illness. She looked at his big hands; they had held her gently and carried the baby so carefully.

'It might . . . be . . . fine . . . Garth,' she said slowly.

And he turned and put his head against her knee as they sat there before the fire. She put her hand on his head slowly, and felt the thick softness of his black hair, and smoothed it from its roughness. Maybe it would all work out.

Chapter 11

It was March, and Laurel would graduate from high school in June. She would be eighteen in April, and she felt quite the young lady in her long skirts and with her hair up in a coronet.

Hazel had matured also, although sometimes she played the tomboy with a giggle. She could play a wild game of tennis, dressed in a red skirt to her ankles, and a red blouse that made her flushed face flame in the sunlight.

Delia would sigh at her and say, 'Hazel, you must act more like a dignified lady!'

Delia was a very dignified lady now. She was engaged to be married, to Norman Cooper, a clerk in Uncle Arnold's dry goods store. Laurel secretly thought Delia was too good for Norman; he seemed as dry and stuffy as the warehouse of the store, where he often worked. Delia was so sweet and gentle, so good-hearted; and Norman was stiff and prim and tight with money. But Uncle Arnold approved of him and said he might make Norman a partner someday.

So Delia was sewing her bridal clothes, a white silk gown with a deep hem of Valenciennes lace, a white lace veil, and all kinds of silken underclothes, and night garments that made all the girls blush to see them.

Laurel had begun to worry about her future. She would not be going on to college, she thought. The Rutherfords did not think much about college for girls because they supposed it gave them foolish ideas about equality and careers. Girls did not need that much knowledge, anyway, to run a house and bring up children.

But Laurel meant to earn a living somehow; she could not forever depend on her relatives. She had begun to cast about for some way to earn money. She painted well now, but women artists were not much regarded. And even men artists had a difficult time and lived in attics, she had heard, and did strange things to earn their daily bread.

So what could she do? She decided to approach Uncle Arnold, who was practical and full of good ideas. She went to his study one evening and asked if she might talk with him.

He laid aside his papers and beamed at her over his spectacles. 'Come in, my dear!' he said kindly. 'Sit down! I see you have something on your mind. Need a bit of funds for a dress length, or shoes?'

'Oh no, thank you, Uncle Arnold,' she said quickly. 'You have been very good to me, and I have plenty to wear. No, I wished to discuss . . . my future, after graduation.'

'Very sensible of you, my dear. You have a practical turn of mind, I am glad to see. Not like – But there, I say nothing about the past.' And he frowned, and hummed and hawed.

'Yes, Uncle Arnold, thank you.' He had been kind, rarely criticizing her father, though he felt deeply about how her father had 'carried off' his sister into a life of recklessness that had brought on her early death.

'Well, Delia will be leaving the store on her marriage in May. Her fiance does not want her to work, and she will have much to do in her new house, which I must say is very fine,' and he looked proud and gratified. He had helped buy a house for the young couple, and they had been most grateful and appreciative.

Laurel looked at him, and suddenly she knew. Uncle Arnold was going to have her take Delia's place in the store! And she felt full of dismay. She had helped out in the store on Saturdays with Hazel, and it was dull and boring, having to have patience with unsure women, totaling up accounts, doing inventory, lifting down bolt after bolt of fabric.

It was not for her; it just was not! She loved the outdoors, and the fresh pure air, and laughter. Not the quiet stifling air of a large warehouse and store, fabric dust, helping try on shoes . . .

'I had thought you could start at the store in June,' said Uncle Arnold. 'Full time, six days a week. Of course, your aunt will want you to help in the house more, now that Delia is to be married. Shall

125

we say, six hours a day in the store, and the rest of the time at the house? You will be paid half-wages, of course.'

Delia had been paid half-wages, half the wages that a man clerk received. Uncle Arnold said that was because Delia received room and board at home, but Laurel felt it was not right. Delia worked hard all the day and evening, doing her share at home, cooking, cleaning, doing the linens and so on. She had worked eight hours a day, though Uncle Arnold had called it six, smilingly, because she came home for lunch, and the walk back and forth took awhile, though it was but ten minutes each way. And in the evening, after the store closed, it took a time to clean up and put things away, and lock up.

Uncle Arnold was good, but he also was tight with a penny. He liked to get value for his money, he said. If his girls had not worked in the store, he would have had to hire two more clerks, Hazel had whispered one day, rebelliously, to Laurel.

Laurel tried to silence the defiance in her mind. He had been so good to her. She had tried to earn her way, yet they need not have taken her in at all.

'So, after graduation, you will work in the store, as Delia did,' said Uncle Arnold, leaning back in his swivel chair and beaming benignly on his niece. 'And don't worry, your aunt and I will find you a nice young man like Norman to marry! We have our eye on a prospect or two! And there is a house near to Delia that may be for sale in the near future! My dear, you have no need to worry about anything at all!'

Laurel gasped in horror! But Uncle Arnold took her surprise for pleasure and beamed all the more, putting his finger beside his nose and nodding his head.

'Surprised you, didn't I? Your aunt and I have our eyes out for you, my dear! We'll settle everything, and make sure you have a solid future. This is what I wanted for Madeline, and it could have happened, if – Well, well, I'll say no more.'

He ushered Laurel out of the study before she could say a word. She rushed up to her room, and flung herself on the bed.

Oh, she could not do it, not do it! She thought of Norman Cooper and his big wet hands when they shook hands, and the lank hair across his forehead, and his mind that thought in dollars and pennies and profit. And they would find just such a young man for her, and stifle her forever!

She shuddered. No wonder her mother had rebelled and had run off with the handsome young artist with dreamy eyes who had lured her to the wide-open spaces and the wilderness of fresh clean air and unspoiled trees and animals such as neither had seen before. No wonder her mother had fled to the West, and then to Alaska, eager to experience life to its fullest, to try her strength against the wilds, to live rough – but free.

'Alaska,' whispered Laurel, and lay back on the bed with her eyes closed. The room had faded away, the neat clean room of her aunt's house, with its cheery white-and-red draperies, and white muslin curtains, with the four-poster bed and comfortable chairs and the desk where she did her homework and painted pictures.

She saw in her mind the tall pointed Sitka spruces, and the pines and hemlocks. She saw the jagged peaks of mountains covered with snow, the blue streams with ice chunks going out in the spring. She saw the thick tundra of grass and wildflowers, the dainty blue forget-me-nots. 'No, I have not forgotten you, my Alaska,' she murmured.

She could see the shaggy bear she had shot, his head weaving, his eyes red with rage, maddened by the bullet in him. She saw her father panning the gold, up to his hips in icy waters, sending her a slow smile when she found a few golden grains in her pan. She remembered running across the plains with Jade, their laughter peeling against the chill air, the puffs of their breaths coming cold and white.

Cooking fish over an open fire, drinking coffee when the icy air made her cheeks rosy. The wind in her hair, the fresh cold breath of the glaciers in her nostrils, the smell of spruce and herbs and flowers and grass . . .

She must return to Alaska, her land, and claim her land and build her house and live her life there! But how?

She had some money in the bank, but not enough. She could work when she got there, any way at all, clerking in a store. She could do it in Sitka, not in Boston!

She could cook, clean, be a housekeeper, teach small children with her high school degree. There was work she could do, and she would do it in Alaska! But not here, not in the East, not in a formal conventional city, where she could not breathe free.

She must go to Alaska.

'Thor,' she murmured. Thor would help her. He was keeping Rex for her! Surely he expected her to return. Perhaps he would advance her the money to come; she would manage somehow! Though young ladies did not travel alone across the country, she would go somehow. There might be a family she could travel with, family with small children; she could help them . . .

She got up and went to the desk to compose a letter. After several anxious attempts, she finally took out clean paper and wrote out neatly what she had composed.

'Dear Thor, I am due to graduate from high school in June of this year. I have done well, Uncle Arnold and my teachers say. Delia is to be married in May. Uncle Arnold will give me a position in his store. However, I wish to return home, to Alaska.'

She paused to consider this, was satisfied and went on.

'I long to come to Alaska. Please, Thor, will you help me? I don't have enough money to pay my way, but I am willing to work hard. Would you advance me the money to come, or tell me how I might earn my way? I would be grateful for any help or advice, and I would quickly repay any moneys you lend me. I would be most grateful to you if you would once again help me.

'Alaska was my home once, and I have longed to return. I think so much of the beautiful land, the mountains, the lakes, the wilderness. I wish to see it again, to live there and belong there.'

She paused; had she stated her case too strongly? Perhaps it was not ladylike to plead so hard. But she felt this way, and she must be honest.

'Please help me and know that I am your grateful friend, Laurel.'

There. She sealed it, and would go to the post office to get the letter on its way immediately. It was early afternoon the next day before she could get there, but she watched the stamps being placed and pounded on satisfactorily by the clerk, and the letter was dropped in the right pile to go to Alaska.

Then she must wait, anxiously. She helped more at the house, feeling vaguely guilty that she was making such plans to get away from all these loving, but stifling, people. She helped Delia sew her

128

clothes; she made new dresses for the wedding for Hazel and herself; and she helped her aunt and uncle all she could.

Delia was married at their church in a beautiful ceremony. She was a pale and quiet bride; Laurel wondered if she was regretting the marriage. But she was always composed and never spoke much of her feelings. She would do her duty and follow her parents' wishes. How sad, thought Laurel, that she was marrying a man who would never really appreciate her fine qualities.

Laurel was all the more anxious about herself. She lived through the days and was tired enough to sleep well at nights. But when her tasks were more monotonous, she would worry over the future. What if Thor did not come, or did not receive her letter, or had no help to offer? What would she do? She must escape somehow; she would not be married off as Delia had been. And she must, must, must return to Alaska.

Then the first week of June, as she looked forward to high school graduation and studies for her final examinations, Thor arrived. She came home from school to find him taking tea with Aunt Gertrude in the parlor. Aunt Gertrude was looking flustered and upset.

'My dear Laurel, come in; you have a visitor!' Aunt Gertrude greeted her and Hazel as they came in the door.

Thor was standing, smiling. He looked taller and more commanding than ever, his blond hair bleached by the sun, his face heavily tanned, his shoulders seeming more broad.

Thor wore a dark blue suit, with white shirt and stiff collar and cuffs of linen. His waistcoat matched the lining of his coat, of a handsome light blue striped silk, and a blue knotted tie at his throat. His green eyes were icy like the northern skies, she thought, when the northern lights were blazing. He held out a large bronze hand to her; she put her slim one in it, and her heart beat like crazy for her joy. Thor had come!

Hazel was admiring him, eyes wide, taking him all in. In her blue schoolgirl suit and white shirt with the middy collar, Laurel felt immature next to his evident maturity and confidence. But she could have hugged him as he smiled down at her.

'Oh, Thor, it is so good to see you . . . so very good.' He squeezed her slim hand in a secret message and nodded his handsome head.

'It is very good to see you, Laurel, all grown up. Your aunt says you have been a good girl, and help much about the house and the store,' he said solemnly. With a rush of joy, she realized he was teasing her.

'I have tried hard,' she said demurely. 'You have come for my graduation? It is in four days!'

'Splendid, I timed my arrival well,' he said. 'I must see several people; then we may depart within a week, Laurel.'

'Depart?' Aunt Gertrude looked faint. Hazel squeaked. Laurel could have jumped up and down with delight.

He meant it! He was taking her home, home to Alaska!

'Yes, Laurel's home is in Alaska,' Thor said firmly. 'It was her father's wish for her to live there,' he added, and none could dispute him.

'But – But – ' sputtered Aunt Gertrude. 'She's going to work in her uncle's store! We have plans – '

'I am sure she would do well,' said Thor. 'But I have come to take her home.'

And Thor was the kind of man none dared dispute for long. Uncle Arnold came home, and waved his hands, and smoked his cigars furiously. But Thor just smiled, and shook his head, and bought two trunks for Laurel to pack her goods, all of them, he had said.

'But she cannot travel alone with you, a young man, to Alaska,' said Arnold, triumphantly. 'It is not done!'

'Not at all. I intend to hire a couple to come with us. I am conducting interviews this week,' Thor said suavely. 'Several persons have already applied to come and live in Alaska. When I find the right ones, they will accompany us, of course. Someone decent and respectable, to work in Sitka with our firm.'

The next day Thor brought a young couple to meet Laurel and her family, to reassure them. Patsy and Mike Dugan were a newly married Irish couple. Patsy's parents had come from Ireland with nothing but their hard working hands, as she said cheerfully. She had worked as a lady's maid, as a cook and housekeeper, and had saved enough to have some laid by when she married Mike, a bartender, a horseman, and a farmer.

Both were eager to make a new start in the land of Alaska, willing and able to do any of many tasks. Thor had hired them to live in the

130

new house he was building, to take care of it, and his horses and dogs. He still lived at home with his parents, but from what little he said, Laurel realized he was fed up with his stepmother. Patsy would take care of the house, train a cook and maids. Mike would handle the outdoor work, and oversee the Indian boys Thor had hired.

They were bright young people, rosy-cheeked, blue-eyed, eager to make a new start in a land where they didn't look down on the Irish, as Patsy confided later.

Uncle Arnold felt a little better about Laurel's going to Alaska with Patsy to chaperone her.

Her relatives wept when Laurel departed. She wept too, for leaving them, but also for joy in the leaving. She hugged them all, thanked them for her care and education, and promised to write. 'And come if you can!' she urged them.

Uncle Arnold looked rather pathetic as he gazed at Laurel. 'But I never wanted the girl to follow in her mother's path,' he cried. 'Madeline died up there in that ghastly land! It is too harsh for a delicately raised female!'

'Laurel is not delicately raised,' said Thor, more gently. 'She is sturdy, tough, determined. She can take it. She enjoys the land, the challenge of it, as men do. Yet we will protect her, Mr. Rutherford,' he added. 'You may be sure of that.'

Uncle Arnold had to be satisfied with that, but he did look grieved, and Laurel was sorry for that.

'It takes a special kind of female to live in Alaska and be happy there,' Thor went on. 'The woman must be courageous, self-sufficient, able to adapt to harsh conditions. It is best if she can ride, shoot, know how to stay alive in snow and rain and cold. She must be able to cook and sew, grow vegetables, and take care of animals if she must. But for those who can manage, it is a marvelous, free life, with challenges that make one grow physically, mentally, and spiritually.'

Aunt Gertrude wept. 'But she could have an easy life with us!' she cried. 'Why should she want to go way up there?' And she never did understand why.

Delia hugged Laurel and whispered that she wished her well. 'I know you will be happy there, Laurel; you have longed for your Alaska,' she said, and Laurel knew that her cousin did understand her. Gentle good Delia, how she wished she could take her along, and make her live a wonderful life!

Thor was gone for several days, returning only just in time for Laurel's graduation. He looked quite satisfied with himself, and later she learned why.

She marched down the aisle of the schoolhouse auditorium, beaming on all her schoolmates who did not have the excitement before them that she did. Happily she received her diploma that signified that she had passed all her courses satisfactorily. Joyfully she accepted the congratulations of the adults. If only they knew how happy she was, that she had finished these preliminaries and could now go on to her real life!

Thor sat with her relatives, and indulgently went through the ceremonies. Her uncle and aunt gave her a sturdy coat and boots for her graduation gift, instead of the bracelet like the one they had given to Delia. She would have more use for the coat and boots, they said gloomily.

She thanked them sincerely for the thought. Thor winked at her, and handed her a small box. She opened it, and cried out with pleasure. It was a delicate gold chain, with a watch pendant on it, of lovely black-and-gold design. Inside the case were inscribed her name and the date, and 'From Thor.'

Hazel gave her a new flowery hat of white straw and blue flowers. Aunt Gertrude wondered when she would wear it. 'In the summer in Alaska,' said Hazel.

'But I thought it was always cold and snow!' said her mother, grimly.

They saw her off at the railroad station. Thor had paid two porters to carry all their trunks and cases and hat boxes. They had a car for themselves, and Thor said when they got to New York City they would change to a private coach. A friend of his was loaning it to them for the journey to Chicago.

Laurel was overawed when she saw the private coach. It was a grand affair, of mahogany paneling and furniture in the Victorian style of red plush. They had a dining table to themselves with a chandelier over it, and huge sofas at the large windows. It was the last coach on the train, and they could look out the rear windows or stand on the back platform to watch the scenery go by.

Next to the private coach was a sleeping coach, and they had that to themselves too. Thor had bought out the space! He had hired a porter just for themselves, who brought their dinners to them, kept the bathrooms spotless and their bed linen immaculate.

Nights, Laurel had a little bedroom to herself, with a cunning bed in it and a chair and wash basin. In the daytime she sat in the parlor coach and luxuriated in the views, the plush chair and sofas, the bowls of fresh fruit, books to read, and magazines and newspapers put on at various stops.

In Chicago they left the train and traveled, in several carriages for themselves and their luggage, across Chicago to take the train across the West. Again Thor had been loaned a private coach, and it was even more luxurious. It belonged to a business friend, he said, and Laurel was beginning to realize that her friend was a very important man, with important friends of wealth and position.

No wonder it had not been a trouble for Thor to come! He had business in Boston, in New York and Chicago, as well as in San Francisco! Some friends of his were on the second train, and during the daytime he often held business conferences with them, and Laurel would sit in the background, meekly, pretending interest in her book. They were always kind, those gentlemen with huge moustaches and some with beards, with their cigars and brandy glasses, talking of margins, and lumber, of silver and stock exchanges, and the future of Alaska.

Laurel sat in her red velvet chair and gazed out at the landscape, which she had traveled once in a wagon with her parents. No wagon and oxen now, or cold beans, and buffalo her father had shot, or rabbits cooked on spits. No sleeping under the stars close to the campfire for warmth and protection from wolves. No cold nights or hot sun-burning days when sweat rolled down her cheeks under the sunbonnet.

No, she had a maid to brush her hair and keep her clothes clean. She wore silk dresses and lace shawls, suede slippers of black or gray or blue, or high-buttoned shoes of the finest leather.

She sat and read, or looked at the scenery or took out one of her sketch pads and filled it with scenes of cowboys, wild buffalo, an Indian riding beside the train shaking his lance, a desolate prairie town with train station, saloon, and a few leaning houses. She sketched the plains, with its thick grasses, its sand, and its cacti. And the high mountains in the distance as they neared the Rocky Mountains. Now she would go to the rear platform and lean on the railing to gaze at where they had been, at the wide ranges unrolling behind them and only the two rails of their train narrowing after them to recede in the distance.

She would secretly watch Thor's intent face as he talked as one among equals with the older businessmen. She noted how they treated him with respect. He was 'Mr. Koenig' to them, and they asked his opinion about Sitka, and Juneau, and Wrangell, and the copper possibilities, and about the gold, and about the Indian labor, and how many prospectors were coming up next summer. What did he think about the Interior, and what did he think the government would do about this, and what were the prospects for statehood, and did they want to be independent, and would Canada try to take them over, and were the gold prospects exaggerated.

Sometimes they remained for dinner, and Laurel would be hostess, and they called her 'Miss Winfield,' and treated her with great respect. She had finished her education, said Thor, and was returning home to Alaska. She was a fine artist, he said of her, and they murmured and looked at her sketches critically and said nice things to her.

And she would wear her blue silk with the gold pendantwatch and chain, or Thor's necklace of pearls that he had given her in Chicago. Or she would wear her dark ruby silk, with the lace fichu. Or sometimes her light rose cotton faille on a warmer day, with a little jacket of white linen. Thor's eyes always shone with approval of her, and he would gaze thoughtfully at the neat chignon of her hair. Patsy had clever hands, and could do wonders with a chignon of Laurel's thick brown wavy hair, and make it look as fine as an opera star's.

And Thor would look warmly at Laurel, and she would blush and feel warm inside. His icy green eyes could be warm as the summer grass, she thought. And he was always kind and courteous to her, sometimes a little teasing, but always nice.

She was radiantly happy. She was going home, home to Alaska! She did not know what she would do there, but somehow she would find a job, and work her fingers to the bone, if necessary. She would repay Thor somehow too, and show her gratitude. But she was going home, that was all that mattered.

'You look very pretty tonight,' Thor said one evening. They were about two days out of San Francisco, and they would remain a few days for Thor's business, then take the ship home! 'You look very happy, young Laurel!'

She shone up at him, her dark brown eyes starry. 'I am so very happy, Thor,' she said simply. 'I am happier than I ever was in my life!'

'Good,' he said, and bent and kissed her lips teasingly. His lips moved slowly on hers, then he lifted his head. 'I'm glad. You deserve to be happy.'

'I'm so glad you came to take me home,' she said with a sigh of pleasure. He must like me, she thought, to have kissed me. And she touched his arm confidently. 'I knew you would come; somehow I knew you would come.'

'How did you know?' he asked, a slight smile on his mouth. He was looking down at her mouth.

'Oh . . . I just knew,' she said, disconcertedly.

'I came because you asked, Laurel. Then I was sure you wanted to come,' he said seriously. 'I had thought you might like Boston and civilization too much to want to leave there. But you didn't. You tasted it well and chose to return to Alaska.'

'Yes, I wanted to come home,' she said. 'I can't wait to see the skies, and the rivers, and the seals, and the northern lights – oh, everything!'

'Good. You've made your choice,' he said, and made it sound very final. She did not have a chance to ask him what he meant, for the men came in then for dinner.

Two days later they arrived in San Francisco. Thor put up Laurel and Patsy at the hotel, and told them to stay there, while he and Mike ran around town. He did take them out evenings, but he did not want Laurel walking around alone, or just with Patsy. San Francisco was a pretty wild town, he said.

He and Mike met some men, and bought some fine riding horses, and transacted business about lumber and silver and a new ship. Then at dawn of a glorious day they boarded one of the Koenig steamers, and started north.

Laurel was at the deck railing much of the daytime. She watched eagerly as they steamed past stands of dark Douglas firs, and tall Sitka spruces, bushes and clearings, a few towns. Then they left towns behind them, to sail in and around the islands of the Inland Passage. The sun shone and the sea was a glorious blue-green, and the waves churned white, and even the birds seemed to sing, 'Welcome home, Laurel, welcome home!'

Thor would come to lean on the railing with her, blowing his cigar smoke away from her. He would talk about Alaska, and the changes, and the many people who had come.

She would gaze at the green islands they were passing, and listen to Thor's deep musical voice as he talked, and think that Heaven could not be more exciting and beautiful.

He would say, 'You may not know Sitka, it has grown so large. I'm glad I bought my piece of land when I did. You should see my house soon. I want you to tell me what to do with the parlor and drawing room furniture. I want to order more made.'

And he would talk about going north to the copper mine. They had added more than two hundred men to the operation. He rarely spoke of Ewan, his brother, and then with a frown. Ewan was neglecting his work at times, and he had gotten a woman in trouble. His father was very displeased with Ewan, he was so wild.

Laurel thought of poor Jade; she hoped she did not still fancy herself in love with Ewan. He sounded like so much trouble.

But she was happy, and troubles seemed far away. The sun was warm, the breeze cool, the islands green and thick with bushes and trees. And they came nearer and nearer to Alaska, and Sitka, her future home.

Thor leaned down, and kissed her cheek quickly as she gazed out dreamily. 'You have grown beautiful, Laurel,' he said, and her joy was complete.

Laurel was abruptly shy with him, and turned her head away. Her heart beat fast. Could he be falling in love with her? She loved him, she felt she had always loved him; he was such a strong fine person, so handsome and distinguished looking. He commanded respect from everybody. He was a wonderful man, probably too wonderful to look at her.

But when he gazed down at her, and his green eyes were gentle, she felt he might . . . possibly might . . . one day fall in love with her. And that would be the most marvelous, grand, tremendous thing in the world, that Thor should love her.

Could such dreams come true?

Her dream of Alaska was coming true, that was certain. Maybe when one dreamed strongly enough, it could happen.

Chapter 12

In Sitka Rex greeted his mistress with some tentative woofs and sniffed around her for a short time. His eyes were glazed with film.

'He's going blind, I fear, Laurel,' Thor said gently, watching their reunion. The dog seemed slower of movement. 'I think he's about twelve or thirteen years old. I take him out daily when I'm here, but he moves more stiffly.'

'Oh, poor darling Rex,' murmured Laurel lovingly as she stroked his fine head and ruffed up the fur around his neck. 'Don't you remember me, love?'

Rex gave a tremendous 'Woof!' and barked a short loud bark, then began to dance stiffly around her, coming back to sniff her hand and lick her fingers.

'You do remember me!' she cried and hugged him. He licked enthusiastically at her cheek and neck as she laughed and half cried over him. 'I thought of you so often!'

Olaf Koenig was happy to see her, greeted her kindly, told her she was beautiful, and beamed on her often.

His wife Sidonie was not nearly so happy. In fact she hinted that Laurel should soon find a home of her own, and a job. But Thor refused firmly.

'No, I want Laurel to relax and have fun. She's been working hard on her studies and in the store. She needs time to rest and do some painting. Laurel, you are not to look for a job!'

'Yes, she's our guest here,' seconded Olaf Koenig. 'My, what a lovely lady she's become! We must have parties for her, Sidonie, to reintroduce her to our friends here.'

That did not suit Sidonie at all, Laurel realized. She was quite the mistress of the Koenig home, and took her position seriously. She

138

liked to entertain the up and coming politicians, including Addison Leverett and his daughter Clarissa. She always had guests there when she could, important guests, she emphasized coldly to Laurel, of the visiting businessmen, wealthy investors, mining executives, an opera singer, an artist.

But Thor coolly gave Laurel the best guest room at the back of the house, overlooking the mountains, and another room next to it for a room to paint in, with a north view. Sidonie objected violently, but he overruled her, and his father said, 'Oh, let it be, Sidonie; there's always plenty of room!'

Laurel had the feeling Olaf Koenig had had his eyes opened to Sidonie; they now slept in separate rooms, and he did not come home often until late evening. And he would take off for weeks at a time, leaving her with no regret. She was a difficult woman to live with, a perfectionist, who hated mud and dust trailed in 'her' house, who wanted people on time for dinner, the best foods served at her table, the best wines, the best guests in her home, the most important people bowing to her. And she had a fierce temper when she was aroused, and a lingering enmity to anyone who crossed her.

Servants came and went there; she never kept any of them for long. She said that they trained under her, then got higher paying jobs. Laurel felt she roused no loyalty in her servants, and they could not endure her spiteful moods and tempers.

Natasha had left; she had gone to work for Thor in his new house. Patsy and Mike Dugan were living there, taking over for him, and overseeing the completion of the house.

Thor soon gave Laurel a guided tour of his new home, and she found it beautiful. He drove her there in a carriage; it was about a mile from his parents' house, and she resolved to walk there other times to see it.

The house was of stone and brick, unlike many of the Sitka houses which were of wood. But fire was a frequent hazard, and Thor told Laurel, 'I want this house to last. I don't mean to rebuild every few years. And I will have treasures in it; I don't want them burned! You will see some of your framed sketches there, and I should like to have a painting from you before long!'

She looked to see if he was teasing her. He was not.

'Oh, I should like to give you a hundred paintings, if you

wished!' she said happily. 'What subject would you like?'

'Whatever you want to paint!'

She smiled, and resolved to watch his tastes and interests in the next weeks. When she had a clue, she would paint what he would like in his home, still lifes, or outdoor scenes, or portraits, or animals.

Mike Dugan and an Indian boy came to take the carriage and horses when Thor pulled up in the muddy lane. The stables had been built in the back, just where Laurel had indicated they should go, and beside them the long kennels for dogs. They were empty as yet; Thor had not moved in, she realized.

Patsy Dugan stood on the balcony waiting to greet them. She was smiling and waving, attractive in a bright blue calico dress and mobcap.

'There now, Miss Laurel! I was hoping you would come over soon!' she exclaimed.

Laurel greeted her warmly. Patsy had won her respect and affection on their long journey together. 'It is good to see you. Are you all settled here?'

'Oh yes, miss! And right happy we are! Such a nice suite already on the third floor, with our own bath and all! And so much to do. It is a real pleasure!'

She opened the front door for them. It was a large double door, of mahogany carved with Indian symbols of raven and eagle, like a miniature totem pole. Laurel admired them before entering into the wide hallway.

In the center of the hall, toward the back, was a beautiful cedarwood staircase, winding up to the next two floors. Under it was a closet for coats and hats and canes.

On either side of the hall were sliding doors, so that the parlor on one side and the drawing room on the other could all be opened up and made into one huge reception area. Laurel, admiring the cunning workmanship, slid open one door and back again, eagerly. Thor watched her with a smile, standing back to let her explore as she wished.

The rooms were empty; there was no carpet on the floor, no draperies and curtains.

Patsy Dugan said in a low voice to Thor, 'Miss Leverett came yesterday, sir, and insisted on seeing over the house. She said you wanted her suggestions for the furnishings.' She looked fussed and troubled.

'Um.' Thor looked thoughtful. 'Well, it was kind of her,' he said. 'I expect she will tell me what she thought.'

'Yes, sir.' Patsy turned back to Laurel, whose heart had gone into her smart boots. So Clarissa had been here to help him choose furnishings! That sounded as though she would be expecting to live here as mistress of the house! Had matters gone so far? Clarissa and her father were often at the Koenig home, but Laurel had thought it was Sidonie's doing. Now it looked as though Thor was involved more with Clarissa than Laurel had feared.

Laurel looked at the wide windows to cover her dismay. She walked over to one of them and gazed out at the sea below. The house was high on a cliff, and the front windows overlooked a wide expanse of sea, and green islands dotting it.

'Do you like the view?' asked Thor eagerly, standing beside her, and looking into her face rather than to the sea. 'This is the way you suggested, for the front windows to overlook the sea.'

'Oh yes, it is beautiful, Thor,' she said soberly. 'What a marvelous view, and it will be even more lovely in the winter, with snow on the mountains, and ice on the beaches, making it all blue and white.'

'Yes, the scene was lovely last winter. I wished you had been here to help me decide on matters. But I followed your house plans exactly, they were so good.'

'My cousins helped,' she felt compelled to add. 'Delia suggested a linen room and big closets. Aunt and Uncle added ideas too.'

'I must thank them in a letter,' he said. 'The plans were so detailed and splendid that the carpenters and I just went ahead as you wrote them out. Come and see the rest . . .'

He took her arm lightly and showed her back through the drawing room to the study behind it. Then they crossed the hall to the kitchen, the dining room, and the front parlor. All was neatly arranged, with the back door at the end of the hall beyond the staircase.

She peeped out the back door and saw that the balconies ran all around the house, just as she had drawn the plans. She smiled at Thor, without speaking, tremendously pleased that he had followed her plans so exactly.

Then they went upstairs to the second floor. At each end of the hallway on the second floor was a window seat to take advantage of the wide beautiful windows looking east and west. Then Thor took her to the front, the west side overlooking the sea.

'This is the master bedroom,' he showed her, and she stepped inside timidly. This is where Thor would sleep! With his wife, whoever he chose! 'Lots of space, a huge closet, and the bed will be there near the north windows. And over here . . . a full bathroom for these two rooms, the west room and the east room. They will cover all this side of the house. I like big rooms.'

'You're a big man,' she tried to joke as she opened the closet door and admired the space. She opened the bathroom door and gasped to see a huge white tub installed, a toilet and washbasin, all the most modern plumbing. 'Oh, this is splendid!'

'No more outhouses,' he joked soberly, a twinkle in his eyes. 'I will be spoiled for my journeys north!'

She laughed and went out the other door to the next bedroom, which also opened into the bathroom. It too was large, with huge windows.

'What a lovely room, and the view of the mountains,' she sighed. She was thinking what a beautiful room it would be to paint in, with the good north light.

She lingered, then went on to the area across the hall, on the south side of the house. There was a matching suite of rooms, two huge bedrooms and a bath between. She silently admired all the space and graciously arranged closets and windows.

Then they went upstairs to the third floor. Patsy Dugan had been waiting for them there, and proudly showed them the large bedroom and bath that was their suite on the northeast side of the house. There was another large bedroom at the front. On the other side of the hall was a large linen room, as Delia had indicated, and two other rooms for bedrooms or storage.

'Oh, this is all just grand,' said Laurel with great glee. 'It's just the way we drew it! All so big and fine, lots of space, and big windows to see the glorious views. Oh, Thor, I'm so pleased with it!' Then she flushed, and realized it was not her house; it was his! 'I mean, I think you will enjoy it very much!'

'Thank you. I'm glad you like it. Come downstairs again and tell me what you think about the furniture. Should it be light wood or dark?'

She walked down the stairs before him. Patsy Dugan disappeared into the kitchen area and was busy with pots and pans for her dinner and her husband's.

Laurel walked slowly in the bare rooms, admiring the floor-boards, which had been planed and varnished. The wood was of Alaska spruce.

'I think I'd like reddish woods for in here,' she said. 'The mahogany like the furnishings on the railroad train would be lovely. I like the deep reddish tones, all varnished and showing the grain of the wood. And some chairs in the parlor could be of Alaska spruce to give a good smell to the rooms; the wood is so fragrant.'

'Good idea,' he said with a nod of his handsome head. She watched the blond hair flop over his forehead engagingly, and felt a lurch of her heart. She loved him so much! And she might be helping him plan a house for another woman to live in with him!

With a little sigh, she stifled that thought and concentrated on the house. 'I would have furniture that could change with the seasons. For example, in the winter one could have dark red velvet slipcovers for the drawing room and parlor, with matching red velvet draperies and white lace curtains. Then in the summer those could be removed and other ones put up, ones more suitable to the warmth.'

'What, for example, for the summer?' He stood with his arms folded, watching her face.

'Well . . . a pretty blue-and-green-and-white print, for example, that would look summery. And plants standing in pots here in the rooms and in the hall, and perhaps on the balcony. Of course you will have a garden . . .' She looked at him questioningly.

'You showed some space for that on the plans,' he said. 'I don't know much about gardens, but someone might make one for me.'

She wondered if Clarissa Leverett knew about gardens. Did she ever put her fastidious white hands in the dirt? Laurel doubted it.

'Oh well, that could come later,' she said hurriedly. 'I think I would have comfortable yet beautiful furnishings, ones that beckoned one to sit down, and grouped so they looked right for conversations. Not too much to be a clutter though. And space for bookcases, here and in the study. And a large table for magazines and newspapers.'

She wandered back to the empty room designed as a dining room, and looked about.

'And here, I would put in a table that could be enlarged. Aunt has one that can be opened in the center and planks added when we had guests. The room is long enough that one could probably seat a dozen people. When you had more guests, one could serve buffet style and have people sit in the parlor and drawing room.'

She looked to him questioningly, to see what he thought. He was still gazing at her consideringly.

'Would you arrange all that, Laurel? I would ask Mike Dugan to help you,' he said unexpectedly. 'I like all your ideas. There's a good lumber yard in Sitka where I have an account. Talk to Mike and make the measurements you want. Would you go ahead on the downstairs furniture and the master bedroom?'

She looked at him blankly. Was he serious? It seemed that he was. 'Oh, I would be glad to, Thor. But don't you want – I mean, other advice?' She meant Clarissa.

'No, I don't think so. People have advised me to send to San Francisco for brass beds and marble-topped tables,' he said without a smile. 'I don't care for that sort of stuff. I like your idea . . . native woods, hand-carved.'

'Then I would be glad to help.'

'I don't want to overwork you; I want you to enjoy yourself, Laurel. But if you would oversee the jobs, plan the tables and sofas and so on, make sure the work is done right, I would appreciate it. And go ahead and choose the fabrics, and have slipcovers and such made up, whatever you think right. And the draperies, of course, and all that,' and he waved his big hand helplessly. 'I have so much to do this summer, have to go away for a time, yet I would like the house to proceed, maybe be finished by autumn.'

Her heart sank a little at the thought of him gone, leaving her to the untender mercies of Sidonie. But she contrived to smile.

'Then I will do it, happily. Maybe I could show you plans from time to time, and swatches of material for your approval.'

'Yes . . . or just go ahead. I feel your taste is fine, much better than mine.'

They said goodbye to Patsy Dugan and returned to the Koenig home in Sitka. Laurel decided to go ahead with his house; it would give her much to do to occupy her hands and her mind. She drew up plans, went to his house and made measurements, began to work with Mike Dugan and Patsy on plans for the furnishings. Patsy was especially helpful, a good seamstress, and she had found some Indian women willing to do sewing and embroidering.

Mike oversaw the carpentry; he chose woods with Laurel from the lumber yards, carried the material back to the house, and hired men to build from Laurel's designs. Soon the interior of the house began to look livable, with several tables in place. Then the men started on the sofas and chairs, and the master bed of beautiful cedar.

Laurel and Thor did not discuss the project in front of anyone, especially his stepmother. Laurel just came and went with Rex, or Mike Dugan, and said nothing about what she did.

She was working in her study one day, painting at the easel, a mountain scene that might be for Thor, when she was shocked. Someone came up behind her and put his hands on her shoulders.

The man bent over her and tried to kiss her neck. She shot off the high chair and off to the side, and turned to face the intruder, the palette knife in her hand, her eyes wide with alarm.

She stared. The man was Ewan, but older, with signs of dissipation on his puffy face. His eyes were red from a hangover, and his jowl was puffed and swollen. He had not shaved for several weeks – a scraggly beard covered his tanned jaw – and his hair was shaggy.

He laughed at her. 'Well, Laurel, don't you remember your playmate, Ewan?' And he reached out for her again. She stepped back, her back to the wide table under the windows.

'Don't touch me,' she said sharply. 'How are you, Ewan? I remember you well.' And don't like you, she added mentally.

His weak, handsome face showed mild shock. 'Come on, now, honey! Give me a kiss. We haven't met for years!' He came closer to her, and she lifted the knife in warning.

He stopped, eyed the palette knife warily. 'Well, Laurel, that ain't a friendly greeting! Come on, now, give us a kiss! It's been quite awhile since we played together!' And he laughed, stepped forward suddenly and wrenched the knife from her, twisting her wrist cruelly.

She gasped in shock and nursed her wrist mechanically. He had really hurt her, and did not care. She watched him as he came forward again, the knife tossed casually to the carpet, spilling paint. He grabbed her waist and pressed himself to her. She smelled the drink on him; the smell of his breath was overpowering. She stiffened, tried to push him away, but he was strong and did not mind hurting her.

'Come on, Laurel, just a kiss,' he coaxed with a mocking laugh. He pushed his face close; her face was scratched by his beard. He tried to put his mouth on hers, but she averted her face in disgust.

'Let me go!' she said loudly, and debated screaming. Was any servant about? 'You let me go, Ewan!' She kicked at him, but her soft slippers made no impression on his booted feet.

'Well, am I interrupting an assignation?' said an amused feline voice. Ewan reluctantly let Laurel go and turned to a laughing Sidonie, who was leaning against the doorjamb. Her face was alight with malice. But Laurel was glad to see her for once.

'She doesn't remember me and tried to pull a knife on me,' Ewan joked rather sulkily. He frowned at Laurel and tried to put his arm about her waist. She sidestepped and slid nearer the door, away from him.

Sidonie eyed her with dislike. 'Can't you welcome your host's brother?' she asked pointedly. 'Thor says she's our guest, and she lays about like a lady!' She laughed. 'She could at least be cordial to you, darling Ewan!'

Her black eyes were narrowed as she took in the distaste Laurel could not conceal. Her black shining hair was like shellac about her well-rouged face. The lines of her silver dress showed her thin, well-corseted figure, the slight breasts, the narrow hips. She moves like an animal, Laurel thought, unease shivering through her.

'She will be, when she gets acquainted again,' Ewan said complacently. 'I bet she met only those frozen gents in Boston, down under, thinking about their money and their dry goods,' and he laughed. 'You're among real men again, Laurel, honey!'

Not you, she thought finally. He could not compare with his brother, so upright and honest and strong. What had caused the difference? Ewan seemed to have only contempt for women; he seemed to feel all must succumb to him.

'Well, we have visitors for tea,' said Sidonie, straightening. 'Come on, darling,' she said to Ewan, 'Mr. Leverett and Clarissa are here, and more people are coming. I want to show you off, now that you're home. Why don't you shave and wear your new black suit?'

Laurel was not invited and did not feel like joining them. They departed, and she slipped away, downstairs, to the housekeeper.

'May I have keys to my bedroom and study, ma'am?' she asked politely.

The housekeeper asked no questions and handed them over at once. Laurel went back upstairs, locked her study, and put on her coat and scarf to go outdoors. She felt sick at heart that in Thor's father's house she should now be unsafe. She would not put it past Ewan to come to her bedroom. She locked the bedroom on her departure and went to the kennels to collect Rex.

She walked to Thor's house and talked to Patsy about their progress. They discussed the dining room; then Laurel whistled for Rex and started home again.

There was one patch of thick trees and brush that she did not like on her way home from Thor's house. It was turning dusk, and she walked faster, keeping Rex at her side.

He was growling softly in his aged throat, and kept pausing and looking toward the brush.

'What's there, Rex?' she asked sharply. She too had heard the rustle in the brush and looked toward it fearfully. It was dark in there. Could it be a bear or a wolf? She wished she had her rifle with her, but one did not carry a rifle on the shoulder around Sitka. Perhaps she should start carrying a handgun.

Rex gave a short sharp bark, then a low rumbling menacing growl. On stiffened legs he raced toward the brush and disappeared inside. She could see only shadows of a large figure, she could not make out whether it was a man or an animal.

There was a low cry, and a deep growling sound from Rex. Then his growl ended in a yelp quickly stopped. Laurel waited, her fist clenched. She heard someone crashing away in the brush; it was not the sound of an animal. It was too clumsy and lurching to be animal.

'Rex!' she called sharply. He did not come. 'Rex! Rex, come here!' She waited in agony, then could wait no longer. She went to the brush and forced her way inside the tearing bushes and thick trees. She stumbled, and almost fell over a body. She looked down, blood freezing.

It was Rex, lying stretched out, blood gushing from his throat. She bent over him, incredulously. She held his head, his eyes were glazed in death. 'Oh, Rex,' she whispered. 'Oh, Rex . . . Rex . . .'

But he did not answer; he could never answer her call again. His thick fur was still warm in her fingers, but he would grow cold and stiff. A knife had cut his gray throat, where she had loved to ruffle and fluff up his fur.

She ran back to Thor's house with tears pouring down her cheeks and blood on her blue dress.

Mike Dugan met her at the driveway. 'Miss Laurel!' he said sharply. 'What happened?'

'Rex . . . my dog . . . knifed in the brush . . .' she said, and began to sob.

Mike and two Indian boys came back with her to take Rex away. Patsy consoled her at the house and sponged her dress. Mike drove her home in one of the carriages, and she slipped inside through the back door and quietly went upstairs. She was heartsick. She could not talk to anyone.

Thor came home, and she went down to the kitchen and told him, fresh tears streaming down her cheeks. He took her in his arms, before the sympathetic cook and the maids.

'I'm sorry, Laurel, awfully sorry,' he said gravely. 'Did the person try to attack you?'

She shook her head. 'No, it was someone in the brush. I wasn't sure even. I don't think it was an animal . . .'

'An animal doesn't carry a knife,' he said. 'Mike went back and searched the ground; he found the knife, and we're trying to trace it, but don't expect much luck. It's the kind most men carry around here.'

Laurel drew back, suddenly realizing she was clinging to Thor's arms and sobbing all over his broad chest. He'd been holding her very close to him.

It had been comforting, like comforting a child. But she was an adult now, a woman. And the way Thor looked at her now was not the way one looked at a child. His green eyes were warm and searched her face. He put his hand out and brushed back a lock of dark hair that fell across her forehead.

'Want your supper in your room?' he asked gently.

'I'm not hungry.'

'I'll send up some soup,' he said. 'You see you eat it. I'll tell Dad when he comes home. You get some rest now, darling Laurel.'

His voice was gentle and sweet, low and musical. She felt better, but when she got to her room and thought of Rex, tears flowed again. She felt as though she had killed her pet, for he had been protecting her, she felt.

He had lived for years while she was gone. But within just weeks of her return, Rex had died defending her, or thinking he was defending her. She wondered what that dark form had been in the brush, an enemy or just a drunken bum skulking about to steal her purse?

She shuddered, and lay back on the bed, exhausted by the day. First Ewan, and Sidonie's malice, then that horrible man, and Rex dying for her. It was all too much.

Chapter 13

Laurel stayed indoors for days. She felt shocked and sick at the incident, and she missed Rex badly. He was such a good and undemanding companion. And he had died for her.

She painted and sketched in the locked study, away from the busy household. She did not bother to come down to tea. She did not care much for Clarissa Leverett, who seemed to come daily, perhaps in the hope of seeing Thor.

Ewan tried to hang around Laurel when she did appear, but she detested him and could not hide her dislike. Ewan seemed to see it as a challenge and tried to put his arm about her waist whenever they went in to dinner or returned to the drawing room.

'Why don't you come out with me in the carriage tomorrow?' he coaxed one evening after dinner. 'I could show you around Sitka, drive you wherever you want.'

'No, thank you. I'm sketching tomorrow.'

'You work too hard, Laurel,' he laughed. 'Come on out and have fun.'

'Work!' scoffed Sidonie. 'You call that stuff work?'

Thor interposed smoothly, 'You would think so, if you tried to paint, Sidonie. I hope we may see some of your finished work soon, Laurel.'

She smiled faintly, and nodded, then left the room as soon as she could.

The following afternoon she had just returned to her bedroom to dress for dinner when Thor came upstairs, followed by two maids and a coachman, all with large boxes in their arms. She stared as he came down toward her room, a broad smile on his face.

'In here,' he directed, and she stood aside in a daze as he directed the procession into her bedroom. Boxes were put on her table, on chairs, and on the floor, and then the others beamed and departed.

He shut the door most of the way and said in a low voice, 'Laurel, I know Sidonie entertains much, and you do not seem to have many fancy clothes. I took the liberty of ordering some dresses for you in San Francisco. Patsy Dugan loaned me one of your gowns and a pair of slippers for size. Now, I don't want Sidonie to know about this. If she should ask, just tell her you ordered them. Let her think you paid for them.'

Laurel was staring at him, wide-eyed. 'But Thor you must not – Oh, I should pay – You should not – '

'Hush!' he whispered in mock horror, his green eyes dancing. 'Don't let them hear! Listen, you're working for me, doing the house. Let this be the pay for it, in part. There aren't enough dresses here . . . But there's a dressmaker in town . . . I'll take you tomorrow. Think what you want . . .'

'Oh, Thor!' she whispered back, flushed and dismayed. 'You cannot pay for my dresses; it isn't proper! And I truly need no more – '

'Yes, you do. Sidonie entertains so much, and their little minds think that a woman should have new gowns often. I won't have you outshone!' he said firmly. 'The dressmaker in town is French, and very clever. Madame Bonheur – '

Laurel shook her head. His eyes glinted with laughter.

'And she and Sidonie detest each other,' he added.

Relieved, she said without thinking, 'Oh, then I don't mind.' Horrified, she stopped herself.

He laughed softly. 'I know. I'll take you there tomorrow; you shall order what you want. And it *is* your money, Laurel, the money I would have paid for all the house plans, the furnishings, and advice. Think of it that way!'

'Thor, you are too generous.' She had felt the lack of fancy dresses, and she was so grateful. But she was troubled too about what Aunt Gertrude would have said, to know a man was buying her gowns.

Thor read her troubled eyes. 'Don't worry, my dear,' he said quietly, 'no one is to know of our arrangement. Think of me as a substitute Uncle Arnold! And you are helping me immensely, you

151

know. I simply don't have time to work on the house as I would wish, and as it deserves. Yet I don't think you want to be paid money for your labors.'

'Oh no, of course I don't!' she protested. 'I'm glad to do it – '

'Then it is a horse-trade, of equal parts,' he said easily. 'We are bartering our labors rather than using cash. All right?'

She had to smile and nod. 'Thank you so very much, Thor; you are so considerate . . .'

He looked satisfied as he left the room; then she turned to the boxes. She opened one after another, gasping over the contents.

She lifted out a rose satin gown with a square décolletage, brown velvet bows at the corners, and balloon sleeves of thin silk. The princess waist and narrow hips flaring into a circle hem would be flattering on her slim figure.

There was a blue satin with overdress of white lace that had her gasping for its delicate beauty. The box also contained a matching blue silk and white lace fan!

Another box contained a yellow silk, with a wide, yellow lace fichu; the sleeves were full from the elbow to the wrist. This would be lovely for summer, as would the peach bouffant gown with its full ruffled hem and matching ruffles on short sleeves.

The ball gown will be delightful to dance in, she thought, holding it to her as she admired it in her long mirror. Her cheeks were flushed pink with excitement, matching its peach color.

Two other boxes of the smart San Francisco dressmaker contained clothes more appropriate for winter. There was a golden brown outdoor costume of silk with matching gold velveteen coat, a double row of buttons down the front. With it was a boat shaped hat of panama straw, meant for autumn and another one of golden brown sable.

There was a ruby velvet dress with black braid, a matching black coat lined with the ruby, and a smart toque with the black braid trim. She popped the hat on her head, admiring it in the mirror.

A bright blue velvet gown for daytime wear, for teas, and a yellow silk with brown braid were lifted out and laid on the bed. And under them was a full-length sable coat, with matching sable round hat! She gasped, eyes round and wondering as she touched the fur. This did cost a fortune . . . oh, could she really accept this?

Another box contained slippers, all to match the gowns, blue ones, ruby velvet ones, silver, gold, black, golden brown. With them were two pairs of boots, a smart black pair, a lovely brown pair. And another box contained more hats, with plumes and flowers and veiling.

She sat down on the floor, contemplating her riches soberly. Could she really, really, accept all this from Thor? Her heart glowed that he had done this generous kind act. But what would people say?

And even more important, could she accept this? Would a lady accept such gifts from a gentleman? What did Thor think of her, that he had gone ahead and bought such intimate garments for her? There were matching undergarments, so frivolous and flimsy that she was glad he had not remained to see the contents of the boxes, light corsets, hose, petticoats, and all that.

'Oh, dear,' she sighed. She could not give them back! He had ordered and paid for them. Was there any way she could pay him for it? She thought of what he had said, that her labors for him had more than paid for the garments.

She could not think that they had. But perhaps she could do more work for him. She might write some letters for him, or do accounts as she had for Uncle Arnold. Or give him paintings. Yes, she could give him paintings; he seemed to value them highly.

For dinner that evening she donned the yellow silk with brown braid and huge puffed sleeves. She put on the matching yellow silk slippers, and glowed to see herself in them. The color set off her dark brown wavy hair and brown eyes, and she felt the bright color suited her mood. She was abruptly so happy, after the down moods of the past days. Thor had been so considerate!

For once there were no guests for dinner. Sidonie's eyes opened wide when Laurel appeared in the drawing room before dinner.

'Well, where did you get that gown?' she demanded sharply.

'The ship came in from San Francisco,' Laurel said demurely, not meeting Thor's bright gaze. 'Some gowns had been ordered, they arrived. I hope you approve of it, ma'am.'

Directly appealed to, Sidonie reluctantly nodded, circling Laurel and studying the gown from all sides. 'Well, well, it is smart, I must say. Let me see the sleeves. Hum. My dressmaker must see them, Laurel. They must be the latest mode.'

Thor winked at Laurel as she went to sit down. She had won — with Thor's aid — her hostess's approval!

'Very pretty, very pretty,' said Olaf Koenig, nodding. 'I like you in yellow, Laurel.'

'She is a pretty girl,' Ewan said as he came over to sit beside Laurel. He reached out to touch her sleeve, his bright blue-gray eyes mischievous. 'Hum, a nice neckline also,' and he reached out to touch her neck.

She jerked away. 'Don't,' she said sharply. Sidonie was watching them alertly.

'Son, don't be fresh with Laurel,' Olaf said. 'She isn't one of your doxies.'

Olaf's sharp rebuke caused a sudden silence in the room. Ewan flushed red, and drew back sulkily. He was silent later at dinner, until Sidonie coaxed him and drew him out to tell some of his stories. Then he drank too much, laughed too much, and later lurched out of the house.

He was a disappointment to his father, Laurel knew, and her heart ached for Olaf. One son, Thor, was everything he could want. He worked hard, he was bright and imaginative, he contributed to the business so much. But Ewan was a constant drag, having to be prodded into working; and one could not trust him to complete a job and not make enemies on the mine sites. Would Ewan ever grow up and mature? Would he ever settle down and be an asset to the company? It was a big question.

True to his promise, the next day Thor took Laurel to the French dressmaker, Madame Bonheur. The woman was a small graying lady, in an unimpressive little black dress, with sharp snapping black eyes. Her quick darting movements about her shop reminded Laurel of a blackbird. She measured Laurel, nodded over her, murmured to herself, then began dragging out lengths of fabric from the back room to roll them out on her large worktable.

Thor did not leave, to Laurel's initial embarrassment. He said to Madame Bonheur smoothly, 'Miss Winfield is doing a great deal of work on my house for me. I wish her to choose some fabrics so that you can make up dresses for her, in payment. She refuses money, as you can imagine, Madame!'

'But of course, but of course!' said Madame Bonheur, her brow

154

clearing. 'It is not proper for gentlemen to make such a gift, but in payment for work done . . . naturally! Miss Winfield must be a very clever lady,' and she looked approvingly at Laurel.

'She is very artistic,' Thor said seriously. 'You should see her sketches and paintings. She will be famous one day.'

'Ah, indeed?' exclaimed Madame Bonheur, looking properly impressed. Laurel thought Thor was teasing her, but he continued.

'Yes, indeed. She shall be one of Alaska's foremost artists. She loves to paint scenes of Alaska and its wildlife. I hope to acquire her paintings and keep them for the future, when she is famous.' And he was serious!

Madame Bonheur treated Laurel with even more respect, and laid out length after length of fabric. Laurel was rather overwhelmed, and Thor had to urge her to choose the ones to be made up. He coaxed her to choose a light rose silk, a lovely blue faille, a white muslin to be made up with blue lace collar and cuffs, a golden brown silk with beige lace trim, a yellow silk (because Thor liked her in yellow, he said).

Madame Bonheur was immensely pleased with their orders, and promised to put her 'little girls' to work on the gowns at once. She herself would oversee the operations and plan the smart gowns in the latest modes. Laurel chose several patterns from the lady's sketches, and the work was begun at once.

'And now for my plans,' said Thor. 'First we will have dinner at a restaurant I especially like. Then I want you to come to the warehouse and choose from some fabrics I had sent up from San Francisco. Will you help me?'

'I would be happy to, Thor,' she agreed happily, in a glow. He was treating her like a young lady, handing her his arm, helping her tenderly in and out of the carriage.

And she noted too that he seemed to be forever watching her today. He would gaze at her thoughtfully as she pored over the fabrics and sketches. He stared at her as she was measured for gowns. His green eyes could be very warm and intimate, she thought, feeling hot all over. She remembered the times he had kissed her, ever so lightly, but holding her so closely she could feel his strong muscular body tight against her own.

Thor escorted her to the restaurant he had mentioned, a fine one in the heart of Sitka. The outside was a crude clapboard and white painted brick, but the interior was splendid.

Inside the plain building, one stepped immediately into another world. The hallway was a glowing mahogany wood varnished to shining soft life. Carpets on the floor were of Persian design, in blues and reds.

Inside the dining room were softly lighted tables, with stiff white linen tablecloths and candles in red glass. The chairs were a thick red plush, and the waiters were well trained and soft moving.

Laurel sank into her chair with a feeling of being pampered.

Thor handed her the long menu. 'What would you like, Laurel?'

She gulped. It was all in French. She had studied it in school, but in her awe she could not remember a word.

'Would you choose for me, please, Thor?' she asked shyly.

He smiled, well pleased, and ran his hand down over the menu. 'Of course. Let's start with Alaska crab, then have salmon steaks. White wine, your best,' he directed. 'Green salad, baked potatoes with sour cream, and blueberries in brandy to finish.'

The waiter moved away, soft-footed. Thor smiled at Laurel. 'You look even prettier in this light,' he said, his gaze going over her, down to the table edge. She felt he approved of her hair in the bouffant style, her rose dress, the V-neck partly filled in with lace, the gold chain he had given her.

She felt marvelous all that day. Thor was treating her like a grown-up lady, but also like a favorite person. He talked or was silent, as they wished, easily sharing the enjoyment of the delicious food, the wines. Then they went on to the warehouse, where he ordered the fabrics laid out for her inspection.

He had sent up so many! She was worried, but he shook his head. 'We shall choose what we want for my house; then the others will go into our family store,' he said easily. 'We get first choice, of course! But the others will not be wasted. They are all fine upholstery and carpet materials; others will be glad to purchase them.'

As Laurel inspected the materials, she silently echoed his comments. The fabrics were of the finest material, beautiful colors, and good workmanship.

She studied them carefully, veered from one to the other, but finally settled on the ones she liked best. And Thor agreed with her choices.

She found just the right color of dark rose velvet for the parlor and drawing room furniture slipcovers and cushions. Then she found a deep blue-bright green-and-white pattern for some bright summer slipcovers. She chose matching blue-and-green curtain material for the summer, and would use the same rose velvet for draperies for the winter.

For the master bedroom suite of two bedrooms and bath, she chose golden brown, Thor's favorite color, and brighter gold velvet draperies with white lace curtains. For the summer draperies she chose light yellow-and-white prints.

The suite of guest rooms across the hall were to be in deep royal blue velvet for the winter, with lighter blue linens for the summer.

The dining room she furnished with fabrics to be made up, of colors of deep greens and brown, in leaf patterns, and the rug of deep green with a border of flowers.

Thor helped her choose carpets, lingering over the fine Persian and French carpets that had been sent up from San Francisco. He took great pleasure in choosing, and Laurel realized he had much more expertise in this area than she did.

He chose for the drawing room an *Aubusson* carpet of deep cream with light bouquets of roses and wildflowers in scrolls of gold. It was very light and pretty, and would go well with the deep rose draperies. For the parlor was a similar *Aubusson* in deeper cream, almost gold, with burgundy red roses and golden swirling borders with flowers in the swirls. Laurel fingered the deep lush piles and drew an ecstatic breath, they were so very lovely.

Thor chose a *Savonnerie* carpet from France for the master bedroom, admiring its deep gold, geometric pattern and key design around the border of gold and deep blue. A similar *Savonnerie* with more rose and floral design in it was selected for the front guest bedroom.

He chose similar carpets for the other rooms, and Laurel could only echo his choice. Then he went 'wild,' as she teased him, and chose several smaller Persian rugs to use as throw rugs on the other carpets, near sofas and chairs, and in the hallways. They were so exquisite, she knew they must cost a fortune. And he bought them so easily, without hesitation, she felt he must be wealthy now.

How nice to have the money to buy whatever one chooses, without counting the price! And Thor had been so generous to her, never speaking of any price when purchasing the fabrics for her gowns.

He was so very kind and sweet to her, she could not help wondering, wistfully, if he might one day consider asking her to marry him. Did he really like her very much? She came home glowing and happy, and went up to her room in a daze after he had helped her down from the carriage.

She did not see Thor later; he was out for the rest of the evening. The next evening, she dressed carefully in a new blue silk and went down to the parlor early. She grimaced as, from the hallway, she heard Mr. Leverett's roughly suave tones. He had a gravely voice, but such smooth manners. She braced herself to meet Clarissa, then went into the parlor.

To her surprise Clarissa was not there, but several other couples had come. And to her disappointment Thor was not there either.

Mr. Leverett turned to Laurel with his usual smile that never quite lit up his small, sharp black eyes. 'My dear Miss Winfield, how charming you look this evening,' he said. He seemed to look right down into the bosom of her low-cut dress.

'Thank you, sir,' she said. 'I can scarcely hope to compete with your charming daughter. Is she not coming this evening?' She hoped he would not guess her motives for asking. She longed to know if Clarissa might be with Thor.

'Ah, no. She and Thor have gone to a concert she longed to attend.' Mr. Leverett smiled proudly, as a fond father would. 'Such a fine couple! Such tastes in common! They are going to dinner in town first, then to the concert. I would trust my Clarissa with Thor anywhere!'

Laurel kept her smile glued on her face with an effort. 'Of course.'

She raised her fan and briskly fanned her face, hoping her cheeks were not as scarlet as they felt. She was brazen to ask, but she wished so much that Thor had come for dinner that evening. And to learn that he was with Clarissa! Worse was to come.

Mr. Leverett leaned closer to her, so she could smell his unpleasantly strong cigar and catch his whiskey breath. 'I have approved their marriage,' he whispered, looking directly into Laurel's startled face. 'It is my deepest hope and most sincere wish for their happiness! Thor cannot stay away from Clarissa, and she adores him of course! A most suitable match!'

Laurel felt she might faint, there in the warm room, with the strong smell of cigar smoke in her nose. Thor . . . married to Clarissa? Had it gone so far? Thor was often gone evenings; did he then spend them with Clarissa?

She did not remember much of that evening. She wished only to escape to her room and be alone. She finally got her wish about ten o'clock, when the men began to play poker and some of the ladies sat in a corner to play whist. She played neither, and excused herself.

In her room, she locked the door and went to the dark window to look out forlornly. It had been such a glorious day yesterday – and now this! She had dared to hope that Thor's gifts and his attentions meant something rich and meaningful to them both.

But he must be just grateful for her aid on his house, as he had said! Yes, he had told her plainly he was grateful. He wished to repay her, but not with money, like a hired worker. She sighed and sighed again, like a great puff of wind. She sank down into the stuffed chair at the window and gazed sadly at the bright crisp white stars in the vivid night-blue sky.

Laurel felt bewildered and lost the next days. She saw little of Thor. By sharp watching and demure questioning she learned that he was often at the Leverett house or out with Clarissa in his carriage. So he did spend a great deal of time with her, and Laurel had not known! Somehow it hurt deeply. She had not realized they were so close.

Had he proposed? She thought the engagement had not been announced as yet, but Mr. Leverett had seemed so complacently sure of the matter.

What would she do? She could not remain on here as Thor's guest, when he and Clarissa married! Or perhaps he meant to move into the grand house with Clarissa as soon as Laurel had completed furnishing it!

But it was so curious that he had asked her to decorate the house rather than Clarissa! Had it been Clarissa who had wanted brass beds and the gaudy San Francisco style furnishings, and he had not approved of that? Still, his bride's wants should mean more to him . . . It was all very curious and disheartening.

Laurel felt sick inside. For several days she could not bring herself to go to Thor's house. She tried to paint, but her brush was not clever these days. She sketched some ideas, idly, but found no inspiration in the July flowers, those heavenly blue ones she usually loved. The forget-me-nots looked up at her from their golden hearts in vain.

Thor spoke to Laurel one morning, privately, after breakfast. 'Would you have time to go to the house today, Laurel? Patsy wants some advice.' He raised his eyebrows significantly. He looked anxious. 'You're not too tired?'

'Oh no . . . no, never, I'll be glad to go.'

'Good. I'll drive you over. Mike will bring you home this evening. Patsy wants you to remain for lunch; she has a stack of questions, she said.'

'I shall be glad to do whatever I can,' Laurel said.

He had spoken to her in a quiet voice. She understood that his stepmother was still not to know that she was helping him with the house. She put on a blue jacket over her blue-and-white linen dress and set out with him. On the way he chatted about the progress.

'The first bed is finished, the large one for the master bedroom. They should deliver it soon, and have started work on the next ones. I think the sofas are a problem. They are made up, four of them, but the women are having trouble with fitting the slipcovers. I know nothing about that.' He gave a helpless shrug of his shoulders.

'I have helped Aunt Gertrude many a time with theirs. I don't think it will trouble us for long,' she said confidently, her spirits lifting with the thought of helping him. 'It's usually just a matter of doing the corners properly.'

'I leave it to your master touch,' Thor said with a smile. In the carriage, as they drove through a forested area, he leaned over and kissed her cheek gently. 'Feeling happier, Laurel?' he asked.

She wondered, startled, if her unhappiness over him had shown. He added. 'The loss of Rex was a sad one, I know. I am on the lookout for a proper dog for you. Of course, it won't be the same, but I hope you'll accept another one. You should have a dog for protection as well as pleasure.'

Laurel managed to smile. 'You are most kind, Thor. And I shall be glad to have another dog. And yes, Rex was special and could never, ever be replaced.'

And he thought her unhappiness was entirely over Rex! Well, best he should think so, and indeed she had wept much for her lovely playmate.

At the house, Thor left them and drove off. Patsy was glad to have Laurel, and the Indian girls were shyly welcoming. They all worked together with a will. Laurel showed them how to turn the corners – that had been the problem – and get the slipcovers to fit snugly. They put on the blue-green-and-white ones for the summer, after the ruby velvet ones had been completed and folded away in storage, in the linen room upstairs.

The rugs had arrived. Laurel helped them figure which ones were for which rooms. Mike would oversee the tacking down of the rugs over their mesh counterparts beneath. Laurel promised to return and see to the laying of the smaller Persian rugs in a few days. She went upstairs then, to help figure out and measure for beds and sofas and chairs for the other bedrooms.

They would not be done until fall; the men had other work to do. Thor had told them the rooms could wait, just so his main rooms were ready. Some work was being completed upstairs, and Laurel admired the way the men worked at the window ledges. The rooms were glorious with the beautiful polished woodwork.

Mike appeared about five o'clock to drive her home. He handled the reins well, and asked her to regard the horses. They had come up on the steamer from San Francisco. They were fine sturdy black stallions, a little frisky but full of energy and able to pull more weight than they were asked to pull. They were handsome too, and she admired their fine heads and shining black hides, and the way their braided tails swished proudly.

'We will have the stable full by next summer,' Mike said proudly. 'Mr. Thor is getting some riding horses also. Do you ride, Miss Laurel?'

'No, I don't. Uncle Arnold didn't teach us. I think he thought it wasn't ladylike. And we couldn't drive the carriage,' she added with regret.

'I could teach you easy,' Mike offered.

Laurel smiled, but she did not take him up on the offer. She thought she would not dare handle Thor's precious and probably expensive horses. She pictured Clarissa Leverett in one of her smart riding habits, riding one of the black stallions, and sighed. She would look so handsome!

On the way Laurel saw a hulking man, bent over, carrying a load of logs. Something about him teased her memory, but she could not place it.

'Who is that, Mike?' she asked curiously, pointing to the man in the distance going to a cabin.

'Him? Oh, that's Herman Ranke. Some handyman for Leverett.' Mike recognized him at once; he seemed to know everyone in Sitka already. 'Mean with horses,' he added with a frown. 'Sort of an odd fellow, just grunts when you speak to him. Don't care for him. Some say he does a lot of prospecting, comes in from time to time to report to Leverett.'

He was silent a moment, concentrating on the horses.

Then he added, 'Miss Leverett, she came over a couple days ago. She was mad as fire when she saw the sofas and chairs. She said it wasn't what she wanted and she would speak to Mr. Thor. Do you know what she meant, Miss Laurel? She doesn't plan to marry him, does she?'

Laurel swallowed and looked into the distance, everything else flying out of her mind.

'Well, I have heard the rumor,' she said bravely. 'They . . . they do make a fine couple.'

'Huh,' said Mike, and clucked at the horses. 'Has a fine temper, don't she?'

Laurel would not be drawn. He pulled up to the house, and helped her down, gallantly. 'Thank you, Mike. I enjoyed the day.'

'We did too, Miss Laurel.' He smiled. 'Hope you'll come again soon.'

He tipped his hat; she nodded, then turned to the house. Sidonie was at the front window, watching, she saw, and Laurel went in to face her questions.

Sidonie came out to the hallway. 'Where have you been, Laurel? You were gone all the day.'

Thor didn't want his stepmother to know too much.

Laurel found it easy to say, 'I went to visit Mrs. Dugan,' she answered. 'We made friends on the trip to Alaska.'

'Friends with a servant?' asked Sidonie, her black eyes sharp. 'I'm sure Thor would not approve!'

'Yes, he took me there this morning,' Laurel said gently, restraining a smile. 'Excuse me, I will change for dinner.' And she went past her and on up the stairs. Sidonie stared after her, but Laurel did not turn around.

She had much to think about, in the privacy of her room. Even the Dugans were afraid that Clarissa would marry Thor. Oh, what would she do if Thor did that? They could never be close again – and Clarissa would not welcome her, she was sure.

Would Thor be lost to her forever? Yes . . . in truth he would be, and Laurel must make some other life for herself. . . .

Chapter 14

Some days later at breakfast Thor said to Laurel in front of them all, 'I've found a dog I think will make a good guard dog for you. Will you come out to the kennels with me this morning?'

'Oh yes, thank you, Thor,' and her face lit up. 'What's his name?'

'Czar,' he said with a slight smile. 'It means king, just as Rex meant king.'

Olaf added, 'As does Koenig. Well, well, quite a coincidence.' He drank his coffee absently, looking from his older son to Laurel. 'Do you feel Laurel must be guarded, Thor?' he asked abruptly.

'Sitka is full of strangers during the summer,' Thor said easily. 'Best to have a dog along when she goes walking alone. They'll take a second look with him growling.'

'Our Laurel has become very pretty,' Ewan said, smiling over at Laurel, his eye admiring her in the simple light yellow muslin gown. 'She's all grown up and handsome.'

'Yes, she is,' said Thor. 'And we won't take any chances with her safety. Are you ready, Laurel?'

'I'll just get my hat and jacket so I may take Czar for a walk,' she said. 'Excuse me, Mrs. Koenig?'

'Of course,' said Sidonie with a nod. 'Thor, I'm having guests for tea today. I do hope you can come home a bit early.'

'Sorry, I'm afraid the days are very busy, Sidonie,' Thor said as Laurel left the room. 'I can't promise.'

'I'll be here, Mama!' laughed Ewan. 'Won't I do?' There was a sulky jealousy in his tone. He resented Thor very much, Laurel thought, as she sped up the stairs.

* * *

164

At the kennels Thor led out a handsome young dog and showed him to Laurel. He was a large dog, with slanted intelligent eyes and gray fur with white trim under his neck and along his belly. He looked much like Rex in coloring but he was much more reserved in manner.

'He's two years old,' said Thor as Laurel studied the animal. 'He's trained as a guard dog, not as a sled dog. He'll get some larger, not much. He'll probably make friends slowly.'

Laurel held out her fist so the dog might smell it, and he finally bobbed his head and looked up at her. She ventured then to rub his head and neck. He permitted that in a dignified manner. He seemed curious about her, sniffing at her dress and inhaling the perfume she had put on.

Laurel used a light lavender water, a distinctive floral fragrance. Hazel had given her a lavish bottle of it on Laurel's leaving Boston. The dog seemed to enjoy it, and Thor grinned down at the two of them.

'He likes your perfume,' he mocked lightly.

'Yes, he seems to.' She gave Czar a few minutes to get used to her, then snapped her fingers for him to follow her slowly on a walk with her and Thor. He came obediently, trailing at her boots.

They wandered over to the stables, where Czar stood at attention, studying the huge horses with absolute quiet. She had not heard him bark yet. Most huskies bark very little; they're part wolf, and more usually they whine or growl low in their throats.

She and Thor walked then for about half a mile, then turned back to the house. Czar followed them obediently, not diverted by tempting chickens in the road or birds flying low. He would look at them, growl and go on.

'Have you heard from the Nolans?' asked Thor, after a silence.

Laurel looked at him hopefully. 'No, I haven't. Have you? I had hoped to go there this summer.'

He shook his head. 'I can't spare the time,' he said. 'I'm sorry.' He seemed to take it for granted that he would accompany her. 'Some friends of mine went hunting in that area. I asked them to look up Tom Nolan. They came back yesterday.'

'Oh, how are the Nolans? And Jade?' she asked eagerly.

'They didn't see Jade, but they found Tom and Miriam in

Wrangell; it seems they spend part of the summer there. Tom and Miriam went back to the cabin with them, and Tom went hunting with them. Miriam worked their furs and got them ready. But Jade wasn't around. I wondered if you had heard anything.'

Laurel shook her head, her eyes troubled. 'No, I haven't. Oh, I do hope she's all right.' Her thoughts went at once to Ewan. Had he been around Jade? Had he caused trouble? Or had Jade become restless in the lonely cabin?

'She would be eighteen. Maybe she got a job,' suggested Thor.

'Perhaps so. Oh, I do wish – ' She stopped abruptly. Thor had already said he could not take her there. She would not beg; he had done so much for her already.

'If I hear of anybody going to Wrangell, I'll ask him to inquire for you.'

'Thank you, that would be kind,' she said soberly.

They had arrived at the kennels, and Laurel ventured to give Czar a good rub and hug, running her hands through his thick gray fur. He submitted to it, nuzzling his head against her once, and then turned to his kennel obediently. 'I think we'll be friends,' she said with relief.

'Yes, he has taken to you, Laurel. But I'm not surprised,' Thor said with a teasing laugh. He went on to the stable to get his carriage; she returned to the house and went up to the study to work.

She pondered about Jade, worrying a little as she sketched some flowers. What had happened to Jade? She was probably all right. But she had lived closely with Jade for several years, and she had this strange feeling that all was not well with her friend. She kept pausing, gazing out the window to the snow-covered mountains, and thinking about Jade. How they had laughed together, played in the snow, sat for hours fishing in the stream. Talked, dreamed, read, wondered about their futures.

Laurel had gone to school because she was a white girl with influential relatives. Jade, an Indian girl, had not had that privilege. Girls much alike, the same age, the same interests, the same quick minds, yet divided by race. It did not seem fair at all. Laurel sighed. The older she became, the more she realized there was not much equality in the world. Not between Indian and white, not

166

between men and women, not between rich and poor, not between talented and plodding.

She thought, that must be the way of the world, and I can do nothing about it. But it did not seem fair at all. She thought then of Delia, and wondered how she was getting along in her marriage. Laurel knew *she* would not have liked being married to rigid plodding clerk like Norman Cooper. But Delia was a good obedient girl; perhaps she had settled down to that life.

Laurel decided to take Czar with her the next day into town to the dressmaker's. Madame Bonheur had asked her to come back for a fitting of her new dresses. And this would be a good test of Czar's obedience to Laurel.

She went to the kennels and took the dog out with her. He followed her obediently, into Sitka and down the streets, his head weaving curiously from side to side as he took in all the people and strange odors. If anyone came too close to Laurel, he would stiffen, come closer to Laurel, and give a short warning growl, and they would step around her cautiously.

Within a block of Madame Bonheur's a big burly prospector crossed the street toward her. 'Miss Laurel!' he called, and waved a big arm in a red-checked shirt.

Czar sent up a long low warning growl, rumbling constantly. Laurel stared at the man, then finally recognized him. 'It's Ben Kennard, isn't it?' she asked.

His bronzed bearded face split open into a wide grin showing gold-capped teeth. 'That's me! Well, well, little lady! You've grown up into a pretty fine lady, that's for sure!'

Laurel stopped Czar's growling with a low command, then shook hands with the prospector. They drew aside from two approaching men, to stand in the shelter of a dry goods store to exchange news. Kennard had visited the Winfield cabin several times, to hunt and put up meat before going up to the gold fields in the Klondike.

She thought by his neat new clothes that he had probably done well, and ventured to ask him, 'Are you prospecting in the Klondike, Mr. Kennard? Did you make a good strike?'

He grimaced widely and shook his graying head. 'No, miss. I broke my leg the first winter! While I was recovering, a couple of men took me in and gave me a job with them, handling stores.

When I was okay again, I went on working, handling a mule team, taking meats and stuff up to the gold miners. It pays more than prospecting, let me tell you!'

'Well, I'm glad for you, Mr. Kennard. I guess it is a more certain living.'

'Sure is, miss. My, you're all grown up and got to be a young lady, for sure! How's your dad?'

Her face shadowed. 'He died, Mr. Kennard. He was killed by someone; we don't know who. Mr. Thor Koenig came and brought me out, took me to my relatives in Boston, where I went to school. Now I'm back in Sitka.'

'Well, well, well!' He seemed not so much surprised as saddened. He was used to sudden death by now. 'Sorry to hear about your dad. He was a mighty fine man, he was. You hear about your friends, the Indians? Those Nolans?'

She started. 'No, I haven't heard much. Have you seen them, Mr. Kennard?'

'That's right. I came out by way of Wrangell this May. Met Tom and Miriam on the street. They live in Wrangell every once in a while; came in to see Jade, they said.'

Laurel lit up. 'Have you seen Jade? How is she?' she asked eagerly.

'No, ma'am. Just heard about her.' He seemed a little uneasy, his face downcast. 'Heard she got married, but lost her young one. A baby, she had, only lived three days, Tom said.'

Laurel stared at him. Jade married . . . losing a baby! 'Oh, I'm so sorry,' she murmured. 'Did they say how she is?'

'Not much, Miss Laurel. Just that Jade is married to some lumberjack, they said; a nice fellow. Had a baby and lost it all at once. Then we talked about trapping, and I'm going back to work with them later this summer, and Tom will go hunting with me. Miriam said she'll scrape the hides and they'll sell them in Wrangell for me. So I'm all set.'

'When will you be going back?' she asked.

'In a couple days, I reckon.'

'I'd like to talk to you before you go. Would you take a letter to Jade for me?'

'Glad to, Miss Laurel! You just write it up, and I'll take it over. Be going in a few days; no hurry.'

'Well, I'll meet you day after tomorrow, near this store. Would that be all right? About ten in the morning, right about the same time as today?'

Beaming, he nodded down at her kindly, his burly hand stuck out to her. She shook his hand, then went on her way. Her heart warmed. Some men were so good and kind they would do anything for a friend, even a casual acquaintance. What good people there are in the world, she thought. And in Alaska, they seemed to come closer, out of a common need. The wilderness drew them together, a bond to help each other against the dangers of nature.

Laurel went on to Madame Bonheur's. The lady greeted her happily.

'Come in, Miss Winfield. Three of your gowns are ready! And the steamer came in, so now I have more lengths for you to see!' She darted around Laurel like the blackbird she looked, picking up bits of material, tossing them on the table, twittering over the lovely silks and laces.

Laurel had to laugh at her ruefully. 'No, no, I must not have more gowns made up!'

'But Mr. Koenig, he said this morning when he went by, Miss Laurel shall have more! He said he liked the new yellow silks!'

'I have so many already,' protested Laurel, but the lady overruled her. Mr. Koenig had said Laurel must have them, and Mr. Koenig must have his way.

Madame Bonheur showed Laurel the new fabrics, just in the day before on a steamer. The ships were coming up almost daily from San Francisco and Seattle, laden with hopeful prospectors. Although the first strikes had all been claimed by now, the gold-seekers still swarmed to the Klondike – the prospectors, their wives and mistresses, the prostitutes, the shillers, the gamblers, the followers, all streamed up to Alaska. And with the ships came more goods, the enticing pretties that the gold-claimers could buy for their gold.

Men like Ben Kennard were the most practical, thought Laurel, as she looked over the silks and velvets. They supplied the gold prospectors; it was an honest living, delivering groceries, meats, canned goods, shirts and jeans and boots, shovels and picks and rockers. They would keep their gold, for it came from supplying and from honest labor.

169

Madame Bonheur persuaded Laurel to choose several more lengths of fabric, the yellow silk with blond lace; a white watered silk to be made up in a grand ball gown; a pale daffodil silk faille for a walking dress; a pink silk to be bordered with bands of sable for an afternoon tea gown; and a splendid golden brown velvet skirt and matching jacket with yellow silk bodice.

They paused in their labors for luncheon. Madame Bonheur took her now-favorite client to lunch at a small French restaurant, where they dined on veal steaks, small new potatoes with chives, green salad, and chocolate ice cream for dessert. Laurel enjoyed the luncheon with the lively lady. She was very experienced in the ways of life, had a rather cynical approach, but was most amusing withal.

She had been born in Paris, and apprenticed at twelve to a dressmaker. At eighteen she had married, borne a son and later a daughter. Her husband had died in one terrible war, as she put it, and Madame Bonheur found herself with a living to make for herself and her children. She had worked hard as a dressmaker, and after her children were grown and married, she had come with a wealthy client to San Francisco to work for her patroness.

'Then I found I could make a living for other ladies and not depend on the whims of one grand lady with a temper,' she said, her black head cocked to one side like a bright-eyed bird. 'So I made my own salon, and it succeeded. Then I sold it, and came to Alaska to start once more. Why, you ask? Because I too, have adventure in my soul,' and she clasped her hand dramatically to her thin bosom. 'I love the new, the different, the wilderness that is my new land. I too am Alaskan!'

Laurel felt akin with Madame Bonheur and told her so. 'I too could have stayed in the East, in Boston, in comfort. But the wildness called me back, the stunning mountains, the sea, the animals, the marvelous skies and stars,' she confided. 'I may not be able to live in the snows and woods, but I can be near them, and see them. And I love the winter skies, the bright white stars, and the Aurora Borealis, all the strange wonderful sights that are only in Alaska. The moose and the deer, the wolves and bears, and the seals and beavers, all the marvelous animals here.'

'I cannot share your liking for bears,' said Madame Bonheur whimsically. 'One startled me once while I was berry picking! I had to give it all I had collected and start over again! However, I understand what you mean!'

Laurel laughed with her, and felt friends with the lively French lady who had such an unexpected love for Alaska. She warmed to her, and they had a good afternoon together. At four o'clock Laurel took pity on the restless Czar, who was tied to the front post of the store, and they went home.

She left the dog at the kennels and told him with a final pat, 'You've been a good dog, Czar! We'll walk again tomorrow,' and left him with the Indian boy.

Laurel went inside through the back door, fearing company. She hesitated at the foot of the wide stairway, listening. Sure enough, voices came from the partly opened parlor door. Then she heard her own name as she was about to speed up the stairs to her room. Curiosity overcame her, and she hesitated again.

'Laurel . . .' came the voice of Ewan, drawling.

'That girl!' said Clarissa Leverett, in an affected voice, rather high. 'She loves to be about servants and Indians! I'm surprised Mr. Koenig permits her to remain!'

'She's an Indian-lover,' Sidonie said with a laugh. Laurel could picture her thin shoulders in a shrug. 'She lived with them, you know! Thor had to take her away; he was outraged!',

'Oh, the Indians aren't so bad,' said Ewan. 'The girl was quite pretty!'

'So you discovered!' said Sidonie. 'Well, Ewan, you might help me get rid of Laurel! If you make love to her and get her pregnant, I'm quite certain Olaf would finally throw her out! Even he would not condone that, much as he *adored* her father!'

'I wouldn't do that,' said Ewan sulkily. 'What do you think I am, calling me – '

Clarissa interrupted. 'You need not go so far,' she said in a cool high voice. 'Just be found in her bedroom; that should be enough to turn men off her. They don't like soiled goods!'

Laurel stood absolutely frozen, with one foot on the lowest stair. She could not believe her ears. That these people, her hostess included, should so plan against her! And laugh about it! Was it a cruel joke? Did they merely mock? Or could they possibly mean what they said?

As she stood there, she heard Sidonie continue, 'I think Ewan could manage it if he wished! She is rather pretty, Ewan. It should not be distasteful! Just sneak into her bedroom some night – I could get a key for you – and seduce her. She cannot deny you – you are a charmer!' And she laughed, in a nasty high-pitched manner.

Ewan protested. 'I wouldn't do it against her will! Really, Mama, you go too far! I'm sure Laurel likes me; she's just an innocent. When I put my arm about her, she shivers! She'll come around . . .'

Laurel, unseen, grimaced horribly.

'Well, do it soon, darling,' encouraged Sidonie. 'I would love to throw her out before autumn. If you do get her pregnant, I would not have to accept any argument of Thor or Olaf to keep her in my house! Out she would go! She can go back to her Indian friends!'

'It should not be difficult, Ewan,' Clarissa said lazily. 'Not from the way you brag about your Indian girls and their babies!'

'It wasn't like that! I'm sorry I told you; I must've been drunk,' protested Ewan, angrily, 'I don't go to just any girl. That Indian girl was a beauty, I tell you . . .'

The two women teased him mercilessly. Laurel did not wait to hear more. She ran up the steps, lightly, avoiding making any noise. She felt cold and shivery, for all the warmth and sunlight of the August day.

She felt they did mean it! And Ewan was so vain, he could not realize a girl like Laurel would be revolted by him! He took her shivers of disgust for pleasure! How could she avoid him?

And would Thor help her, or would he care? He seemed blind to the malice of Clarissa. If he loved her and wanted to marry her, planned to marry her, Thor would not care what happened to Laurel! If Ewan caught her unaware, and seduced her, raped her, who would protect her then?

In her room, the bedroom door locked, Laurel sat and looked at the door. If Sidonie gave Ewan the key, could he get in if it were locked from the inside? She went up to the door, examined it, thought he could probably get in. The door lock was fragile. She needed a long bolt over the door. How could she get one without causing a commotion in the house?

Laurel sat on the bed, feeling cold and frightened. She was terrified for herself. Would Thor let them do this to her? Could he even prevent it if she complained and appealed for his protection? Where could she go? She was alone for hours during the day, and all night as well. Would they try to accomplish their vile plan behind his back?

And then she thought about Jade Nolan. Was she the Indian girl who was 'a beauty,' according to Ewan? Had he seduced her; was Ewan the father of Jade's baby? What had happened to Jade?

And what would happen to Laurel? She felt a prisoner in this beautiful large house, which she had so admired. Olaf and Thor were so kind and thoughtful, but they had much work to do. They were even gone for weeks and months at a time.

How happy she had been today, with her new dog Czar, the warmth of Thor's thought of her, the friendship of Madame Bonheur, the pleasure of seeing Ben Kennard again.

And then this – this horror! Could they possibly have been maliciously teasing, not meaning a word? Or did they mean it? Ewan had certainly thought they meant it; he would not hesitate to seduce her. His vanity would not permit him to believe Laurel detested and feared him.

Laurel felt fearful and hysterical. It was a terrible situation. She felt helpless too. She did not have a gun now. Her rifle had been given to Thor long ago, and her handgun that had been her father's. Could she ask for them back? She had best get a handgun at least. Perhaps she could buy one tomorrow in Sitka, and some ammunition. She had not fired a gun for years, but she had been expert once.

Yes, she must get a handgun, a revolver, and keep it loaded beside her bed.

Yet, how could she stay awake for hours, or come awake should Ewan enter her bedroom? What if Ewan crept in, overpowered her, raped her, and she could not even scream, much less use a weapon on him?

She shuddered, and wrapped a blanket about her, thinking, thinking. What could she do? She felt insecure and terrified. Oh, if only she could go back to the old days, with her father nearby, with Tom and Miriam Nolan to run to for help. They would help her; they were her close friends. Indians they may be, thought Laurel, bitterly, but they were dear friends, and she could trust them.

Chapter 15

The following day Laurel went out to the stores with Czar. Exercising the dog was a good excuse for her to go into Sitka. She went directly to a hardware store and bought a Colt revolver, a six-shooter, and a box of cartridges.

'Do you know how to use this, miss?' asked the proprietor, dubiously.

'I think so. I did years ago,' she said. 'Would you go through the loading for me?'

He did, and took her out back to practice at his small firing range. It did not take her long to get back into the procedures, and she impressed him with her accuracy.

'You have a good eye,' he praised her.

She bought a trade blanket also, and a tarpaulin, and a canvas bag to carry them in. 'You going hunting, miss?' he asked curiously.

She smiled. 'Just a little trip with a friend,' she answered. She carried the packages back to the house without difficulty; she was a sturdy girl for all her small neat figure. She stowed them in her room. Then she picked out a skirt, long and practical, some underclothes, boots, shoes, stockings, and packed them all in the canvas bag.

She loaded the revolver and kept it on the bedside table that night. The following day she went to Sitka again, and met Ben Kennard.

'Your letter all ready, Miss Laurel?' he said in friendly fashion. Czar accepted him today, but watched him alertly.

'Yes, here it is. But Mr. Kennard, I have another favor to ask you.' She did not hand him the letter.

'Whatever you want, Miss Laurel! Glad to do it,' he said cheerfully.

'I'm anxious about my friend, Jade. And I want to see the Nolans. They're practically my family, you know. Would you take me with you to visit with them?'

He scratched his head, pushing back his limp hat. 'Well now, miss, that's quite a journey, you know! I'll be going by an old boat with some pigs and things on board.'

She shuddered a little, but would not be deterred. 'I can stand it,' she insisted. 'I'm very anxious to go. And I feel I can trust you, as I would my own father.'

That got to him, and he beamed down at her appreciatively. 'Well now, miss, I must say, you could trust your life with me,' he said gallantly, blushing. 'Reckon Mr. Koenig won't mind?'

'He won't mind,' she said, crossing her fingers behind her back. 'He would go himself, but can't spare the time.' And that was true, although it gave the wrong impression.

Ben's brow cleared. 'Well then, Miss, it's all right, if you don't mind sleeping on deck and all, and it's a bit primitive, you know.'

'That will be all right,' she said bravely.

They shook hands on it, and he said he would set out in two days. That pleased her. He would have Indians with him to help sail the boat, but she could do the cooking for herself and Ben, to help out. That satisfied her; she would be paying for her way.

He promised to get the food, and would be ready to start out about nine in the morning from the wharf. She would be there. 'Well, well, you'll have a good visit with your friend.' 'Spect someone will be glad to bring you back again, from Wrangell to Sitka,' he concluded cheerfully, and went on his way to make preparations for the journey.

Quite pleased and relieved, Laurel went home again. She double-checked her supplies, put in a gift for Jade, of tablecloth and matching napkins, some candles and matches, two dress lengths, and thread and braid, and a blue skirt that matched her own.

Thor and his father were not home for dinner that evening. Ewan seemed restless; it was just him and Sidonie and Laurel there. He sat beside Laurel on the sofa in the parlor, and under Sidonie's amused eye, he tried to make up to her.

'God, Laurel, aren't you even going to be friendly?' he reproached as she moved over to a chair.

'I am friendly,' she said quietly, taking out her embroidery once again. She kept a sharp needle ready, in case he came close again. She was not averse to sticking him 'accidentally' with the needle!

She stuck the needle in and out briskly, eyeing the pattern carefully. She was making smocking for a blouse in a Russian design of red and white. Ewan eyed her.

'Will you go out with me to dinner tomorrow?' he asked, warily. 'There's a new French restaurant.'

'No, thank you,' she said without excuses.

He seemed startled. 'Why not? You'd go with Thor.'

She did not try to answer that.

'Oh, go ahead, Laurel. I am having guests, and you don't enjoy them,' urged Sidonie. 'Why don't you go out with Ewan and have fun? You're only a girl yet.'

'My aunt and uncle would not approve,' said Laurel, demurely.

Sidonie gasped, 'But they're in Boston!'

Mock-earnestly, Laurel replied, 'But they were very strict with us girls, ma'am. None of us was permitted to go out with a young man alone. Even my cousin Delia, after she was engaged, only sat with her fiancé in the parlor!' Industriously she embroidered stitches, aware of the looks going on over her head.

'But you went out with Thor!' Sidonie said. 'I know you have, several times.'

'In the daytime only,' said Laurel. 'And he is sort of my guardian. He promised Uncle Arnold to take care of me and protect me.'

She suppressed a nervous chuckle at their disgust. 'Well,' said Ewan, 'I must say, I can't picture Thor as a guardian of the morals of young girls!'

Laurel gave him a wide-eyed look, full of shocked innocence. 'Oh, but he has a fine character, Ewan! I'm sure of it, and so was my father!'

Ewan presently gave up and went out on his own amusements.

Sidonie watched Laurel sewing, then said, 'Really, Laurel, one would not believe you like Ewan! And he is such a fine young man!'

Laurel gave her a level look. 'Really, ma'am? I had heard rumors about him in Sitka. I do hope they aren't true.'

Sidonie bit. 'What kind of rumors?'

'About Ewan . . . and women.'

'Oh – Well, one cannot believe all one hears!'

'Where there is smoke, there usually is fire,' quoted Laurel, virtuously. 'Please excuse me, ma'am, I believe I will go to my bedroom now. I have some more sketching to do.'

She departed, troubled. Sidonie seemed intent on throwing her at Ewan, maliciously, just as in the conversation Laurel had overheard. She shivered. Would Ewan really rape her? She believed he would, given half a chance.

It made her all the more anxious to get away for a time. She longed childishly for the protection of Tom Nolan, so solid and good. She wanted to lean against the breast of Miriam Nolan, to feel the motherly arms go about her and hear the reassuring croon of her voice.

And she wanted to be with Jade, her dearest friend. They had been so close for years; they had exchanged thoughts, secrets, ambitions, wishes. They had giggled together, wept together, hunted together, enjoyed the wilderness and hunting, and animals, the snows, the skies, everything. She had longed to see Jade again. And she felt Jade needed her.

Laurel's anxiety to see her Indian family made her gloss over her rudeness in not telling Thor she was going, and her recklessness in going. Thor would understand, she told herself as she wrote the note to him that he would receive well after she had departed.

She knew Thor would be gone two days, and so she left the note on the desk in his bedroom. Then she quietly left early that morning and stole out the back way. She walked into Sitka, then down to the wharf, wearing her stout boots, her red-checked shirt and navy serge skirt, with a parka carried in one arm and her canvas bag in the other.

Ben Kennard met her at his boat, beamed at her, and tossed the canvas bag to one of the Indians on the deck. They were Tlingit Indians, and she knew them both. She greeted them in their language, and they gave her shy smiles and nods.

'How are you, Miss Laurel? Good weather for sailing!' Amos said. The other one, Job, ducked his head, the younger brother.

'Yes, it looks good. May we have good sailing,' she answered. 'Good hunting and good fishing to us, with the help of the Raven and the Eagle.'

'Yes, yes, with their aid we will do well,' the older replied.

'Say, Miss Laurel,' said Ben. 'Didn't realize you knew their lingo.'

'Yes, from the Nolans,' she replied, stepping aboard cautiously. She looked with approval at the 'old' sailing boat, was pleased to find it well-repaired, painted, caulked, and seeming in good order.

The pigs were surprisingly clean, to her relief. Ben explained, 'Yes, pigs don't usually like mud; what they like is keeping the mites off themselves. So I keep them well-washed down days, and they are happy. Stubborn, though. I'll leave them in Wrangell for the summer. Then when I go up to Dawson City in August, I'll be driving them up. Reckon folks there will be mighty pleased to pay high for animals to breed and kill for food.'

Laurel had the run of the front half of the boat; the pigs were corralled in the back half. She slept on board rolled up in a blanket, with a tarp over her when it rained, as it did half the time. She made no complaints, to Ben's praise, for she felt no hardship. She was used to sleeping out under the stars. The fresh air was keen in her nostrils, and the stars were white and brightly shining out in the open. The skies in summer were not very dark, and she loved the deep blue of them . . . and sometimes she was treated to a display of the gray-green flares of Aurora Borealis.

When the nights were fine, they went ashore, and the Indians made a campfire. Laurel would cook for them all; she volunteered, and the Indians were quietly pleased with her. They brought her the fish they had caught, carefully cleaned, and she roasted them over the campfire in their own manner, split on sticks and turned slowly on willows. They had baked potatoes baked in the coals, sourdough biscuits, and cranberry jam. In the open air the hot food on the cool nights, and their own appetites, made it a feast for a king.

The Indians felt she was one of their own, as she spoke their language, as did Ben. Amos was quite a storyteller, and he would tell stories of the Tlingit myths – all about the smart Raven and his adventures with people; how the earth was invented; how people began, their relations with animals and the stars and the waters of the earth. It was an enchanted time, that hour or two before their bedtime. Then they would all roll up in blankets and go to sleep.

She had no fear at all with them; they were her friends and would protect her with their lives. They all carried rifles and were good shots. She carried her handgun openly. They had encouraged her once to shoot rabbit for dinner, and praised her enthusiastically for her skill. She had her old touch with the gun back again in short order.

They traveled slowly, but in ten days they were in Wrangell. Ben Kennard went ashore with Laurel to help her find the Nolans. He found them at their cabin, and Tom and Miriam greeted Laurel emotionally. They held her and hugged her, and Miriam wept over her, slow tears rolling down her cheeks. Miriam sighed, 'And our Laurel is such a young lady, such a fine young lady!' she said proudly.

'Oh, Miriam, I'm so glad to see you. It is so good to be with you. Oh, Tom, I have missed your wisdom and goodness!' and she hugged Tom again.

Ben Kennard finally left her with them assured she had a place in their cabin. She thanked him, shook hands with him, and said, 'Nobody could have been kinder. You are so good to me. May you have a good time this summer with the Nolans.'

'I'll do that. Just let me get my pigs settled, and I'll come back to go hunting,' he said.

'First I will take her to Jade,' said Tom Nolan. 'She wishes to be with her friend. They will have good talks. Jade has spoken often of Laurel.' And he looked solemnly pleased.

After Ben Kennard had left, Laurel asked them, 'And how is Jade? Where is she?'

They both looked pleased, to her relief. 'Jade has married a white man! He is a good man, he works hard, he keeps her well. He works with the lumber. He is kind, he is fine man!'

'Oh, I am so glad. What is his name?'

'It is Garth Fleming.'

'I hear she had a baby, but lost it,' Laurel said. She looked from one to the other. Miriam nodded, Tom held his head in his hands in a gesture of unhappiness.

'I tell you,' Miriam said slowly, 'she is with that too bad Ewan Koenig one summer. They are alone together, to my shame. She makes baby. She comes to Wrangell, works. Ewan Koenig, he comes. He is angry, he shoves her. He does not want her and baby. She is just an Indian girl, he says.'

'Oh no,' breathed Laurel, her worst fears confirmed. 'What did Jade do?'

'Garth Fleming, he takes care of her now. He married her. But baby come, lungs no good. He die. Poor little one. Jade stay with Garth. He take care of her.' Miriam sighed and shook her head. 'And they not always happy, but the gods will be kind. Both good, though Jade bad girl for a time.'

Laurel thought about it that night as she slept in their cabin. She hated that Ewan Koenig. He had played around with Jade and got her pregnant. She clenched her teeth. And he would have done the same to me, she knew it. She bet Thor didn't know about this – or did he? Did he guess that Ewan played fast and loose with Indian girls?

Did Thor think it was all right, so long as Ewan let white girls alone? Did he have any idea that Ewan was after Laurel now?

How could she go back and live in the Koenig house? She was afraid of Ewan now, deadly afraid. If he came near her, she would shoot him in the leg, she decided. Shoot him enough to incapacitate him! That would stop him for a while.

The next day she went up the Stikine River with Tom and Miriam Nolan. They too had decided to go visit Jade. They traveled three days, resting nights on the shores, thick with Sitka spruce and hemlock, shrubs and flowers. The grassy banks of the Stikine were beautiful in the summers, though covered with ice and snow in the winter. She saw several abandoned cabins and wondered what had happened to the former inhabitants. Gone on to the gold fields? Or driven back to Wrangell or Sitka by fear and loneliness? Or killed by bear or wolves?

It was so good to be with Tom and Miriam once more. They talked much of the time, unusual for the stolid Indians. All were eager to get up to date with what had happened during the three years Laurel had been gone.

Laurel told them about her relatives, how good they had been to her. She told them about Aunt Gertrude, and how she had trained Laurel in housekeeping.

'A good woman, a fine woman,' pronounced Miriam in satisfaction. 'She treat you like her own daughters!'

'Yes, she did,' said Laurel. 'And Uncle Arnold was good to us. I worked in his store; it was good training. But always I longed to return to my home, Alaska.'

'The wilderness called you back,' said Tom, nodding his shining dark head. 'There is no sound like the voice of wildness that calls and calls, in animal tongue, return to me. Return to me. Like the howl of wolf at night, the sound of the wolf god in him. Like the call of the Raven, the maker of the earth, from whom we are all descended.'

'Yes, it was like that,' agreed Laurel, happy that they understood. 'The call of the wildness. I thought of the skies and the streams, the wildflowers and the animals, the stars and the fish, all of them calling me to return. So I had to come back.'

Miriam pressed her brown work-worn hand on Laurel's fingers silently. She knew. Her brown eyes glowed like jewels.

Late afternoon of the third day, they came to the lumberjack camp. Tom tied up the boat, they all stepped ashore eagerly.

Tom led the way to Jade's cabin. There was a settlement of cabins in a rough clearing, around a central oven and camp-fire. All the houses were similar, of logs and a single room, or of two rooms, with an overhang above the front door to keep off the snow.

Jade saw them coming and stepped out the door. She ran to her parents; then she saw Laurel. She stopped, she stared, her black eyes opened wide in amazement. 'It is – Laurel!' she gasped.

Laurel laughed and cried. She hugged Jade, they hugged each other and danced around, while Tom and Miriam silently laughed and laughed until they shook with it. 'It is a much big surprise!' cried Tom at last, wiping tears of joy from his eyes. 'What do you think of this big surprise!'

'Oh, it is wonderful! It is wonderful!' cried Jade, smiling while the tears ran down her tanned cheeks. She was more lovely than ever, thinner; her high cheekbones more sharp and poignant, her mouth full and deep red, her slim form in a crisp red-and-white checked dress to her ankles. Her hair was braided and wound in a coronet, much like Laurel's.

Miriam volunteered to begin the dinner; the men would come home from the lumbering at dusk. Jade and Laurel sat on a bench outside the cabin, held hands and talked and talked.

Jade told Laurel all that Miriam had said, and more. 'I loved Ewan so much,' she said sadly. 'And he only played with me. I am sick with it. I was so fooled.'

'But now you have a good husband,' Laurel said encouragingly.

Jade looked down at their hands, folded together. 'He does not love me,' she said somberly. 'He married me because he was sorry for me. He had a wife, she died in childbirth. So he felt sorry for my child and for me. Now the child is gone, and he does not want me.'

Laurel hesitated delicately, but Jade finally went on.

'He does not sleep with me,' she said in a low tone. 'He sleeps in a blanket before the fire, not in the nice bed with me. We have two homes, here and in Wrangell. He treats me with courtesy and with honor. But he does not touch me in love.'

'But surely, Jade, he must like you very much and . . . you are so very lovely . . .'

Jade bit her full red lips and finally confessed. 'I dream of Ewan,' she said. 'I think I do not love him, but I do not know . . . I dream of him . . .'

'You still want him?' Laurel tried to conceal her distaste and gently asked her question.

'I don't know. I dream of him . . . I speak his name in my sleep. Garth said he hears me say the name of Ewan in my dreams, and I still love him, that is what he says,' Jade said desolately.

'Are they . . . good dreams?'

'I dream of the time when we lay in the fragrant grass, and he loved me so much. He was so good, Laurel. Our love felt so very good . . . never did I feel anything like this,' said Jade, flushing red. 'It was the best time in my life, the most exciting time. Ewan . . . he is good lover, I guess. He makes me feel . . . oh, so good, so hot and fine. We make love on the beach, we make love in the waters of the stream. Always he is fiery hot and make me feel like on fire. Yes . . . I still think about him.'

Laurel was silent, troubled. She did not know what to say. She loved Thor, but she could not imagine making love with him. His kisses had been gentle and made her feel protected, excited, sweet. But she had not known the erotic love of a man. How would it be with Thor? She tried to put the thought from her; it was forbidden for her, a girl.

'You do not love Garth, your husband?' Laurel asked.

Jade drew a big sigh. 'I don't know. He does not let me come close,' she said. 'I like him, I respect him. He is a good man. But I think he is sorry he married me. He is very sorry for me. He will not discard me, but I think I should leave him.'

'Oh, Jade,' Laurel said sorrowfully. 'What will you do then?'

'Work in Wrangell. I was cook and waitress in a restaurant there. Maybe I go back.'

'Don't do anything of a sudden,' advised Laurel. 'Wait . . . maybe Garth will love you.'

'Maybe,' said Jade, bleakly. Her head turned, and her black eyes sparkled. 'They come home!' she exclaimed.

Laurel had been absorbed in their conversation and had not heard any sounds. Now she heard the jingle of mule bells, the sound of men's heavy voices, and laughter. Then men came into the clearing from the west and started scattering to their cabins. One of the cabins was a long bunkhouse; she watched as many men went there, to come out again with basins of water to wash up for dinner.

A very tall man stalked toward Jade's cabin. He was so black-haired, Laurel thought at first he was an Indian. Then he came closer, and she saw his features those of a white man, with lighter brown eyes. Tom Nolan walked with him, carrying a load of wood for the fireplace. They paused to speak to Jade and to Laurel.

The wood was dropped outside the cabin; the man whipped off his big hat, to reveal a taciturn solemn face with a square jaw.

'This is my friend, Laurel Winfield,' introduced Jade.

Laurel held out her hand. It was swallowed up in a huge brown hand with firm fingers. He squeezed it very gently, as though afraid to hurt her, then withdrew his hand from hers. He eyed her solemnly, thoroughly.

'How do you do, Miss Winfield,' he said in a low musical voice.

'How do you do, Mr. Fleming?'

'Oh, call him Garth, Laurel,' urged Jade. 'She is my best friend,' she said happily to her husband. Laurel noticed how her eyes lit up and shone when she saw Garth. Hmm, thought Laurel, I wonder.

'I hope you do not mind if I visit with Jade for a few days,' Laurel said to him. 'We have not seen each other for three years.'

'And you will catch up with three years in a few days?' he asked solemnly.

Laurel stared at him, and finally saw the twinkle in his brown eyes and a slow curve of his mouth. Then she smiled back at him. He was gently teasing her! And she liked him from then on.

'Well, maybe more than a few days,' she admitted with a little laugh. 'Jade and I were very close for many years; she and I always told each other all our secrets,' and then she blushed for her words.

'That is good, to have a good friend,' he said. Miriam had been watching, and now she called them for dinner. He excused himself, and he and Tom Nolan went to wash up. He and Tom presently appeared with shining faces and slicked-back hair, hands scrubbed clean of the dirt of the forest.

Both brought with them the fragrance of the Sitka spruce. The fire burned in the fireplace, giving off a pleasant smoky fragrance of more spruce. The food was simple, but delicious – venison steaks, boiled potatoes, greens, sourdough bread with cranberry jelly. They ate hungrily, almost in silence. Miriam and Jade spoke briefly; Laurel mostly listened and watched as the men stoked themselves, then sat back to light up pipes.

After dinner, Laurel brought out her gifts to Jade, and she exclaimed rapturously over them all. They planned at once how to make up the dress lengths, and Laurel glanced over at Garth. He approved, smiling, his glance tolerant of women's foibles. He did not seem jealous of his wife; he happily shared her with her family and friend.

Then the girls talked and talked, while the others were silent, listening. Laurel told about Boston and its wonders, of carriages with fine horses, women dressed in silks and furs and lace; concerts of thousands of people, stores with many floors. She told about riding on the train, and they wondered about that – all but Garth, who seemed to know about trains.

When she ran out of breath, Jade told about her adventures with her husband, hunting last summer. Tom Nolan told about some hunting he had done, how many bears were about. He had caught three already this summer.

'I think it is very cold in the mountains,' said Garth in his slow calm way, knocking out his pipe. 'The bears come down for berries and fish. More hunting this summer will be good; we will put up much dried meat for the winter.'

'You come in the autumn, we hunt,' said Tom, satisfied. 'Women gather berries then, make jam, put up much for winter. Another cold one, I think.'

The talk of the men turned to lumbering, how well it went, how soon they would finish in the autumn. While the men spoke, Laurel noted how Jade's gaze went to her husband, proudly; a shine glowed in the brown eyes of Garth, a shine in her black eyes. Did they not love each other? Laurel wondered.

Yet Jade had said, several times, sadly, 'He is only sorry for me.'

Laurel had much to think about that night as she slept in the large bed with Jade. Tom and Miriam Nolan had rolled up in the blankets before the fire, to sleep on the wooden plank floor, as did Garth. Was it a courteous gesture on his part to Laurel, their guest? Or could it mean that Garth never slept with his lovely young wife? She thought maybe Jade was right; maybe Garth did not love her. But how could he resist her?

Chapter 16

Thor's anger had died somewhat during the long journey from Sitka to Wrangell. But it flared up again as he finally turned the bend and saw the lumbering camp in the midst of deep forests along the Stikine River.

That Laurel had dared, dared!, to come here practically alone! That damn fool girl, that daring stupid silly irrational impetuous crazy girl! And against his wishes! He had told her he could not spare the time to come this summer! And then he had had to leave all his work, leave his father to go up to the copper mine, and take off to rescue Laurel!

He was tired, for all the good sleep under the stars these nights. From Wrangell, he had come alone three days to the camp, pulling the boat with long strokes against the stream. He had left the two Indians with the huge sailing vessel in Wrangell, for them to stock up against the return. He meant to go right back; he could spare no more time on this silly venture.

Damn the girl, anyway! Never a word to him or anyone, just a note left for him to find at the end of his trip north. Everyone wondering where she was, Sidonie malicious about some boyfriend, his father upset and tired from searching the town.

The day was almost at a close, and dusk was closing in when he pulled up at the crude wooden dock at the lumber clearing. A man passing by came to the dock, caught the rope he tossed, and helped pull him in.

'Thanks very much. Is Garth Fleming around?'

'Sure. Hey, Fleming! Visitor for you!' he yelled, and a big man in a red-checked shirt lifted his arm and strode down to them.

They measured each other, as Thor stepped ashore. He tossed out the box of provisions, his canvas bag, and Garth Fleming caught them.

'I'm Thor Koenig,' he said, offering his hand.

Fleming took it in his big rough hand and shook hands gravely. 'Garth Fleming.'

Thor eyed him critically and liked what he saw. A big man, with a steady brown gaze. Big build, powerful, more than six foot tall, his own height. Dark blue jeans, checked shirt, clean-shaven, clean hands, square jaw. About thirty or so. Well, Jade had fallen soft, he hoped.

'I came to get Laurel Winfield,' he said bluntly.

'She is staying with my wife at our cabin,' Garth said. He picked up the canvas bag and led the way uphill to a rough cabin at the edge of the clearing.

Even before Garth opened the cabin door, Thor heard the sound of women's chatter and soft laughter. The door opened, and Thor stepped in to meet Laurel's startled gaze. Her brown eyes opened wide; she paused in setting the tin plates on the table with its neat embroidered tablecloth. She and Jade were dressed alike, in long blue skirts, blue-checked blouses, with their hair fastened in braids down their backs.

She looks young and girlish again, was his first thought. In Sitka she had been all dressed up and adult, now she had reverted to girlhood, and he was not sure he liked it. His anger flared up as she continued to stare.

'Well, you have led me on a merry chase,' he said grimly, without greeting. He set the box of provisions on the floor and put his hands on his hips. Garth set down the canvas bag, and stood in the background, waiting. Jade watched them all with fascinated black eyes, a bowl of salad in her hands.

'Uh . . . Thor . . . how . . . how nice to see you,' said Laurel, faintly, the plates still in her hands.

He ignored that. 'Do you know what happened after you left? Father chasing all over Sitka, up all night, thought you were raped and killed! Sidonie furious as hell, thinking you had run off with some man. Nobody knowing what had happened. Someone saw you on a boat, said you had been forced aboard . . .'

Laurel set down the tin plates with a clatter. 'Oh no, no! I came with Ben Kennard, a prospector – I knew him; he is ever so nice – and two Tlingit Indians I know. We had ever such a good time –'

'How nice for you,' Thor said between tight lips, 'How very nice for you . . . when everybody was thinking you were killed and lying in some grave! I dropped everything and took off for Wrangell with Henry and Billy; we came all day and all night, sailing like crazy and with little rest. I could only hope we would find you, not killed.'

'Oh, Thor, I am ever so sorry.'

He ignored the words. He was so blazing angry, he was hot as fire. 'If you ever, ever!, pull such a stunt again, – going off alone – I'll tan your hide till you don't sit down for a month! We'll go back to Sitka tomorrow, and set off for home. And you don't stir ever – not ever! Do you hear me? You don't stir away unless you ask me first, and then I will probably tie you up and keep you tied!'

She swallowed, her eyes wide and frightened. She was staring at him, unable to believe he could be so furious with her. Well, let her listen, and listen good! He didn't mean ever to be so frightened about her again! She was no independent young girl, she had better know that!

'You're no child,' he said, biting off the words. 'You are a grown-up young lady, or should be! You're eighteen years old, and you better start acting your age! You're very beautiful, and you cannot run around the world pretending nobody can see you! Some man is going to grab you and rape you and murder you – and you won't be able to squeak!'

'I have a Colt revolver,' she said seriously, pointing to the gun lying with a gun belt on the table on the side of the room. 'I can shoot, Thor –'

'Much good it would do you if you were caught asleep! Now, listen to me, Laurel – don't ever pull such a stunt ever again in your born days! Do you hear me!'

He expected a meek obedience. To his amazement, she lifted her head and shook it violently.

'No, Thor. I am grateful to you, but I am my own person! You don't own me; you are not my guardian. You have been kind, but when I feel I must do something or go somewhere, I shall do it! I have a mind of my own and –'

He broke in violently, going up to her, putting his hands on her slim shoulders, and shaking her. 'God damn it, Laurel! You will not defy me! I may not be your legal guardian, but I am responsible for you, and you will listen to me and obey me!'

She looked him bravely in the eye. She said gravely, 'I will try, Thor, but when I must do something –'

'Damn it!' he yelled, and shook her again.

'Uh . . . excuse me,' Garth said, coming up to them. 'I think you're both tired, too tired to be rational. Suppose we postpone any more discussion for now. I believe Jade has dinner ready.'

Thor's hands fell away from Laurel's slim shoulders. 'Well, you haven't heard the end of this, young lady,' he said ominously. 'You pack your gear, and we'll set out tomorrow morning, about nine. If you aren't ready, I'll drag you along by your hair!'

He turned away, then said, more calmly, to Garth, 'If you'll show me where the outhouse is . . .'

'This way,' Garth said in relief. Jade let out a slow cautious breath and set the salad bowl on the table. Laurel set the plates around as Thor went outside the cabin. When they returned, there were two basins of warm water on the bench at the front door, and two towels. The men washed up in silence, and Thor ran water over his burning head and face. He was still mad.

Jade set a good table. They had bear steaks, boiled potatoes, green salad with vinegar and sugar dressing, blueberry jam for their sourdough bread, and a yellow cake that Laurel had made. Garth kept the conversation flowing quietly; he had a deep calming voice.

After dinner Jade cleared out Thor's provision box, and said, 'I'll fill it for morning. We have some chunks of bacon and there's a loaf of sourdough –'

'I'm not ready to leave yet,' Laurel said stubbornly. 'I'm making a dress for Jade.'

'I can finish it,' said Jade hastily, her cheeks flushed. 'We have had a good talk –'

'We haven't finished talking,' said Laurel, her small round chin set in a way that Thor had not seen before. Her brown eyes flashed. 'When I am, someone can take me back to Wrangell, and I'll find a ride back to Sitka – if I go. I may get a job in Wrangell.'

189

There was an instantaneous silence as the others stared at her. Thor's eyes flashed green fire.

'Like hell,' he said shortly. He got up. 'I'll appreciate the food, Jade. I'll be catching some fish, but we should be at Wrangell in less than three days.'

She put in the food, soberly, two small towels, some salt, and then put his shirts in water to soak until she could wash them. Later she washed them out and hung them to dry before the fireplace. She was a good neat housewife, thought Thor, and he hoped Garth appreciated her. They spoke little to each other, but they seemed to rub along all right.

Later the men talked lumbering and mining while Laurel worked on the red dress she was making for Jade, whipping up the seams as though her life depended on it. Jade finished the laundry, hung up the shirts and a pair of trousers, and came back to work on another piece of sewing. They worked in silence while the men talked.

About nine, Garth knocked out his pipe, and Thor took that for a signal. The girls went to the small bedroom, and prepared for bed. He could hear their voices, low and soft, a little laughter as they went to bed. Garth got out more blankets.

'May be cold tonight; the wind is keen,' he said.

Thor rolled up before the fireplace and went off to sleep. He could still hear the girls talking softly when he drowsed off.

Garth got up in the night; Thor wakened also, his nose cold. Garth got out still more blankets and went to the bedroom, softly. He returned, chuckling.

'Sleeping like two kittens, all curled up,' he reported comfortably. 'Want another blanket?'

'If you have an extra one.'

Garth leaned to spread one on Thor, then put one on his own space. He got into the space and seemed to sleep at once. Thor lay awake a few minutes, thinking of Laurel, all curled up.

Thor wakened in the first light to see Garth already up, putting wood on the fire. He had water boiling in the pot and in the coffee kettle, while Thor washed and got dressed.

They were drinking coffee when Jade came out, dressed and

yawning. She gave them a sleepy shy smile and went to the kitchen to start breakfast.

Laurel came out then, dressed in a sturdy dark blue skirt, a light blue shirt, and boots. Thor was relieved to see her dressed for traveling. He did not relish another fight with her, but they were going today.

Garth went out. When he returned he said, 'I smell rain.'

Laurel looked at Thor. 'We'll start out anyway, get as far as we can,' he said.

Thor knew this time of year the rains could be heavy, but they would chance it. He packed up his clean clothes, thanked Jade for them. Laurel brought out her canvas bag, and Garth lugged them down to the boat. Thor carried the heavier box of provisions; Jade had been generous.

Jade followed them down to the boat. She and Laurel hugged and kissed each other.

'I'll come again,' said Laurel, a hard note in her voice.

Garth interposed hastily, as Thor was about to blow up.

'I'll try to bring Jade to Sitka this winter,' he said in his slow calm way. 'When the lumbering stops for the snows, we could travel.'

'You'll be welcome to stay with us,' said Thor. 'Hope you can come.' They shook hands. Thor bent and kissed Jade's cheek. 'Thanks for your kind hospitality, Jade.'

'You are welcome. It was a good visit,' Jade said, her hands folded shyly in her apron. She gave them smiles, her eyes dark and haunting. 'Tell my parents, if you see them, I hope to see them in Wrangell in October.'

'I'll do that.'

Garth helped shove the boat into the water and held the rope until Thor got in. Then he helped Laurel into the boat. Thor steadied her until she got to the seat in the front. She took a paddle, and Thor let her. Let her work off her anger, as he would work off his! Paddling could be demanding work in such a river as the Stikine.

They said goodbye again, then started out. Soon the bend in the river hid the lumbering camp from sight. Thor did not try to talk; he concentrated on keeping the boat from the little rapids and eddies, and to the center of the stream. When the river widened in places, he paddled along the shoreline, warily.

191

The skies had clouded over. By noon it was raining lightly. The skies in the West were a darker gray. Thor frowned. It would be his luck this trip to be in for a genuine storm. They were due for more rain. Alaska could be mighty rainy in the Southeastern Panhandle where they were.

They did not stop for lunch; he wanted to get as far as possible. He paddled while Laurel ate a hasty meal of cooked bacon and bread; then she passed some food back to Thor. He ate while she kept the boat steady in the middle of the river.

By mid-afternoon the rain came down harder. He began to look for shelter. Laurel turned around cautiously, and spoke for almost the first time.

'There's a deserted cabin by the bank, about two miles farther on.'

'Right, I saw one coming up.'

She turned back to sit, and paddle in front of him, a brave small figure, sturdy and dependable. Except when she took off on her own! He felt admiration for her in all his anger; she was a strong little person, unafraid and determined. She was the true daughter of pioneers, who had gone west alone, had come to Alaska alone, had endured, had died for their wish to live in the wilderness.

But Laurel would not die for her daring, not if he could help it. She said he was not her guardian, but she had no one else. And he would protect her in spite of herself!

They turned another bend in the river, and he saw the deserted cabin, gray against the green of the trees and brush. There was a dilapidated wharf there, its wooden planks broken and splintered. He turned the wooden boat toward it, and Laurel helped with her paddling on the other side of the boat.

They drifted toward the wharf, and the boat bumped gently against it. Laurel sprang out, without being asked, and Thor tossed the rope to her. The bank was slippery with mud; the rain was beating down. She blinked to clear her vision, and held tight while he went ashore and tied the rope to a stake.

He tested the stake, pounded it down more into the bank, then pulled the boat up onto the bank. He didn't want to risk losing the boat, their only means of getting out. They might be rescued in time, with all the traffic on the river, but it might be an uncomfortable and long wait.

He passed the box of provisions to Laurel, then said sharply, 'Wait for me!' when she started toward the cabin.

He left behind one canvas bag, picked up his rifle and the other canvas bag, and preceded her to the cabin.

'Wait outside,' he said shortly. She nodded, set down the box, then drew her pistol, rain running down her fresh cheeks.

In spite of his repressed boiling fury, his soaking wet clothes, and water-logged boots, Thor could not repress a grin at her readiness for what might happen. What a practical outdoors girl Laurel could be! Ready to shoot a person or a bear, she drew her pistol and kept herself in readiness.

He shoved open the creaking cabin door and looked inside. Nobody there. No large form. A small mouse did dart between his legs in alarm, and shoot out into the rain.

He stepped inside. The cabin was small but neatly built, with a good stone fireplace. A small stack of firewood was set in one corner. Near the fireplace was a battered pot. The long rod coming from the fireplace had a hook on the end, in event of needing to hang a pot from it – good. The only furnishings were a bench, a table, some chipped porcelain basins, one broken oil lamp. Evidently someone had moved out and had been kind enough to leave a few supplies for strangers.

'Okay, Laurel, come on in,' he called.

She stepped in after him and set the box of provisions down on the table. 'Mice?' she asked in interest as he kicked at the firewood.

'Yep. Scared?'

'Only of bears and snakes,' she replied soberly.

'No snakes here, or the mice would not set up housekeeping,' he said as he stacked some wood into the fireplace. He searched in his pocket for dry matches, and set one to the wood. A warm fire soon blazed up.

Several mice ran about, squeaking indignantly at the intrusion. Thor brought in their canvas rolls, then took the pot and two basins outdoors. He rinsed them in the steady downpour of rain, then set them where they would be soon filled with water.

When he returned, Laurel had set out the food, and was slicing bread on a towel on the table. She had taken off her parka and had dried her wet face.

193

'Best change your wet clothes,' he said briskly. 'I'll do the same.'

She gave him a quick shy look, then nodded. She took out a dry skirt, her shoes, a blouse. He turned his back to her, then changed his shirt and trousers and put on dry stockings, as she did the same. He heard the rustle of her clothes.

'All right now,' she said in a muffled tone. Her face was flushed as she returned to the table.

He set the bench beside the fire and spread out their wet clothes carefully. With luck they would soon be dry; wool dried out fast, but these things were soaked through. Her parka was waterproof on the outside, and she had sat in the boat with the tarp over her while she rowed; she should not be too chilled through.

'How long do you think the storm will last?' Laurel asked presently. 'Food's ready.'

Thor came to the table, and helped himself to bread, cold meat, cranberry jam on the meat. 'No telling,' he said. 'Could let up by morning, could go on for days.'

The rain beat on the roof in a steady monotonous downpour. They finished eating, and she put the food away carefully against the mice, and then scattered some crumbs beside the woodpile for them. 'Might keep them away from our food,' she said with a smile. Her eyes sparkled. She was enjoying this, damn it, he thought, half amused.

She spread out the tarp before the fire, set a blanket on it, and sat down. He sat down beside her and folded his arms around his knees.

'Are you still angry at me?' she asked seriously.

'Yep,' he said.

'Oh.' She stared at the fire. Her face was grave, the outline pure against the dark walls of the cabin. Her cheeks were a healthy pink, her eyebrows definite on her light face.

'Don't you realize what could have happened to you, Laurel?' he said more calmly. 'You could have been raped, or even murdered. You cannot trust just anybody here.'

'I could have been raped in Sitka,' she said half under her breath.

'What did you say?' he rapped out, turning to her.

'I could have been raped in Sitka – in your home,' she said more clearly. She turned to look at him, and their faces were close. He could see her in the firelight, she was looking frightened and intent.

'What are you talking about?' he snapped.

'Ewan, your brother,' she said. 'Do you know he was the one who seduced Jade? It was her baby that died. His baby, Ewan's also. But he shoved her away, he called her names, and he abandoned her, because she is an Indian girl.'

He felt kicked in the stomach. 'Ewan . . . did that?'

'Yes. She told me. I hope you won't tell Ewan about the baby,' she said more quietly, turning back to the fire. 'I don't think she wants him to know. He knew she was expecting one, but not about the dying and all that.'

'He doesn't know, then? He left her . . .' He was trying to adjust to the thought, about his brother. Ewan, arrogant, flirtatious, charming, yes. But getting a girl pregnant, knowing it, shoving her away . . . 'What do you mean, shoving?'

'He shoved her into the river. Garth rescued her. She was injured; her back was hurt, and she was badly bruised. The baby was probably injured too. She had the baby, but it didn't live long. She didn't blame Ewan, but I do!' added Laurel hotly. 'I think he was cruel and unfeeling – first seducing her, then not being responsible at all. If it hadn't been for Garth, and her nice employer, Jade could have died!'

Thor was silent, trying to get over the shock of it. Then he remembered what else she had said. 'What did you mean, *you* might have been raped in Sitka. Ewan would not –'

'Yes, he would. He has tried to kiss me, hug me. I overheard him talking about me. He thinks I'm attracted to him,' she said with vast contempt. 'Him! His ego is so big – I despise him. And now I hate him after what he did to Jade.'

'He wouldn't touch you –'

'He has touched me! And he would rape me! I know it! That's one reason I ran away!'

She blurted it all out. Thor was shocked, bewildered by her charges. Was she hysterical, or trying to justify herself? No, Laurel was not a hysterical type of girl. She was very practical and had common sense. So she must mean it. Damn it, he had been away too much from home, and not kept an eye on Ewan. The boy had been allowed to run free too much – boy? Hell, he was a man of twenty-five. Old enough to know better. Old enough to be responsible for his deeds. And to try to rape Laurel, a guest in Thor's home and under Thor's responsibility . . .

'I'll see to Ewan,' he said harshly. 'I think it's time he moved out. Father shall know about this.'

'About Jade also?' she asked.

'Yes, about Jade too! He owes her plenty.'

'I think Garth will take care of her now,' said Laurel. 'Just so Ewan stays away from her.'

'He wouldn't dare go about her now!'

'You don't know Ewan,' said Laurel. 'You don't know him at all. He's sneaky, and thinks his charm forgives him everything in the world. He thinks women fall at his feet!'

'Do you fall at his feet?' Thor asked harshly, hating that picture. Was Laurel so hard on Ewan because she was attracted to him?

'Never,' she said decidedly. 'I hate him for what he did to Jade.'

'That's no reason for you to run off from home,' said Thor, returning to the prime subject of interest to him. Jade had someone to look after her now; Laurel was still Thor's job. 'I don't want you doing anything like that again.'

'I was perfectly safe,' she said defiantly. 'Ben Kennard is a fine man; he took good care of me.'

'How did you know he would?' snapped Thor, exasperated again. 'God damn it, listen to me! You cannot trust men! You cannot just go off sailing with any man who comes along!'

'I don't,' said Laurel. 'But I'm here with you now! Can I trust you?'

'Well, if you can't –' he began; then he looked at her. There was a demure smile on her lips. She was teasing him!

He grabbed her and pulled her to him, meaning to shake her. She fell against him, taken off guard. He put his hand around her face, bent down, and pressed his mouth hard to her half-opened protesting lips. The kiss burned all through him, the feel of her soft warm lips, her smooth cheek.

He went a little crazy. He had been anxious about her, scared to death when he thought of what might happen to her, angry with her. He had been tired, chilled, worn out with the effort of getting to her in that damned small rowboat. And now here she was,

196

mocking him, teasing him, and they were alone, alone in the world, a wilderness around them, nobody for miles . . .

He pushed her over onto the blanket before the fire, and followed her down, still kissing her. His mouth blazed on hers, his big mouth on her small sweet lips. His hand sought her blindly, and found her waist, and moved up to her small perfect round breast. She gasped, and he kissed her lips shut.

He fondled her, savagely, wanting to feel all of her. He was not thinking, just feeling, knowing the perfection of a woman's body beneath his. He opened the wool, checked shirt she wore, and beneath it found her naked; she had taken off her wet petticoats to dry them. He cupped the round breast in his big palm and squeezed it gently. He put his lips on the taut red nipple, and found it sweet and hard in his mouth.

She was gasping, trying to roll away from beneath his body. He followed her, mercilessly, wanting to have her, punish her, shake her up, shock her. She had thought she was not in any danger! Well, she should know better. He was a man, and he wanted her, and they were alone.

Despite his burning anger and passion, he heard a small voice. 'Thor . . . Thor, don't!'

He ignored the voice. He wanted her; passion blazed up in him. Masculine need was blazing in him; his flesh was hard and hunger rampant in him. He had not had a woman in a long time; he had worked hard to forget his needs. He had wanted to wait until marriage, but he was a man, very much a man, and he wanted this soft woman's body beneath his, so sweet and young and smooth and silken beneath his hands.

He pushed up her skirt, and she squirmed and pleaded with him. 'Thor . . . don't do . . . this! Thor . . . don't! Oh, God, Thor –'

He tried to ignore the pleading voice. Her cheeks were wet when he pressed hot kisses on them. His hand was searching for her belly, her thighs; he felt her, all soft and wet . . . He pushed down his trousers, and she fought against him; she scratched his back where he had opened his shirt. He felt her hands on him, and it increased his desire. He rolled over on top of her, put one leg on her and held her under him.

He was gasping for breath, passion burning him to a hot fire; he wanted her, he must have her –

And she was crying out, screaming at him as she scratched and shoved at him. 'Thor . . . don't rape me! Thor . . . please don't . . . rape me!'

He hesitated at that horrible word. Rape!

She felt him hesitate and gave him a hard shove with her little fists. He rolled over on his back, and lay there, fighting himself.

Laurel jumped up, shaking, stumbling over the blanket. He looked up at her, at her naked shoulders and breasts, so white and pearly beautiful, with the red nipples a beautiful rose, and the small belly and little navel. She was pulling up her skirt to cover her, and crying, and trying to pull on her shirt. Tears rolled down her cheeks; her brown eyes were wounded and frightened.

'That was close,' he muttered, and struggled to sit up. He shoved his hair back, and put his hand on his face.

When he got up, she backed away clear to the wall, her face white and terrified. He had frightened her half to death.

But she had kept on fighting him.

'Don't worry . . . it's over, Laurel,' Thor said gruffly, and went outside to walk around and around the cabin. It was not until he was soaked through that the chill wind and driving rain drove him back into the cabin.

Laurel was sitting on the blanket, huddled there, her frightened, defiant face peering from the heap of blankets she had pulled tightly around her as though for protection.

'Coffee?' he asked. He had brought in the rain-filled battered coffee pot with him.

'Yes, thank you,' she said in a soft voice. She eyed him warily as he put the coffee pot on the wood piece in the fire. He waited until it boiled, removed it from the flame, then poured it out into the two tin cups.

He handed her the cup, from his height staring down at her on the floor. 'Sorry, Laurel,' he said. 'It won't happen again.'

She nodded, her face down, sipping at the coffee. They drank in silence. She rolled up then, and seemed to sleep by the fire. He thought by her breathing she was not asleep, but he said nothing to her.

Presently, he rolled up also, on the other side of the fire, facing her. Her face was pale and quiet, the eyebrows dark on her forehead, her mouth a soft rose. How sweet her mouth had tasted. He shut his eyes determinedly. He could hear the timid scrabbling of the mice coming out as all became silent. The rain beat down steadily.

Next day the rain was still coming down; the sky was almost black with clouds. They were holed up all that day. Thor went out and got a couple of rabbits, brought them back, cleaned them. Laurel cooked them on the spit over the fire.

That afternoon the rain did not let up. He went out with his string and hook, and caught fine trout. He cleaned them, and Laurel cooked them for supper. They would not starve here, the wilderness was lavish.

She made sourdough biscuits for supper, patting them out on the table, and baking them in a pot. She was resourceful in the wilds, he thought; she was used to this life. What a wife she would make for a woodsman.

But Laurel was too smart for that. She could live anywhere, make a home anywhere. He brooded as she prepared supper. She was happy, he decided, singing over the food, over the setting of the meager table. He moved the bench over to the table, and this time they sat down for supper. The clothes had all dried; Laurel had kept turning them on the bench all afternoon.

Thor had cut fresh firewood, searching out partly dry pieces in the underbrush, among fallen trees. He had a goodly pile in the corner, spread out to dry thoroughly, for themselves, or the next party that came along.

Laurel put a tarp over her head, and went outdoors with the pans, scrubbing them in the rain. She came back, still humming, and set them on the table. Then there was nothing else to do. It was about six. He lit his pipe, then sat on the bench before the fire. Laurel came to sit beside him, leaving a careful distance between them.

'Now is the time for a good book to read,' said Thor. He rather regretted her aloofness because of his attack on her; he had really scared her. And yet, he may have awakened her to him, and that was all to the good.

'On the trip here,' said Laurel, 'Amos told us some Tlingit stories about the world. Would you like to hear one?'

'Might as well.'

Laurel settled herself again, and folded her hands in her lap. They were red and work-worn, but pretty hands, he thought.

'In the old days the world was made mostly of water,' she began. 'One day, Raven, the smartest one in the world, was flying over the waters, when he saw a beautiful mermaid swimming in the waters. Raven fell in love with the lovely mermaid and asked her to be his wife. First, she said, make some land for me, so I may dry myself.'

Thor listened, half smiling, for he had heard the old tale before, but it meant more in Laurel's musical low voice and her vibrant way of telling it. She raised her voice in the mermaid's tone, lowered it in the Raven's *klawock, klawock!*

Laurel went on, about how Raven approached Seal, and then Frog, to enlist their aid; and about how he received the sand and scattered it on the waters to make islands, so his mermaid could sit on land and dry herself, and he taking her for his wife. And from them, all men descended, especially the powerful Raven tribe of the Tlingit.

After that Laurel told another story, and then they began to talk about the history of the world. She talked of her history courses in high school, how inadequate they were, 'all about wars and such, and not much about people,' was how she put it. 'I learned more, reading biographies about famous people from the library. That made more sense. People in the world achieving things, and not wars to destroy people.'

Thor talked about the books he had read, and promised to find them for her in his library. So the evening passed pleasantly. They turned in, rolling up in their blankets, about ten o'clock by his turnip-shaped gold watch.

Next morning it was still pouring down, so they decided to remain for another day. By evening it was beginning to clear.

'Some hope for starting out tomorrow,' Thor said, eyeing the sky at dusk. 'The clouds are breaking in the West.'

By morning the rain had stopped. They packed up, scrubbed the pots and pans to leave for the next stranded persons, doused the fire well, and shut the door on their temporary home.

He was glad to get out the boat and load it. Laurel got in, and they started out, to reach Wrangell in one long day of travel. They got in after dark, and went to Mrs. Simpson's boarding house. She gave them a hot meal, and separate rooms. She also gave them a long look, as she realized they had been traveling alone together for some time.

Thor thought, after he had turned in and lay sleeplessly in an unfamiliar bed, there's bound to be talk about us. What shall I do about it?

But he thought he knew what he would do. Gossip spread in Alaska and the wilderness as quickly as in any town in the States. And he would not have Laurel talked about as Jade had been.

Chapter 17

Back in Sitka Thor soon heard gossip about them, unpleasant gossip. Men whispered in the saloon; he heard them as he sat at table with one of his men. Sidonie reported to Olaf that everybody was talking about Laurel. She had the gall to tell Olaf he should throw the girl out of the house.

'She's a troublemaker,' said Sidonie to Olaf in front of Thor. 'Taking Thor away from his duties, running off to her Indian friends! She is no better than a savage!'

'That will do, Sidonie,' snapped Olaf, but he was troubled too.

Young ladies were not supposed to go off on their own with strangers, as Laurel had done. And Thor had brought her back, spending time in the wilderness alone with her. How that had gotten out, Thor could only guess. Sidonie had known; she must have gossiped to her friends.

And then there was Ewan. Thor sat back in his chair as his father questioned Ewan sternly. 'You knew Jade Nolan was pregnant, by *you*, and you deserted her?'

'It might have been any man, she was willing enough,' said Ewan sullenly, his face flushed.

'Nevertheless, you could guess it was your child,' said Olaf, stern anger in his face and eyes. Ewan was twenty-five, when would he mature? 'You're old enough to know better. A young girl like that – And her parents had been good to us. You abused their hospitality as well as betrayed their trust. And to take a young girl –'

'Only an Indian girl!' Ewan said with contempt.

There was a short silence as his father stared at him. Thor thought, So it is true, what Laurel had said. Ewan has only contempt for Indians, and any Indian girl is fair game. But what about Laurel herself?

'You didn't offer to help her? You ran off?'

'I walked off!' said Ewan, offended. 'She wasn't my responsibility!'

'Whose, then?' snapped his father. 'If you could not do the decent thing and marry her, you should have given her money.'

'She had a job,' said Ewan, with a shrug. 'And her parents. Why should I?'

'Because you were the man who made her pregnant!' Olaf said flatly, and his big hands spread out as he looked to Thor. 'How can I tell my son he owes something to honor? My God, have I taught you so poorly?'

Ewan was flushed and sullen. He hated being scolded and told he was in the wrong. He liked being charmed and liked, smiled at and petted.

'Well, at least Jade is all right now,' Olaf said with a sigh. 'No thanks to you, Ewan. She has married a decent man –'

Ewan interrupted. 'Wh – an Indian?' he asked sharply.

'No, a white man. Garth Fleming. A lumberjack. Thor met him and likes him.'

'A good strong man, decent; he'll go far,' said Thor, watching Ewan squirm. 'They make a fine couple.'

Ewan looked thoughtful, frowning.

'At any event, I'm sending you north for a couple months, to the copper mine,' said Olaf, bruskly. 'That should keep you out of trouble for a time.'

'Thor is supposed to go this trip!' blustered Ewan. 'I spent months there last spring.'

'You'll go where I tell you, Ewan,' Olaf said wearily.

'About Laurel,' added Thor. 'You'll keep your hands off her. I don't want you fooling around Laurel!'

Olaf looked shocked. 'Laurel! Ewan, you haven't tried to bother her! A guest in our home, a fine young girl!'

'No, I haven't –' began Ewan.

'Yes, he has,' Thor interrupted bluntly. 'She has complained about you; she locks her door now. If you go near her, I'll break you in half, Ewan! And I'm not fooling.'

Ewan sulked, 'She likes me, she likes fooling around, she showed that when she went off with that man –'

Olaf blazed up in a rare fury at him. His green eyes snapped fire at his younger son. 'You'll keep your tongue off the subject of Laurel! And you'll stay away from her. By God, if you do one thing . . . I'll disown you! Here you are, twenty-five, and no common sense of decency! What do I have to say to you, boy! She's a fine young girl, a good girl. And you would hang around her skirts! Now, off you'll go to the North, and I may not bring you back for a year!'

Ewan for once looked rather shaken. He slammed out of the room, and his boots pounded on the stairs. Olaf looked at Thor.

'You're sure of this? He made advances to Laurel, in my own house?'

'Yes. She asked the housekeeper for the keys to her bedroom and study and had an Indian boy put bolts on her doors because of him.'

'Why didn't she tell me?' Olaf stood up and paced the floor, running his hand through his graying hair. 'By God, I wouldn't have anything happen to her! I liked and respected Jim Winfield – and his daughter not safe in my home!'

'There is no longer reason to worry, Father. I'm going to take care of Laurel,' Thor said calmly, leaning back in his chair.

Olaf paused to glare at his son, then the glare faded to a smile. 'Like that, is it? Well, good luck, my boy! She's a spirited lass!'

Thor and his father discussed the rest of the summer plans for an hour or so, until about three-thirty. Then Thor took off for the office, to get some work done. When he returned that evening, Sidonie was full of wailing and fussing at his father.

Ewan had complained to Sidonie about being sent away. The evening meal was painful with her complaints about her favorite stepson being sent away 'for no reason at all.'

Olaf finally shushed her, sternly, and then there was silence at the table. Thor watched Laurel's face thoughtfully. She was pale and quiet, no sign of the young spirited girl who had told him Tlingit stories as the firelight lit her bright face and shining brown eyes. The gossip was getting to her.

If he didn't look out, she would take off again, to get a job or seek refuge with one of her many friends. She makes friends as easily as a bird sings, he thought proudly. She would pause, smile and talk to someone, and he or she would be a friend for life. She took such interest in everyone, remembered his name, was concerned for him, white or Indian, young or old, man, woman, or child, or dog.

Trouble was, Laurel seemed to trust just about anybody. Except Ewan, and Leverett; she didn't like Leverett at all.

Thor wondered with a frown if Leverett had tried to make advances to Laurel. Surely not; yet he was a strange man at times. And having the needs of a older man, probably. He had a grown daughter older than Laurel, but odder things had happened. He would not have Leverett hanging around Laurel.

After breakfast the next morning, Thor went looking for Laurel. He had worked in his office for an hour; now he was ready to talk to her. His plans were made. Now she must fall in with them.

He heard voices in the parlor, women's voices, raised, and he walked quietly along the hallway. The maids were in the kitchen clearing up the breakfast dishes, talking about the work for the day.

He paused outside the parlor door, unseen by the two women inside. He caught Sidonie's clear cold voice.

'. . . go off to your Indian friends!' she said. 'You're not wanted here. Your shameless behavior –'

'I am Mr. Koenig's guest,' said Laurel slowly, wearily. Thor wondered if she had argued with Sidonie before. 'When *he* says so, I will go.'

'My husband was stupidly fond of your father!' sneered Sidonie. 'He doesn't realize what a little bitch you are! Well, you can just take off! I don't want you around! You can fool the men, but you can't fool me! You're a little harlot!'

'You would like to believe that,' Laurel said bitterly. 'Encouraging Ewan to make me pregnant, like Jade Nolan! Well, he won't, he won't! I despise him. I'm going to get a job and leave here. You won't have me around for long.'

'Good! You can go back to your Indian friends, and live like the savage you are!'

Thor stepped inside the door, burning inside. He kept his face under control. Laurel saw him first, and gave him a shocked, startled look. Sidonie saw her face, turned around, her furious face smoothing to a bland smile, rather uneasily.

'Laurel, I want to have a talk with you. We'll take Czar for a walk. Get your hat and jacket, if you will.'

She started at his firm tone, then nodded. She sped past him and up the stairs. Ewan had left, reluctantly, that morning. He had no fears of Ewan upsetting his plans or making trouble.

Thor said evenly to Sidonie, 'I will not have you speak to Laurel again like that, ever. You will be respectful to her, and polite, if it kills you.'

'You don't give orders to me in my house!' she blazed her face white. The enmity between them blazed into the open. He had hated her ever since she had first married his father and had dared to make a secret advance to him. He had pushed her from him, utterly repelled by her. Ever since then, only politeness had kept him from striking her, from telling his father. That and his love for his father.

'I'll be moving out soon,' he said quietly. 'You can live for that moment! But from now on, living here or not, I'll tell you, you will be polite and courteous to Laurel! No more remarks like the ones I just heard. No more sneaky plans to encourage Ewan – My God, you can certainly stoop low.'

'Ask your girlfriend Clarissa about that!' she flung back at him. 'It was partly her idea! She doesn't want that savage girl around either! You better think about her feelings! She could marry anybody she chooses! Think about that!'

Thor eyed her curiously. Clarissa? Had she been in on plots against Laurel? He had always thought Clarissa was quiet and kind, but then a woman did not always show her true nature to a man who seemed to enjoy her company. He had escorted Clarissa about, enjoyed her company, her flattery, her interest in his work, her intelligent mind. She had been well educated in Boston, she knew Alaska now, and she and her father were interested in politics.

He wondered how true Sidonie's remark could be, and put some of it down to spite. She would like to come between him and Clarissa – if there was anything to ruin, he decided, she would do so.

He turned and left the room abruptly, and waited for Laurel at the foot of the stairs. She soon came down, half running, her face anxious. She wore her jacket, and swung her hat by its ribbons.

As they went out the back door to the kennels, Laurel said, 'Czar was glad to see me home. We went for a walk yesterday.'

She was obviously making talk. Thor nodded, his mind on the conversation to come, turning over in his mind just how to approach her.

Czar came from his kennels, led by the Indian boy in charge of them this morning. He came up to his mistress, and rubbed his big gray head against her fondly. She petted him, rubbed up his fur, greeted him with loving low words.

'Oh, you're a good dog! You're a splendid dog! Czar, we are going for a fine walk, and you shall sniff out rabbits and all kinds of goodies! But you're not going to catch anything, because you are such a good obedient dog!'

Czar whined, and snuffed and ruffled at her in a low growling joyful tone. Thor could not help grinning at them both, at the nonsense she talked so lovingly, at Czar's happy response to her. Czar gave a last whoof at her throat with his cold nose, then settled down to walk beside them, padding quietly at Laurel's heels, putting his nose into her palm when she held it out to him from time to time. He loves her already, thought Thor.

They walked in silence for a short time, toward Sitka. He noticed that Laurel kept turning to look across him at someone. 'Who is it?' Thor asked.

'I think his name is Herman Ranke. Do you know him?' She sounded fearful, and shrank behind him.

He glanced at the hulking figure of the man going into the woods. 'Oh, yes, he's a handyman of Leverett,' he said impatiently. 'Don't worry about him.'

'He looks . . . so strange.' Laurel said.

'He can't help his looks. He's harmless, Leverett says. Does odd jobs around.'

Laurel glanced again at the man, frowning slightly. Even Czar was growling slightly. Thor, however, had his mind on other matters, and went on.

'I have been thinking, Laurel,' Thor said when she caught up with him. 'What you said – that I am not your guardian, that I am not responsible for you –'

'You aren't,' she said. 'But I was rude about it. I am truly grateful to you for all you have done,' and she sounded prim and schoolmarmish.

'Including bringing you back from Jade's, I suppose,' he said grimly. He had not forgiven her for running off. 'Well, that is neither here nor there. I think we should make our relationship definite.'

Instead of asking him what he meant, as he had hoped, Laurel went off at a tangent. 'I think I should move out to a boarding house and get a job,' she said. 'I can teach small children. I can housekeep. I can cook and sew. I should not have trouble up here.'

'Those are nice accomplishments,' said Thor, with a slight grin despite his grim purpose. 'They fit into my plans for you, I'm glad to say.'

This time she bit. 'What plans?'

'I want you to marry me, Laurel, and soon. There has been talk about us, and you running off. That should silence it.'

'M-marry you!' she gasped. 'That is . . . rather drastic, isn't it? The gossip will die down soon. For you anyway. For me, when people see in a few months that I am not pregnant, then the gossip about me will die down!' she added bitterly, her face flushed and her brown eyes flashing with anger.

'I won't have you talking that way!' he scolded her furiously. 'We know nothing happened –' And then he remembered that night when something had so nearly happened, and he too flushed. It was dangerous to be alone with an attractive young woman like Laurel, and he could very well have made love to her.

Both were silent. He stalked along wishing she was a good obedient girl who did not ask questions. But that was not Laurel. He set himself to persuade her.

'Now, Laurel,' he said more gently – he must use a mild tone to her, she flared up when pushed – 'I have been thinking for some time about this. We suit each other very well, and you do want to stay in Alaska, don't you?'

'Oh yes, I want to live here forever!'

'Of course,' he said, encouraged. 'But you are young and attractive. I expect men will nag you until you marry one of us,' he said to make her smile.

The corners of her rosy mouth curled up a little, he noted with satisfaction.

'So, why not marry me? You like me, don't you? We always got along pretty well.'

'I do like you,' she admitted in a low tone. 'But Thor, haven't you been thinking – I mean . . . don't you like Clarissa Leverett awfully well? You go out with her a lot.'

He shrugged. 'I have gone out with several young ladies, but I have never proposed to any of them,' he said. 'You are the only one I have considered living with, Laurel. We like the same kind of life, the same people, hunting and fishing, books, and so on. We have the same tastes; I even asked you to decorate my house because we like the same colors and such.'

He glanced down at her sideways, to see how this took. She was frowning slightly.

'I wondered why you didn't ask someone else,' she admitted.

'Because I like the colors you do, like the furniture, and so on,' he said with forced patience. 'So, Laurel, what about me? Will you marry me?'

'I don't see the need,' she said stubbornly, her chin set, and he could not see her eyes because of her hat.

He sighed in exasperation. 'Well, we *are* going to get married,' he said definitely. 'I can't have you running off whenever you choose. And you complained about Ewan. Other men could be the same way. I won't have a peaceful moment until you're settled! So we are going to get married. All right?'

She turned and looked up at him, her worried brown eyes pleading. 'Thor, it isn't necessary,' she said slowly. 'We know the gossip is wrong about us. I could get a job –'

'No, you are not,' he said, and caught at her hand, 'Come on, Laurel, give in! You might as well marry me, because I'm going to pester you until you do! I want to take care of you, and you do need a man to look after you. You like me, don't you?'

Slowly she nodded her brown head, her eyes still troubled. 'But Thor –'

'No, no buts; we'll do it. Now, what shall you wear? Do you have a fancy white dress?'

It seemed an effort for Laurel to turn her thoughts to clothes. And she knew that he had done it deliberately to make the marriage a fact. 'Well,' she said, 'Madame Bonheur is making a summer gown for me now, in white taffeta . . .' They were in Sitka now, walking down the street near the dressmaker.

'Good,' he said. 'Let's go see her now. There is time before lunch. Want to be married in church? We'll arrange it,' he said firmly as she opened her mouth to say something in protest.

He led her to the door of the dressmaker's and pushed open the door. She turned and tied Czar to the post; he gave her a reproachful look, so eloquent that she laughed softly, and bent and gave him a hug.

'Now, Czar, you be a good dog! I know you don't like this, but we won't be long!'

She went ahead of Thor into the shop, the smile still on her lips. Madame Bonheur was already coming to them.

'Miss Laurel! I have been worried about you! I heard you were lost in the wilderness!'

'No, no, that rumor is wrong, Madame!' Laurel assured her, a little pink flush in her clear skin. 'I went off to see some friends in Wrangell, that is all. Thor got worried and came after me, and brought me back in his ship.'

'Oh, so, so; that is good,' said the Frenchwoman. 'And now you come to see about your dresses? They are all done. Voilà!'

She pushed back the curtain that covered a row of gowns on a rail. Thor looked past the yellow gowns, a rose silk, and a golden brown one, to see the white, watered-silk taffeta gown, long-skirted, formal, and with a beautiful heart-shaped neckline.

He shoved the other dresses back and looked at it more closely. Laurel stood in silence.

'There, that will make a fine wedding dress,' Thor said. He could just see Laurel in it. 'Can you make a lace veil, Madame, with a little crown on it?'

'A wedding dress!' gasped Madame Bonheur, eyebrows raised, hands up. 'You are getting married?'

'Yes, Madame, quite soon,' Thor said cheerfully. 'How about a veil, and some white satin slippers?'

Laurel gulped. She seemed incapable of saying a word. Madame brought out some lace veiling, and Thor chose the most fragile of the soft laces and held it out.

'This . . . I like this. And some little pearls on it,' he said. 'Here . . . like this on her head.' He removed Laurel's bonnet, tossed it onto the counter, and draped the veiling over her head so that her face shone out pearly white and cream and rose from the lace. Laurel was so lovely, he had all he could do not to grab her and kiss her senseless. But that could wait.

Madame Bonheur shoved him politely aside, and adjusted the veiling more closely, studying the effect. 'Yes, yes, this will be most beautiful,' she breathed. She opened a drawer, shoved around some trinkets, and brought out a little circlet of pearls. 'And this to hold it down,' and she put it softly on Laurel's braided coronet of hair.

'And now the slippers,' and she bustled around and brought out some white shoes. Laurel sat down and tried them on, her little feet so small and fragile. Thor looked at them wondering how she had managed to keep up with him in the wilderness, when she had gone hunting with him, and fishing, and paddling that rowboat against the rapids. She seemed so small and fragile, and was so sturdy and determined. What a mate she would make!

Madame Bonheur promised to wrap up everything, and send it to them in a carriage that very afternoon. And if they wished anything else, they must tell her at once. She would work her fingers to the bone, 'to do everything for Miss Laurel's wedding. And when is the fine event to be?'

'On Tuesday morning,' said Thor, disregarding Laurel's gasp. 'We're going to the church to arrange it now. I hope you will be able to attend, Madame?'

She beamed, having fished for just this. 'Of course, of course. I shall be delighted! Good wishes, every best wish to you both, good fortune always!' She came to the door with them, still calling down blessings, in English and in French.

After the door was closed, Czar untied and at heel, Laurel whispered desperately, 'But Thor, not so soon! It does not need to happen so soon. I am not ready!'

'Might as well get it over with,' he said, cheerfully callous and knowing full well she might think of a way out or escape on someone's boat! He was not having that. 'I hate ceremonies, don't you?

And we can move in to my house at once. The house isn't finished, but enough rooms are ready. I want to be in before winter. I'll tell Mrs. Dugan to get our rooms ready, and get more supplies in. She has been training some maids and houseboys. And they will be glad to have us to fuss over.'

Laurel was silent – she looked rather overwhelmed – and marshalling her arguments. He did not give her time to think. He marched her to the minister's manse, and they talked to the preacher and his wife. He had them sign the register, talked to them for half an hour about the ceremony, promised to have the license made out for them to sign the next day, reminded Thor to purchase a wedding ring, and beamed them on their way. He had known Thor for years, and had met Laurel in church many a time this summer.

Thor led Laurel to luncheon, talking very fast so she could not make up any arguments. After lunch they went to the jeweler's and Thor chose their rings. Laurel seemed numb.

He chose simple gold rings for their wedding bands, a delicate slim one for Laurel, a wider one for himself. For her engagement ring, he chose a beautiful sapphire surrounded by small diamond points. It looked lovely on her hand.

'Like the forget-me-nots,' he murmured to her, and won a smile from her, the first in a while.

As they left the jeweler's, Laurel looked at the large ring on her hand soberly. 'You shouldn't have done it, Thor,' she said.

'Don't you like the ring?'

'I mean, the wedding and all. I don't think we –'

'I'm going to marry you, Laurel, and get you tied up fast,' he said quietly. 'No more running off, no more talk of getting jobs. You're eighteen now, and I'm twenty-eight; maybe that seems a bit old for you –'

'Oh no, not old . . .'

'Good,' he said. 'Let's go home now. You get some rest. I have a bit more work to do. I'll tell the boys to get out your trunks and some cases. The maids can help you pack up to move out to our house.'

She just looked at Thor, numbly. He grinned, and held her arm lightly on the way home, Czar snuffing at their heels. At the kennels he left the dog and escorted Laurel inside. He spoke to one of the maids, to a houseboy, and saw to it they started immediately on Laurel's room and her study.

It was Thursday. He went to his house and notified Patsy and Mike Dugan of his plans. They were in a flurry of excitement and pleasure, for they liked Laurel immensely. Then he went down to the office, put in a few hours of work, and returned home.

All was silent. Sidonie had been out to tea and knew nothing. He told his father, and Olaf promised to make the announcement at dinner that evening. Olaf chuckled and chuckled with glee.

Thor stopped at Laurel's room and tapped on the door. She opened the door, and stood there, a little forlornly. The trunks were half filled, the wardrobe was open, half the clothes packed.

'Coming along? Fine. Wear a blue silk tonight, will you, honey?' And he kissed her cheek lightly.

'Are you – Will you tell – I mean –'

'All taken care of. Just look pretty and smiling, and wear the ring, Laurel!' He turned her head, and kissed her deliberately on her soft mouth. God, she was sweet! Her mouth tasted of something like honey, and she smelled of lavender.

He stopped at the study door, made sure the boys were handling the paintings and easels carefully. He told them to take them in his carriage over to Mike Dugan. Mike would put them in the study that would be Laurel's on the second floor, opposite the master bedroom.

He showered and put on a blue silk suit, with a ruffled, white linen shirt. Might as well do it up fine. He went down early, on the alert for Laurel.

Thor greeted the first guests, Clarissa Leverett and her father, cordially. He liked talking politics with Leverett, for he knew plenty about Alaska and its potential. He wondered again why Laurel did not like the man.

Sidonie came in, splendid in her black silk and lace, with her black lace fan, which she used idly to her advantage. Her long dangling jet earrings set off her white face and red mouth, her black silky straight hair. Thor could see why his father had been attracted to her, she was a handsome, poised woman. One had to live with her to see the restless craving for excitement, the domineering

213

passion for attention, masculine attention. The malice in her came out also when she was off guard. She could be a cruel enemy.

He would see that she did not harm Laurel. He could not get Laurel out of there fast enough. He should have seen sooner that any woman like Sidonie could not stand the competition of being next to a young, innocent beautiful girl like Laurel. The contrast would be too humiliating to a vain woman like Sidonie.

Laurel came down the stairs. Thor was there at the bottom, waiting for her, and took her white arm. She trembled a little. 'You look glorious,' he assured her softly.

Laurel was so beautiful in the blue silk, with her radiant, rich brown hair and the golden chain on her white throat. Her ring shone, but she tried to hide her hand against her skirts as they went into the parlor. Clarissa saw them, and her eyes narrowed as she swished up to them and took Thor's other arm insistently.

'Come along, Thor. Daddy wants to talk to you,' she pouted.

'Of course,' Thor said pleasantly, and took Laurel along with them. He held her at his side, though he could feel her stiff resistance, her desire to move away.

Clarissa completely ignored Laurel. Mr. Leverett spoke pleasantly to her on greeting, but then he too ignored her. Thor had not noticed before how they treated Laurel, how most of Sidonie's friends treated her, as a nonentity. They made no attempt to engage her in conversation. Yet Laurel could be a most interesting conversationalist. His eyes opened, he watched how she was ignored, shoulders turned to her, glances flicked past her face. He was furious inside, but kept on smiling grimly. They would soon have to change their attitudes about her! His wife would not be ignored by Sitka society, even that little bit that Sidonie's patronage encouraged.

Laurel was loved in other places in Sitka, and those people would be their guests. When we are settled in our own home, Thor silently promised. His lovely and intelligent and good wife would not be treated so in their own home!

Thor had stolen into the dining room and changed the place cards. He escorted Laurel into the room, and set her at his father's right, and himself at Laurel's right. Sidonie glared at them in displeasure, and frowned along the line of guests. She would probably blame the maids until –

Thor sat through the courses, the conversation. He talked to Laurel encouragingly, and she smiled timidly in response, but said little. He realized it was her habit to say little at Sidonie's table. How could he have been so blind? He had been absorbed in his work, impatient with Sidonie's guests, absenting himself from her tables often. Poor Laurel, how she must have suffered!

As dessert was brought on, the houseboys brought around the bottles of champagne Thor had ordered put on ice. Sidonie was now very perplexed. Olaf stood when all had been served, and waited for the boys to stand back. They all knew – word had gone around quietly – and they all liked Laurel, who treated them with respect.

Olaf beamed at all his guests. 'I am very happy to make this announcement. I have long wished to do so. I am asking you now to drink a toast to my son, Thor, and to his bride-to-be, Miss Laurel Winfield! Ladies and gentlemen, their health!' And he raised his glass and downed it heartily.

Some glasses were raised more quickly than others. Sidonie sat transfixed, her cheeks burning with a spot of red in each, her hand gripping the stem of the champagne glass. Addison Leverett burst out angrily, 'But this cannot be! I was sure – My God . . .'

Clarissa put her hand on her father's arm, she was sitting next to him, by Thor's planning. 'Father, hush,' she said, her mouth tight. She drank the toast, but she seemed to choke on it and began to cough.

Only Olaf seemed pleased, Thor was quick to note. He smiled grimly, and took Laurel's cold hand in his. He stood up, still holding her hand.

'And I would like to make a toast to my beautiful bride-to-be, and to invite all of you to the wedding on Tuesday next, at the church in Sitka,' he said, still smiling and glancing around at them all. His free hand held the glass high. 'To my Laurel!' he said in ringing tones, and drank the champagne right down.

Chapter 18

During the few confused days before the wedding, Laurel kept thinking of Jade's poignant words. 'Garth married me because he felt sorry for me. He does not love me.'

Laurel felt that Thor was doing the same thing. But she could not seem to stop him. She tried to protest; she even went to Olaf, to plead for a time to let them think it over.

Thor was furious with her. Olaf beamed at her and said, 'You just have wedding nerves, dear girl. I'm sure you will both be very happy. You are well suited to each other. You will allow me to give you away, won't you?'

She had to give in. Sidonie was furious, but kept her mouth clamped shut, Laurel was amazed to find. Thor rushed her through everything, the rehearsal, the fitting of her clothes, the plans for the church ceremony. He had arranged a reception and luncheon at the restaurant she liked, with the red plush fittings.

Laurel just had not time to make Thor stop and think. She felt it was wrong, but Thor would not listen. She scarcely had time to go for walks with Czar. The rest of the time she was packing her clothes, her paintings, supervising their removal to Thor's house, getting her easel set up in the beautiful room with the north light.

There was no need for wedding invitations. The minister invited everybody at church that Sunday, and everyone was welcome to come. Word went out through the community, and the Tlingit Indians heard about it as soon as everyone else.

On Tuesday morning Laurel wakened after a disturbed night, to find that the fatal morning had indeed arrived – and she was not ready at all. Patsy Dugan came early to help her. Patsy put up Laurel's hair in a soft bouffant style that did make her look older.

After a breakfast that Laurel scarcely tasted, Patsy helped her dress in the full white petticoats, the corselet, and the white, watered-silk brocade wedding dress that fell softly from her tight waist to her heels.

Then Patsy fastened the broad collar of pearls that Thor had given Laurel last night. They had been his mother's, he said. It fit her slender neck, and gave her dignity. On went the little pearl earrings, her ring of sapphire and diamonds. Then the veil, of lace and seed pearls. Patsy sighed in rapture.

'You look like royalty, miss!' she said. 'Just like a princess!'

Me? Laurel stared at herself in the full-length mirror, and did not know herself. Her insignificant five feet three looked taller, somehow, and her face solemn behind the lace veil. But where was the girl Laurel, who had run free in the meadow grasses, and waded in streams, and fished with her bare hands, laughing?

She put on the little half gloves that left her fingers free. Those hands that had cleaned fish, and skinned rabbits and deer, that had cooked over an open fire, washed dishes in cold rain. All hidden now in white silk.

Olaf Koenig was waiting for her at the foot of the stairs as Laurel came slowly from her room. He gazed up at her, and his face became solemn and moved. His green eyes misted, his big Scandinavian frame stood erect and proud.

'My dear,' he said as he reached up a hand to help her down the last steps. 'You are radiantly beautiful. Your father and mother would be so proud of you! I only wish they could be here today to see you.'

'But they are here, sir!' snapped Patsy Dugan, her Irish blue eyes frankly streaming. 'In spirit they're here, both of them, God love her!'

Olaf nodded, and then put into Laurel's arms the wedding bouquet he had been holding. 'From Thor, with his love,' he said. The bouquet was of white roses and blue forget-me-nots, tied with a broad white satin ribbon. The roses were in the center, surrounded by the blue small flowers of Alaska. She held them to her, and put her lips to the little blue flowers.

Mike Dugan had driven the carriage around to the front door. Patsy, splendid in her best blue silk dress, sat beside Laurel. Her husband was at his finest too, with the reins of the two black stallions in his hands; he was dressed in his finest gray silk suit, with a gray top hat.

Olaf Koenig was in a dark blue that set off his fine blond good looks. Laurel kept thinking of other matters. Czar and Thor's other dogs had been transferred to their new kennels at his house. The horses and carriages that were his had been moved. Patsy told her the master bedroom was ready, her study next to it, with her easel and paintings and study table and chair, all there waiting for her.

Their wedding supper would be in Thor's new house. And then . . . And then – Her mind sheered away in fright before the night that would come. Miriam had told her things when she was twelve, and that was all. Oh, dear, what was she going to do? She was so ignorant. Delia had whispered a few things, and Hazel had guessed. But what really happened?

She must not think about that, or she would faint. She felt dizzy already. She felt as though she were outside her body, floating above herself and looking down in pity and wonder. She felt two persons, one in a white-clad body, waving at the people and smiling. The other was detached, aloof.

'Look at all the folks turned out!' gloated Patsy Dugan, frankly enjoying herself. 'Guess everybody in Sitka and miles about must have come for your wedding!'

Laurel woke up sharply, and realized people were lining the plank sidewalks of Sitka, waving and smiling at her! She recognized some red-checked-shirted prospectors; and the waitresses at the coffee shop, clad in blue dresses and white aprons. The clerks at the hotel. The proprietor of the dry goods store across from Thor's store. Men came out of the saloon and waved their bottles.

And at the church a small crowd had gathered in the yard. She saw Tlingit Indians, and others she thought she knew. She waved at them, smiling, and they waved back, dark faces lighting up in beaming grins. They called to her, in English and in Tlingit, 'Good wishes, Miss Laurel! Good wishes, good life, happiness! A long married life, many fat children!'

She blushed and laughed, and waved again. Olaf Koenig helped her down, a broad grin on his face for he knew what they had said. Somehow it helped her bear up as she went slowly through the crowd. She greeted the ones she knew by name. 'How are you, Bennie? Good morning, Minnie. It is so good of you to come, and here is little Jimmie and Sue. Hello, Fred . . . thank you for coming . . . Amos and Job, hello, Joe, hello, Billie –'

They showered good wishes on her head, blessings in English and Tlingit. Other townspeople were there too, and they crowded after her into the church in friendly fashion, settling themselves in the pews, satisfied they had welcomed her heartily.

Laurel waited in the small vestibule as the pianist began the wedding march. Now there were butterflies in her stomach. The music, like Delia's wedding, in the solemn Boston church with the organ . . . And here was her church, lovely in Sitka spruce and pine and hemlock, with the plain windows letting in the sunlight.

Tuesday, August 29, 1905, she thought. She must put it in her family Bible. It would go after the entries about her father and mother's wedding, her birth, their deaths. Were they present, as Patsy Dugan said? Did they look down on their daughter today, proud of her, hopeful for her, blessing her?

Tears stung her eyes, and her hand shook as she put it on Olaf Koenig's dark blue arm. He put his other hand over hers, then, and led her solemnly down the aisle toward Thor.

There was a low murmur in the church as she walked past. Murmurs of love, of approval, of awe as they saw the girl in the white brocade gown and white lace veil, with the flowers of blue and white on her arm.

She saw Thor before her, turning to look at her. He looked so solemn. Did he regret it? Oh God, what if he regretted it?

Is it too late to stop it, she thought, and her mind seemed fuzzy and unsure.

His green eyes, warm today and kind. He was kind to her. He's only sorry for me, she thought in a panic. Oh, she could not go through with this!

He was so tall and strong. Strong, she could cling to him. He was strong inside and out, a man to lean on. A man to depend on, to trust. She trusted him, she respected him, she loved him. Was that enough for him? Did he need to love her? He had never said he loved her. No, he was sorry for –

The minister had begun the words. She listened, raptly. She

must listen.' 'Love and honor and obey . . .' Yes, she could do all that. 'Cleave only to him . . .' Oh, yes, yes. Always.

'Until death do you part.' May it be a long, long time away.

Laurel put the ring on Thor's finger, he put the ring on hers, and then he leaned to her. He put back the veil, and bent to kiss her lips. She felt his strong hands on her shoulders; they felt so slim and breakable in his hands. He put his lips on hers, gently, reverently. Not like the night in the cabin, when his lips had been hot, passionate. Today they were cool, gentle.

It was done, and she had not cried out in panic. It was done, and they were married. She turned, dazed, and felt Olaf Koenig put his arms about her and kiss her forehead. 'My dear girl,' he murmured, 'you are my daughter now.'

They signed the registry book, and walked out of church together, man and wife, Laurel and Thor, Mr. and Mrs. Thor Koenig. She saw people smiling, waving; some threw rice, and some threw confetti. She saw Madame Bonheur beaming and throwing rice at her. Then Thor picked her up and put her in the carriage, bouquet and all.

'Oh . . . my flowers!'

'Keep them,' he ordered bruskly. 'You should have them, they are you and your love for Alaska, white roses for the snows, blue forget-me-nots because you never forgot to come back.'

And he leaned and kissed her before them all, there in the carriage, and his mouth was warm now.

He did understand her, he did understand her! Her frozen heart melted, and she held his hand as Mike Dugan drove them to the restaurant for the reception. His big strong hand, folding around hers, so warm and strong, so strong, strong . . . She smiled more freely now, and waved and laughed at the people lining the street. The veil was flung back; they could see her face now, her smile.

'God bless you!' cried one woman. 'God bless your bonny face!'

She smiled and smiled, and laughed with Thor, and held his hand, and she was so happy.

The wedding reception was beautiful. She stood near the table of the huge wedding cake, and shook hands and accepted warm kisses and best wishes. Everybody is here, she thought, everybody but the

Nolans. All her friends in Sitka were there, beaming and leaving wedding presents, which piled up and piled up, spilling over tables and chairs onto the floor.

Even Sidonie was smiling, widely, as though this was her own idea. Laurel thought maybe she was reconciled to this, now it was done. She hoped so. Anyway, Sidonie liked being in the center of Sitka's biggest wedding of the year.

Laurel cut the cake with Thor's help. It was a huge seven-tiered cake, and she could scarcely reach the top. Thor lifted her up, his hands on her slim waist, and held her until she could cut the top layer and carefully remove one piece. She set it finally on the plate, and everyone applauded. Then Thor put her down, and turned over the knife to the beaming chef. He cut the rest, and put slices on plates and into boxes, for girls to put under their pillows.

She ate a piece of cake, and it tasted of almonds, delicious. She faintly remembered later, drinking some champagne and eating some finger foods. She remembered snapshots, Thor looking like a Viking prince, his blond hair ruffled, laughing as he drank down a glass of champagne. Madame Bonheur in unaccustomed pink ruffles, instead of her dressmaker black, telling about French customs.

She remembered Olaf Koenig booming, in his big voice, his toast to her and his son. He clapped his son on his shoulder, and almost knocked Thor down. The minister's wife kissed her cheek, and murmured a tender blessing, and Laurel remembered how kind the woman had been to her when she first came to Sitka, a frightened girl of fifteen.

All the kind, kind people. Patsy and Mike Dugan, watching over her for anything she might want. The clerks in Thor's store, with a gift of white silk printed with forget-me-nots. Several women telling her they were going to piece a quilt for her, and what patterns would she like? She told them, 'Anything about Alaska!' and they beamed, and nodded.

Finally it was late afternoon, and Thor was impatient to get her away. He rushed her out, and lifted her into the waiting carriage. People cheered and flung more rice and confetti, and good wishes, as they drove away and up the hills of Sitka to Thor's new house, her new home.

She said, seriously, 'I wish some of the Indians could have come to the reception, Thor.'

He grinned down at her, understandingly. 'They're having a party of their own on the beach. Salmon and plenty of drinks. It is all arranged!'

'Oh, Thor!' She slipped her hand into his arm. 'You are so kind! Thank you!'

'I wanted to do it. They're my friends, too. I wish they could have come to the reception, but the Indian wars are too fresh in people's memories,' he added quietly. 'Someday, we can all be friends.'

'I hope so,' she said.

At Thor's huge house, she looked from the carriage to the brightly lighted windows. It was to be her home! This lovely place she had helped design and furnish. If she had only known then . . . but it was a lovely surprise for her, that she would be mistress here.

Thor lifted her down, and Mike Dugan drove the carriage around to the back to put it away. She walked up the steps to the veranda with Thor, then turned to look out over the sea.

'How lovely it is here,' she murmured. 'You can see the ocean, and the mountains with snow on them, and the green islands with the spruce . . .'

'Umm, and smell the spruce and hemlock, the bushes and flowers. And in the winter, this will be snug, while the rains and snows come down.' He hugged her. 'May you be very happy, Mrs. Koenig,' he said, kissing her cheek.

'And may you be happy, Thor,' she whispered. She felt rather awed with her new responsibility, to be mistress of his house, to greet his guests, and to keep everything beautiful for him and make him happy. Was it too much to expect of her? She would try very hard, she vowed.

They moved to the door, Patsy held it wide for them, her grin beamingly happy. 'Welcome home!' she cried, and gave a flourish as Thor picked up Laurel in his arms and carried her into the hallway.

He let her down, and she blushed at his look. She smoothed her skirts with one hand, the bouquet in her other one. Patsy reached for the bouquet. 'I'll put the flowers in water, Mrs. Koenig,' she said.

'Oh, you must call me Laurel,' she protested warmly. She moved into the drawing room. 'Everything is here!' she cried.

The sofas were in place, the chairs with their blue-and-green-and-white slipcovers. The precious carpets and rugs were in place, giving a warm glow to the room. And in the dining room, the tables and chairs were all set . . . and two places for dinner, with shining tablecloth, silver, and glass.

'Everything possible,' said Thor. 'There are still several rooms left to finish, but no hurry. You must choose what you wish,' he said, his wide arms gesturing all around. 'Why don't you change and be comfortable? Patsy will probably have dinner ready soon.'

'I'm not sure I could eat another thing,' Laurel confessed.

Patsy pretended to look crushed. 'Sure, and I have a foine meal for ye,' she exaggerated her accent, and they all laughed.

Laurel excused herself, and went upstairs shyly to the master bedroom. There she found Natasha, the Indian girl who had left Sidonie Koenig to come to Thor's house. The girl had a dress laid out, a simple blue dress of linen, and Laurel changed quickly, removing the white brocade dress, the veils and pearls, the thick petticoats and corselet. She felt much better without all the finery. A photographer had come to the wedding and taken her and Thor's pictures. She hoped they would turn out well.

Laurel went downstairs then, to find Thor stretched out comfortably in one of the big chairs. 'Say, these are very comfortable, Laurel!' he said.

'I'm glad.'

He looked so handsome, with his devilish green eyes gazing up at her – and the thought of the night to come before her. She was glad when Patsy called them to come to dinner.

Laurel did not taste much of the venison steaks, the rice and shrimp mixture, salad, fresh blueberries, and wedding cake. She drank some champagne, but it made her dizzy, so she refused a second glass. She had had more champagne this week than in all her life before.

After dinner Patsy served their coffee in the drawing room. Laurel could not think of anything to say. Thor said small things like work going at the office, the weather, winter to come, Czar settling down in the kennels with his favorite kennel mates.

Finally all too soon it was ten o'clock. Thor let her go upstairs by herself. Natasha was there, and she had laid out a new nightgown of white silk and lace, and a negligee to match. Laurel had a sudden absurd recollection of going to bed in the cabin she had shared with her father. The huge cotton nightdress that had been her mother's, long socks on her feet to keep her legs warm, snuggling down into the bunk with blankets and quilts piled over her.

Could this be the same Alaska?

Soberly she changed into the nightdress, used the huge white shining bathroom, and padded back to the bedroom in the white silk bedroom slippers with the white pompons on the toes. She slipped off the negligee, and slid into the huge bed. Then she did not know which side to sleep on, the left or the right. Did Thor want the side near the window, or didn't he care?

She propped herself on her elbow to gaze out the wide windows to the sea below and beyond. How beautiful it was at night, with the white foam moving to shore and melting on the sands. Out to sea would be the giant whales and the seals, and the sea gulls with white on their wings. She started when Thor came into the room.

'Do you like it here, Laurel?' he asked in matter-of-fact tone.

'Oh, it is lovely, Thor. I know I am going to enjoy the view from this window,' she said nervously. 'Can you see whales from here?'

'I don't know. This is my first night here too,' he said. 'It will be fun to wake up to that view, won't it?'

'Yes.' Shyly she slid down into the bed and put her head on the pillow. Primly she asked, 'Do you want this side or the other?'

'You have first choice,' he offered solemnly, a twinkle in his green eyes. Then he blew out the lamp, and a soft blue dimness filled the room.

As he undressed, she could hear him moving about, taking off his pants and shirt, his shoes and socks. She did not hear the rustle of a nightshirt, but she kept her eyes firmly closed. He went to the bathroom, returned, and slid into bed.

She drew a deep ragged breath. Now the pain, the fear. Thor put his arms about her and drew her close. And he was not wearing anything at all.

He was slow and calm. She was grateful for that. He bent over her and kissed her cheek, then her mouth. She tried to respond, but nerves kept her tense. 'Remember the cabin?' he whispered. 'Don't you wish we were there, with only the scrabbling mice for company?'

She giggled, and relaxed a little. He drew her against his long warm body, and she felt the hardness of his muscles. How tough he was, how strong. She felt very weak and silky next to his hard flesh. He put her head on his shoulder, and gently brushed out her long dark curls on his arm. He buried his fingers in her thick hair, and caressed it with his lips.

'You smell good,' he murmured. 'Lavender?'

She wanted to say he smelled good too, of fresh soap and his own masculine smell. He smelled of spruce and pine, and all outdoors, and maleness. She rubbed her cheek timidly against his chest.

He lifted her head, and their lips met, slowly, long. He kissed her softly at first, then more and more deeply, until the long kiss made her breathless. She broke away, and dug her head into his chest to get her breath again.

She felt his fingers in her hair, caressing her. Then he put her down on the pillow and bent over her again. He put his mouth on hers again, in a long kiss, and while he kissed her, he moved his hands over her body, slowly, from her shoulders to her breasts. He fondled her breasts, and she remembered how he had done that the night in the cabin, when she had become so hot and flustered. She shifted under his hands, yet they followed her body relentlessly, and held her still while he bent his big head and kissed her breasts. He held the little points on her breasts in his lips, each in turn, until they were hard and aching.

Then his mouth moved lower as his hands moved lower on her She felt his lips kissing her waist, and then her thighs as he moved down in the bed. She wriggled as he lifted the nightdress and took it off her completely, then flung it to the foot of the bed. She gasped as she felt her nakedness under his body, as he moved over her.

He was hard and hot now, and passion filled him. His moves were harder, more reckless. He kissed her more passionately, and she felt afraid as he went on and on. He lay between her slim legs, holding them apart. She was getting soft and warm, and wet and feeling strange – so strangely hot and funny.

Then he pressed to her, and she was abruptly terrified. He was so very big. And he was doing something to her . . . she knew what is was, but it was odd, and frightening. She cried out, 'Thor, please . . . don't. Thor –'

'Let me, darling . . . for just a minute –' he said breathlessly, his voice deep and dark and low. 'Laurel, darling . . . just a . . . minute . . . now . . .' And he shoved hard, and she cried out with the sudden pain. Tears rolled down her cheeks. He didn't seem to notice as he shoved in and out, wildly, as though he had to have this, had to do it. Something drove him furiously, and he drove at her so, she could not move. She must lie still, while he filled her with his bigness.

His body jerked hard as he held her, and it filled her so she could not move. She was sure he would kill her, rip her in two . . . Then he was drawing out, and she could breathe again.

Oh God, was she alive?

He lay limply on her, his weight heavy. Then he shifted off with a big sigh, and lay beside her, his arm across her.

She was breathing hard, so was he. She could not move. She hurt, and yet was at peace; it was over. She felt someone new and different; she was a woman now. Not the girl Laurel any longer. She was someone new, though she was not sure who she was.

His arm lay across her, and his breath became even once more.

'Darling Laurel, I hurt you,' he said, his voice low in her ear. 'I'm sorry, my love. It had to be, but I'm sorry.' There was such remorse in his tone.

He must not feel sorry about loving me, she thought. He can do whatever he likes with me . . . I love him. She put her hands on his thick hair, and moved her hands on him softly.

'It's all right, Thor . . . it's all right . . .'

'Darling . . . love,' he murmured sleepily, and his lips touched her cheek. She held her hands on his head, and moved her fingers through his hair, and caressed his strong thick neck. He went to sleep against her.

She lay awake a little longer, then slept against him, the sound of the sea in her ears. There was the low, sighing, sloughing of the waves, again and again . . . it was so peaceful.

She wakened in the night, slid out of bed softly, and padded to the bathroom. She lit the lamp, and gasped to see herself; there was

226

dried blood on her thighs. She washed quickly in the warm water from the tap. What luxury, like in the other Koenig house, to have water from a tap. How had Thor endured the primitive life of the cabin where she and her father lived, and Jade's cabin? But he was used to the wilderness, as she was.

She returned quietly to the bedroom, found her nightdress, and slipped it on again. When she got into bed again, Thor's arm reached out and came around her in his sleep. She smiled. It was strange, but she thought she could get used to this. It was sweet to wake up next to his hard body and feel his flesh next to hers, his warmth warming hers.

Laurel slept again, to waken when the dawn came. She opened her eyes and saw the ocean spread out before her. She watched the waves for a while, then far out to sea, she saw a sudden huge form rise out of the waves. Her eyes widened, and she stiffened as the whale rose up, splashed down. A huge blast of water rose up where it had been as it blew again.

'Wow, did you see that, Laurel?' Thor's low voice murmured against her head.

'Oh yes, wasn't it marvelous?'

They watched in silence then, as though words would spoil it. Another whale, a smaller one, blew and came up rising like some unearthly creature from the sea.

Finally the show was over, and the whales moved on, lazily. She sighed. 'Do you ever see seals?'

'I think not here. We'll go round to Seal Point sometime.' He nuzzled his nose against the back of her neck, brushing aside her thick hair.

He turned her around, and their eyes looked at each other as though they had not truly seen each other before. She gazed into his green eyes, so deep and fathomless, so like the Viking he was. He reached out his finger and gently traced her nose, her cheeks, her lips, her soft round chin.

'Sorry that I hurt you, Laurel,' he said quietly.

'It's all right, Thor. I expected it.' She blushed, then looked away.

'It'll be better next time. I'll give you time to heal first.'

His frank speech both embarrassed and relieved her. She nodded, flushed. He yawned, stretched. 'Come on, let's get up. I'm hungry! Let's take Czar and Jamie out today.'

'Jamie?'

'A new pup, good one. He'll make a good dog someday. Czar can teach him manners.'

He kissed her nose, then left the bed. She heard him humming in the bathroom as he showered; then he returned to dress. He grinned at her primness as she put on the negligee to go to the bathroom.

He had gone downstairs when she returned to the room. She chose a pink-checked dress to wear, and got out a jacket and a pink hat to match. Then she went downstairs, her first day as a wife, to have breakfast with him. Her husband.

And then she realized, and paused on the stairway, smiling all to herself. She was no longer the girl Laurel, alone and rather frightened about her future, but determined to make a go of it alone.

She was Laurel Koenig, Thor's wife. And that was who she was now.

Chapter 19

Jade anxiously smoothed down the skirt of her new bright green cotton dress with the white collar. It was her very prettiest dress, and she had just finished making it from a length of material Garth had given her.

Would he like it? Would he even notice it? She did not know. There were such long silences between them. He was so quiet, so aloof. They had been married more than a year, but he had never made love to her. Didn't he like her? Didn't he want her?

She had almost forgotten Ewan, even though she felt an odd yearning for him now and then. He had been so sweet and loving that summer. She could close her eyes and remember how he felt against her, his long length naked against hers in the tall summer grass.

Then she could remember the bitterness, how he had flung her away from him, cursed her, his face sour against her. He had rejected her and the baby they had made together. Poor, poor little baby, all waxen pale and quiet, to live only a few days. It had been so little, so tiny in her arms, too weak to live. Would she ever have another little one, one that would grow and laugh and be strong?

Would Garth ever know her? He was so strong and kind, and he gave her everything she could want, materially. Once when she had timidly said she would like some books to read, he had had a trapper bring some from Wrangell for her, for a surprise. Now they both read evenings, when the silences got too long.

What else? She surveyed the table, with its white cloth, the tin plates, the mugs. Yes, flowers. She would put flowers in the pottery vase her mother had brought for her. It was of red clay and baked, and her mother had made signs on it, the raven and the eagle, and some other signs of their clan. It was a lovely big vase, and Garth liked it too.

She went outside then, leaving the cabin door open. She had seen a patch of flowers near the trees, some September flowers, the showy orange-yellow monkey flower with its bright blooms, the tall spikes of the glorious blue swamp gentian, and a few deep pink swamp laurel. There, that would fill the vase with color.

Her hands full of the long-stemmed flowers, she moved back to the cabin. The first men had come from the forest, Garth would come soon. Her steps were eager, her face flushed with anticipation, and she stepped into the cabin carelessly.

A man stood inside, grinning at her. She started violently, stiffening, staring. 'God, oh God,' she whispered. He had scared her close to fainting. No man dared step inside their cabin without invitation. Garth was respected and feared.

Only one man would have the crass gall to do that. And he stood there – Ewan Koenig.

After the first shock she moved past him and set the flowers down on the table beside the dry sink.

He moved to face her. 'Hello, Jade. You look mighty pretty today!'

She drew a deep shaking breath. 'Hello, Ewan. Now get out of this cabin. I'm married, you know.'

She lifted her head bravely and faced him. He is handsome as ever, she thought, fighting down a touch of longing. Blond, his hair ruffled and long on his neck. Blue-gray eyes smiling, his broad mouth smiling. Handsome, too handsome, in the dark blue-checked shirt and blue pants that fit his form snugly.

She had to force herself to remember how he had rejected her and turned her away. But she kept thinking of him pressed against her.

'I just heard about that, Jade,' he drawled. 'You don't think it will make any difference between us, do you? I had you first, and I'll have you again!'

She caught her breath at his brazenness. Anger stiffened her spine. 'You have your gall!' she snapped. 'I'm married, I tell you! My man is twice what you are!' And she thought so, too. Garth was twice as big, twice as fine, twice as good.

His eyes narrowed and his cheeks flushed with temper. His

mouth took on the sulky look of a mistreated child. Chilled, she stared at him. Had he always been so . . . so like a boy? Garth was so grave, so mature, she had forgotten what Ewan was like. She had remembered the good feelings, the embraces. She had forgotten how he always had to have his own way and sulked when things went against him.

She felt years older now.

'That why you don't have his child?' sneered Ewan. 'We made a baby fast, you and I!'

'You killed him,' Jade accused swiftly. She had never said the words, even to herself, but she said them now. 'You killed the baby pushing me into that icy water. I never was right after then, until long after the baby came. He didn't have a chance!'

Ewan went pale. He stiffened, stared at her. 'The baby . . . died? He was a boy . . . he died?'

Jade nodded. 'Just a little waxen baby boy,' she said sadly. 'Never had a chance. I wonder that you dare to come around me, Ewan Koenig!'

He frowned. 'Thought you would welcome me,' he said deliberately. 'We had something going that summer. Have you forgotten all about that, the way we kissed, the way we were together?' He laughed when she flushed hotly and shook her head with the long braid swinging.

He stepped toward her, and she backed away warily, realizing her mistake as she backed away from the door. She should have run screaming, not stayed in there with him.

She watched him. The kitchen knife was too far from her hand. He backed her into a corner of the cabin, and suddenly jumped forward at her and caught her in his arms. She fought and kicked, but he pressed his kisses on her, his mouth biting at hers fiercely.

He laughed as she fought him. 'Come on, Jade honey. You were willing once,' he mocked her. 'Come on, give us another kiss!'

He pressed his body against hers deftly, so she felt his masculine hardness against her thighs. She was held in the corner so she could scarcely fight, and his arms held her so tight she could not lift her fists to hit him. Her foot kicked out at him, but she was wearing moccasins, and the soft leather did not hurt.

He kissed her again, his mouth pressed tight on hers, his face scratching her soft cheeks as he rubbed roughly against her face.

'What the hell –' said a voice, deep and masculine.

Ewan let her go, slowly, and turned to face Garth Fleming towering in the doorway. Jade almost fainted at the look on Garth's face, shocked, accusing, his brown eyes so dark.

Ewan stepped away from Jade. His hand went to the belt he wore, and she saw with a jolt that he carried a Colt revolver. Oh God, and Garth was unarmed except for his hunting knife.

'I'm Ewan Koenig,' Ewan said, sounding as though he were saying he is a god, Jade thought with contempt. 'I'm renewing acquaintance with my girl, Jade.'

'You damn . . . damn –' sputtered Jade, furiously. 'He come in here, Garth. He was here when I –'

Garth waved his arm, briefly, not looking at her. His attention was on Ewan. He stepped inside the cabin, leaving the door open. The men faced each other.

Jade shut up and pushed herself back into the corner, out of the way. Her hands pressed so flat against the walls of the cabin, she felt the sharp bark of the logs.

She knew, she knew. Ewan had come deliberately when he knew Garth would be coming home. He had seen the lumbermen returning home. He knew damn well Garth would come in and see them kissing. Knew how it would look. He had done this to her, to Jade, to make her husband hate her.

Jade felt sick to her stomach at his treachery. It was as bad as Ewan's turning against her when he saw she had his baby in her stomach. It was just as bad, his malice and treachery, coming here to make trouble between her and her husband.

Why had he done such a thing to her? He had said he loved her that summer. This was not love, this was hate.

'She is my girl,' Ewan said deliberately, watching Garth, a big grin on his face. 'I had her first, and I'll have her again! I put my mark on her,' he said.

Garth did not smile, he did not frown. He just stared at Ewan, waiting for something. Ewan eyed him, like a boy challenging another boy. But Garth is not a boy, thought Jade; he is a man.

'I'll have her again,' repeated Ewan, his hand near his revolver. 'I don't know why you married Jade. She can go to any man. But she still belongs to me, because I had her first. She is an Indian, and she goes to any man who beats her! But she belongs to me, and I'll claim her any time I want!'

He was goading Garth into fighting him, Jade knew it. Oh God, don't let Garth get hurt, she prayed frantically. Please God, keep Garth safe. He is so good; he is my man.

Turning her head slowly she looked about for a weapon, any weapon. Garth said at last, quietly, 'Jade, stay out of this. Stay there.'

He was her man, she would show him so. 'Yes, Garth,' she said in a low voice. And she stayed still there in the corner.

Ewan's smile went away; he looked sullen and furious now, his face red under the tan. 'She's my girl, and I'm claiming her again!', he said to Garth, watching him alertly.

'No, she is my wife, she is my woman,' Garth said softly. 'You betrayed her. You hurt her. Jade is a good fine woman, too good for the likes of you.'

Jade savored his words, even though she knew Garth said that to take Ewan off guard.

'I'll take her away with me, anytime I like!' boasted Ewan, and his hand went to his gun.

Garth moved like a panther, like one of those great lynx cats, thought Jade afterwards. He struck Ewan in the head, and that handsome blond head snapped back. Ewan was still trying to pull the gun.

Garth struck him again. Blood began streaming from Ewan's nose. It distracted him. His hand went to his nose. Garth pulled the gun from the holster. Jade's hand went to her mouth, but Garth tossed the revolver away into the corner, where it slid under the stove.

Then Garth worked on Ewan. He knocked him down, pulled him up again with one fist closed on the blue-checked shirt. He knocked him down again, methodically. He hit him in the face, in the chest, in the eye, and Ewan could hardly fight back. He was whimpering, trying to hit, blindly, blood flowing down his face from his nose, his eye rapidly closing. He was no match for the big lumberjack.

Then Garth picked him up by the seat of his pants and literally threw him out of the door of the cabin. Ewan landed with a thud about ten feet outside the cabin. Garth followed him out. Jade dared to move to the door to watch, fascinated.

Several men had gathered at a respectful distance from the cabin, the sounds of the fight having drawn them. They watched, open-mouthed, quiet, as Garth stood over Ewan and spoke to him.

'You will get away from this place tomorrow morning,' said Garth, dispassionately. 'I wouldn't send a sick dog out on the Stikine at night. But you will go at first dawn. And you will stay away from my wife!'

Ewan struggled to his elbow, his hand at his face, panting for breath. 'But she is . . . no good . . . no good . . .' he panted. 'I'll have her . . . again, by God! I'll have that bitch –'

Garth kicked Ewan in the side to shut him up. Jade winced at the blow, involuntarily. 'And you will keep your filthy tongue off my *wife.*'

Garth stood back, his arms folded. His hands were bloody, Jade saw, but he kept his dignity. Ewan scrambled to his feet and backed off, fuming, humiliated, frantic with rage. 'I'll have her! I'll have her!' he howled.

'Goddamn,' muttered one man in disgust. The other men were not looking at Jade, she realized. They were staring at Ewan. He had broken the law of the wilderness; he had shown great disrespect to a woman, another man's lawful wife.

And she realized, Garth had given her respect. No matter what had happened in her past, Garth had given her respect, the position of his wife. And they respected that and despised Ewan for what he had tried to do to her.

Jade had shown no favors to any man but her husband. She had kept herself to herself, she had kept his cabin clean, she had prepared his food well, and she had tried to be his wife honorably.

Her heart swelled in her, for what Garth had done for her. And she now hated and utterly despised the man who had once had her love and adoration. She watched in silence as Ewan stumbled away. He went near his boat, sat down, and tried to wash the blood from his face. No man went near him to help him.

One man came up to Garth, the lumber boss. He said in a low tone, 'I'll have him guarded, sent on his way in the morning, Fleming.'

'Thanks,' said Garth, and turned and stalked back into his cabin. Jade stood aside to let him enter, then followed, and he shut the door after them.

Garth stood there, his arms hanging at his sides, and looked at her. His brown eyes were angry with her.

'Why did you let him in?' he asked in a level tone.

Jade started. 'I did not!' she exclaimed, horrified. 'I went out to get flowers – ' She indicated the flowers wilting near the dry sink. '– and when I returned, he was inside the cabin!'

'You invited him to come.'

'No!'

'Why did he come?'

'He – I don't know,' she said miserably. He seemed to think it was all her fault. She drooped like the flowers.

'He is a child,' Garth said finally, wearily. 'He takes the toys of others and breaks them. You are too good for him, Jade. Stay away from him.'

'I will stay away, Garth. I don't want him. I –' How could she convince him that she did not love Ewan? How could she say 'I love you' to Garth, when he did not invite the words?

'I'll wash up,' he said, and went out. His hands were bloody, one fist of Ewan had hit his dark face, and a bruise showed now.

Jade poured some hot water in the basin, and put that and a fresh towel on the bench outside the door. She returned to the cabin. The flowers reproached her. She picked up the top ones, and mechanically put them into the pottery vase.

The orange-yellow and then the blue ones, and the pink swamp laurel – she arranged them carefully, and the flowers began to revive and lift up their heads as their stems drank in the water. She set the large vase on the table, to the side where it would not come between her and Garth. She wanted nothing else between her and Garth, nothing more to separate them. Too much stood between them already.

He returned, wiping his face with the towel. He set the towel on the sink, then sat down at the table. She placed the hot platter of roast venison beside him, for him to carve, and served the baked potatoes and steamed corn.

They sat together, and ate in silence. Finally he spoke, and she was so glad she could have smiled at him.

'Winter will come soon. We'll go down to Wrangell and clean up the cabin there. Reckon your folks will come in for a time before the snows?'

'Yes, I think so. Mother wishes for a visit. We will can blueberries and cranberries together.'

'I have some hides to finish tanning. And your father will have some, probably.'

'Yes, he goes hunting with several men this summer.'

'I've been thinking, Jade,' he said.

'Yes, Garth?' She almost held her breath, waiting for the slow deliberate words.

'I've got some money saved. We could buy a piece of timberland and work on that ourselves. I could hire some men to work it with me, pay them wages. We could build up a business, send lumber to Wrangell and Sitka.'

He paused and looked at her. She listened, wide-eyed. He would be a businessman! How wonderful! It's what he always wanted, she thought.

'Or . . . I thought we could go to Sitka. Buy a house. I could get a job there, working lumber in the mill. You could be near your friends . . . people. Women. What do you want, Jade?'

She studied his face, shocked. He was asking her, his woman, what she wanted? He had a seeking look on his face, a troubled look.

She shook her head. 'How can I say? It is what you wish, Garth. You are the man.'

'I want to know what you want,' he said stubbornly.

She thought about it. It would be nice to live in Sitka, have a nice house, be near to Laurel and her man. But Garth – she could not see him working in a mill, not when he could work in the forests as he liked to do.

And besides, she was an Indian. She would not be accepted by Sitka society, probably. And she also felt more free and easy in the wilderness; it was her life, and she enjoyed it.

'I want what you want, Garth. And we both like the Stikine River, and the forests, and the outdoors. You would not like working in a mill, and keeping to the hours, and doing that work, I believe.'

'I would do whatever makes you happy, Jade,' he said, so quietly she had to strain to hear what he said. 'This is a hard life for a woman.'

She smiled then, and shook her head with decision. 'No, it is not hard, it is easy. My mother works hard, tanning the skins, living in the snows sometimes. I have an easy life, she tells me, and it is true. You are very good to me, Garth . . . very generous and kind.'

'No gratitude, Jade!' he said, suddenly harsh and frowning. 'I do not want gratitude!'

What did he want? If she knew, she would give it to him. Maybe he wanted nothing from her. She wished she had more wisdom. Maybe her mother would know and could tell her. He did not want her in bed, it seemed. He accepted the food, the clean clothes, the clean cabin, the flowers, all in silence.

Ewan was very possessive and mean. He did not want her to be happy with anybody. He had come to claim her again after discarding her. All because he had probably heard that she was married!

But Garth – Garth was a good man. He was a strong man, inside and out. She wanted to make him happy, and be happy with him. Was it too much to ask?

At least Jade could help him in his work life. She knew what he liked; he liked timber and everything about it. Cutting down the big trees in a neat and clean fashion, not ruining the land and trees around them. Replanting the small trees. Clearing space for the young sprouts to grow. Leaving the land as beautiful as when he had found it.

'I would be proud,' she began slowly, 'if you buy land and clear it, that you would be a lumberman, a businessman. I would want to help you, and I would want to live in a house with you, and make food for you and keep all clean. I know you would succeed; you would be a good boss. And I like the smell of the lumber, the feel of the forest, the living in the wilderness by the rivers, where all is sweet smelling and the life his good.'

His face relaxed, and he leaned back in the chair. He nodded. 'You would like that, Jade?'

'Yes. And maybe sometimes we would go on visits to my friend Laurel and her friends. And we would visit my parents, and our friends in Wrangell. But always we would come back to our home in the wilderness and our work. That would be very good, I think.'

It was the longest conversation they had had for quite a time, and it seemed to clear the air.

He nodded again. 'When we go to Wrangell I will talk with the land men and see about where to buy. Or maybe when we go to Sitka, there will be a good man to discuss this with us. Maybe Mr. Koenig will buy our timber and ship it for us. He has many ships now. And it would be good to work with a man I can trust.'

Jade's face shone with pleasure. He had said 'our timber' . . . he had included her.

And she would visit Laurel, as she wished. Garth already accepted her parents without reserve, and they adored him. It could be a good life – if only Garth would someday want her as his true woman. She did not ask, wistfully, that he love her. He was a strong man, and he had given his heart once to another woman, his first wife, and had lost her. Maybe he could not love again.

But she could love him, silently, and serve him in the ways that she knew how to do. She could keep his clothes clean, the cabin clean and fragrant, herself clean and well dressed. She would cook his food well, and served him the meals he enjoyed. She would support him in all his ventures, and be loyal to him. And one day he would desire her and want to make a baby with her. She would adore his son, and he would too, she hoped.

She could look forward to that.

Jade got up, brought the hot coffee pot to the table. While Garth poured out the black coffee, she sliced the blueberry pie, and ladled a huge piece onto a plate for him.

'That looks good,' he said, and dug in with his fork.

She smiled proudly, and ate her smaller piece happily. She could do this for him. Maybe her mother could tell her of more foods to cook for him. Maybe Mrs. Simpson at the restaurant could tell her foods. When a man is well fed, he is often happy, thought Jade wisely.

She would do anything for him, however humble, however simple, however difficult. She loved him, and he was her man. And he was her protector. She felt proud that he had showed that so clearly before everybody today.

Nobody could insult Jade now.

She flinched as she thought of Ewan and his crude vulgar words about her. Garth had not allowed those words; he had said Ewan must keep his tongue off Jade. Ewan, such a boy! How could she have loved him! Such ego, such selfishness!

Garth was such a man; he was twice what Ewan was. No, more than twice – a dozen times, a hundred times.

Jade cleared the table, and Garth spread out a hand-drawn map before him.

'Jade, these are the timberlands around the Stikine,' he said, his head bent over them. 'Now, the lands I marked in slashes are the ones taken over by the timber companies.'

She bent over his shoulder to study the map keenly. 'Yes, that is the land beyond the mountains,' she said. 'The British, they claim all that.'

'Yes. But here . . . here are lands not taken. It is government land to here, but I think I might be able to claim some over here. I must ask the government agent if I may buy the land, or must rent it, or lay claim to the timber, to do some clearing. Yes, I will ask the men at the office in Wrangell when we go next month.'

Jade sat across from him while he studied the map, and her heart swelled with pride in him. He was so strong, so smart! She had a fine husband! What a lucky girl she was!

She sat with her hands folded on the table and saw the glint of her gold ring on her hand. No, not a girl, she thought. She, Jade Nolan Fleming, was a woman now. She was a wife, even though Garth had not claimed her physically. She was a woman, and she would help her man all she could. He would be proud of her one day, she vowed it.

Chapter 20

The first few days of her marriage, Laurel busied herself with getting settled in her new home, and she and Natasha finished unpacking.

Thor was so very busy! He worked at the office in town most of the day, from morning to night. He would check the stores, meet the ships that came in, straighten out scores of matters. And Laurel knew, from what Mike Dugan said, that many of the new men coming into Sitka went right to Thor Koenig to ask for help.

Prospectors, businessmen, importers, all came to Thor Koenig, many had his name from friends and associates in the United States. They would come to his office, show letters of introduction, or just say someone had said to ask Mr. Koenig. Then they would ask favors, or advice, or both.

Could Mr. Koenig help them set up a store. Could he find a man to direct them to the gold fields. Could he sell them the right supplies. Could he find a home for their families while they went off to the gold. Did he know someone in Dawson City, or Fairbanks, or the Yukon, or Nome. Could he help them, please?

And he did, patiently, over and over, he and his father also. Those two men were busy six days a week.

Thor said he would be glad when winter came, to slow the tide of new people. It was like the California Gold Rush all over again, with folks not knowing what they were doing.

He had not time to unpack his boxes and trunks. When Laurel offered to do it, he accepted gladly.

'I have no skeletons in there,' he teased her. 'You are free to look through everything.'

She laughed, and wrinkled her nose at him, feeling more free with him. She liked being able to help him, being important to him. It made her feel good, like the way she felt when he was hungry and she fixed a fine meal for him.

Mrs. Dugan did most of the cooking, but Laurel liked to keep her hand in. Often both women worked in the kitchen, and talked away all the time. It was almost as good as being with Jade, Patsy Dugan was so nice and friendly and chatty.

Laurel asked Natasha to help her unpack. She agreed happily, and came upstairs to the linen room with Laurel, where Thor had piled all his trunks and boxes. Mike came up also, to open the boxes that had been nailed shut. Some had been shut for years, it looked like, they were all so dusty, and the nails looked rusted.

Mike worked away at them, while Natasha and Laurel opened the trunks and took out his clothes. Natasha carried them to the bedroom, and hung the suits and shirts in the closet. It was a fine big closet, just the way Laurel had designed it.

It took several days to get everything out of the boxes. Thor came and looked at the stuff on Saturday afternoon, when he took a few hours off.

'My glory, I had forgotten I had all this.' He fingered some red felt banners. 'This is from college, my school banner. This is from my fraternity. What's this?'

He pawed through a pile of albums and a small box of photographs. He picked up one, gazed at it, and his face went soft and tender.

'Mother,' he said quietly. He handed the picture to Laurel. Laurel studied it; the picture was in black and white, but she could see the pale hair, the soft serene eyes, the light material of the dress. 'She was about thirty then, Laurel. I remember her that way. That was her favorite blue dress that matched her eyes.'

He picked up a small miniature, studied it, then handed that to Laurel. It was the same woman, younger, with laughter in her deep blue eyes, the hair soft blond, almost ashen. He had other pictures of her too, and of his father. They sat on the floor and looked at the pictures together.

'I wish I could paint her portrait, and your father's,' Laurel said impulsively. 'I'd like to do their portraits, in twin sizes. I wonder if I'm good enough.'

Thor's face lit up, his green eyes shone at her. 'Laurel, I wish you would! Do you have time? There would be no hurry about it. I would like immensely to have portraits of my parents to hang in the house here. Maybe in my study.'

It was something unique that she could do for him. She had been longing for some such project. She nodded. 'I would try, Thor. May I borrow these pictures?'

'Of course, all of them.' Tenderly he gathered them together and gave them to her. She studied them all again, then took them to the fine large study he had assigned to her, next to their bedroom. It had good north light, and magnificent views of the mountains, which almost kept her from her work.

She set the pictures on the table to look at later. She would study them and study them, and then figure out what to do. She longed to paint these portraits, and do a very good job of it, for Thor.

They sorted out what they could, and Thor closed the boxes loosely, to continue later. She could see he did not want to throw out things. She decided when the bookcases were made for his study and the parlor, she would sort out his things and put some in there, his schoolbooks, his photo albums and mementos of college, his souvenirs of his hunting, the ivory figures carved by Eskimo friends.

The second week of their marriage, Laurel had an unexpected caller. Patsy Dugan came to Laurel as she was sketching in the upstairs study, and practically wrung her hands.

'It's his stepmother,' she whispered, though no one else could hear her. Her blue eyes rolled upwards, expressively. 'All dressed up fit to kill, and says as how she wants to leave her card!'

Sidonie! Laurel felt revulsion for a moment, but manners forced her to go downstairs. Sidonie was still sitting in her carriage, her expression haughty.

'I merely wished to leave my card. They do not understand!' she sniffed. She glanced curiously toward the house.

'You are my first guest, Mrs. Koenig,' Laurel said, and managed a smile. She was proud of the house and longed to show it off. 'Won't you come in for a cup of tea?'

'Well –' Sidonie visibly hesitated, then nodded. Mike Dugan had come out, and he helped her down carefully. Laurel led her to the house as the coachman followed Mike out to the stables. They could have a comfortable talk there, while Mrs. Koenig visited with Mrs. Thor!

Laurel was remembering what her Aunt Gertrude had told her years ago. 'When you want to make a friend, ask her advice!'

She showed Sidonie the view from the balcony, out over the sea.

'Very lovely,' admitted Sidonie. 'Thor chose well.'

Encouraged, Laurel led her around to the other side to show her the view of the mountains. Sidonie praised it.

Then she led Sidonie into the house and showed her the drawing room, the parlor, the dining room and kitchen. By this time Sidonie had thawed.

'Very fine proportions,' she said critically. 'And you have decorated very well, Laurel, for a girl your age. Do you plan to have these colors permanently?' She indicated the drawing room where they were seated.

'No, ma'am. Next month, when it turns cooler, we will put on the other slipcovers and hang the draperies. They are warm colors, and thicker materials for the winter.'

Sidonie approved graciously. Natasha wheeled in the silver tea cart that had been one of Sidonie's gifts to her new daughter-in-law. Sidonie watched the maid in silence. Natasha was accustomed to her former employer, and watched her every mood, taking the coffee to Sidonie first, serving her napkin properly, offering her the tray of small sandwiches, and the plate of little cakes.

'I wondered if I might ask your advice,' Laurel began then, sipping at her coffee carefully and neatly.

'Advice?' Sidonie looked up quickly. 'What advice?'

'Aunt Gertrude taught me about menus, as I believe I told you,' Laurel said carefully. 'And we were taught about seating at the dining table, and in the parlor. But Thor says he may soon invite the Governor of Alaska to dine. I confess I feel a bit nervous about that.'

Sidonie's face, under the severe smart black hat with black plumes, brightened visibly. She sat even more erect, her spine not touching the back of her chair. Her black frilled skirts were precisely set about her thin legs, and not even her black-stockinged ankles showed, only the tips of her black shining boots.

'My dear Laurel, I should be happy to instruct you,' she said, and perked her head like a blackbird. Laurel was reminded of Madame

Bonheur. 'I admit, I would hate to be mortified in my son's house by anything going amiss! Now, when you send out the invitations, you must address them so . . .'

And she proceeded to go right through all the procedures, from invitations to greeting them at the door, to seating them in the parlor, to conversation.

Then they went to the dining room. Patsy Dugan came in from the kitchen curiously, as Sidonie stood behind Thor's chair, and told Laurel in detail, just where everyone should be seated. Natasha came out also, in her black dress and neat white apron, to listen and take it all in. Sidonie, aware of her alert audience, was at her best.

'The Governor will be seated at your right, Laurel. The wife of the Governor will be at Thor's right. The next most important guest, for example, the minister, will be at your left. His wife will be at Thor's left . . .'

Sidonie Valin Koenig had been thoroughly trained by her mother in every nicety of etiquette, and she showed it. She was passionately fond of company, and the proper procedure was her delight. And she could teach well; she gave examples, and she explained over and over, in interesting terms, just what must be done.

'Now, if your guests are the Governor of the State of Alaska and a United States Senator from Massachusetts, you would do this . . .' She went on and on.

Laurel absorbed it all, memorizing it as Sidonie continued.

'But this is all very much to learn,' Sidonie said with a frosty smile. 'When the occasion arises, I wish, Laurel, that you would come to me for advice.'

'I would be happy to do so,' Laurel said promptly. 'If you are sure it would not be too much trouble. I am sure you are the one person in Alaska who is thoroughly conversant in every detail of etiquette.'

It was a sincere compliment and Sidonie accepted it graciously as such.

The hour grew late, so Laurel invited her to remain for lunch. 'Thor will be home soon, and he will wish to thank you for your kindness in coming and your advice to me.'

Sidonie looked gratified, and finally agreed to remain. Thor's face was a study when he came home and found his stepmother in the drawing room. But he was always polite and at ease. He greeted her, then excused himself for a few moments. He returned from upstairs, to converse genially.

In the dining room, with Sidonie at Thor's right hand, Sidonie chatted pleasantly about events in Sitka. The town was growing rapidly.

'I am quite overwhelmed with my social duties, Thor,' she said. 'When you and your new bride are quite settled in, I will be happy for Laurel to take over some of those duties. She must entertain the Leveretts, the Prices, the new banker, Mr. Custis.'

'I was rather planning a dinner before long for Mr. Leverett,' agreed Thor, glancing at Laurel. 'What about next Saturday evening, my dear? Leverett had been hinting he would like to come and discuss politics.'

Laurel managed a smile, though she disliked Leverett. But this must be part of her duties, to entertain Thor's associates, even when she disliked them. And she must hide her dislike.

'Of course, Thor. Who else would you like to invite?'

Tactfully he turned to Sidonie. 'I would like you and Father to come, our first dinner in our new home. Are you free that evening?'

'Yes, we shall be happy to come.' She preened herself, almost unconsciously it was so natural for her. 'And I think Mr. Custis too; it will be a good introduction for him. I was planning to have a dinner for him, but this would be even better. I am sure everyone longs to see your new home, and Laurel has made it look elegant.'

Thor soon excused himself to return to the office. 'I'm so sorry, Sidonie. I would like to remain, but Father is not even taking off time for lunch.'

'I know,' she said with a grimace. 'I can scarcely get him to come home for dinner. I shall be glad when winter comes and he can let up. I don't like to see Olaf going so hard; he looks tired, I think.'

Her sharp voice was unusually concerned. Laurel and Thor exchanged speaking looks. Was Sidonie truly fond of Olaf?

'We must try together to get him to let up. I wish Ewan could be made responsible,' Thor said frowning.

'He will grow up sometime,' said Sidonie, nodding. 'He must. But he is . . . rather spoiled. I admit I helped. He can be so charming.'

'Charm chops no wood,' said Laurel, quaintly. 'My Uncle Arnold used to say that.'

Even Sidonie laughed aloud. 'Too true!' she commented.

Thor went off to work. Sidonie remained long enough to assist Laurel in drawing up a guest list for the next Saturday and helping her compose a brief note of invitation. Then she departed, smiling and waving briefly.

'Well, I never,' said Patsy Dugan.

'I was surprised too,' Laurel said reflectively. 'However, she does have a position to uphold. I guess now that I'm married to Thor, she has decided to accept me! I hope so, anyhow.'

'Yes, I reckon so,' said Patsy. 'She won't ever be sweet and kind-natured, but you won't have to watch for poison in the food!'

Natasha giggled and giggled over that one, doubling up and putting her hands on her mouth to hide her laughter, politely.

Laurel and Patsy discussed the menu for Saturday night. There would be a dozen guests, so they would open the table to its full width and put in all the boards. They would use a white lace tablecloth over white satin, and have a low epergne full of fall flowers.

Patsy would serve hot spicy shrimp as the appetizer, then a course of cold salmon with peas, followed by a roast beef platter with baked potatoes. For dessert there would be blueberry pie with ice cream, Thor's favorite.

Once that was settled, Laurel set herself to try her new painting project, the portrait of Thor's mother first. She tried several sketches before she decided on a pose from head to waist, to show the lovely long slim hands. She showed it to Thor, and he liked it very much, so she transferred it with charcoal to a canvas on her easel.

Mr. Leverett did not wait until Saturday to talk politics again with Thor. He came over on Wednesday evening, after dinner, full of enthusiasm and a big black cigar. Thor took him off to his study.

Laurel found a fan and started waving it around the drawing room to get rid of the foul cigar smell. She didn't mind pipes, they could have fragrant tobacco – but cigars! Well, she hated them.

Patsy took over, and shooed her outdoors for a time.

Laurel wandered to the veranda and leaned on the railing, contemplating the scene before her. It was past dusk, and the night-dark sky was filled with stars.

Some of the stars were reflected in the black ocean, and white waves rolled up on the shore. It was beautiful, and she was leaning there, enjoying it, when she suddenly felt uneasy. Someone was staring at her.

She looked about, feeling chills going down her spine. Was it an animal? Then she saw the dim form of a man, near Mr. Leverett's carriage, where it stood on the gravel drive. The horse was standing quietly, the coachman stood nearby, half hidden by a tall bush.

She peered at him; he was stooped and his head was shaggy. Then she realized who he was – Herman Ranke, the odd-job man of Leverett's. She shivered. She disliked the man, felt uneasy around him.

Abruptly she turned and walked inside. She felt silly, the man stood perfectly still, but she felt so odd near him. Was it the smell? He was unwashed, and had a piggy smell. But it was not just that. He stared at her from under shaggy brows, and she could not see his eyes. She felt . . . unclean.

Once inside she shut the door, and went on out to the kitchen. Patsy swung around and surveyed her.

'What's wrong?' she demanded with the familiarity of an old servant.

'That man . . . Herman Ranke. He must have driven Leverett over tonight.'

'Yes, he did. Mike despises him, horrid old man. Mean, he is,' said Patsy, vigorously scrubbing a pan. Natasha was wiping dishes for her, cleaning the shining glasses carefully with a linen towel.

'He is a strange one,' agreed Natasha. 'He comes from nowhere, he goes to nowhere. He has a hut in the woods; he does not sleep at the Leverett house. He goes off in his boat, alone. He carries a rifle and a knife, and some say he kills little animals with his hands.' She gave a shudder, shaking her shining dark head.

'I wonder why Leverett keeps him around. Mr. Leverett is so civilized, and a fastidious dresser.' Laurel frowned over her thoughts. She picked up a glass. 'I like this pattern, let's use these glasses Saturday evening, Patsy.'

'Yes, Miss Laurel. And what china do you want?'

They looked over the three lavish sets of china, one of them a gift from Thor's parents, and the other two chosen by Laurel.

'The gift ones are the most elegant,' she decided. 'Simple, but effective. Sidonie has good taste. Yes, let's use these. The white ones with gold rims, they will go well with these glasses.'

They discussed the silver to be used, the flower vases for the drawing room and parlor, what flowers would be available. Natasha offered to have her brother gather flowers from the woods, some of the lovely autumn flowers growing lavishly in the marsh lands.

Laurel agreed, and went back to the drawing room, to read a magazine of fashion that Madame Bonheur had given her.

Mr. Leverett remained until past eleven. When the men emerged from the study, Laurel thought Thor looked exhausted, unusual for him. They said good night, and Leverett departed in a satisfied, expansive mood.

Thor flung himself down in an armchair, reached for his pipe, and began to fill it. 'He wants Dad and me to support him in a race for governor,' he said. 'Next year, the governor may be elected, instead of appointed. He thinks he can be effective.'

Laurel felt shocked. 'A governor? Mr. Leverett?' She could not believe he would feel compassion for people or be willing to stand up for other people's causes.

Thor shrugged. 'As a politician he could be good. He knows everybody, and he has his fingers in a lot of pies. And he's a wealthy, distinguished-looking man. He could make a lot of friends for Alaska. If the governor is not elected next year, but still appointed, he might get the bid. I just wish –' He hesitated, then finished his sentence in a low voice. 'I just wish I knew more about him.'

Laurel looked at her husband sharply. 'What don't you know, Thor?'

'His past,' said Thor. 'Don't pass this on, my darling.' Reflectively, he pulled at his pipe, and he looked older and tougher somehow, like his father, she thought. 'I wish I knew where he came from, what he did before he came to Alaska. He keeps his mouth shut about that, says it doesn't matter.'

'Lots of men come from nowhere to Alaska,' she said at last, thinking about it. 'They leave the past behind, and they're accepted here for what they are, Thor.'

He nodded his appreciation of that. 'Yes, but Leverett . . . he wants us to support him knowing absolutely nothing about him. His daughter supposedly went to a good school in Boston, but Laurel, when I picked you up in Boston, I checked on that. No girl's school in Boston had a Clarissa Leverett registered.'

Laurel stared at him, wide-eyed. He stared back at her. 'But Thor – ' she began.

'Either she did not go to school in Boston – and she does have something of a Boston accent, though you do not!' and he grinned at her. ' – or she went under another name. Perhaps the name he used to have.'

'Oh . . . my goodness,' she gasped. 'He might have changed his name!'

'Yes. To conceal anything . . . parents he was ashamed of . . . or a past he had to hide, with something like a crime in it. What crime? Well, maybe stealing money. He has plenty now, with no known occupation. He owns a lot of gold claims, but how did he get them? Any man locating a gold claim has the right to stake two claims on any one creek. What claims did he find? Or did he buy other claims? He doesn't say; he just grins, and shakes his head, and implies he has plenty of secrets.'

Laurel digested that in silence. She thought of her father's claims, all unworked. She had never filed on them; she wished she could do so soon. Perhaps she would go to visit the Nolans, and register the claims in Wrangell. Jade and Garth might help her do that.

'Well – ' Thor knocked out his pipe. 'I told him I would discuss it with Father and let him know. He has a silver tongue, I'll say that for him. And he knows about Alaska's problems. We ought to have more say in what laws are passed up here. Those folks in Washington don't know our problems, or our potential. We need a senator, a representative, who can speak up for us, and who can know what is going on up here. That might do more good than electing a governor.'

'Yes, we have a right to decide things for ourselves,' Laurel agreed seriously. 'How can they know in Washington just what

249

timber ought to be cut, or what mines should be leased to whom. And when outsiders come in and pay to have the minerals taken out – and they don't even care about us – I think that is wrong! We Alaskans ought to have the right to make our own decisions!'

'Hear, hear!' applauded Thor, with an affectionate grin. 'You're right, Laurel. Don't get mad! I just like to hear you sound off like that!'

She almost punched him, but she laughed at his teasing, and he put his arm about her to lead her upstairs. In their bedroom they forgot about the future of Alaska, and thought of their own future, together. She was not accustomed to his caresses, not by any means.

She lay in bed, having undressed first and used the bathroom. From her side of the bed, she could watch the stars, white in the night sky. And she would listen to the sound of the ocean waves slapping lightly up on the sandy beach. All of nature seemed to surround her, the ocean, the sands, the mountains. How good it would be in winter, to hear the ocean, the rains, the winds . . . and be inside in comfort, watching it, enjoying it.

Thor padded to the bed, then blew out the bedside lamp. He crawled in and reached for her. She turned to lie there, looking up at the dark face dimly seen. She put her hands on his face and felt the scratchy beard; he had shaved that morning, but by evening he could have shaved again.

He kissed her mouth, slowly savoring it. She lay quietly, her hands slipping around his head to clasp him closer to her. His arm went under her body, as he leaned closer and kissed her more deeply. His other hand was caressing her body, from her breasts to her thighs. Excitement began to build in her. He was so slow, so gentle, teasingly so.

He pushed up her nightdress and came over her. Abruptly he wanted her, and passion made him hot and full of need. She felt the change in him, and it thrilled her and made her afraid all at once.

He put his leg between her thighs and pressed to her. She had healed, and he had had her twice since then. But it was still so strange, so odd. She stiffened as he came slowly to her, pressing into her.

He kissed her lips and teased her into opening her mouth. His tongue slid into her mouth, and he touched her teeth and her tongue. Absorbed in this new sensation, she forgot what he was doing to her. He came into her, easily, slowly, carefully. He was inside her, up in her, before she knew what he had done.

'Oh . . . oh,' she gasped, as his bigness filled her.

'Easy, honey, darling,' he whispered. 'Easy, take it easy. Just relax.'

She relaxed with an effort as he kissed her throat, her breasts, still holding tightly in her. She felt her body soften, moisten. Then it was easier for her, and he began to slide back and forth inside her. The excitement built up and up swiftly. She was gasping, and she felt her heart pounding with mounting thrills. Then it happened.

He was moving back and forth, and something thrilled in her, and she convulsed. She cried out, softly, against his mouth. 'Oh – Thor – Ohhhhhh . . . ohhhhh . . .' She felt her hips lift to his spasmodically, involuntarily, and inside her something tightened, loosened, tightened, in a series of thrilling spasms.

He felt it, and he groaned, 'Oh, Laurel – darling – darling – oh, love . . .' And he was moving faster and faster, and it make her convulse harder than ever.

She was pressing him, and her hands went to his back to pull him closer. Her hips surged up to his, and his hard body held her gently but possessively. All the time those thrills shaking her, racing through her, making her dizzy, making her faint with the sweet wild passion of it.

Then it faded, slowly, like a sunset fading in the night-blue sky. She saw stars behind her tightly closed lids. Thor sighed, and lay drained beside her, his arm still over her.

He went to sleep, effortlessly, lying half on her. She closed her eyes again, and her hand smoothed his ruffled hair softly. It had happened, and she felt strange and new and happy.

Laurel thought about it all the next day, dreamily, as she went for a walk with Czar. She scarcely paid any attention to where they were walking. She strolled down the hill, past the bushes and a little street that came into the main road. They were walking along the trees now, and it was dark, but she did not notice.

It had been so marvelous. Was this what being a wife was all about? She knew it could mean having a baby. Thor's child! What happiness and joy could there be in a life! She could think of nothing more exciting than being Thor's wife, and having his child.

A boy. She would like a son. Thor's son! Big and handsome, blond and laughing, with green eyes.

Czar growled. She said mechanically, 'Quiet, Czar.'

He growled again, more loudly. She stopped, said uneasily, 'What is it, boy?'

Before he could growl again, an arm slid about her neck. It jerked her backwards against a hard smelly body. She could not cry out, though she struggled against it. She was too frail against the man who had caught her.

She tried to pull on the arm. Czar had gone quiet. He was panting, snuffing, no growl now. Only an ominous nosing around her. The man kept her between him and the dog. She noticed the smell, a piggy smell.

Then Czar got around Laurel, with a swift lithe move of his magnificent half-wolf body. He sprang, without a sound, at the man and got hold of his shoulder. The man gave a muffled cry. He still held onto Laurel, swinging her desperately between him and the dog. Czar had hold of a sleeve, and tore it. Then he got flesh, for the man screamed and let go of Laurel.

The man flung Laurel face down on the ground. She lost her breath and rolled over trying to get away. She was in a bunch of fallen leaves, half smothered by them.

The man ran away; she heard his booted feet pounding on the gravel, then fading into the grass. Czar was after him, grabbed him again by some cloth, it tore.

He would die as Rex had died!

Laurel screamed at him, 'Czar, come back! Czar! Come back. Here, Czar, here! Come at once!' Somehow she had authority in her shrill scream.

The dog returned to her, reluctantly, snarling low in his wolflike throat. He crouched by her, his head swung to her, then longingly to the deep dense trees. He longed to disobey her, to return to his prey. She dared not touch the animal. He was like a savage, his mouth drawn back to bare sharp teeth.

'Good dog . . . good Czar,' she managed to say, crouched on her knees beside him. There was blood on his muzzle; he looked like a

252

wolf. 'Good, good dog; good Czar. Calm now, calm.

He was rumbling in his throat; he was still dangerous. She fought to calm herself, half-hysterical tears streaming down her face. Her lace collar was torn half off, and her dress lacked two buttons. Mechanically she groped among the leaves to retrieve the bright gold buttons, then found them and picked them up.

She stumbled to her feet, dizzy with fear, sick with it. She must get back to the house. It was half a mile. She started out, the dog waited, looking back to the woods, into the dense thicket of trees and bushes.

She said sharply, with authority, 'Come, Czar. Come! At once!' She snapped her fingers.

He turned his head and looked at her, the black eyes still blazing with fury. Then slowly, he calmed, and he dropped his head and came. He followed her as she started up the road.

She kept saying, 'Good dog, good Czar. Come along. Good dog, good dog.'

He followed her, finally coming to her hand and walking near to her, his head pressing against her. There was blood on his muzzle, and a growl still ripped through his throat at times. But now she dared to touch him, and she put her hand slowly on his head, and he accepted it.

At the kennels, Mike Dugan came out, smiling, to see her. His smile faded when the Indian boy said something sharp in his tongue and pointed to the dog.

'No, he protected me,' Laurel said at once. 'A man attacked me . . . in the trees.' She took a cloth, wet it, and knelt to wash off Czar's nose. She still shook. 'Good dog, good Czar, let me wash off that blood . . . good dog.' He was slowly quieting, the rumble finally stopped.

She put Czar in the kennel herself, not trusting him to anyone else. 'Let him alone today; don't try to touch him,' she told the Indian boy. 'He attacked a man, drew blood. He will be wild for a time.'

The boy agreed, his look respectful on the big dog.

When Thor came home and learned what had happened, he was furious and concerned. 'Laurel, you are not to go out alone any longer!' he said. 'Even with that dog, you are not safe!'

She had had time to calm down also. 'Nonsense, Thor,' she said briskly. 'I need my walks. And Czar protects me with his life – just as Rex did,' and she shook her head as she remembered how Rex had died. 'But I won't let Czar die.'

Thor's jaw went very tight, his eyes icy green. 'You are not going out alone, Laurel! There must be a killer about, and I won't have it! When I'm not here, you take the carriage, with Mike driving. I'm giving orders, and that is that!'

In vain Laurel protested. She resented his commands, though she loved him. And he was trying to protect her. But she disliked the loss of her freedom. She fumed, but even Patsy was against her going out alone.

'Do you have any idea who did it?' asked Thor, then.

'I think – It smelled like – Herman Ranke,' she finally said.

'It smelled like? Honestly, Laurel!' he said in exasperation, 'Didn't you see the man?'

'No, he attacked me from behind. Then when Czar grabbed him, the man knocked me into the leaves, and I was blinded for a minute. Then he ran off, Czar after him. I called Czar back. The man was hidden in the trees, and I was afraid he would knife Czar. Thor, Czar is a well-trained dog; he came at once!' she added proudly.

Thor groaned, and put his hand over his face. He seemed pale and strained. 'Laurel, you will never go out alone!' And he meant it.

'But I'm not afraid with Czar!'

'You'll go with Mike Dugan and with Czar, both of them!'

He let the subject of Herman Ranke drop; he felt her evidence was too flimsy. But Laurel did not forget. She was deathly afraid of that man now. She kept remembering how he watched her, stared at her. Maybe he was crazy.

Chapter 21

All day Saturday Laurel was so busy she hardly had time to turn around as her Aunt Gertrude used to say. She had the Indian girls clean the house again thoroughly, so not a speck of dust could be seen by eagle-eyed Sidonie. She set the table herself, studying every plate to see there was no chip or crack. She went over and over the arrangements with Patsy and Natasha.

Natasha's friends had brought in flowers from the swamps and marshes. And Sidonie came over too, in the early afternoon, offering assistance and bringing more flowers 'in case they are needed.' She graciously offered to arrange the flowers, and Laurel accepted. She could do it herself, but Sidonie wanted to help, and her flower arrangements were always exceptional.

For the silver epergne at the dining table, Sidonie arranged a beautiful low setting of deep red roses from her own garden, a few perfect blooms floating in the water of the silver bowl. For the parlor and drawing room, she filled several green vases with the tall orange-yellow monkey flower and several cream vases with deep blue swamp gentian.

Sidonie had looked critically at the flowers Natasha's friends had brought, but finally conceded, 'They are lovely, though wild-flowers. And the colors are splendid,' and she set them about.

She must have ravished her own gardens, for she had brought an armload of red roses, a basket of purple iris, and a few rare gladio-luses of beautiful scarlet. When she was finished, the rooms looked glorious. She stayed to approve the table, made suggestions about ashtrays and demitasse cups for coffee, then departed.

About five o'clock Laurel went upstairs to bathe and change her dress. She donned the new white brocade with the pale silver stripes

255

in it, and put on Thor's collar of pearls and the long dangling pearl earrings.

Thor came home just as Laurel was coming down the stairs. He stared at her, came and kissed her. 'You look like a bride again, my darling,' he said. He put his hand on her soft throat, gazed at the upswept hair and the pearl coronet on the bouffant style. 'Glorious,' he said.

Laurel was so pleased and relieved, she felt new confidence. He approved of her! She was able to smile at Mr. Leverett and Clarissa when they arrived, the first guests.

Clarissa was elegantly beautiful in a gown of her favorite lavender, with a diamond necklet about her slim throat. About her wrist she wore a splendid barbaric bracelet made of huge gold nuggets, reminding Laurel of her necklace, which Clarissa had scorned! Remembering that, and how Clarissa must have demanded something like it from her father, amused her.

Sidonie and Olaf Koenig arrived right after the Leveretts. Sidonie was gowned in her sophisticated black, this time of silk spotted with silver butterflies. Laurel complimented her on the gown, and Sidonie smiled happily.

'New this week,' she murmured. 'Olaf brought me some lengths from the ship arrived from San Francisco and Paris!'

'Stunning,' said Laurel. 'The butterflies are so dashing and yet so lovely.'

Laurel found herself able to give out compliments that she meant, give praise where it was due, make her guests at ease. From where did her new confidence come? Probably from Olaf and Thor, she thought. They both seem to think so highly of her.

Mr. Custis arrived, as well as several others, and the party was complete. Natasha served drinks in the parlor, then they moved to the dining room, and Laurel smoothly seated them all, smilingly indicating their places. She was aware of Sidonie's tenseness as Laurel went through her paces, and her relieved soft sigh when all had been seated. Sidonie took all this so seriously!

Mr. Custis, the new banker, was a wealthy bachelor in his thirties and a handsome, suave man. Laurel had decided to seat him next to Clarissa and see how that worked! The banker was clearly delighted; Clarissa gave him enigmatic smiles and gazed at him over her lace fan.

Sometime during the meal, Mr. Custis said, 'I must confess, I did not expect to find such elegance in Alaska!'

Laurel stiffened and retorted at once. 'And why not, sir? Alaska has everything!'

They all laughed, as though she had said something supremely clever. Thor's green eyes shone approval on her.

'Including beautiful ladies who say intelligent things,' Mr. Custis said gallantly, and raised his wineglass to her. 'It is fascinating to me that the conversation at tables, in elegant saloons and elsewhere ladies gather, is so filled with ideas of the future of Alaska and its potential. Nowhere is one blasé, bored. All are eager and alive to the present and the future, full of suggestions for improvement. All it takes, one lady said to me, is courage and strength! I would not hear that in New York, I am sure.'

'Here, here!' said Olaf Koenig, his ruddy face beaming. 'Our ladies are as alert as the men to our fortunate position, the pioneers of a glorious territory.'

'To the future of our Alaska,' said Thor, raising his glass, and they all drank to that.

'The trouble is,' Mr. Leverett said thoughtfully as the glasses were set down again, 'the politicians in Washington do not see it this way. It is not so long ago that Alaska was called "that icebox," and Mr. Seward was derided for managing its purchase from Russia!'

'And now it is repaying that money over and over, not only in gold and silver, but in copper, timber, homesteads, and other wealth we can only guess at,' said Olaf, enthusiasm in his voice and his face. 'Gentlemen and ladies, we are seeing only the beginning of the great wealth that is coming from Alaska to the world!'

Laurel found herself saying, 'And it is not only the timber and minerals that make Alaska wealthy. It is the magnificent mountains, the valleys, rivers and streams, the wildlife and wildflowers – all the beauty that is our land! No place I have ever seen – and I have seen much of the United States – can compare with the awesome splendid scenes I have witnessed in Alaska! No place draws one again and again to the glaciers, the whales, the huge Sitka spruces, the glorious wilderness that surrounds us.'

There was silence at the table, all faces turned to her as they absorbed the passion with which she spoke. Thor's gaze was on her

257

face, as was that of the others. She felt warm and flushed, excited, exalted by speaking of her great love of the land here.

Mr. Custis finally spoke. 'I honor you, madam,' he said respectfully. 'There speaks a true citizen of Alaska. I hope one day to see these scenes of which you speak and come to know and to love Alaska as you do.'

Sidonie smiled approvingly at Laurel. Olaf encompassed her with his beaming grin. The atmosphere at the table was even more relaxed and genial as the meal was completed.

Thor led the gentlemen to his study for more serious discussion, port and cigars, and pipes. Laurel led the ladies to the parlor, where they spoke of more frivolous but important matters, dresses and styles from the United States, vegetable gardens being started just outside Sitka by a firm, the flood of newcomers to Sitka, another gold find up north.

Then the gentlemen returned to the drawing room. Some ladies stayed in the parlor and some went into the drawing room. The doors had been opened wide on their sliding rungs, so that the entire front area of the large house was one huge room. They mingled freely and strolled about to admire the furniture, the view, the ladies' gowns, their own conversational tidbits.

Clarissa had somehow managed to acquire Thor's arm and was clinging to him, smiling up into his face. Laurel hoped Thor would feel uncomfortable, and she glared at him. However, he did not seem to notice; he looked at ease. Maybe he enjoyed her attentions! Why hadn't he married Clarissa if he liked her so much?

'Daddy wants your advice on Anchorage,' said Clarissa. 'Don't you think he would be wise to open an office there? Should he make a tour of the North, become known there?'

She gazed up at Thor worshipfully, hung on his arm and his words. Laurel finally turned from them. She would growl like Czar if she continued to watch them together.

Mr. Leverett strolled over to her. 'A handsome house, Mrs. Koenig, and you grace it.' He smiled.

'Thank you, Mr. Leverett.'

He bent to her ear. 'I think they are a fine couple, eh?' he murmured, nodding to his daughter and Thor. 'I had high hopes for them, they were so devoted to each other. But the gossip about you and Thor came first, eh? He is a gentleman, after all. He couldn't do anything else, unless he sent you back to your relatives!'

Laurel stiffened and gave him a frosty look, like one of Sidonie's when someone spilled cigar ash on her Persian carpet.

Laurel was about to blurt out something rude, when she noticed his small blue eyes surveying her shrewdly. Yes, he would love for her to make a scene! She clenched her small fists in her full skirts and changed the subject.

'Do you intend to tour the North, Mr. Leverett? You would see stunning countryside.'

'I am thinking of beginning a tour in the spring, yes. No point in going now, the snows have started.'

'Yes, of course. They begin early up near Fairbanks.'

'I was over near your father's old cabin last spring,' he commented. 'The cabin has fallen down, too bad. I went up the mountainside, looking for deer. I was surprised to find a gold claim there, thought it might be your father's when I saw the stakes.'

Laurel stiffened again and could not conceal her interest and anxiety. 'Oh yes. Did it have his initials on the stakes?'

He shook his gray-blond head slowly, fixing her with his stare. 'No, no, Miss Laurel, it did not. Right near your father's cabin and all, I thought it would. Didn't you say he had found gold up there?'

'A small amount,' she said cautiously. 'He found some gold nuggets, then nothing more.' She looked down for fear her honest face might betray her. She rarely lied, but she had no intention of telling this man of the gold there.

'Indeed. A pity. It might have financed your education. I understand Thor paid for you.'

'No, sir. I went to my uncle and aunt in Boston, my mother's brother.'

'Indeed?' He was still smiling politely while she burned. 'I thought you might have made a deal with Thor. Your education and travel in exchange for your father's gold claim.'

'What? I don't understand you, sir.'

'The name on the stakes was Thor Koenig.'

She gasped, unable to conceal her shock. 'Thor's name on the stakes?' she whispered.

Leverett nodded, smiled, seeming to appreciate her surprise.

'That amazes you, does it not? Me too. Was it your father's claim that he stole?'

'He would not steal anything,' Laurel said hotly, even while she began to doubt.

'No? I went over to the land office at Wrangell later. The only claim on that stream was that of Thor Koenig.'

'Did you file a claim next to his?' Laurel managed to ask.

'Me? No, didn't seem any other claim was worth taking.' He shrugged. 'The only gold around lay in his land. Ah well, he may have some explanation.' The snide remark was covered by his gleaming gold-toothed smile.

Laurel was speechless as Leverett smoothly moved away and began to speak to Mr. Custis. Her mind was churning. Her father had set stakes on the land; she herself had helped him measure them out. He had put up stakes and had put his name on them. And he had meant to file on them; only, he had been killed.

If only she had filed her claim . . . but she had not. She didn't know how to go about it. And Thor . . . Thor had a claim up there! It had to be her father's claim. There was none other around.

The law of the Klondike, she knew, said that no man might remove another man's stakes once the claim was filed. And no man of honor removed any stakes, even without the filing. Had Thor done this? If he had, how dared he!

He could have claimed beside her father's land. But he had evidently not done so, not finding other gold. It had been a narrow streak on a cliff. She remembered so well. She had enjoyed gazing out over the valley below to the blue streams as her father dug and shovelled gravel into the rocker. Why had her father's stakes been removed and replaced with Thor's?

Or had Leverett lied?

Her guests began to leave. The carriages were rolling up for them, driven by their coachmen. She fastened a false smile on her face, disturbed and upset.

Sidonie swept up to her, followed by Olaf. 'My dear, it went well,' she praised in a low voice. 'For the first time, you showed remarkable poise.'

'Thank you, Mrs. Koenig,' said Laurel.

'Please! Olaf may prefer to be called Father, but I hope you will call me Sidonie, as Thor does.'

'Thank you very much . . . Sidonie,' said Laurel, with a more genuine smile. Olaf was clearly listening to them. 'And thank you again for your help. The flowers were gorgeous, and your advice made me feel more . . . self-confident.'

Sidonie gave a side glance to Olaf, as though to make sure he heard. 'Anytime, my dear. You must feel free to call upon me!'

'I shall, you may be sure.' Laurel turned to Olaf. 'Father? Thank you for coming!'

He bent unexpectedly and kissed her soft cheek. 'I enjoyed the evening, my dear. You and Thor must come to us soon. Sidonie will arrange it. We don't see enough of you!'

Laurel laughed. 'You two men are the busy ones! Sidonie and I will be only too glad to tear you away from your work for an evening of entertainment!'

'You are right, Laurel,' Sidonie chimed in, pleased, 'Shall we say a week from Sunday? Just the family!'

Thor had come to Laurel's side as the last words were spoken. He agreed to the evening and assisted Sidonie to her carriage.

Then Clarissa and her father departed, all smiles. Laurel wondered if the man had meant to make her angry with Thor. Well, he had succeeded. But surely he did not think to part them and give his daughter a second chance! He was not so silly, was he? Or was he more shrewd than she thought?

Laurel did feel boiling angry, and could scarcely contain her anger until her guests had left. Mike Dugan saw the last ones into their carriages, and Patsy Dugan closed the front doors and began to clear the drawing room of ashtrays.

'There now, a success, I'd say,' said Patsy, happily.

'Your dinner was splendid,' Thor said smiling. 'And I must compliment Natasha. She served perfectly.'

Laurel echoed his words and started up the stairs. She would not quarrel with Thor in front of anyone.

In the bedroom Laurel unfastened her jewelry and laid it on the dressing table. Thor had gone to the bathroom, and returned to take off his jacket and yawn. She began to unfasten the small pearl buttons down the front of her gown. Thor sat down on a chair to pull off his dress boots.

'Thor? I was amazed at something Mr. Leverett told me,' she began as she removed the dress.

'Oh, what was that? Something about his past?' he asked alertly.

'No. About *our* past.'

'You intrigue me, Laurel,' he said, smiling. 'What does he know about our past?'

She took off the full petticoats. She had refused to wear the corselet. She hated the confinement of the whalebones. Her waist was quite slim and she did not feel the need of such.

Now Thor was watching her figure as she removed the clothes. Irritated at his inattention to her words, she turned her back on him to remove her camisole and pull on the full-length cotton night-dress. From under its voluminous folds, she pulled down her pantalets.

'He said he was over near father's cabin in the spring,' she told him. 'He went hunting up in the mountain near the cabin and found stakes near a gold claim. He went to look at the stakes, thinking they would have father's name or initials on them. Instead . . . the name was yours.'

Laurel turned around to face her husband, her face serious. Thor nodded. 'That's right,' he said placidly.

She gasped. She had thought he would deny it vehemently. 'Right! Your name . . . on father's claim? Thor, how could you?'

He looked puzzled, standing up in his bare feet. 'Why not, Laurel? He didn't live to file the claim.'

'And you took it from him . . . from me!' she gasped. 'I had meant to file on the claim one day. I wanted it . . . it was mine by inheritance! I helped father dig on that claim, I found some gold there, I dug in the cold water . . . I . . .'

'Why, Laurel, what difference does it make now?' he asked. He seemed genuinely surprised by her attitude. 'It belongs to us both now. Everything I have is yours, and what you have is mine, isn't it?'

'But it wasn't then, Thor! What would have happened if I had never returned to Alaska?'

'But you did return, honey!' he said reasonably. He stared at her

262

stained angry face. 'What are you upset about? You wanted to return, I helped you return, it all worked out.'

'But it was Father's claim! It was *my* claim! How dared you file on it – for yourself!'

Now Thor began to get angry. She knew by the white line about his mouth, by his tight lips as he spoke. He seemed to bite off the words. 'Damn it, Laurel, I did the best I could. Your father didn't live to file on the claim. I didn't want men coming in and filing. When I learned there was a gold claim – you told us about it, wore the nugget necklace – then I went back there . . . I made a quick trip, I'll tell you, raced back and forth. I filed on it, after changing the stakes.'

'You changed the stakes!' she accused, wildly. 'You dared to change the stakes! How could you!'

'Dead men . . . cannot . . . file claims! Damn it! You know that, Laurel! And you were only fifteen. You were leaving Alaska! How could you file? I did it to protect the claim . . . for you, Laurel?'

That was not what he had said before. He had said he didn't want men coming in and out, trying to file on the claim. He had taken it from her, without telling her!

'Where did you file?' she asked in a strained voice.

'In Wrangell. I went over and looked at the claim. There was nothing more showing in gold upstream. His two claims were the only color showing. And there was some good stuff there, by your nuggets. I meant to get back and do some digging the next summer, but I got too busy. It will keep.'

Laurel rubbed her face with her hands. She was sleepy, she was weary; was she being stupid? It seemed to her that he had cheated her and her father; he had filed on their claims by changing the stakes, putting up his own stakes, and filing under his own name. But he made it sound so reasonable!

'For God's sake, Laurel, don't you trust me?' he yelled.

She didn't know, but how could she say so? She could destroy their fragile relationship. He had married her because he was sorry for her, hadn't he? Or had he had some deeper motive . . . such as a gold claim he knew might pan out rich?

She went to the bathroom and washed her flushed face. In the mirror she looked at her face. It was angry, and her eyes were wide and hurt. She had leaned on Thor – he was strong, he was fine, he was dependable . . . or was he? Why had he filed on her claim? Laurel had wanted her own piece of Alaska land. She had thought of that land on the mountainside as hers, her piece of Alaska. And she would rebuild the cabin . . . and live there one day . . . or could she?

Her life had not turned out as she had hoped and planned. She had married Thor. He was sorry for her . . . he did not love her; he wanted her gold claim. He concealed things from her . . . he trusted Leverett, while she hated him. Leverett had deliberately told her about this, to make her distrust . . . Leverett still wanted Thor as his son-in-law. He had practically thrown Clarissa at Thor . . .

And Laurel had just wanted her own land, her own piece of Alaska, to belong somewhere beautiful . . . to belong to Alaska . . . But instead she belonged to Thor! And he had taken her over, her and her dreams and turned them to his own purposes! She had never wanted to live in a huge mansion and be a stylish hostess! She had never wanted to be a light of society! She had never wanted to entertain Thor's guests and make them happy while she chafed in her layers of fashionable clothes!

By the time Laurel returned to the bedroom she had worked herself up to a fine temper. Partly because of weariness, she was ready to fight Thor, to argue with him, to yell at him. He was not the only one who could cuss and swear! She had heard plenty of words in her short lifetime!

He was lying in their big bed, waiting for her. She took the brush and began to brush out her long thick curls. 'For God's sake,' said Thor. 'Forget the routine and come to bed!'

The brush dropped with a clatter on the marble-topped sprucewood table. She turned on him, flaring.

'Thor, you don't own me! You don't tell me what to do every minute of the day! You don't tell me not to brush my hair! You don't tell me not to walk my dog! You don't tell me to give up my claim!'

He sat up with a jerk of surprise. 'Laurel, what's got into you, damn it?'

'And you don't swear at me!' she cried. She stood up, raging, and pointed at him with a quivering finger. 'You don't cuss me, unless you want me to cuss too! I've got plenty to cuss about! Why didn't you tell me about my father's claim? Why didn't you just tell me? I was feeling so grateful to you for all your help . . . getting to Boston . . . coming back to Alaska . . . and all the time, you were taking my land!'

Thor was out of bed, hopping about in his bare feet on the cold floor, even more furious than Laurel. 'Damn it to hell, what are you talking about? Yes, I took your goddamn land! It belongs to both of us now!'

'Yes, now, now! If you share it with me! If you tell me about it, which you did not! It took Leverett to tell me about it, and you would never have said a word! '

'That is hellish unfair!' he yelled at her. His voice bellowed through the rooms. 'I never had a chance to tell you! How long have we been married, huh? I ask you?'

'Would you have told me if I hadn't married you?' she yelled back, enraged again. 'If I had not returned to Alaska, if I had stayed in Boston, would you have written to me and told me?'

'Why should I?' he yelled again, bluntly. 'If you didn't care enough to return, why should I have broken my back digging out some damn yellow metal to make Boston rich?'

Laurel stared at him, chilling. No, he would not have told her. He would not have told her! He would have kept it all for himself!

Not realizing the thoughts that went through her head, Thor scowled at her. 'The gold belongs to Alaska and Alaskans,' he said pointedly. 'If you had not wanted to return, why should you have a part of Alaska? But you did, Laurel, you did return. Like the forget-me-nots, you didn't forget.'

Laurel turned to the door. She was tired and confused, and very angry.

'Where are you going?' he barked.

'To sleep in the other room,' she said and opened the door to the hallway. They had recently installed the beds in the guest suite across the hall. She would put linens on one and sleep there.

'The hell you say!'

Thor had followed her, and pounced on her. He picked her up, kicked the door shut with one bare foot, howled 'ouch!' and carried her, kicking and hitting him, back to their big bed.

'You let me go! I don't want to sleep with you tonight!' she yelled, and hit him in the chin with one square fist.

'Ouch, damn it!' He bounced her down on the bed and followed her down, breathing hard. Then she was afraid. He had always been gentle with her, even that first night when he had to hurt her to take her maidenhead. But now he felt angry and hard and tough, and his green eyes flared in the darkened room. He blew out the lamp beside the bed, and it was pitch dark to her until the faint light from the window took over.

Laurel wriggled and squirmed and hit at him again until he caught both fists in one of his huge hands and held her hands above her head. She still kicked out at him, until his one long leg pressed down both of hers. He held her down and began to kiss her fiercely.

His mouth bit at hers, and he was not gentle. She felt the teeth marks of his mouth as he pressed his lips on hers. She would be bruised tomorrow.

He pulled down the loose neck of the nightdress with his lips, and pressed rough kisses on her soft small breasts. He was panting, excited by their anger. She was afraid of him, with a sort of scared excitement. Would he hurt her?

Laurel was out of energy. She gave up, sagging against the mattress as he pressed his big head to her breasts, kissing her in a mingling of rage, desire, and angry passion. He felt her giving-up and he could have softened, but he did not. He kept on kissing her, one hand moving over her bared breasts down to her waist, his lips following. He pulled the nightdress down to her thighs, and he kissed her from her breasts to her hips.

Then he lifted up, and yanked the nightdress off completely. He flung it away onto the carpet somewhere. He had not bothered with a nightshirt, and his naked, hard body pressed down on her soft, trembling bare body.

Thor's arms wrapped about her softness. He lay back and deliberately rolled over with her so she was above him. His mouth was on her throat. She lay on him helplessly feeling the hard masculine flesh rising in his passion. Her legs sprawled apart on his thighs, and he was between her thighs, his hands on her soft hips, pressing down.

She moaned, and he thought she was becoming more passionate. She felt his lips opening and smiling against her throat.

'Laurel,' he whispered, coaxing, bullying. 'Laurel, kiss me . . . kiss me.'

She held her breath, shocked now. She had never done that. He pressed her face to his face, insistent. 'Come on, honey . . . darling . . . kiss me . . .'

She kissed his cheek obediently, but resisted when he pulled her lower.

'No . . . I don't want – Thor . . . please – Don't make me . . .'

'Kiss my body . . .' he urged. 'I want you . . . to know me . . . as I know you – '

He was passionate, possessive, urging, wanting. She could not hold out against his strength. He pressed her down on his body, so she lay with her head against his chest. His heart was beating rapidly. He put his hand behind her head, urged her face to his chest. She timidly kissed the hard chest with its mat of tangled thick hair.

Her touch excited him the more. She felt his masculine hard thighs pressing upward to her soft ones. He urged her lower, so she kissed the lean waist. He put her hands on his thighs. She flinched from the touch, but he insisted.

'Yes, go on, darling . . . do it . . . touch me there!'

'Oh, Thor . . . no! It isn't . . . I can't . . .'

'Yes, we can do anything together. Go on, darling . . . Oh, yes, hold me there . . .'

He was so excited, she feared him. He groaned and rolled over so she was beneath him again. He came to her, pressed hard, urgently, and the familiar motions began again. Part of her stood off and watched them coldly. Was he doing this to make her forget their argument?

The other part of her was hot and as passionate as he was. He excited her so. Soon her hips were moving with his; she groaned with him, and when he finished in her, her soft body was quivering with his. Again she felt that strange wild thrill, the ecstacy of almost blacking out with desire.

He lay still then, half on her, sighing with pleasure. 'Now,' he said softly, 'you do believe me, don't you? You love me, don't you? Laurel, say it!'

Her hands ruffled through his thick wet hair, smoothed his damp face. He urged her again.

'Say it, say you believe me, say you love me!'

'I love you, Thor,' she said. And he was satisfied, and muttered against her body and fell asleep, exhausted with his pleasure.

But Laurel had not said she believed him. For she did not really believe him. She lay awake for a time, troubled and brooding. And in the morning it all came back to her, the worry and the mystery. Why had Thor changed the stakes? Why had he claimed her father's gold claim for himself?

Chapter 22

Winter was coming to the Stikine. In the early morning ice had formed on the edges of the stream. The bare limbs of trees crackled in the wind, their music a warning of the cold to come.

Garth would waken early to get up and start a fresh fire in the fireplace. Then he would return to his blankets, to drowse while the cabin warmed.

Jade would hear him and also waken and lie there, wishing he was in the big bed with her, holding her, warming her, wanting her. But he never came.

Then one morning she did not hear him stirring. She finally wakened completely to see the dawn light creeping into the dark cabin. The fire crackled in the fireplace, the cabin was warm, but she heard no sound.

She got up, and peeked out into the other room. Garth was stirring, yawning in his blankets.

'Garth? I think it is late! I'll hurry!' She was surprised because he rarely overslept. He was usually up and ready for breakfast before she was, and off to work eagerly.

He smiled and shook his head, his eyes crinkling to see her in the cotton nightdress, rubbing her bare foot against her other ankle.

'Not going this morning, Jade. Reckon lumbering is finished up here for the winter. There's ice on the grass and the horses would slip. We'll be bringing in the wagons and folding up.'

He got up, stretched, and she could scarcely keep her eyes from his tall firm body in the loose nightshirt. He had a strong broad neck, and his face was tanned to his chest. She blushed and retreated as he lifted his shirt to undress.

She waited until he had gone outside, then scurried to wash and dress. She pulled on her long woolen stockings, the long cotton petticoat she had made, her thick, blue wool skirt, and the green checked shirt. Her hands flew through her hair, brushing it, braiding it into a long plait down her back. Then she went out to the outhouse, returned, washed her hands and arms, and was ready to fix breakfast.

Garth had filled the stove with wood and had the fire going. He had put the water on in the coffeepot and was setting the table. How good he is, she thought again.

Since they both had time, she fixed sausages and eggs for breakfast, and sourdough pancakes with the last of their jars of blueberries. Garth ate hungrily and appreciatively. He seems more relaxed lately, she thought.

Then he leaned back and stretched, took out his pipe and filled it. 'Reckon we'll go down to Wrangell soon, Jade,' he said. 'Want to stay awhile?'

'Whatever you want, Garth. I'd like to visit with my folks. Wonder if Mother wants help with the tanning.'

'I can help out there. For the winter I'll just be chopping wood for folks, probably. Or we could go to Sitka for a spell, and talk to the Koenigs about my lumbering.'

Jade nodded eagerly, her eyes sparkling. 'Oh yes, if we could, please!'

He seemed happy with her and smiled at her. She began to pack that day. After the sunshine had melted the ice, the men went up to the camp with the horses and began to pack up.

Garth returned that evening and reported, 'A man came through last night from up north. Says snows have come, been here two weeks. It'll be a hard winter. Boss has sent for a steamer to come and get us and our gear to Wrangell. The ice will be forming hard on the Stikine within a week.'

It was important to get out from their northern post before the ice formed. When the Stikine froze, it didn't unfreeze until spring, and they would have to go out by walking or dog sled.

Happily, ready for the next part of their lives, Jade packed for them both while Garth helped close up the lumbering operations. Within three days the steamer chugged up from Wrangell. They loaded her that night, and early the next morning they went aboard. The horses were loaded on and their neighing at the distress of sailing filled the steamer.

'Poor animals,' murmured Jade.

'They'll live through it,' Garth comforted, his arm around her shoulders as they leaned at the deck rail. 'I sent word down to Mrs. Simpson to have the cabin cleaned up for us.'

'Oh, Garth, I can do that,' she said, turning her head to look up into his face. 'I wanted to scrub it and make sure it was really clean.'

He chuckled, and his eyes crinkled. Her heart turned over in love for him. 'I know it, Jade. That's why I told Mrs. Simpson to find someone to clean it. I know you'll go after the dirt again, but the first layers will be off. Besides, I'm looking forward to your good meals when we can get some fresh supplies in. We haven't had veal steak for a month.'

She smiled, and leaned against him contentedly. They were closer, and she would be happy if . . . if one day they could be very, very close. He was such a wonderful man, and she was proud to be his wife.

They arrived in Wrangell late that night; the steamer had made good time. Garth had pointed out the ice forming at the sides of the river and around the boulders in the stream. It would sure freeze up soon.

The next morning after their arrival, Garth went uptown. He returned with Miriam and Tom Nolan. Jade squealed when she saw them and flung her arms about her mother.

'We heard the steamer come in late last night,' said Miriam, smiling. 'We said we will come over today, but here come Garth for us!'

'We had a good summer, lots of hunting,' said Tom equally happy. 'That Thor Koenig, he sends lots of his friends to come hunting with us. Got lots of deer, moose, a fine bear. Make lots of skins, got lots of money!'

'A man is lucky to have a rich father-in-law,' said Garth, and they stared at him, open-mouthed. Then Miriam began to laugh. She laughed so hard, she had to sit down hard in a chair, holding her plump sides.

Tom Nolan was laughing too, rare for him, and leaning against the cabin wall, wiping his eyes from gales of laughter. Garth was grinning at his joke, and Jade just had to shake her head and join in the laughter.

When they had stopped laughing, they sat down to talk and exchange news. Tom Nolan told of the hunters, counted out the skins he had taken. Miriam had tanned many of them, but the rest had to wait for the winter.

Miriam had canned many many blueberries and cranberries. 'Mrs. Simpson at the restaurant wanted all I could put in jars,' she said proudly. 'She said, "I'll buy all!" But I said, "Yes, yes, madame. But I will keep some for us and for my Jade, because my son-in-law, he loves our berries!" '

'I'm relieved to hear that,' said Garth. 'I thought I might have to go hungry!'

And again they laughed. Then the two men went off to inspect the skins and talk man-talk. Miriam and Jade also set to their talking while they cleaned the cabin once more until the windows were sparkling and shining in the frosty sunlight and you could have eaten off the floor boards.

They had the veal steaks bubbling in the pot and potatoes baking in the hot ashes when the men returned hungry at noon. Miriam took down a jar of blueberries; she had stocked Jade's shelves liberally in Jade's absence.

Garth was carrying a large cold bucket. 'Found some ice cream in town!' he announced triumphantly. It was the first they had had for months. They poured blueberries on the vanilla ice cream for dessert and ate until they were stuffed. Then they sat around drinking coffee and talking idly. Miriam turned serious and looked at Tom.

'You never guess who is in town, all of the month,' she said.

They shook their heads.

'That Ewan Koenig!' said Miriam, frowning heavily. 'He works all day, then he comes back and drinks all the night in the saloons. I am surprised at him. I think maybe his father doesn't know where he is.'

Garth had turned sober, and he was angry inside. Jade knew by his eyes.

'You stay away from him, Jade,' he ordered brusquely.

She nodded shyly, her eyes drooping. Would he never forget or forgive?

'I see him out near the old cabin of Jim Winfield,' Tom said. 'I think he sleeps in the cabin nights. I think maybe he is hunting. He shoots the rifle sometimes.'

They were silent, thinking about that. Garth stirred. 'I think we may go to Sitka pretty soon. Jade wants to visit with Laurel again. I will talk to Thor Koenig about my lumber plan. I told you about it,' he said to Tom.

'You think you would like to be your own boss,' Tom said scratching his chin. 'That is good, maybe. But you need wagons, horses, and many men to work the lumber.'

'Yes. I have some money saved. The trouble is, to find the right place, rent or buy the property. And have the good way to sell the lumber where it can be hauled away.'

'Thor Koenig will help you. He is a good man,' Miriam said with conviction. 'He makes a good husband for our Laurel. I am happy he marries her. He keeps her safe, I think maybe.'

Jade stared at her. 'Laurel is married . . . to Thor Koenig?' she cried. 'When did this happen?'

'Oh, you did not know? Ewan Koenig has word from town. He has letter from his father. Anyhow, he stops me on the street one day – he is nice that day – and says Laurel married his brother; he is happy for them.'

Jade was so excited she got up and danced around the room in her pleasure. 'My Laurel got married – and to Thor! Oh, that is wonderful. We must see them! Oh, I wonder what happened! You know, when he came to get her at our place, I thought – he cares what happens to Laurel!'

Garth nodded, rubbing his chin. 'Yes, he cared,' he said. 'Hmm, I thought they might marry one day. But I did not know it might be soon! She is very young.'

'We are the same age,' Jade said indignantly. 'And I am eighteen now, so is Laurel.'

'That's what I said,' he teased, 'very young!'

She wished she dared come to him and pummel him for his teasing. But she contented herself with wrinkling up her nose at him while her mother chuckled.

Jade offered to go to her mother's cabin the next day and help her with some fire work on the skins. Jade liked brushing the skins and making the furs shine. Garth agreed and took her over there in the morning, then went on to talk to his boss about lumbering.

At about four in the afternoon, Jade was tired. She was not used to this work now, and her arms ached. 'You go home,' her mother said affectionately. 'I stop now and get supper for Tom. You go and get supper for your man.'

'All right, Mother.' She put down her brush and washed her hands and arms, then brushed her dress where the fine hairs clung. She put on her red wool cloak and pulled the hood over her hair. The October air was chilly.

It would be darker soon; dusk came earlier now, for winter was not far off. She would see the white stars shining in the purple skies, and the soft lights of the aurora borealis, the beautiful northern lights. Then would come the snows to whiten the world, and the ptarmigan would turn white from its autumn golden brown.

How beautiful were the seasons in Alaska! How could anyone live anywhere else? Laurel had told her about the American West, the plains and deserts. She had told about Boston and concerts and streetcars in New York City. Surely they must be ugly and plain compared with Alaska!

She was humming to herself, smiling, thinking about getting supper for Garth. He would be full of his plans, and she would listen and think of their winter together, when he had more time for her.

'Jade!' Someone caught her arm roughly and flung her around. Jade gasped, gasped again as she saw Ewan Koenig frowning down at her. His face was flushed red with drink; he staggered before her, planting his legs wide apart, to keep his balance. 'Jade, what're you doing here?'

'I . . I am here with my husband,' she said with dignity. 'You are drunk, I think. Excuse me!' And she tried to go on her way, on the plank sidewalk.

He must have just come from the saloon behind him. She glanced about, but saw nobody she knew. A little desperately, she tried to move out of his path. He could be ugly when sober; he would be worse when drunk.

'No, you listen . . . you listen to me,' Ewan said and held her arm

274

tightly. He was holding her so hard, half to keep himself upright, she realized. Her mouth tightened with disgust.

'You let go of me, Ewan Koenig! If my husband saw you, he would knock you down again!'

'Yeah, yeah,' he said, and she realized he did not know what she was saying. His blue-gray eyes burned down at her. 'God . . . you're lovelier than ever, Jade. I was . . . was a fool . . . '

She stiffened, but he made no move to kiss her. 'I got to go home now, Ewan,' she said carefully, as to a child. 'You let me go. I have to go home now.'

'You listen . . . to me. You listen. Listen. Tell Laurel . . . gold claim . . . her dad's claim. Good stuff.'

Jade stared at him, puzzled. Why was he talking about that old claim of Jim Winfield? Had he been hunting around there?

Ewan's voice went lower. He lurched against her and she steadied him automatically with her hand on his arm. He was still clutching her with the other hand.

'Leverett . . .' he said. 'Tell Laurel. Herman Ranke – God knows he's a mean bastard. Tell her Ranke is here . . . and Leverett. Never should've got mixed up. You tell Laurel her gold claim . . .'

She could make no sense of what Ewan was saying. She only half understood his words.

'What are you talking about, Ewan Koenig?' she snapped.

'You listen . . .' he repeated, swaying with the drink. 'I gotta go. Go to work . . . work, huh!' And he began to laugh as he swayed away from her, lurching down the plank sidewalk.

Jade stared after him. Someone caught her arm, and she jerked and turned about again. This time it was her husband, Garth, blazing down at her.

'I told you to stay away from him,' he growled. 'What're you doing, talking to him on the main street? Don't you know I mean what I say?'

'Garth,' she said. 'He was drunk –'

'All the more reason to stay away from him! Why didn't you wait for my coming for you? Your mother said you went on, seemed in a hurry! Did you arrange to meet him?' His voice, so angry, hurt her.

'No, no, I ran into him. Garth, he said –'

But he would not listen to her. Anger burned in him, and he

caught her by the arm and turned her toward the cabin. He did not hurt her; he never hurt her, she thought. But his hand was firm on her arm, and he compelled her to come with him.

Once inside the cabin, he shut the door. 'Now, Jade, I told you to stay away from Ewan Koenig! Do you still love him? He is no good! I won't have you throwing yourself away on the likes of him!'

She stood before him, her red cloak tossed back from her shoulders, her hands on her hips. 'Garth, I don't love him! I haven't since . . . since the baby died. What I felt for him seemed to die with that poor little one. It is just gone. I feel sorry for him, though. And I want to tell you what he said to me. Will you please, please listen to me?'

Garth stared at her from her black hair to her heels, then up again at her flushed face and sparkling eyes. Finally he nodded in silence.

Jade expelled a breath. 'Well! He didn't make sense, but I think it is important. He said something about Laurel and Jim Winfield's gold claim. And he said something about Mr. Leverett and Herman Ranke –'

'Wait a minute, wait a minute. Who is Leverett, and that other man?'

Jade began to tell him, but it took a long time. She told him about how she and Laurel had discovered Thor and his brother being mauled by a bear, how Laurel had shot the bear, how Clarissa Leverett and her father had come, all that.

She removed her cloak and sat down at the table to continue. Garth sat down in his big chair with the arms that he had made and listened in silence, except for a brief question to keep her talking.

She sighed at the end, and got up to begin supper. It was growing dark. Garth lit the lamps, and brought fresh water for the coffeepot.

'Then Ewan said I must listen to him.' She frowned, trying to remember his exact words. 'He said, "Tell Laurel . . . gold claim . . ." something about her father's claim. "Good stuff," I remember he said.'

'Jim Winfield discovered gold?'

'Yes, and he made Laurel a big necklace of nuggets. Whoever murdered him took all the gold in the cabin, but she still has her gold necklace. And then Ewan mentioned Leverett. I don't know why. I wonder if he has been around Wrangell? He lives in Sitka. I think.'

'Did Laurel work the claim after Jim died?'

Jade shook her head. 'No, we never did. Dad thinks gold claims are unlucky. I'll tell you about that another time. Anyway, Thor came and took her off to Sitka; then she went to Boston.'

'And that other man, Herman Ranke . . . he works for Leverett, you said.'

'Yes, Laurel told me about him. She dislikes him. I think she is afraid of him, and that is odd. Laurel does not fear much of anything, not even bears.'

'And Ewan implied there might be claim jumping at Jim Winfield's claim.' Garth poured out their coffee and set the sugar before her.

'Yes, I think so. Anyway, it was "gold claim" and "good stuff," and then he spoke of Leverett.'

Garth sliced the berry pie and gave her a piece first. Then he sat down again at his place. 'Do you think Ewan might be involved with Leverett? Would he go behind his father's back? I thought he worked for his father?'

'I thought so too.'

'It's too much for me. I don't know these people. But I have a feeling Thor and his father ought to know about this. Let's go over to Sitka soon, Jade.'

Jade nodded eagerly. 'I would like to, Garth. Not only to tell Thor, but to see Laurel and see if she is happy in her marriage.'

'You think she may not be happy?'

'I hope so. I want to be sure. She and I are like sisters. We grew up together. We are close.'

And, Jade thought, Laurel had been so concerned about me that she came a long way to see me and make sure that I was happy. Jade in her turn wanted to be sure Laurel was happy. The marriage had been so sudden; that was what worried Jade.

'I think I'll get your father to take me over to the gold claim,' Garth was saying as he finished his coffee. 'We'll take a look, and see if someone is working the claim.'

'Garth, that could be dangerous!' Jade said sharply. 'Prospectors are usually honest. But if someone is jumping that claim, he won't want to be seen! And he'll be carrying a rifle, likely!'

'So will I,' he said. 'Don't worry. I have field glasses, and I'll take those also. We'll have a look-see from a distance and size up the situation.' He stood up and tested the side of the kettle lightly. The water was just beginning to boil. 'More coffee? The water isn't hot enough for the dishes yet.'

'Thank you.' She decided to say no more about Garth's trip to the gold claim. He would go if he thought best, and she didn't want to quarrel with him.

'Are you sure you are over Ewan?' he asked abruptly.

'Yes, Garth,' she said. 'More than anything I want to make our marriage work well,' she added shyly. 'I want to be a good wife to you . . . in every way.'

There! She was brazen, but she was also desperate! Couldn't he see that she loved him? Couldn't he see that she cooked for him, cleaned for him, sewed for him, made herself pretty for him? Did she have to come right out and beg him to take her to bed?

Garth was silent, his dark tanned face brooding. She got up, washed the dishes. He dried them and tossed the water out in back.

Then he took out his map and spread it out. Part of it he had made himself, and part the prospectors had added to for him, so he had a good map of the entire southeast section of Alaska.

'Show me where the gold claim is, and Jim Winfield's cabin,' he said.

She bent over his shoulder and studied the map on the table with care. 'There is a stream here, leading from the bay inland toward the mountains. It rises in the top of the mountain and flows down to the valley and to the bay,' she said.

'Draw it in as you remember it,' he invited, handing her the pen.

She drew carefully and showed the curves of the stream. 'This is where Laurel shot the bear. This is where we often waded, for it is shallow. This is where the fish are best caught.' The pen drew up toward the mountain until it ended in a little line. 'And right about here is the cliff where Jim Winfield found gold. He and Laurel took the rocker up there, put gravel in it, and found nuggets.'

'Lots of gold?' he asked.

'I don't know. I did not often go there,' she said.

'And your father did not file a claim beside that of Winfield?'

'No, he will not. He despises gold and its false promise of happiness,' Jade said simply.

She did not know what Garth would say. Most white men respected gold and money in banks.

He said, simply, his head bowed over the map, 'Your father is a wise and good man.'

Jade caught her breath, then bent and kissed his forehead where the dark hair grew back from his ear.

'Thank you,' she whispered.

He raised his head; their heads went very close together. She could see deeply into his dark brown eyes, the white around the brown, and the dark eyelashes above them, and the wrinkles around his eyes where he gazed into the sun. What did he see in her eyes, that he gazed so deeply into hers?

He shoved the chair back from the table and held out his arms. 'Jade,' he said.

She let him draw her down to his knees. It was where she wanted to be, close to him, leaning her head against his shoulder. She pressed against him, feeling his warmth, hearing his soft breathing near her ear. His arms had closed about her body, and his hand stroked her back ever so gently, ever so softly, sending thrills down her spine from her shoulders to her thighs.

His lips touched her hair. She turned her head, and he kissed the tip of her ear. A chill went right down into her heart, a delightful feeling, like the feel of the frost on the windows on a winter morning, all pretty and gleaming in the sunshine. A lovely chill, an exciting chill.

He just held her for a time, his lips against her cheek, on her chin, on her ear, on her mouth. Finally she turned, shyly, ever so carefully, and put one arm on his hard broad shoulder, on the thick red plaid of his shirt. Her arm curled about his shoulder, and her hand rested on the thick strong neck. She lifted her face to see his eyes. The brown eyes gleamed down at her, glinting in the firelight, shining at her.

She looked at his eyes, then at his strong long nose, so straight and fine, and then daringly at his broad mouth with the wide lips, and the big square chin. She reached up, she was only inches away, but such a distance! What daring it took to move that distance!

279

She reached out, one inch, another, another, and finally her lips were just a breath from his. He did not move. Her hand urged at his neck. He must come down just a bit! He must! Her hand moved again, pressed, pulled. And his lips were on hers. How delightful, how delicious, his strong mouth, with the soft clean breath of his mouth, the warm touch of his lips, the hard teeth . . .

Their lips clung for a time; both were hungry for this. She lifted off a moment, and then with shy desire she kissed him again. She nibbled at his lips, softly, and he let her, just holding still while she tasted him.

'I love you,' she whispered shyly.

He did not speak; he was gazing down at her. Her heart hurt with its painful beating, its hope reaching up, the longing in it.

She pressed her chest to him and felt the hard strength of his chest against her soft breasts. Was she pleasing to him? Did he at least admire her, if he did not love her? Would that be enough?

'I love you, Garth,' she said again.

'Why?' he asked hoarsely.

She thought of his goodness to her these months, this year and more. She thought of her gratitude for his kindness. She thought of all he had done for her, marrying her, nursing her, caring for that poor little one. But it was not just that.

'It is . . . everything, Garth. You and your goodness, and your kindness, and your strength. And you will fight for me,' she said. 'I do not want to live without you at my side.'

He let out a long relieved breath and gathered her up. 'Oh, Jade, I love you so much!' he said hoarsely, and stood up.

Surprised, happy, she lay in his strong arms as he carried her to the bedroom. He laid her gently on the bed, then stripped off his clothes. His eyes shone at her, his brown body was big and powerful in the dusk of the bedroom.

When he was completely naked, he sat down beside her on the bed. Gently he drew her to sit up and began to unfasten the buttons of her red dress. She helped him, her head lowered, and then he drew off the dress. He looked a little helplessly at all the clothes, and she laughed a little in sheer nervousness.

She took off the petticoat, and the pantalets, and the stockings, and threw them recklessly at the end of the bed. He drew back the heavy quilts and blankets, and she slid into bed.

'The fire,' she said breathlessly.

'Later,' said Garth. He always put down the fire at night, in the stove and in the fireplace. But tonight, it seems that must wait.

He lay under the covers with her, but he did not grab her and maul at her. His arms went around her, and he drew her to his shoulder and let the warmth of their bodies mingle. She felt so good, so content, so happy. Yet she wanted more, and her body was hungry with its urgent desires.

She stroked her palm softly on his chest, and he moved his hands down her back, slowly to her hips, then up again. They felt each other, learning each other, silently communicating their passion to each other. Heat was building up in Jade, and she curled closer to him and pressed her face to his neck. His strong hard neck, his strong shoulder, the hardness of his chest – all were so delightful to her.

How slow he was. He did not seem impatient, as Ewan had been. He did not pull at her or hurt her in his wildness. Garth was slow and sweet, kissing her all over her body, moving his lips from her mouth to her cheek, to her throat, to her breasts. He lingered long at her full breasts, and she remembered the sting of the milk in her when the baby had died.

She and Garth would make a baby between them, and the birth would be good, and they would love the child they had made, and he would grow up strong and fine. She promised that to herself, joyously.

Her hand stroked over his shoulder, down his back, and he moved onto her. She delighted in the width of his body over hers; he made her feel small and precious. He was so tall, so big, and he would protect her.

Slowly, slowly, Garth came to her . . . and gently, carefully entered her body. Passion was building up in her, and the heat made her burn with delicious ecstasy. Before he was finished and in her, she was moving her hips impatiently. She had wanted him for so long, had dreamed of him, longed for him. And he must have wanted her too, because his hands knew just where they wanted to go, and he caressed her with long stroking caresses.

She was wet and soft for him, and he was moving more and more swiftly. She cried out softly against his throat; the thrills were making her almost black out. She was so excited – and he was moving faster and faster – and his big body was so hard and masculine and possessive, and she wanted more and more . . .

'Oh – Garth!' she gasped against his throat. 'Oh, Garth – My love . . . darling . . . love . . .' and she said words in her native Tlingit, not able to think of English, though she knew it so well – the words of love, and husband, and adoring devotion . . .

He groaned, and his love burst in her, and filled them both with shaking passion and such ecstasy that they could not speak again; he was shivering with it, and so was she.

He fell over on the bed, drawing her against him, holding her still as his masculinity satisfied itself. And then they were quiet, drained, sinking back to reality again, which was a warm bed, a dark room, and their aloneness with love and each other.

Garth got up after a time and banked the fires, then returned to bed. Jade welcomed him back and warmed his chilled naked body with her warm hands and legs. She chuckled against his chest. 'I must warm you up,' she said complacently, and stroked her hands over his chest.

'Is that what you are doing?' he murmured, a chuckle in his voice. He warmed his hands on her body, and she half shrieked a protest at the coldness. He apologized swiftly. 'I'm sorry, Jade . . . I should not have done that . . .'

'No, no, I am only teasing. Warm your hands on me.'

But he would not, warming them in the blanket first, before drawing her to himself again. How considerate he is, she thought sleepily as she curled herself against him.

How good a man, how fortunate she was. Life looked very good to her now, after the sorrows and despair that had come before. Garth had restored her to life. He has saved her life in more than one way, she thought, not just the icy river and her baby's birth, but also her soul and mind. Her ability to laugh and love again. He gave her real life – the life of joy and peace and contentment.

Chapter 23

The Indians drew up their boat to the dock in Sitka, and one jumped ashore to take the rope and tie it up. Garth leaped out after him and helped tie it up.

Then Garth came back and carried Jade to shore. He set her down on the dock, and turned to catch their gear as another of the men tossed it out to him.

'I think there is a boardinghouse down the street,' said Garth. 'It was a good one, if I recall.'

'That is fine,' said Jade. She felt rather shy now in the strange city, with men staring curiously at her. She picked up one of the rolls of her clothes. Garth took two of the rolls and the Indian carried the rest, following them down the street.

At the boardinghouse, Garth signed them in at the register with a bold black handwriting: Mr. and Mrs. Garth Fleming. The woman stared at Jade again, curiously, as though she did not believe the words. Jade put her left hand on the desk, carefully turned so her hand showed the gold ring on it. The woman nodded and said, 'Room ten, upstairs on the second floor,' and gave Garth the key.

'Do you serve meals?' asked Garth.

'Yes, sir, five to seven, the dining room is through that door.'

'Fine, we'll be down about six.'

'I'll send up hot water,' she said.

'That would be kind of you,' he told her, and the Indians padded after them upstairs, taking their gear. He unlocked the door and they took their things inside. Garth paid them, and thanked him for the journey.

'Anytime, Mr. Fleming. You go back to Wrangell before the winter?'

'I don't know yet. I'll see you around the docks,' he said.

'Okay, Mr. Fleming.' And they went away.

Jade was curious, but she did not question her husband. Miriam never questioned Tom; he was the boss. That was the way Jade felt usually. Now she washed up, changed her muddy dress to a clean one of blue stripes, and was ready to go down to supper.

They both ate hungrily. The food was hot, good, and served quickly by an Indian girl. They had venison, baked potatoes, the first greens in a time, and ice cream. It was a feast.

Afterwards, in their nice white-washed room, Garth said, 'I think I'll go to the Koenig offices on the docks come morning. Want to come along?'

Jade nodded. She felt shy about meeting the Koenigs. They would know what Ewan had done to her, probably. Olaf Koenig had seemed like such a nice man, she wondered if he thought whatever Ewan did was all right, so long as it was to an Indian girl. Yet he had been courteous to her and to her mother when they had come hunting years ago.

She and Garth went to bed and slept hard. It felt good to Jade to sleep in the room after the days and nights on the boat. It had rained much of the time, and they had not slept on shore.

She felt dry and warm and cozy there in the room, with the fire crackling in the fireplace. And Garth sleeping next to her, with his warm solid body for her to cuddle against.

They both awakened early, washed, and dressed. They ate breakfast in the dining room – bacon and eggs, pancakes and maple syrup, coffee and fresh cream.

When people started moving on the streets, Jade and Garth put on their coats and went down to the docks. Garth had located the Koenig warehouse the night before as they went by.

The main office seemed to be in the big central building. Garth opened the door and Jade followed him inside. It was a huge room with clerks on their high stools working at their desks, and beyond, more doors into the back.

One clerk put down his pen and came forward. 'May I help you?'

'I'd like to see Thor Koenig,' said Garth. 'Tell him Mr. and Mrs. Garth Fleming have come from Wrangell.'

'Yes, sir. Have a seat there.' He indicated one of the benches near the door.

They had scarcely sat down when Thor erupted through the back door and came to them, beaming. 'Say there, this *is* a grand surprise!' he declared. Garth and he shook hands; Jade stood shyly waiting.

Thor turned to her and put his big hands on her shoulders. He bent and kissed her cheek lightly. 'Good to see you, Jade! My word, Laurel is going to go right out of her mind! Where are you staying; when did you arrive?'

'Last night . . . boardinghouse down the street,' said Garth, with a little grin at Thor's excitement.

'Well, we will gather up your gear and take it home. I'll get the carriage,' declared Thor.

'Oh, no, we're all settled at the boardinghouse,' Jade said nervously. Sitka was different. People were so fancily dressed, and women stared at her with their noses in the air. She was an Indian, after all.

Thor gave her a look, then turned to Garth. 'How long can you stay? Made any plans?'

Garth hesitated. 'It depends. We have a lot to discuss with you,' he said seriously.

Just then Olaf Koenig came from the back and approached them. The clerks were watching curiously from behind their desks.

'I heard you had come, Jade,' he said simply, and shook her hand. His eyes were curious and sad. He knows, she thought. He knows about me and the baby and Ewan.

Thor introduced Garth. 'My father, Garth, and this is Garth Fleming, Dad.'

The men shook hands and measured each other, Jade saw. And they seemed to like what they saw. 'Good to meet you. You're a lucky man, marrying a fine girl like Jade Nolan,' Olaf declared too emphatically.

Jade was flushed and warm.

'How are your folks, Jade?' asked Olaf.

'Just fine, sir. Father did lots of hunting last summer. He said to thank you, Mr. Koenig,' she said, turning to Thor. 'You sent many men to hunt with him. He had a very good summer.'

'I know the men appreciated his hunting ability,' said Thor. 'Now, how about it, let's get you moved to the house.'

'We would not wish to impose,' said Jade, primly.

Thor's blond eyebrows shot up. 'As I imposed on you two at the cabin?' he asked quietly. 'Nonsense. I'll be glad to have you, and Laurel will be over the moon.'

'We are not sure how long we will stay in Sitka,' said Garth.

'Look, Garth,' said Thor, 'if I don't bring you home, and Laurel learns about this, she'll give me a lot of trouble! I'll have to go out to the kennels and tell one of the dogs to move over!'

Olaf gave a big booming laugh. Garth began to smile slowly, starting with his dark brown eyes.

'Then we had best come,' said Garth. 'All right. We'll go back and pack up.'

'Good. I'll come with you, and we'll get you to the house,' declared Thor with satisfaction. 'Father, don't expect me back today. Tell them to wait on the orders for Bob Price. And tell Jim to hold off on the lumber orders. I'll have to figure out something on that.'

'Right you are, Thor,' Olaf said and went to the door to bid them goodbye. 'I'll expect a dinner invitation this week!' he called after them.

Thor got them organized and into the carriage. Garth paid their bill and they were on their way, Thor facing Jade and Garth, with their gear all piled in somehow. 'The bedrooms are all fixed up just in time,' said Thor. 'We moved in before the house was complete. Laurel decorated it, and in fact she planned the house!'

'That was fast work,' said Garth, gazing about with interest at the new houses and stores on the streets of Sitka. 'Say, this town is booming. I'll bet there are twice as many buildings as when I was here four years ago.'

'I wouldn't be surprised,' said Thor. 'We can't keep up with the housing. More newcomers keep pouring in. I'll be glad for the winter to come, to let us get caught up with the lumber. Our yards are empty.'

Jade and Garth exchanged a look. This is good news for Garth, thought Jade, with keen satisfaction.

As they came to the top of the hill, the horses strained to pull the carriage up the last steep ascent. Then the big house was in view, a huge house overlooking the sea. Jade stared, her hopes sinking.

Laurel and Thor lived in a mansion! She could not stay here. She would be out of place. She was Indian, she was not society, she was . . .

But there was the house, and the carriage had already pulled up. Thor jumped down. Jade whispered to Garth, 'It is too grand. Laurel will be changed . . .'

He squeezed her hand, shook his head, and got down to help her out. The door flew open, and Laurel came running down the steps, her face radiant. She called, 'Jade, Jade! You came, you came!' Her arms were out, and Jade forgot her doubts and ran to meet her. The two girls met, laughing, calling, then hugging each other.

A big red-faced man came to take the carriage. Indian boys lifted the gear out of the carriage, and Garth directed them.

'It is so big, your house,' Jade gasped as they entered the hallway.

'You'll get used to it,' said Laurel. 'I think I am, finally. Mrs. Dugan, this is my very dear friend, Jade Nolan – I mean, Mrs. Garth Fleming!' and she laughed at herself, her face shining with happiness.

The housekeeper ducked her head, wiping her hands on her apron. Jade nodded shyly and shook her hand.

'Pleased, I'm sure,' said Mrs. Dugan. 'Miss Laurel has talked of you often!'

Thor directed the luggage to be carried upstairs. 'I'll show you your room, Jade,' said Laurel. 'We just finished decorating it. I do hope you like it!'

Arm in arm the girls went upstairs. The men had already put down the gear and the Indian boys passed them on the stairs coming back.

Jade gasped again at the room. It was so huge, bigger than her whole cabin at the logging camp. Beautiful draperies and white lace curtains, precious deep rugs on the fine shining floors.

Laurel opened a door at the far side of the room, showed Jade the huge bathroom with the white shining porcelain fittings. It was so . . . so elaborate! Like a mansion, like a palace from one of Laurel's storybooks.

'Laurel planned the whole house,' said Thor, proudly.

'In just a couple months?' asked Garth, puzzled. 'That must have been fast building!'

287

'Oh, no,' and Thor shook his big blond head. 'I wrote to Laurel in Boston, when she was only a schoolgirl, and asked her to draw a house plan for me. She did, and this is the result! I had it almost ready when I married her. In fact, when she came to Sitka, I put her to work decorating it to keep her out of other mischief!'

Laurel was gazing at him soberly, a little frown between her eyebrows. Jade wondered. There was some other meaning between them. She would have a long talk with Laurel and make sure she was happy. That marriage had been very, very sudden! And Laurel did not seem all that comfortable with Thor.

On the alert Jade watched them carefully through the morning. The men talked; she and Laurel talked.

Stretched out in chairs in the fine drawing room, Jade felt ill at ease at first. But Laurel was her old self with Jade, bubbling with laughter, serious, then asking about the Nolans, then her words running over each other as she tried to tell all that had happened to her that summer.

At a pause in the conversation, Jade turned to her husband. 'Garth, should we tell Thor and Laurel . . . about Ewan?'

Thor started, Jade noticed. And Laurel looked puzzled. 'What about Ewan?' barked Thor. 'Has he been bothering you?'

Garth answered. 'Yes, he has. But I sorted him out. Then just recently, he came up to Jade on the street in Wrangell. Why don't you tell them what happened, Jade?'

'He was drunk,' said Jade, simply. 'He came up to me, and I was afraid of him. But he said that I should tell Laurel something. About her father's claim; he said it is ''good stuff.'' And he said Leverett's name, and that of Herman Ranke. ''Tell Laurel,'' he said. And that is it.'

'My father's claim?' repeated Laurel, and looked to her husband.

Thor was frowning heavily. 'And Ewan was in Wrangell?' he repeated incredulously. 'But Father sent him to the copper mine in the North! What in hell is he doing in Wrangell?'

Garth continued, 'I asked Tom Nolan to take me over there, to see if someone is working the claim. He refused. He said he had seen two men working there. They carried rifles, and one day when he came closer, one man fired at him. He has stayed away from there. They have been there more than one month, he said.'

Jade explained quickly, 'Father did not wish to be disobliging to my husband. However, he is afraid of the gold claims; they make death, he says. And the men did fire at him, and he went away quickly.'

'Damn it! And Ewan is involved. What did he say about Leverett?'

'That is all,' Jade told him.

'Well, Leverett can't be involved. He's here in Sitka. In fact he is coming to dinner on Saturday. He wants us to back him in politics.'

'Mr. Ranke has been gone for a time,' Laurel said quietly. 'Mike Dugan told me he went away on a boat several months ago, soon after his attack on me – I mean, I think it was him . . .'

'What do you mean his attack?' Jade asked in alarm.

'I was attacked by a man near the woods and brush you can see on the way up here. My new dog Czar attacked him . . . bloodied him. He finally ran off. Thor doesn't believe it was Herman Ranke . . .'

Jade was quick to note Laurel's defensive accusation. She looked at Thor. He was frowning again.

'Honey, you never saw the man. You can't accuse him like that,' said Thor. Laurel set her mouth, but did not argue with him.

Garth turned to Laurel. 'Did your father work the claim during the winter, or was it frozen up?'

'He worked it until late November, then quit when the weather got bad,' she explained. 'But often, he could work it all the winter. Whenever the snows let up, he would go again. If the ice was not too slippery, I went along and helped with the rocker. He enjoyed working outdoors, and he always got excited whenever he found a good nugget. And he said the gold would help give me a good education.'

She was silent then, evidently thinking of how her father had died. Jade would never forget the evening when Laurel had come back, her face chalk white, and told them her father had been murdered. And that walk in the snow and finding Jim Winfield lying across the cabin threshold, all bloodied and stiff.

She moved over to sit beside Laurel on the couch and take her hand in a silent sympathy. Laurel squeezed her hand convulsively and swallowed hard. Jade looked anxiously at Garth, silently begging him to change the conversation.

Thor said, 'Well, I'll have to go up there and see what's going on,' so casually it took Jade a minute to realize he could get into danger! Just as Garth could.

'I'll go along,' said Garth. 'If there are two of them claim jumping, you'll need help.'

'Thanks,' said Thor, nodding. 'If the winter stays open, I may go in a couple weeks. They'll be working the claim as long as they can.'

'Wonder why they started now?' Garth frowned. 'Didn't Jim Winfield die four years ago?'

'Three and a half years,' Laurel said quietly. Her fingers were almost crushing Jade's. Jade squeezed back in sympathy.

'Laurel came back,' said Thor. 'I wonder if they thought they had plenty of time with her gone?'

'Hmm. Then someone in Sitka may be the one who is doing the claim jumping,' said Garth.

'Not necessarily,' contributed Jade. 'She must have been seen in Wrangell when she came. And she came up to our lumber camp, then down to Wrangell again.'

'That's right.' Thor sat frowning down at his boots. Laurel was watching him intently, and her hand felt tense in Jade's. Jade wondered what she was thinking about.

Jade decided to change the subject herself, since the men did not. 'Garth had an idea, Thor,' she said brightly, then realized she was using his name in a familiar way. She flushed. 'I mean, Mr. Koenig,' she said.

'No, you must call me Thor,' and he smiled at her, his face softening wonderfully. He was a hard tough man. She liked it when he smiled because he didn't look so formidable.

'Well, Thor . . . Garth and I – I mean, Garth thinks – he is interested – ' Then she floundered, glancing at her husband. Maybe he didn't want to bring up the subject now.

'What Jade wants me to talk about,' said Garth, with his slight grin at her, 'is lumbering. I'm thinking about leaving the company and starting my own. I wondered if you might have ideas about where to go, what forestry claim to file, or if there is land for purchase. I have some money saved to buy horses, wagons, and so on.'

Thor brightened up, leaned forward eagerly. 'I say, is that what you want to do? That's great! The Koenig company can use a lot more prime lumber, especially spruce and pine. We're trying to supply firms building houses and stores in Sitka, and in the North. And we ran out early in the summer, had to buy at high prices, and import some from San Francisco. What had you been thinking – what capacity?'

'I thought of starting with half a dozen good lumbermen; several of the men offered to come with me. I'd like to do prime lumber. I like working with spruce. There is some land near Wrangell, but I thought I might move further up the coast. However, there is a problem of transport, have to get some ships.'

'We would supply ships,' Thor said promptly. His green eyes were snapping. 'Got a map?'

Garth pulled the map from his pocket. It was never far from him.

'Wait a minute, I'll get a map from the study,' and Thor went next door and returned unfolding a large sheet of paper.

Thor spread out his map on the coffee table, and Garth put his next to it. 'That's a good one,' said Thor, with keen interest. 'You must have more information than I do, especially here,' and he indicated the points.

The men studied the maps. 'I know there is spruce along here, but I don't know if it is claimed,' said Garth.

'I don't think so. I've seen it going up north to our copper mines. And nobody ever seems to be working it. Good timber, tall stuff, looks like virgin forest. And there is a lot of pine around here, just north – through the Tongass Forest. Our ships go up weekly, taking supplies and bringing copper out. We could pick up whatever you have.'

Jade and Laurel exchanged happy looks as the men discussed the prospects eagerly. They evidently liked each other, wanted to work together. That would mean the girls could get together more often!

'Could you get a house in Sitka?' whispered Laurel.

'Maybe we might,' Jade returned.

Garth heard them, looked up, and gave Jade a wink. He looked happy and eager, not the same somber silent man she had met two years ago in Wrangell that unhappy winter. Had she helped put that happy look on his face? She hoped so. He seemed contented now, with her.

'Well, let's talk to Dad about this,' concluded Thor, folding his map. 'He'll have ideas about the land. And we will want a contract with your company for all the prime timber you can give us. And . . . there's a steady market for the poorer wood too – for firewood. And the carpenters will want some for shacks; the quick ones for the newcomers to Alaska. Should be able to take all you can drag out of the forests.'

'That sounds good to me,' Garth said with satisfaction. 'Know a good lawyer? I'll talk it over with one –'

'Not Leverett,' Laurel said quickly. 'I don't trust him!'

'Now, Laurel.' Thor rebuked her mildly. 'Don't prejudice them against Leverett just because you don't like him.'

Laurel looked stubborn, her lip out as it rarely was. Jade could remember half a dozen times that Laurel looked like that, and it usually meant Laurel was fighting mad inside.

Garth asked, 'Why don't you like him? I feel a woman has ideas about men, and is often right. She has a feeling, not from what he does, but from what he is inside.'

That was unexpected, coming from Garth. Jade watched him as Laurel answered.

'I can't explain. I just do not like him, Garth. He smiles and is pleasant, but all the while he does, he puts in little jabs and says things that make trouble for people. I think he enjoys making trouble.'

Garth nodded. Thor looked like he would protest, then he shut up. Mrs. Dugan had come to the door.

'Miss Laurel, would you like to come to lunch now? I've got it about ready.'

'Oh, Mrs. Dugan. I was going to help set the table,' and Laurel jumped up, looking young and confused.

'Never you mind. Natasha fixed it all up pretty,' Mrs. Dugan said.

Jade got the idea that Mrs. Dugan liked Laurel immensely and would do anything for her, and that was good. She herself would have been scared to death to have a housekeeper!

They went to the table. Jade was seated at Thor's right, and Garth at Laurel's right. They were rather far apart at the ends of a long table.

Jade would have felt confused and unsure of herself, but Thor turned to her and asked her about the summer, her life there, and her family. Soon she was chatting away about Mrs. Simpson and the boardinghouse, her mother and the berries, her father and the hunting.

'What do you think of Garth's idea, of the lumbering? Would you want to live here in Sitka while he goes out?' Thor asked her pleasantly.

'Oh, no! I go with my husband,' Jade said positively.

Garth looked over at her, his eyes dark and unsmiling, but glowing. 'Yes, you come with me,' he said.

'But I thought you might live in Sitka,' said Laurel. 'Oh, Jade, you will be far away again.'

'We would come back when the autumn winds begin and the ice forms,' said Garth. 'I think we will build a house in Sitka this winter and have a home to come back to, eh, Jade?'

She drew a deep, happy breath, and nodded. Even a cabin would be grand, just so they would be near Laurel!

'We will be rich, a family with three houses,' Garth said solemnly, but with a twitch at the corner of his mouth. 'We have a cabin in Wrangell, near to Jade's parents. We will have a cabin at the lumber camp and a house in Sitka. What wealth!'

Jade laughed out loud. 'Oh, Garth, will we really? How mother will laugh!'

'But of course you will want to go visit your parents, Jade!' said Laurel. 'I'll come with you sometime!'

'With me,' said Thor.

She wrinkled her nose at him.

Jade watched to see how they were with each other. That gesture had looked quite natural. But Laurel had always liked to do whatever she liked, and her father had not bothered to check her, so long as she was safe. She must chafe at being held in by a husband, Jade thought.

'We must see my dog Czar,' Laurel said to Jade. 'Let's go for a walk after lunch. You'll like him!'

'Not far,' Thor said sternly. 'In fact I'll go with you girls; so will Garth. We'll look at places around here, Garth. I bought fifty acres. If you like some location, I'll sell you a piece of my land. Then you could build next door; that should please Laurel!'

Thor had spoken quickly, as though to head off any protests from

Laurel. Did he not allow her even to go walking alone? Perhaps not, if she had been attacked.

They went around to the kennels, and Jade admired the dogs extravagantly. Most were guard dogs, not trail dogs. 'They're used to guard the property,' Thor said casually. Jade wondered in awe at their wealth. She remembered the silver centerpiece at the table, filled with red roses. And the fine silverware, knives and forks and spoons, and the serving bowls. And the fine china with gold rims, and so thin you could see through them – no pewter mugs for them.

And Laurel was wearing a silk dress with gold jewelry, a beautiful rich rose silk with gold lines in it. Over it, she wore a light fur wrap of mink skins. Jade had helped trap mink. And they brought high prices. The wrap was a short one, to Laurel's waist, but she wore it so casually. Jade abruptly felt her own position; she wore a cotton dress she had made herself and had wrapped a woolen shawl around her shoulders.

An Indian boy at the kennels brought out a fine gray dog and Laurel fell to her knees to hug him and brush up his fine hair around his throat and muzzle. He muttered to her in a low caressing growl, and she said love words to him. 'Oh, you fine dog, my fine Czar, you lovely thing. Did you want to come for a run?'

Thor watched her indulgently, and they all went off for a walk with Czar. Laurel ran ahead, teasing the dog, clicking her fingers at him, and he raced along, bounding ahead of her, then turning back to wait, panting, his mouth open as though laughing.

Jade ran with them lightly, keeping up with Laurel, laughing with her. But once, she caught Thor's words, 'Laurel is too reckless; she would walk anywhere, in spite of being attacked, twice. Her first dog was killed defending her.'

Jade raced on and caught up with Laurel, still pondering the words. Why would anyone attack Laurel? Just because she was a woman, or because she wore jewelry – or why? And someone had killed Rex! She would ask Laurel about that. Her friend was not completely happy, and Jade meant to find out why.

Chapter 24

In the next several days Laurel and Jade had opportunities for good long talks and walks together. Czar always accompanied them on those walks. He permitted Jade to pet him, but Laurel was his mistress, and he was devoted to her. He would walk close to her, so close his fur brushed her skirts, and when ignored too long, he would poke his muzzle into her loosely swinging hand, until she turned and petted him and talked to him.

The dog's devotion was comforting to Laurel. She felt puzzled and confused these days. Thor's filing on her gold claim had shocked and stunned her. And his defense of the man she detested, Addison Leverett, dumbfounded her. Could Thor not see that the man was crooked? And he was mean as well. She thought even Clarissa Leverett was afraid of her father. She had cringed once when he snapped at her, and had fawned over him the rest of the evening. Laurel had been sure there was fear in those small blue eyes of the beautiful woman.

It was good to be able to talk to Jade. Jade questioned her gently, thought over the answers. Jade had matured with her experiences and her marriage. She was much more sensible and practical, and not so scatterbrained and giggly.

They discussed who the two men might be who were working the claim. 'One might be Ewan Koenig,' said Jade. 'I am afraid he is doing something he should not. And Thor said he was supposed to be up north, supervising the copper mine.'

'Yes, he and his father discussed it. Olaf . . . Father . . . is most distressed, and speaks of going after him and bringing him back. Thor said he would do that, maybe soon.'

'Well, if they go, they may run into trouble,' sighed Jade. 'My father is worried about that, especially after the rifle was fired at him. He says also that your father's cabin is being used by someone. There are signs someone lives there.'

Laurel turned and stared at her. 'My father's cabin – Jade, are you sure?'

'Yes, of course! My father said so!' Jade was puzzled by Laurel's excitement. 'Why not? You have no need of it.'

'No, no, I'm not angry about it. Anyone may use the cabin, as long as there is need; that's the rule in the wilderness. But . . . Mr. Leverett told me he was over that way and found the cabin very run down, almost falling down. I forget his words, but he meant it was no good anymore!'

'Leverett said that? But it is a lie!' cried Jade. 'Why would he lie about that?'

'I don't know,' Laurel said slowly. Czar poked his nose into her palm as she stood there, and she bent to hug him and ruffle up his thick fur, running her hands through the gray fur. 'But maybe to keep me from going over there. Maybe to keep me from renting it to hunters. To keep me away. So I would think there's nothing to go back for.'

'Laurel, are you sure you do not simply distrust everything Leverett says? Did you misunderstand his words?'

'No, Jade,' said Laurel.

'Umm.' Jade looked into the distance, to the sea, and the slowly moving blue-gray waves of the dark October day. It would be November soon, and the ice would be formed on the lakes and streams further inland toward the mountains. 'If Thor and Garth do not go soon, they may be snowed out.'

'Yes, there is ice on the creeks now.'

Both girls strolled on, thinking. Thor and Garth were so busy with the lumber projects, planning the future work. And Laurel thought that Garth was planning to build a cabin for himself and Jade for the winter. She hoped it would be close by, but Garth was reserved about that.

'I want to go along when the men go,' Laurel said suddenly. She had been thinking about it for days. 'I want to go with them. I want to see the claim for myself. I think there was lots of gold there. Dad found a thick seam. I told people there was little to throw them off, and keep the men away. They would pile all over the creek if they thought there was lots of gold.'

'Yes, Father was relieved that no gold prospectors filed nearby.'

'But I have the nugget necklace,' murmured Laurel. 'You know how large the nuggets are.'

'Yes, and there must be more.'

Laurel and Jade became silent again, as they used to do when thinking along the same lines.

'Yes, we must go and see for ourselves. I am sure Thor would not cheat you, Laurel, however –'

'He filed on the claim in his name, Jade! As I told you, he said my father could not file, and I was too young, so he did. But why – Why didn't he tell me what he had done? Why wait, until I found out accidentally from Mr. Leverett? Would he have ever told me?'

'Surely he would,' Jade looked distressed, and caught Laurel's hand to comfort her. 'Surely he would. He has been very busy all the summer and autumn.'

'Too busy to tell me in a few sentences, that he had filed on my claim, on my land, and would work it when he had time? No, I cannot understand that,' Laurel said bitterly. 'It was my land, and he took it. My land . . . my Alaska and . . . I had so hoped –' She stopped abruptly.

'But now you own it together. He is your husband, you are his wife.'

'A wife owns nothing; you know that, Jade!'

Jade sighed and nodded. 'Yes, but my husband is generous –'

'And so is mine! He gives and gives to me, and wants only to know that I am pleased. But nothing is *mine!*'

Jade was frowning. Laurel thought she did not understand. Then her friend of years said quietly, 'Yes, that is true. Men own everything. They keep the money, and they say how it is to be spent. If they are generous, the woman is fortunate. That is the way of the world. The woman must obey her man.'

'I don't like that,' and Laurel tossed her head restlessly. 'Father left me to myself much of the time. And I am used to doing what I wish! It was difficult, in Boston, to follow the commands of my uncle. If he had had his way, I would have worked for low wages in his store and married the man he chose! So I came up here – only to have Thor tell me what to do, and that I must marry him!'

'Are you not happy, then?' Jade asked very gently.

Laurel brushed back her hair; the stray strands had blown loose in the wind. 'Yes – at times,' she admitted slowly; 'He is good, and I love him. I think he loves me. But when I think I could have been independent with the gold of my claim . . . I could have worked as a teacher . . . But Thor took me over and told me I must marry him. When I do what he wishes, he is pleased with me. When I go off, for a long walk with Czar – *only* that – he is displeased and scolds me like a child!'

'But you were attacked. He worries about you.'

'Yes. Yes. I know that,' said Laurel, impatiently. 'But why, why did he file on my claim?'

'It always goes back to that. I think men feel women are incapable of doing such a thing,' said Jade, wisely. 'Maybe he did feel he was keeping it for you.'

'He said . . . if I had not come back to Alaska, it would not belong to me . . . because Alaska belongs to the Alaskans. I think he would have kept it and said nothing!' Her bitterness spilled over in her furious words.

'And now two men are working the claim. Well, I wish we could go with the men and see for ourselves what is happening,' said Jade. 'You would feel better then, to know someone is trying to rob you and that your husband will protect you and the property.'

Laurel stopped and turned to face Jade, to look in the deep dark eyes of her friend. 'Jade . . . what if . . . what if Ewan Koenig is over there, working the claim . . . for his brother Thor? What if Thor sent him, without telling me?'

Jade stared at her, and put her hand to her mouth. She gasped in horror. Laurel flushed; she felt so awful putting the words into speech. But she had to say it, she had to. The thought had been haunting her for weeks.

'Why would he do that?'

'Why did he file on my claim?' Laurel asked fiercely. Then she shook her dark head despairingly. 'I don't know. I don't know. Sometimes I hate myself for doubting Thor. He has been so good to me. But I felt he had to marry me . . .'

'That is what you said because you were alone so long, and people gossiped. But Laurel, if he had not wanted to marry you, I think he would not have done so,' said Jade, nodding. 'He could have found you a job in San Francisco, or sent you back to Boston. He knew you had done no wrong. There would be no baby, no need for gossip. But he married you, and he seems happy with you. He praises you for the house and your paintings, and all.'

Laurel was silent. As they walked on, she turned it all over in her mind. She felt better for having said this to Jade. Jade would keep it to herself. Unless she told Garth . . .

'Jade, don't tell Garth!' she said swiftly. 'Please – do not tell your husband! I am so ashamed of my thoughts; I had to speak to see how empty they were.'

Jade slipped her arm about Laurel's waist. 'I will tell no one, not even my husband,' she promised. 'It is like the old days, I will not tell even my parents! You know we kept each other's secrets, you know it, Laurel. I will not tell.'

'Thank you. I am ashamed, yet the fears and worries puzzle me and haunt me nights. I tell myself, Thor is too honorable to do this. Yet . . . he did file . . . and now Ewan is over there. He may be working the claim . . . for Thor.'

'Let us go over there and see,' said Jade.

'We will have to ask the men to let us go along.'

'We can say that I wish to see my parents and that you wish to visit them also. After all, my mother was your mother.'

'Yes, and I long to see her. Yes, yes, let us say we long to visit your parents, so we must go along.'

Satisfied, the girls returned to the mansion on the hill, Czar bounding ahead of them, turning to wait, then impatiently bounding on again, delighted with the winter wind, the leaves that tantalized his nose as he pawed the thickets, the freedom of running after long hours in the kennels.

Laurel had been planning the dinner for Saturday evening. Leverett had wanted to talk politics again with Thor, and Thor was too busy during the week. Thor told Laurel he had a feeling Leverett was going to announce for some political office, perhaps a representative or even the governorship.

'He's a very ambitious man, and of course he has presence, knows many important men.'

Laurel could not like the man, but she agreed to plan the dinner. What worried her more was the matter of Jade's clothing. She had seen her friend's wardrobe, and while the gowns were attractive and neatly made, there was nothing but wool and cotton. She should have a silk gown. Thor had sternly forbidden Laurel to offer her one.

'Her husband has the right to provide. It would humiliate him, and I won't have that.'

'You are right, but I would so like to give Jade a gown, or a length of silk, to have Madame Bonheur make it up. She would look so sweet, and . . . and Sidonie and the others could not snub her!'

Thor had looked briefly like a Viking prince about to do some despoiling. 'There will be no snubbing of Jade and Garth in my home!' he said fiercely.

That evening Thor and Garth returned home early, and brought some packages into the house where Jade and Laurel were talking in the parlor.

Each laid a paper parcel before his wife. And Thor gave Laurel a large significant wink. Laurel tore open her parcel, delighted to find two lengths of silk.

'Oh – I'll bet a ship has come in, Thor! How lovely, how beautiful!' And she slipped her fingers into the lengths of silk, one of white with a blue forget-me-not pattern, and one of a delicate, green floating pattern that looked like the northern lights. 'These look like Alaska. How could it be done!'

Thor smiled. 'I had a friend describe this for me to some people in San Francisco, and they were made up in Paris. It took long enough to get here, I must say!'

Laurel jumped up and hugged him spontaneously. 'You are the best man in the world,' she cried. 'I love the material! I must have Madame Bonheur make them up at once!'

Then she went over to see the contents of Jade's parcel. Garth was beaming. He must have bought it, thought Laurel in relief.

One pattern was of white with a jade green design of leaves, delicately worked in embroidery on the white silk. The other was of rose silk with a network of delicate silver embroidery.

Jade was speechless, caressing the silk with her pretty fingers and looking at Garth with her heart in her eyes. 'I never saw such beautiful fabric,' Laurel said sincerely. 'Oh, let us make up the green ones in identical modes, for us to look like sisters!' That pleased Jade, and the men as well.

Madame Bonheur set to work on them the very next day, and they chose gown designs of tight bodice, neat waist, and full skirts to the tips of their toes. The neckline was of a heart shape, the sleeves full at the shoulders narrowing to the elbow, and tight at the wrists. Floating from the shoulders were lengths of the same fabric, in the effect of a soft scarf waving down their backs.

When Saturday evening came, the gowns were finished, and Laurel and Jade wore their matching dresses. With hers, Jade wore her green jade raven on a thong, and a gold bracelet from Garth. Laurel chose her gold nugget necklace, and the barbaric splendor of it complemented the delicate shimmering green of the northern lights to make a picture of Alaska for her.

The girls came down together, to see the proud lights in the eyes of their husbands. Garth was speechless. Thor lifted his glass of sherry to them and said, 'To the two loveliest girls in all of Alaska!'

Laurel was so proud of her best friend. Jade looked like a fine lady, which she was, but also according to the lights of Sitka society. Her hair was brushed into the same bouffant style as Laurel's, and the deep glossy black set off her lovely high-cheekboned face, the beautiful black eyes. And her gown shone in the candlelight, with all the lights of the sky when the northern lights glimmered.

Jade and Garth stood with Thor and Laurel to receive the guests. Sidonie looked a bit tight lipped, but said not one ungracious word. Clarissa drifted about for a time, until all the guests had arrived. Then she came over to Thor, clung to his arm, asked him questions, and made Laurel furious. Jade noticed also, and so did Olaf, disapprovingly.

Did Clarissa Leverett really think she could get Thor back again? Her father beamed on them, cigar in his mouth, his narrowed small blue eyes enigmatic.

Defiantly Laurel seated Garth at her right hand, and Jade at Thor's right hand, signifying they were the honored guests. She placed Leverett with Sidonie, and Olaf with Clarissa. The others were scattered about, a full dozen at the table.

The table was set with candles, as most of the flowers were gone. Laurel had chosen a deep red tablecloth, covered with a sheer lace one of white. In the center was the silver epergne, with only its own swans for centerpiece. At either end of the table was a branch of silver candlesticks with red candles in them.

Jade spoke only when she was spoken to, but her soft voice was calm, and she smiled often. Garth was rather quiet also, but he knew the lumbering business, Sitka, Wrangell, hunting, so he made a hit with the men.

After dinner they adjourned to the drawing room and the parlor. Leverett presently stood and tapped a cigar cutter to his sherry glass.

'May I have your attention, ladies and gentlemen?'

Laurel turned from speaking to Sidonie, in surprise. She watched as Leverett expansively made his speech. Thor was standing nearby, his hands in his pockets, his face impassive. Laurel could not tell if he knew what Leverett was going to say.

'In response to many inquiries from my friends and neighbors, I have decided to enter politics! Some have been kind enough to suggest that I should express my willingness to become governor of Alaska,' he said, and beamed at them all. He seemed all smiles, and geniality tonight.

But Laurel could not help remembering the times when he had seemed more like a cruel monster, whispering nasty things. And she remembered when they had first met, how indifferent he was when Thor and Ewan were both gravely injured. With a friend like that, one did not need an enemy.

Somehow Clarissa had managed to make her way to Thor's side. She put both arms in one of his and cuddled to him.

'I am sure that Thor will support my daddy,' she said coyly, her lashes fluttering at him. 'They have been close friends for simply years!'

Everyone clapped, except Jade and Laurel. Laurel simply could not. The men clustered about Leverett, asking about his politics, his attitude toward different state and national matters, the territorial issues.

'I plan to leave this week for Anchorage and Fairbanks,' he

announced. 'It is not too soon to begin my campaign, to become more acquainted with the problems of the North as well as the Alaska panhandle. My lovely daughter will remain here, and I hope Mrs. Koenig will keep an eye on her in my absence.'

Laurel thought he meant Sidonie, and looked at her mother-in-law. Sidonie looked blank, and then Laurel realized Leverett was staring right at her. She could say nothing; she was so stunned at his effrontery. He meant that *Thor* would keep an eye on Clarissa!

'Of course, we will be happy to do so,' said Thor for Laurel, giving Laurel a cold look. She glared back at him. 'We plan to get together this week . . . shall we say on Monday?' he said to Leverett. 'If you wish to set out soon for the North . . .'

'Yes, yes, a week today at the latest. If we could meet on Monday . . .'

'Why don't you come to the house Monday evening, say about eight o'clock?'

'Fine, splendid,' and Leverett pulled at his waistcoat and patted his stomach in a satisfied manner.

Clarissa still clung to Thor. For goodness sake, couldn't he push her away? Annoyed, Laurel went to the kitchen, spoke to Patsy Dugan about more coffee, then returned to the drawing room. And still Clarissa clung!

The guests finally left at eleven. Laurel was in a mood to hurt! They relaxed in chairs for a final talk before retiring. Jade and Laurel sat on the sofa together, Garth and Thor had taken the large armchairs in front of the fire.

Laurel said deliberately, 'When you and Garth go to Wrangell, Thor, Jade and I would like to come with you and visit with her parents.'

Thor, looking weary, began to speak in annoyance. 'This is no trip for you girls, Laurel! It is already winter, there have been snows, and it may rain heavily. No, you stay here in comfort –'

'I wish to see my parents,' Jade said gravely. 'I do not mind the weather. It is all one. I am used to it, and so is Laurel.'

Garth scratched his chin reflectively. 'Well, as for me, I would rather take Jade with me. I don't wish us to be parted for weeks on end.'

Thor gave a gusty sigh. 'In that case, I will not be able to refuse Laurel! Are you sure you want to face wind and rain, open seas and seasickness?'

'I never get seasick,' said Laurel, her voice clipped. 'And I should like immensely to visit with Miriam and Tom. They have been my parents, you know.'

Thor was not pleased with her, she could see that. But after an evening of Leverett and daughter, Inc., she was *fed up*, as Hazel would have said with her usual vigor, though her father deplored the slang.

However, when Garth added mildly, 'And I believe we can find a comfortable boat in which to take the girls,' Thor had to agree.

'We'll take the family ship, the *North Star*. That has two bedrooms and ample space. We can go to Wrangell in that.'

So it was set. Thor had reluctantly approved the journey, and Laurel and Jade were to go with them. They briefly discussed when they would leave, and Thor frowned over his schedule.

'I can probably manage to go in about two weeks,' Thor said finally. 'How about you, Garth?'

'Anytime is all right with me; my time is yours,' said Garth, pleasantly. 'Jade and I will look at house sites and do some planning. That's all I have in mind.'

When Laurel went up to bed, she looked out the window at the stars. She felt dissatisfied with herself and how nasty she felt inside. She was scared, afraid to trust Thor, and hating herself for that. Why couldn't she relax and trust him?

She looked out, and then remembered . . . Leverett had been in a carriage tonight, with an Indian coachman. Where had Herman Ranke been? Come to think of it, she had not seen Ranke in town for weeks. In truth it had been more like two months since she had seen him lounging at the swinging door of the saloon. She had noticed him and flinched from his lowering look at her. She wondered now if he had gone away. She hoped so. She would feel more free to walk with only Czar.

She undressed and slipped into bed. Thor came up presently. She pretended to be asleep, and he walked around noiselessly, to slip into bed after her.

Thor kept sighing. He turned over and punched his pillow and lay down again. She could not pretend any longer.

'Thor, can't you sleep?'

He turned to her at once. 'No, maybe too much coffee and sherry.' He sighed. 'It was a splendid occasion, however, and you are a fine hostess, Laurel.'

'Thank you. Mrs. Dugan does everything, you know!'

'Oh, of course, and talks to everyone, and pays compliments, and listens as though fascinated, and knows all about Alaska and the best sites for fishing!' he teased her, and she loved it.

She laughed softly.

'Thank you for letting Jade and me come along,' she said impulsively.

'I didn't know I had a choice,' he said drily, but put his arm about her. 'I feel as Garth does. I don't want to leave you for weeks! But you *will* stay put in Wrangell with the Nolans, you know that. I'm not having you shot at!'

'I would rather not be shot at,' she replied demurely, and he laughed and drew her close to him. His regular breathing soon told her he had gone to sleep. And she too finally drifted off, in spite of the worries that plagued her.

Chapter 25

On Monday evening Addison Leverett's carriage rolled up promptly at eight o'clock. Thor went out to greet him and show him inside. Laurel smiled, shook his hand, said all the proper things. Yet Thor knew that Laurel detested and feared the man. It showed in her dark brown eyes, in her shrinking from the touch of his hand. It showed all too well in her betraying face.

Thor quickly took the man to his study behind the drawing room, and they settled down with port and cigars.

'I'll come to the point,' said Leverett, after some polite nothings. 'I want to go into politics. The governorship will enable me to do some things for Alaska. Things you want done, and your father wants done.'

'I'm interested in your career,' Thor said carefully. He looked at the glowing tip of his cigar. 'I don't have time for politics, yet Father and I feel we need to have friends at the highest level. We have been in Alaska for years, since 1896. We feel kin to Alaska and we want the best of it – and for Alaskans.'

'Of course. I feel the same way. I came up in the Gold Rush of '98, and have been here since. Made my fortune, and now I want to give something back to Alaska, in the way of service.'

His small eyes were close together. Otherwise he was a handsome man, with graying blond hair, a fine figure, always dressed suavely in black or gray suits and white ruffled shirts. The image of Herman Ranke came to Thor – dirty, smelly, crouched over. Why were those two so close? They had been together as long as anyone could remember.

Perhaps Herman Ranke had saved Leverett's life; maybe Leverett felt he owed him something. Otherwise it was very strange and unaccountable. The men were complete opposites.

Leverett had gone on speaking.

'Our ideas about the future of Alaska are similar. We don't want the Federal Government interfering with our plans. We want Alaska kept open and free, not bound with their regulations. We want hunting and fishing open, lumbering open, mining open. And we don't want people from the States to come up here and rape the land and leave!'

'That's correct,' said Thor. 'My ideas exactly. Alaska for Alaskans. We pioneered the land, it is ours. Yet Washington seems to feel it can run us as it pleases, even when the officials know nothing about the land and have never been up here.'

Leverett was pleased with Thor's words. His face shone as he took another sip of the ruby red port. 'Good, good. You know, you could help me write my speeches, Koenig! We think along the same lines, and *you* have the gift of eloquence!'

Thor could not help feeling flattered at Leverett's praise. He was an older man, experienced, and would be powerful someday. Even Olaf had said it might be well to get in with Leverett from the ground floor on.

'I plan to go north at the end of the week, as I told you,' Leverett continued. 'I want to visit Anchorage and Fairbanks, some other cities, as long as the snows make traveling by dog sled feasible. If it storms,' – he laughed, shook his head – 'well, I'll hole up! I'm an old hand at that. Can you imagine some nosy official from the States trying to cope with our weather?'

They both laughed, comfortably.

They discussed various issues. Thor found he agreed with Leverett on most of them. Where they disagreed, Leverett was eager to listen to Thor's arguments.

'Well, well, I think you have something there,' Leverett would say. 'I'll check further, I appreciate your views.'

They finally got around to talking money. Thor expected to help pay for the campaign; it was the usual practice now. A contribution, generously made, could ensure the 'friendship' of the politician, and Thor could expect to have contracts sent his way and his views respected.

'I'm not asking many men to contribute to my campaign,' said

307

Leverett. 'Frankly, I don't want to be obligated to a crowd. There are a few of us old-timers, old Alaska hands, who should be running Alaska. I mean to keep the club exclusive, you see what I mean?'

'I believe so,' Thor said drily. 'Father and I will want to contribute, of course; that is, if we decided between us that you are the best candidate for the position.'

He had practically made up his mind to do so. If he didn't like the man – well, that was politics. You didn't have to like someone to work with him.

'I'll need about fifty thousand dollars from each of you, you and your father, Koenig,' Leverett said. 'I plan to do a lot of traveling, and I may have to grease some palms, you can understand that. What do you think?'

Thor had lowered his eyes to study his empty port glass. He was in shock. Fifty thousand from him and his father – a total of one hundred thousand dollars! That would wipe out all their savings in one blow. It might mean he could not finance Garth Fleming this year. Not until another year, when he could build up again. Could he put off Garth? He didn't want to. He liked the man, believed in him. Garth Fleming was a hard worker, a quiet man with sound ideas. And he was married to Jade. They owed much to Jade, the Koenig family. Owed her a big debt, though she would never say so.

Leverett saw his hesitation and leaned back in the chair, grinning. 'A big amount, huh Koenig? But I'm making big plans. There are minerals in this state, not just gold and silver . . . but copper! And you already have a hand in that. And there's other stuff up north, more gold, probably. Whoever throws in with me will be in pretty, because we're going to have the minerals for ourselves. No allowing others to come in and take it out, huh?'

Behind the words, Thor read the message clearly. If Thor did not turn over a large sum of money to Leverett, he would not be in with the politicians of Alaska and he would not get the mining concessions he and his father wanted and had counted on. They might even be cleverly forced out of the copper mine in the north, and have to fight for the gold and silver they had.

They could not expand and grow, and Thor wanted that. He wanted to build an empire, a Koenig empire, for himself and his sons.

'You want to discuss it with your father?' For the first time, Leverett sounded patronizing, as though Thor had not any authority of his own, but must run to papa.

Thor fought to remain cool. 'Yes, of course, I must do that,' and he managed to sound calm and slightly surprised. 'Father and I run the firm together. And of course I have no authority to commit his funds. I'll have to speak to him.'

'Why don't you do that tomorrow?' Leverett was beginning to exert the pressure, to sound like the politician. 'Then we could meet on Wednesday and discuss it again. I must leave by the end of the week, and I want your commitment and half the money by that time.'

Thor was silent. No way was he going to turn over twenty-five thousand dollars of his own, and a like sum of his father's, in one week. He had other uses for the money. And he had only just begun his investigation of Leverett, and so far, he did not like what had been dug up.

'I cannot promise that, Leverett,' he said politely. 'There are other issues . . .' He let his voice trail off.

Leverett must know that Thor had talked to two other men about the governorship. Not that Thor liked them any better, but they were rivals, and possible governors.

'Well, well, think it over, talk it over. You know, Thor,' and he leaned forward confidentially and lowered his voice to speak secretly, 'you could be a governor one day! You've got the makings of a statesman, I don't mind telling you! When you are a few years older, more mature, with more experience under your belt, you might take this very job I'm going to have! With my grooming and influence, you would be at the top!'

'It is immensely flattering to have a future governor say this,' Thor said quietly. And to have Leverett call him by his first name, talk confidentially to him. Yet he did have those lingering doubts.

He could not really like the man, and Laurel detested and distrusted him. He remembered what Garth Fleming had said about how women had feelings about people, deeper than what men did, and could see through to their natures. Garth had implied that Laurel saw straight and clearly, and Thor thought maybe she did.

His own deep feelings for Laurel blurred his vision at times. He saw her as a beautiful girl-woman, his wife, her beauty and sweetness drawing him to passion. He loved her, and he was coming to adore her. Yet she was very young; how was her judgment?

'I would want not just your financial backing,' continued Leverett. 'I would want your public support, dinners given for me, speeches around the States when you go down there, especially in New York City and in Washington and San Francisco. You could do me a lot of good. And do good for yourself, become better known, draw men to you, get your name known. That's a lot of power, Thor Koenig! And you could have it. I only wish –'

'Wish what?' asked Thor.

'Wish you had married my daughter Clarissa,' Leverett said earnestly, putting his hand on Thor's knee as they sat facing each other. The man was gazing into Thor's eyes, his hand hot on Thor's silk-clad knee. 'Thor, you made a bad mistake marrying a green girl with no training. She won't be the hostess you will need in your career. You should divorce her, discreetly, pay her to go away. You married her because of some silly gossip, that was a poor move!'

Fury tore in Thor, but was concealed. He wanted to know how far the man would go. To hide his feelings and his disgust, he got up and moved away, pacing the room, from windows to fireplace and back again.

'My wife is learning well,' he said with reserve, his face turned to the fire. 'Sidonie is teaching her. She speaks well for Alaska!'

'Koenig, she talks like a native, and she makes friends of the Indians!' Leverett dared to say sharply. 'That won't do; it won't do at all! Whites won't like it, and let's face it, whites run this place! There's a lot of talk already. No, get rid of the girl, and marry my Clarissa! She will do you proud, Thor. She's well trained, went to a special school in Boston –'

'Which one?' asked Thor, as though idly making conversation.

Leverett hesitated, then shrugged. 'Sacred Heart Convent, a Catholic school, but good training. They taught my girl well, I can tell you! She has served me as hostess for every important man in the United States, and several from Europe! She can talk some French and German, she can listen prettily to any man . . . and let me tell you, she does what I tell her! She toes the line! A valuable trait in a wife, huh?' And he laughed.

Thor was stiff, remembering the times he had seen fear flare in Clarissa's eyes, fear of her father. It had puzzled him, but now he realized. Leverett ruled her, controlled her, and to him she was but a weapon in his fight for the top position in Alaska.

And Thor had gone to Sacred Heart Convent, there had been no one enrolled for the past twenty years by the name of Clarissa Leverett. Was Leverett lying, or had another name been used? What was Leverett's real name; had he changed it?

Too many questions and too many problems. He did not like Leverett, and now he distrusted him. Thousands of dollars *demanded*, not requested. Promises hinted at, of copper mines and gold mines, if he went along – and ruthless dismissal if he did not. Maybe this was the political method, but Thor could not persuade himself that it was.

'Shall we say Wednesday?' Leverett was smiling, standing. He had thrown out his promises and his threats, and Thor was not a stupid man. 'Let us say . . . the French restaurant, at one o'clock? I'll ask Clarissa to be hostess for us, and you will see how well she does it! Get rid of that Indian-loving wife of yours, Thor. She can only hold you back!'

Thor was boiling inside now. But he hid it. Politely he opened the study door, and they came out. Laurel had disappeared; she probably had gone up to bed, it was past eleven. He was glad of it. Leverett might have made some remark, said some insult, and Thor would have knocked him out.

No, he must play this hand coolly and carefully. Too much was at stake.

He showed the man out to his carriage. The Indian driver helped him up, sprang up to the driver's seat.

'Well, see you on Wednesday.' Leverett smiled and waved his freshly lit cigar as he rolled down the driveway to the road. He sounded complacent, sure of himself. He had Thor Koenig in the palm of his hand, he thought. Thor stood, hands in his pockets, watching the carriage roll away. His thoughts were somber and confused.

He stood there for a time, disregarding the chill wind. He gazed out at the silent ocean, the waves swelling and bursting on the pale creamy sands and the white foam splashing up. The stars shone whitely in the purple sky; it was a glorious night.

Finally he moved on around the side of the house, out to the stables. Mike Dugan came out.

'Did the Flemings come back, Mike?'

'Yes, sir, that they did. About nine o'clock.'

'Thanks, all right then.'

'Good night, sir.'

'Good night, Mike.'

Thor went back to the house and inside. He blew out the lamps in the front rooms and went upstairs. Mike would check around one last time, then turn loose two Indian boys with the guard dogs to patrol the area. One of the penalties of being wealthy was that thieves prowled. Another was that politicians figured you were a natural source of their income.

He didn't know what to think, and that irritated him. He usually felt very sure of himself and knew which way to go. He and his father had talked about Leverett, decided he had a chance of becoming governor, and discussed contributing to his campaign. But Leverett had just about talked blackmail. 'Contribute, and give the amount I ask or else.'

Thor prowled up the stairs and silently entered his bedroom. The guest room was still. The lamp still burned in his bedroom, and Laurel was sitting up in bed, a book in her hands. She set it aside on the bedside table on her side of the bed, the one near the window. How she loved to gaze out at the sea and the mountains.

She gazed at him expectantly. He took off his black silk jacket and put it on the back of a chair to air out from the thick tobacco odor.

'What did you decide, Thor?' Her voice was low and tense.

'I haven't decided yet,' he said carefully. 'I have to talk it over with Dad.'

'But you may back him, that crook, that sneak?'

'Come on, Laurel!' His own doubts made his tone the more sharp. 'Most politicians are somewhat crooked. That does not make them less effective! They know how to make deals work out, they know whom to approach. And favors breed favors.'

She stared at him. 'And you, Thor . . . you would work that way?'

312

His mouth tightened. He disliked it, but he felt he had to go along with the system. If you wanted the copper mines, the permits to operate, the claims, you had to know the right people. He gave fair work for fair pay, fair wages for fair return, he was honest with men. That was as far as he could go, and much further than some.

The trouble was, he did not know whether Leverett worked on these principles. There was fair dealing and paying out; and there was blackmail and under-the-table payoff. He had a bad feeling in his stomach that the latter was Leverett's mode of operation.

'Laurel, stay out of this,' he said brusquely. 'You don't understand men's dealings. And I don't want you involved with this.' He meant, it could be dangerous.

Laurel took it badly; she stiffened right up, and her brown eyes flashed in shock and anger. 'Thor! How can you say you don't want me to understand? Don't treat me like a child! Don't tell me to close my mind!'

Her voice rose. He frowned. 'Hush, Laurel. I don't want to rouse the whole house! Go to sleep.'

He pulled off his trousers and hung them up. He finished undressing, pulled on his nightshirt, and went to the bathroom. When he returned, the light was out, and Laurel lay rigidly on the far side of the bed.

He slid into bed, sighed. In his temper he had handled this badly. 'Come on, honey, don't be upset. There are just some things you should not get involved in. Come on, Laurel, please try to understand –'

'No, Thor, you don't want me to understand,' she said tightly. 'I'll close my mind, and let you manage everything! Only, don't expect intelligent conversation from me at your table with your guests! Just wind me up and make me sing a tune!'

It was so funny he had to laugh. He lay back, still chuckling, and Laurel flounced over in bed and lay with her back to him, stiffly. She did not laugh, and Thor realized she was furiously angry.

He reached over and pulled her to him. 'Now, don't act like this! I don't mean to insult you, so don't take it like that! Of course you're smart and sweet, and you're a marvelous hostess!' He thought of Leverett's cruel remarks and burned once again. His arms tightened protectively around Laurel. Divorce Laurel and

313

marry Clarissa because she was a better hostess and did whatever Leverett ordered! Like hell!

Laurel struggled in his arms and kicked him. 'Let me go! I don't want you to hold me!'

At the opposition he held her the more tightly, and she scratched his chest and kicked out the more viciously. 'Ouch! Quit that! You little hellion, stop that!'

'You let me go! I don't want to sleep with you!'

Her voice rose again. Embarrassed, because the guests in the room across the hall would hear if they were awake, he pulled her around and put his mouth on hers forcefully. This would shut her up!

She bit at his lips, and he kissed her the harder and held her more tightly to him. He was much stronger than she was, much taller and bigger.

As he held her and she struggled against his body, desire rose up sharply in him – and would not be denied. He wanted her, and she was his wife, by God!

He pulled up her nightdress, and his big hand moved over her smooth round thigh.

'No!' said Laurel, outraged. 'How can you – Thor, don't do that – Don't! I'll be mad at you . . .'

'You'll get over it,' he muttered against her throat. 'God, I want you, Laurel. Lie still!'

He rolled over on her and forced her to lie under him. He wanted her passionately; his instrument was hard and taut, and his heart was thumping wildly. He held her roughly, and she cried out.

'Don't – Don't do that!'

He pressed his mouth again on hers. He held her under him, and came between her thighs. He was mindless, wanting, his masculine urges making him deaf and blind. He did not think of her needs, only of his own. He moved on her smooth slim body, felt the soft silkiness of her, muffled her cries with his urgent lips, forced his tongue into her mouth. Oh, God, she was sweet and smooth and fragrant . . .

He moved his hand urgently on her thighs, until the warm wetness came and she lay quiet for him. He did not want to hurt her, but he had to have her – now! – now she was ready. Passion was blazing high in him, making him urgent and hard.

He thrust into her, slowly, forcing himself to move gently. She was small, slim, sweet. She lay still, and he did all the moving, back and forth, faster and faster, until the ecstasy burst in him, and he cried out, muffled, against her throat. He shook in rigid excited release, and then lay still.

He gasped for breath and rolled back over. She lay quietly beside him, her head turned away. She had not enjoyed it, he knew that, but he could not do anything about it. He was limp and exhausted.

He remembered thinking, Laurel did not enjoy it; she was not with me tonight . . . another time . . . another time . . . I will make sure she enjoys it . . . But he fell asleep before the thought was fully formed.

Chapter 26

Laurel was so hurt and so angry with Thor she could scarcely bear to speak to him. And it made her the more furious that he was too busy to notice!

The two couples had breakfast together on Tuesday morning, and Jade and Garth spoke of their plans. Garth had found some old friends in town, several prospectors and lumbermen, and he and Jade had a luncheon engagement with a man and his wife. They were also looking at house sites and studying plans for a house or cabin to build in Sitka.

Thor kissed Laurel briefly on the forehead and went off in the carriage. Jade and Garth soon followed in the carriage that Thor had loaned them. Laurel went upstairs to her study, and worked furiously on painting. She had to think about something else or go mad!

Thor treating her like a child. Telling her she would not understand. Telling her she did not know men. Telling her to stay out – to stay out of his life! And then his taking her like that, like an object, like a wooden doll with no feelings! That had been the final blow. She was outraged. And this morning he had acted just as usual. This would be their life. Outrage at night, indifferent during the day.

Laurel knew that when she was more calm she would see that she had exaggerated the situation. Thor was usually kind and considerate, and he would be again, when the work slowed down. But last night had dumfounded her, infuriated her.

Thor knew she despised and distrusted Leverett, yet he would not listen to her. She knew it was wrong – and dangerous – to get involved with Leverett. One would get tarred with the same black pitch, as Uncle Arnold would say.

She had been thinking about her Boston relatives recently. They were so decent, so good, so honest and honorable. They worked hard, they owed no man anything, they were generous, and they had treated her like their own daughter. She had written to them several times since her return to Alaska, and they had responded, all four of them, with generous, loving eager words. Was she well, was she happy, did she wish to return? She would be most welcome.

Laurel had written following her marriage to Thor. They had replied recently, in an overflow of loving messages and several thoughtful gifts. White Irish linens from Boston shops, a short broom of special make that she had always liked, a box of fine kitchen pans for baking and stewing, and two recipe books. All practical, thoughtful, and showing much loving care for her.

Delia had written a long letter of advice to a new housewife, evidently thinking Laurel would be doing her own housework. Laurel had laughed and cried over that letter, thinking of Delia and how good she was to her. Delia was expecting a child – she mentioned it carefully in prim words – but one could tell she was joyous over the occasion. Dear Delia. Laurel hoped she was happy with staid Norman Cooper.

Should Laurel have remained in Boston?

Her brush paused in a stroke; she remained staring in space, then shook her head. No, Alaska was her land, her homeland, her strength, her joy. And Thor was all bound up in Alaska in her mind – his Viking strength, his outdoor quality, his wild moods and courage, his booming laugh so like his father's, and like the boom when a blue-white ice chunk broke off from its glacier and splashed into the sea.

How could she *not* come back to Alaska? No, she had had to return. This was her habitat, as much as it was the habitat of the seals, the wolves, the moose, the otters, and all the creatures of the wild. Like her own husky dog, Czar, one could not imagine him anywhere else but in Alaska.

She sighed deeply, and dipped the brush in blue. She was painting the portrait of Thor's mother, Brianna. She had died when Thor was sixteen, but she lived in his memory. Laurel wanted this portrait to be extra special.

The portrait was coming well. Brianna was shown seated in an armchair, as in one photograph in black and white. She wore a blue silk gown with a white lace bertha. Her eyes were as blue as the blue silk, and her mouth was a sweet curve of a half smile. She had strength, that woman; it showed in the directness of her gaze, in the hands, work-worn and rough, folded in her lap. It showed also in the chin, firm and uplifted, in the broad forehead under the folds of the blond waves of hair.

Strength and sweetness. A wife and mother, an intelligent woman, who loved working at her husband's side. A patient woman too, thought Laurel, from Thor's stories of her. What had it cost her, that patience? With three big men in her life, her husband and two sons, wanting their own ways.

Laurel did not go down for luncheon. Patsy Dugan sent up a tray, a roast beef sandwich, a dish of canned peaches, a pot of Russian tea. She ate and drank and went on with her painting. By dusk she had much of the dress completed, and the hands. The face was outlined, and she would be ready to continue when she had time. She knew now how she wanted the painting to be. And then she would start the matching portrait of Thor's father as a young man, the same time period as Brianna's picture. It would make a fine matching pair of paintings, Laurel hoped.

She washed off the paint and put her brushes to soak. Then she went downstairs, swung on her red cloak, and went out to the kennels. Czar was brought out, and he rumbled his pleasure at seeing her and the prospect of a run. He curled his big body around and around her legs, rubbing against her, begging for a hug and a good rub of his thick fur.

Laurel hugged him, told him how good he was, and then ran off down the gravel walk. Mike Dugan followed them at a more sedate pace. He must have his orders, she thought.

She and Czar raced across the lawn in the front of the house, back and forth. He was too dignified a dog for stick throwing and retrieving. He was not a plaything, but a working guard dog, the descendant of man's companion and friend in the wilderness. And the descendant of wolves, which had roamed the Arctic lands for many centuries.

Then finally she went inside, and Czar was returned to the kennels. She had no freedom with Mike trailing them always on the lookout to protect her. Not that he wasn't a good man and a decent man. He was. But she could never be alone, by herself, with only her dog.

Laurel worked herself into fresh anger over that. Her life had changed completely since Thor had taken it over. She felt a prisoner in her own land. His wealth and lack of trust were making her feel inside a cage.

Someone had sent word that the Flemings would not be back until nine or ten o'clock; they were dining out. Then Thor sent word from the office that he was 'tied up.' Laurel wondered if he was tied up with Leverett; she suspected so.

She ate a lonely dinner in the parlor, with another tray of food. This time Patsy insisted on a veal steak, baked potato, canned peas, salad, and a dish of canned strawberries for dessert. Laurel sat over her pot of tea until Jade and Garth returned. They talked a little time, but Jade was weary, and she and Garth soon went up to bed, his arm protectively around her.

Laurel felt more alone and resentful than ever. Thor had not returned by ten o'clock. She went up to bed.

In the morning she found that he had slept in one of the other bedrooms, so as not to disturb her. At breakfast she was very cold and chilly to him, and it finally penetrated. He frowned at her, as though saying it was her fault somehow.

'What are your plans for the day?' Thor asked.

'I have a fitting by Madame Bonheur this morning,' she said.

'Well, have Mike Dugan drive you. I'll speak to him.'

Thor then turned to Garth and asked, 'Any luck on the house site?'

Garth smiled slowly. 'I think so, Thor. There's a fine site about five miles outside Sitka, on a spit of land reaching out to sea. Jade and I like it immensely, and it isn't owned. The next cabins are owned by some prospectors; you know one, I believe, Hank Mullenberg. He made a little pile, and retired; does some wood cutting now. I'm interested in hiring him to run an office here in Sitka, while I'm out at site.'

'Hank Mullenberg? Say, that's fine. He is a good fellow. Known him for years.' Thor seemed to be thinking something deep. 'I'd like to talk to him too, about another matter. Would you ask him to drop by the office this morning if you see him? Or tomorrow morning, either one is fine.'

'Sure, I'll do that. We're going to see him again today. He has a carpenter friend, a good worker; we may have him build our cabin.'

They discussed briefly a site for an office and lumber yard, if Garth decided to go on his own. Thor wanted him to join with him, but was not insisting; it was all to be settled later, evidently. Laurel was silent; she was stunned by the fact that Jade would be five miles away. She had wanted her next door!

Had Thor made them feel they would not really be welcome nearby? Garth had said something last evening about the wealthy neighborhood she and Thor lived in, and he had not been jesting.

By the time they had all departed and left, Laurel felt thoroughly depressed. Maybe Thor had, for once in his life, she thought bitchily, made a mistake. He had married her, and she was the wrong wife for him.

Mike brought the carriage around; then Laurel went out and he helped her in, with a glance at her grave face.

'Now, Miss Laurel, 'tis a fine day to be sure!'

She glanced about. The skies were dark in the west – it was sure to rain or snow later – and the sea boiled with the winds. Gusts of sharp cold air struck her face.

'It is? I hadn't noticed!' she said tartly.

He grinned his big Irish grin. 'Now, Miss Laurel, you ain't been looking rightly! See the mountains and how grand they are with all their snowcaps. And the trees, so tall and fine, nothing puny like in Boston, belike! Ain't you glad you're here in the grandest land ever, in Alaska?'

There was anxiety as well as humor in his honest red face. Laurel smiled and nodded. 'Yes, I am glad, Mike Dugan. Very glad, as I hope that ye are as well, begorra!'

They both laughed aloud, in a welcome gust of laughter, and Laurel felt the lighter of heart for it. She looked about as Mike drove her down into Sitka, at the bare trees, stark against the purple-gray sky, their limbs twisted and torn by the winds. There were the evergreens, dark green now, almost black, some bent double by their struggle to survive in spite of winds and snow and driving rain. The flowers were gone, the gardens in tatters. Now Alaska showed starkly its own courage to survive in the Arctic air, the bare bones of its land ripped from the flesh of summer beauty.

Yet Laurel loved it still. In all its grim courage, it showed the beauty of an aging man or woman, cheekbones shining in taut skin, hair gray and thin, eyes fading but still glowing with the joy of a life lived with courage. A walk that's a little stiff, limping from old injuries, slowed to a painful pace, but still moving on.

'My Alaska,' she whispered, and looked out to the rolling seas, the gusting waves of whitecaps, the bleakness of the beaches. She would look, and love, and paint it one day, not just in summer brightness, but in winter's grim struggle for survival. She could picture how she wanted that scene, the sea, a lone boat and a fisherman, head bent against the driving rain storm, the high waves almost swamping the boat, but he was persevering.

Mike stopped the carriage in front of Madame Bonheur's, and Laurel stepped out with his aid. She went into the dressmaker's salon with relief. She liked the lively Frenchwoman, and they had much to talk about, as well as have dresses fitted.

Madame Bonheur was bustling about, beaming, with more lengths of material spread on her worktable. 'Come, come, Mrs. Koenig, I have a surprise for you!'

Laurel looked from her face to the table, and could have wept. More lengths of material, silks, faille, and brocade, in glowing colors.

She knew even before Madame said, 'Your good husband, he stopped in yesterday afternoon with two clerks. They have such glorious materials for me! And he said that you must have the first choices, and that I may have the rest for my most valued clients! What a pleasure, and how good he is!'

Laurel had to smile and express joy, when her heart was like lead. How he bribed her, how he dressed her like a favorite doll! Only, she must keep her mouth closed, and not presume to have opinions!

'And I have so many dresses already, Madame,' she said ruefully.

'Can a lady have too many gowns?' laughed Madame Bonheur, her skillful hands clasped before her. 'Now, come look with me, Madame! I thought this rose, embroidered silk with the silver spiderwork lace . . . and the blue silk like the summer skies with the little white threads of flowers . . . and the fine black silk with gold dragonflies . . .'

Laurel lifted the black silk in her fingers; it was soft as a fluffy cloud. 'You know who this looks like? My mother-in-law, Sidonie Koenig,' she said thoughtfully. Madame Bonheur could not repress a grimace. 'Yes, she goes to another dressmaker, but Madame, if she knew of this fabric, she would not be able to stay away from your door!'

They looked at each other, and both smiled. Madame Bonheur gave a brisk nod. 'Yes, yes, I will send her a note. She must look at it. If she wishes another lady to make it up for her, *eh bien* . . . it shall be done. But I would make it up for her, if she so wishes.'

'Good.' Laurel looked through the other fabrics. 'You know what I really need is a good day dress to paint in! I shall ruin my other dresses; the aprons are not thick enough.'

'Oh, I have the solution for you!' Madame Bonheur lifted down a length of light blue broadcloth. 'This gown of blue and some aprons of sturdy cotton to cover your dress completely – eh, how about that?'

'Perfect.' They measured, and talked, and looked at patterns until it grew one o'clock.

Madame Bonheur invited Laurel to lunch with her. 'There is a new French restaurant, not two blocks from me. It is called the Red Mill, and the food is not bad. Will you come?'

Laurel did not want to return home to another lonely luncheon on a tray, nor did she want to lunch alone in a restaurant. Besides, Madame Bonheur was good company with her lively chatter and gossip.

They strolled over to the Red Mill. The restaurant was crowded, many wanted to try out the new place. Mrs. Laurel Koenig was bowed in, however, and with Madame Bonheur they were shown to a table at the side, in a discreet corner away from the louder gentlemen in the middle.

Laurel sat down, and looked about curiously. The decor was noisy – bright red plush, bright golden lamps, brass rails on the bar at the other side of the room. But there was a lively Gold Rush quality about it that made it a cheerful and timely place. It did not look like the Red Mill in France, but it suited the brisk Sitka atmosphere.

'One hopes the food is decent,' sighed Madame Bonheur. 'Let

me see . . . trout, salmon, shrimp, crab, prime rib of beef, and venison – Madame?'

Laurel had let out a gasp of shock. She had seen Thor at the other side of the room; he was half turned away from her. And beside him was Clarissa Leverett, facing Laurel, but leaning to Thor, her face smiling, her eyes flashing. They were sitting comfortably, wine glasses half filled before them.

As Laurel watched, her eyes wide in disbelief, Thor flung back his head and let out a boom of laughter, his big hearty laugh. And Clarissa was laughing too, softly, her hand on his arm.

It was like a blow, that laugh, and Laurel flinched. She could not believe it, Thor there alone with Clarissa Leverett! Having luncheon and drinks with her!

It confirmed all her fears. Clarissa was fond of Thor, and Thor liked her immensely. Perhaps it went deeper. Did he love her? Did he regret marrying Laurel?

Laurel was very sensitive to the fact that Thor had been forced by gossip into marrying her. Before their marriage, she had been sure that Thor was practically engaged to Clarissa; they were seen everywhere together. And Leverett had been promoting it, and had wanted Thor to back him, financially and personally.

Did Thor regret marrying Laurel? Did he wish he had married Clarissa? Laurel knew then the agony of rejection. What if Thor had come to despise her?. He called her a child, he told her to grow up, he told her not to try to understand his business! But Clarissa was mature, Clarissa understood, Clarissa was very grown up!

Madame Bonheur's mouth was set in disapproval, and her black eyes flashed. Laurel turned slowly back to her. 'Madame, would you like the crab?' the older woman suggested.

'Yes . . . fine,' Laurel said dully.

Madame chatted about clothes, the decor of the room, foods of France, snails, lace – Laurel did not hear a word. From time to time Madame Bonheur darted a frosty look at Thor and Clarissa, and gave a tiny shake of her head. How could they? And in public! An unmarried woman dining with a married man!

Then Madame relaxed. 'Ah, here comes Mr. Leverett, the papa!' she said in great relief. 'He must have been delayed. No, no, he would not permit his daughter to dine alone in public . . '

Laurel glanced over there also. It was quite half an hour that she and Madame Bonheur had been there, and Thor had been halfway through his luncheon when they arrived, which meant that he and Clarissa must have been alone for an hour or more. Mr. Leverett had done this deliberately, she thought, let the world see the closeness of Thor and his daughter. Thor was standing to greet him; they shook hands in very friendly fashion, and Mr. Leverett clapped Thor on the shoulder. People were staring at them curiously, and a few near to Laurel, knowing her, glanced sympathetically at her.

Laurel scarcely saw them, she was suffering so. Was Thor seeing Clarissa in private as well as in public? Was he sorry he had married Laurel? Even worse, did he plan to discard her, and marry the woman of his choice, Clarissa? So much more suitable a wife, and a hostess! So politically wise, so well trained, so well educated . . .

What if Thor had married Laurel only out of pity and compassion, and now regretted it? The gossip had been wicked, he had been furious and had married her in haste. Marry in haste, repent in leisure, that was usually for women, but it could be for men too. And Laurel had been so cold to him, and she was so unskilled in lovemaking. Thor must long for a more experienced woman like Clarissa – had he made love completely to Clarissa, did he know what it was like to lie with her in his arms, in bed, did Thor long for an expert mistress such as Clarissa might be?

Beads of sweat stood out on Laurel's forehead by the time the long meal was over. She had had no wine – she could not drink any for fear she would be sick and dizzy, more dizzy than she was already.

Madame Bonheur rose from the table. Laurel stood also, and followed the older woman from the room. She glanced once at Thor; he did not turn around – he had not seen her. But Clarissa and her father had, and they sent curious looks at Laurel.

Laurel was furiously jealous, and curiously forlorn. She had been angry with Thor over the gold claim, over Leverett, over so many other matters. But at the thought of losing him, of being discarded, she felt sick.

And it was then that she knew how deeply she loved him. She could not imagine life without him. Life without Thor – without his holding her in bed, without his protection, heavy and dogmatic though it was . . . She could not endure it. She would be only half alive after that. If he left her – if he threw her away –

Mike came with the carriage; she did not know how. Madame Bonheur must have sent for him. He drove her home in silence, respecting her white face and shocked eyes. He helped her down from the carriage, then into the house.

Patsy Dugan came to the front hall. Mike growled, 'Get her upstairs and some hot tea into her, woman! 'Tis shocked she is, and one can see it plain. Cold and bitter the day.'

'Aye, that it is, Mike. Come along with you, Miss Laurel!' And Patsy helped her up the stairs to the bedroom. She took off Laurel's shoes, and helped her lie down, and put a blanket over her, the pretty quilt the church women had made for her.

Laurel's fingers went aimlessly over the quilt pattern, the square of the Russian blockhouse, the one of seals, the one of wolves, the one of mountains, glaciers, forget-me-nots . . . How the ladies had worked, and stitched with such skill and care.

Jade came in about mid-afternoon, tiptoeing into the bedroom, her face concerned, and red from the wind. 'Laurel, darling? How are you? Mrs. Dugan said you got chilled.'

Laurel nodded, and lifted her heavy head. Jade exclaimed over her, and came to sit beside her on the bed, her eyes anxious, her hand on Laurel's.

'What happened? Are you still cold?' Her hands fondled Laurel's and rubbed at them briskly.

At first Laurel could not tell her. But Jade just held her hands and rubbed them, and encouraged her with soft words. The door was shut.

'Where is –'

'Garth is talking to Mike Dugan, out at the stables.'

'I had luncheon with Madame Bonheur at the new place, the Red Mill,' Laurel began dully. 'Thor was there – he didn't see us come in . . . he was sitting with Clarissa Leverett.'

'Waiting for her father, I'll be bound,' Jade said quickly, her black eyes worried.

'Well, Leverett came in another half an hour. But Jade . . . Thor and Clarissa, they talked and laughed, and she put her hands on him – all the time – oh God, Jade . . .'

'That Leverett fellow is always hanging around Thor. What does he want?' asked Jade.

'Politics. He wants Thor to back him, financially and with speeches, Thor said. But Thor told me to keep out of it; he said I didn't understand,' Laurel said bitterly. 'Called me a child when I said he should not go in with Leverett. Said I didn't understand politics. Oh, Jade, he despises me.'

'Leverett?'

'No, Thor!'

'Now, Laurel, you're overwrought. Thor is crazy about you! He cannot keep his hands off you!' Jade said vigorously.

'Oh, that way, yes! But not – not me, Jade. He does not love me, or what I am inside.'

Jade was silent, distressed.

Laurel added in a low tone, 'Remember when you told me Garth had married you because he was sorry for you?'

Jade's head tossed, and her dark hair shone in the dim lamplight. 'But he loves me now!'

'Yes. But I think Thor married me because he was sorry for me. The gossip about us was bad when we came back from your place; we had been alone together for a long time – in the cabin and all – and there was talk. And he married me fast because people whispered.'

'But he did marry you, and he loves you,' Jade reassured her.

'He was going all the time with Clarissa. Sidonie, my mother-in-law, she said he and Clarissa were practically engaged. They were alike, she said. And Clarissa is a fine hostess. She knows how to dress, she knows everything . . . about politics, and mining . . .'

Laurel looked at Jade anxiously, wanting her friend to repudiate that and vigorously defend Laurel's ability. Instead Jade was silent, her face troubled. Laurel felt she was sinking into a deep dark pit in which she would drown. Her fears were being confirmed by her own dearest and closest friend. She was not suitable as a wife for Thor.

'What I cannot see,' said Jade, in a very low voice, 'is why Thor hangs about that slimy piece Leverett. We know how he was, when Thor and Ewan were mauled by that bear. We know how he and Clarissa were about to take off without them, saying it was no good to stay, they were dying? Remember?'

Laurel nodded, remembering. She and Jade had been fourteen, so young, so green, so carefree. 'Thor says that Leverett might become the next governor of Alaska, if he can get appointed. And if he is, he and Olaf will benefit, because Leverett will throw business their way – contracts and such – and help them with mining claims.'

'I'd rather starve than be beholden to a creep like Leverett!' declared Jade. She sounded like her old self, young and sure of herself, and jaunty.

'Me too. But rich men don't feel like that, Jade. They get money, and want more, and more. And Thor is talking of expanding, and hiring more men, and opening more mines, and getting Garth to haul timber for more houses, and building a village on the mainland – Jade, it scares me how much he wants.'

'Yes. Even Garth,' murmured Jade, distressed at her own disloyalty. 'I was so happy at the lumber camp. And Laurel, I want only his good. But will he be any more happy with more work to do, more men under him, more worries, and more money? I don't think I will!'

The two girls looked at each other, and Laurel squeezed Jade's hand. 'I guess men are like that and women just have to go along,' she sighed. 'But oh how I wish I knew the truth about the gold claim. It's horrible not to trust Thor! And then seeing him with Leverett and Clarissa . . . and wondering and being sick at heart – Jade, I can't take it for long!'

Chapter 27

Thor got up to prowl the large office he shared with his father at the warehouse.

'It sticks in my craw,' he said bluntly. 'I don't like it at all. It's practically blackmail.'

Olaf Koenig leaned back in his large armchair, his big hands folded on the thick ends of the arms. He watched Thor prowling about; his green eyes were troubled, his Viking face strained.

'You saw him off this morning?'

'Yes. Leverett was at the wharf about eight o'clock. He had his own ship. I made a point to go over and tell him we wouldn't have the money for him for a time.'

'Did he yowl?'

Thor's mouth curved reluctantly, in spite of his fury. 'Just about. Said we had better come up with it. I told him we had no plan to cripple our operations by giving him all the loose money we had in hand. In order to raise that sum, we would have to sell off properties.'

'And what did he say?'

'He had the nerve to tell me to sign over the properties to him, and he would handle them!'

'By God, he has such gall!'

Olaf pounded his fist on the huge spruce desk before him.

'Yes. He does. Question is, will he get the appointment? He knows plenty of powerful men. But if this is the way he begins, he will continue in this way. He'll bleed us dry, Father. And he'll ask for more money every time we want to file a claim, set up another business, expand in any direction. He means to make the governorship his personal step to being a millionaire.'

328

'And that's not the kind of man we want as governor of Alaska,' said Olaf. 'He isn't trustworthy; he's a man of no background; what we know of his achievements is little. I don't trust him, Thor.'

'That's what Laurel says,' Thor said impatiently. 'But she has no reason either. It's just what she feels; and she's furious with me for dealing with Leverett at all. It drives her wild when I speak of him as governor of Alaska. She seems to think he can't be trusted to care for Alaska, and she loves the land.'

'Yes. And Laurel is a smart woman, Thor. You should listen to her,' declared Olaf.

Thor swung on his father in surprise. 'What? She's only a child, only eighteen!'

'A child in years, but those years have been more full of experiences than the usual girl, Thor, my lad! Take that into account. Her mother's early death, all their travels, and her father was an unusually learned man. He may have chosen to live away from mankind, but he knew people. He was a sensitive artist, and as such could often see into the souls of mankind – and see much more than we ordinary mortals,' and Olaf gave his booming laugh. 'Aye, I'd have made him an adviser in the warehouse, if he had lived. Just to look at people and tell me what he thought!'

Thor was frowning in thought. 'And Laurel's just like him, an artist, and very shrewd about people too,' he sighed. 'I guess I was mistaken – and too quick of temper.'

Olaf looked at his son. 'Have you been fighting with the girl?' he asked. 'Thought I felt some troubles between you. You treat her good, Thor; you have a rare jewel there.'

'I know, I know. But she is immature . . . and quarrels with me.'

Olaf grinned. 'Courageous girl! You make three of her! Come on, now, Thor, admit it. She's a fine woman.'

'She's a little wildcat,' Thor grumbled, but he had to smile. She was courageous . . . to fight him, to glare at him, even when he roared. But she was so damn cold these days. He could shake her! He didn't have time now to give attention to her, but later this winter they would spend time together – and he would get her shaped up!

Thor thought of her warmth in bed, the way she curled up against him on a cold night, her passion when he stirred her, her little kitten-cries when she was moved to ecstasy. She was just beginning to learn her own potential in love-giving. And one day she would satisfy him herself completely. He looked forward to the lessons he would give her.

'Well, about Leverett,' Olaf said briskly. He leaned back again in the chair, and it creaked under his weight. 'Let's add up what we know. He came to Alaska in the Gold Rush of '98, so he says. But we didn't know him then.'

'Right. He surfaced in Sitka about 1900, with wealth and a beautiful daughter in school in Boston. He brought Clarissa up here, set up a big mansion, made her his hostess.'

'Clarissa. And she's not registered by that name in any Boston school.'

'Right. I checked. He said the name of the school, finally. I sent word south right away to my agent in Boston. He should get the letter in about two weeks, go over to the school, and paw their records. He has a contact there, one of the nuns.'

'Umm. You know, Sidonie said something the other night. Surprised me a bit. But Sidonie is sharp.'

'Yes. What did she say?'

'Said that now she knows Clarissa better, she thinks the woman is scared to death all the time now. Shakes, looks petrified of her father. I wonder what's happened.'

'I've been thinking that also. Whenever Clarissa is with Leverett, she keeps looking at him, as though hoping she's not putting her foot into it. She didn't used to be so unsure. Now she does seem – yes, Sidonie is right – petrified. Her hand was shaking –' Thor frowned, thinking of that luncheon in the Red Mill.

He had had an appointment to talk politics with Leverett. Unusual for him, the man was very late. Clarissa had appeared, apologized for her father, and had luncheon and wine with Thor. They had talked and talked, and Thor had been about to give up and return to the office, when Leverett arrived, full of apologies, and sat down with them. They had waited while he ate, and then there wasn't much time for talk. In fact they had talked little of politics at all. Leverett had seemed pleased that Thor and Clarissa had been alone for a time – in a public restaurant – with people staring at them. And Clarissa had been nervous, her voice high, her

330

hand shaking. She had clutched at his arm again and again.

'Sidonie says she scarcely knows Clarissa for the same girl. Odd. She now says she's glad you married Laurel. Says Laurel has a great deal of common sense, and some presence. I think your little girl has handled my wife very well!'

Olaf watched Thor with bright green eyes.

'Handled Sidonie? What do you mean?'

'Didn't think you really noticed, Thor,' Olaf said with satisfaction. 'Sidonie can be a bitch. Yes, she's my wife, but I had gotten pretty angry with her; she was riding a high horse. Fancied herself the Queen of Sitka society, I think. We quarreled some, about this and that, and she was spending money like water. Well . . . no matter. But Laurel asked her advice and took it. Sidonie took to carrying flowers over there, fixing up the table, loaning Laurel etiquette books –' Olaf broke off into a chuckle.

'But that's Sidonie being gracious,' said Thor, cautiously. 'What has it to do with Laurel? She doesn't handle Sidonie.'

'Open your eyes, Thor! Laurel got the upper hand. She has Sidonie licking her hand! Now Sidonie cannot say enough good things about Laurel. Guess it woke her up, your marrying Laurel and turning down Clarissa.'

'I never really considered Clarissa,' Thor said shortly. 'I was waiting for Laurel to grow up – not that she has!'

'Don't be fooled by appearances, Thor! Laurel may wear her hair in a schoolgirl braid, but the head underneath that mass of lovely hair is a sharp one. You have a fine wife, there, a fine hostess, a fine helpmate for your life. You cherish her, hear me? She reminds me of Brianna.'

Thor studied his father thoughtfully. Olaf was very prejudiced in favor of Laurel, he knew that. Did his father see clearly, or was he trying to force Thor to accept Laurel as a very bright mature woman? Or was Thor so blinded by love for the girl he had known these years, that he could not see she had matured?

At any rate, Thor was pleased that relations between his father and stepmother had vastly improved. His father was happier, and much more relaxed now. He even went home for dinner these days, and often for luncheon and a rest.

Sidonie was a shrewd, practical Frenchwoman. She had seen her marriage deteriorating and did something about it. Thor had an odd thought – he wondered if Laurel had had something to do with that.

Thor could not really like Sidonie, but he could respect her and appreciate her if she settled down and made his father happy.

'Is Hank Mullenberg coming over today?'

Thor returned to his own desk and sat down. 'This morning, I hope. He's rather a casual customer. A good prospector, and shrewd, but no sense of time. I guess that comes from his years in the wilds. One doesn't pay much attention to a clock there.'

'No. Well, *he* should know about Leverett. They worked together up north –'

'Maybe so, maybe not. He doesn't seem to like Leverett. We couldn't talk. We met in a restaurant, and he seemed to be reluctant to say much there. That's why I want him at the office.'

'You talked to other prospectors?'

'Yes. Nobody remembers Leverett working any claims or mucking about in the streams. They just said he appeared one day with title to several claims. They got the impression he had bought out other men who got fed up with working and not finding much. He'd file on the claims, put the stakes in, and then hire an Indian or two to work the site for him. Then he'd disappear.'

'With Herman Ranke about?'

'Yes. Everybody remembered that. They made an odd couple. Leverett was always suave and well dressed, wore suits and white frilled shirts even in the mud. Herman Ranke was always filthy and peculiar. Yet they palled around together, and Leverett even backed down one time when Herman growled at him.'

'Oh?' Olaf looked up alertly at that. 'Tell me about it.'

'Seems Leverett got into an argument with him over a claim, didn't want to work it then. He said to Ranke, 'If you don't like it go off then, you scum.' Ranke turned on him, growled, had a red look about him, the prospector said. Everyone was staring, waiting to see what would happen, if Leverett would throw a punch.'

'Leverett? I can't imagine him in a fight; might get his white hands dirty!'

'Me too. But they all agreed Leverett could fight, had a hard fist, and kept a knife up his sleeve! That surprised me. Explains how he stayed alive in the gold fields, I suppose.'

'And then Ranke challenged him?'

'Yes. Pulled a knife, held it, looked at Leverett. Leverett turned pale and backed down, but he was furious as hell about it. Took it out on another man that night – gambled at the tables with him till morning, then he wiped him out and laughed at him. So they fought; the other man got a slice cut out of his arm and a friend carried him off.'

'Well! That is another side of Leverett! Gambling all night, fighting and knifing!' Olaf bit his lip, gnawing at it. 'What about this gambling? Does he still gamble?'

'Yes. Says he does it for relaxation. Goes to the saloons at nights and plays for hours. But he's a gentleman about it; I never heard anything about cheating or getting in an uproar about losing. In fact he doesn't often lose. Seems smart about it.'

'Keeps it quiet too. I've never heard about it, and I thought I heard gossip. Backrooms?'

'Yes. Usually at Benny Chin's place or Mr. Sato's joint. The Chinese are hot for gaming, you know, and their places usually have the fastest action.'

'Maybe that's why I didn't hear. I never went there, feared a knife in my back! Not that any Chinese was enemy with me,' said Olaf, scratching his chin. 'Well, well, you have learned a lot more about Leverett since you started digging.'

'It was all there, Father. I just didn't bother to dig before,' Thor said frankly. 'I'm surprised too. Thought he just went in for the society bit, entertaining at his mansion, playing the expansive politician. I don't like what I find when I turn over the stones and find worms underneath.'

'Neither do I. I'm glad we didn't turn over money to him. I was ready to do so, but Sidonie said no, she didn't like the smell of the set up. Glad I listened to her!'

'I learned something else, Father. Guess I had better tell you; it's part of the pattern, I'm afraid.'

'What's that?'

'Ewan gambled with him and lost – often.'

Olaf shot right up off his chair. He stood, glaring, furious. 'What the hell? Ewan, gaming and in those places? The hell you say!'

'I know. That's what I said. But Mr. Sato confirmed it. Straight fellow, though undercover about his dealings too much to suit me. Looked me right in the eye and said, "Mr. Thor, you ought to speak to your brother about his matter of the gaming with Mr. Leverett. He gets in very deep, that brother. He drinks too much for a gambler." Well, I said, the hell you say, and he said, "Yes, the hell I say. But it is not mine to concern with, Mr. Thor – except you better get smart, huh?" And he shut up.'

'God. Ewan involved with Leverett, and gaming! Do you think that's why he disappeared?'

'Maybe. Garth told me he was drinking heavily in Wrangell, and when he spoke of Leverett – Well, now I'm putting the pieces together, and I don't like it at all. He seems to owe money to Leverett. I wondered why he ran through his pay so fast.'

Thor was sorry he had had to tell his father about that. Olaf had spoiled Ewan and Sidonie had completed the process. Yet . . . Ewan was good underneath. It was the women who spoiled him thoroughly, and the easy money. He had never had to work hard, the way Olaf and Thor had in the early years. And he seemed to have something about women, some deep contempt for them, that made him fool around too much, and then walk away. Like the thing with Jade. No decent man would have walked away from Jade, expecting his child.

'Well, well,' Olaf repeated unhappily. 'Got to find Ewan, straighten him out. I hate that he went over to Wrangell when I sent him north to the copper mines. I'll tell him a thing or two when I get him by the ear.'

A clerk knocked at the door; Thor called, 'Come in!'

The door opened, and the clerk said, 'Mr. Mullenberg here to see you, sir.'

'Yes, yes, show him in.'

Thor went to greet the big man. Hank Mullenberg was a burly man with a long bushy red beard and long red curly hair showing a little gray. He wore a red-plaid lumberjack shirt that strained his broad chest, jeans that were the worse for wear, and a thick parka over all. Thor took the parka, hung it on a chair, and motioned him to a seat.

'How are you, Thor, boy?' Hank Mullenberg had a grip like a

334

bear trap. Thor eased his fingers out of the grip and straightened them again. Hank was shaking hands with Olaf, and Thor grinned behind his father's back to see him furtively smoothing his fingers with his other hand after the grip had let go. 'Howdy, Olaf. Long time no see.'

'Right you are, Hank,' said Olaf. 'Sit down, sit down. Want a drink?'

'Not in the morning,' and the burly man rumbled a hearty laugh. 'Got to keep my wits about me in the big city!'

'Right you are,' repeated Olaf. He looked at Thor.

Thor came to sit down too. 'What we were talking about the other day, Hank . . . Addison Leverett. You were to tell me something.'

A shadow darkened the red beefy face of the prospector. 'Sure thing. You was asking did I know Leverett from the old days. Yes, I sure did. Never did see him work a claim, like I told you. But he always come up owning claims, even several on one stream. You know, you gotta file one on a stream, that's all, 'cept the finder gets two claims.'

'Right.'

The old-timer brooded, an unaccustomed gloom on his weather-beaten face. 'Well, Leverett, he hung about with Herman Ranke. No-good customers, both of them. In those days both of them carried great knives as long as they was, and six-guns, and rifles; they looked hung about with weapons. Nobody messed with them, let me tell you. Come and go, secretly like; and nobody liked them much. Shut them out, sort of.'

Thor listened patiently. The prospector looked like he had settled in for a long spell of storytelling.

He shrugged himself deeper into the big chair, and resumed his story.

'I had a good buddy then. Name of Jim Knowles. Everybody called him Packy Knowles. Reason was, he was a short guy, yet wide, and he carried a bigger pack than everybody ever seen. Weighed him down; he looked like a funny sight, let me tell you. All bent over with his pack. Everybody called him Packy. Nice fellow. Honest. Close-mouthed, until he got liquor in him. Then he would spill everything. Talk? You never hear anybody talk like Packy with the liquor in him.'

Olaf was tapping his fingers on the desk, but he did not interrupt. The big redhead was leading to something.

'Well. We was all looking up and down one creek and another, up

335

on the Klondike, where she meets the Yukon. In and out, in the gravel and in the mud, and even in the mountains. And one night Packy come in from about a month in the hills, and he yells and screams, "I got a strike! I got more gold than you ever seen!" he yells.'

The burly man was panting with the memory, and sweat stood out on his shining face. He pulled out a red kerchief and wiped his face all over.

Then he resumed. 'Strike! – we all come running. We been finding yellow, and we was busy. I had me a nice little claim and was taking out maybe five hundred dollars a day. But you know how it is, we're all looking for the big nuggets. Packy is sitting on a bar stool and yelling about his claim, and how we all got to come along next day and file a claim with him. And we got to see the nuggets, he says, and he yanks out a poke that would choke a horse, and he takes the strings and rips it open, and spills it out on the bar. God, they was big! One as big as my fist!' and he closed the fist and held it up. He shook it menacingly.

'With regular prospectors that would've been okay,' Olaf said quietly. 'They would've celebrated with him, and gone out on the claim next day and staked what they could around him. Right?'

'Right. But you know he – I guess you heard about Packy Knowles, huh, Olaf? You know he died.'

'The word came here, yes.' Olaf's face was dark and gloomy. 'That was bad, everybody said so.'

Thor was silent. He was remembering years ago, when word had come about the prospector murdered on the Klondike. A vicious crime that had shaken them all.

'Yeah. Packy drank that night, and someone got to him, and shook him down, and found out where his claim was. In the morning we found him in a ditch south of town. All beaten up, bloody, his head bashed in, arms broke, knifed and slashed up – God, I still get bad dreams about that,' and he shook his heavy head and the red hair blew about his thick shoulders. 'All the gold was gone.'

'You ain't connecting it with Leverett, are you?' Olaf asked sharply. 'Was he about?'

'Sure he was about. Him and that Herman Ranke pal of his. Listening and taking it all in, and drinking with him that night, along with others.'

'That's not evidence enough.' Thor put that in.

'Yeah? Well, we went up to stake claims on the creek, after giving him a fine funeral. And Leverett and Ranke were already up there, with claims; said they had known about it before. They took two claims each and worked it for a time, got out the big stuff with some hired Indians. Then they took off; they never cared about working hard for the little grains later. They just took the big stuff and cleared out. And then they'd turn up somewhere else, poking about.'

'What about Packy Knowles and his stakes, didn't they show up? Hadn't he staked it?'

'Sure, probably. He was an old-time prospector. But we never saw any stakes with his name on them. Leverett said there wasn't none on the creek when he come up to claim his. Said he had found gold on his own, never heard where Packy said his claim was. Said he had discovered the place and took his two claims, like Ranke took his two, both discovering it, you see. Filed claim right off, before we got there after the funeral. Leverett, he didn't care about attending any old funeral, you can bet your boots!'

Thor was silent as Olaf questioned the prospector further. Leverett was callous, but was he crooked, was he a murderer? Probably he had gone up to the creek, found some gold and no stakes – and had staked his own. Or was Hank Mullenberg right? The old-timer was brooding over the death of an old pal of his, and his grievous anger had settled on Leverett. Yet, there was no proof; however, Hank was a shrewd man, and he knew men . . .

'Well, I'm going over to Wrangell next week with some friends,' said Hank, rising. 'Want me to look up Ewan when I go?' His shrewd blue eyes surveyed them both. 'I'm going hunting, don't mind doing a favor for ya!'

'No, best not,' said Olaf. 'We'll handle it ourselves.'

'If you go over to Wrangell, though, would you look up Tom Nolan and Miriam? He'll do you good in hunting; there isn't a better man. His girl Jade married Garth Fleming; they're guests of ours. Tell Tom I mean to come over, and Jade and Laurel, my wife, are having a grand time talking.'

'Tom Nolan, huh? Sure, I'll do that. I'll look him up. And his girl is Jade . . . seems to me I met her once, a pretty girl. And you

337

married Laurel . . . that would be Jim Winfield's girl? Well, well,' and he beamed and wrung Thor's hand even harder. 'Congratulations, you old scoundrel! Fine girl, that.'

'Thanks very much.' Thor straightened out his fingers again. 'Drop in anytime. Any favor I can do, mention it. And if you don't mind, would you take a package to Tom? When are you taking off?'

'A pleasure. I'll be going on Monday, likely. I'll stop in the warehouse and get your package for Tom. He need more ammunition?'

'Yes, probably. I'll put some in for the rifle and shotgun. And we got more Colts. I'll stick in a couple with some ammunition.'

Thor took Hank out to the store and stocked him up with goods, giving him a good price mark-down for his information.

Neither mentioned the fact, politely, but Hank understood he did not get a good price just for the quantity of the order, but for the favor of the information. And he would keep an eye out for anything further about Leverett. That was the way it was done in Alaska.

Not by blackmail, the way Leverett wanted. A slow anger was building in Thor. Out and out asking for one hundred thousand dollars for future political favors! No, he didn't like it at all. It left a bad taste in his mouth.

Before Hank left, he said, 'Say, Thor, you ought to talk to Mr. Sato. He knows about some gaming of Ewan and Leverett. Did Leverett go north, or did he go somewhere else?'

Thor studied the blue eyes. 'I talked to Sato. He didn't say much. What do you know about it?'

The big shoulders shrugged, and his voice lowered. 'I heard just a bit, something about a debt that got too big. Some work he wanted Ewan to do for him. Ewan didn't want to, but Leverett just said, "You'll go, by God." Ask Sato about it.'

'Thanks, I'll do that.'

Hank Mullenberg nodded, satisfied, hitched the pack on his shoulder, and pushed his way out the swinging doors. On the street he burst into lusty song, 'Oh, I'm a big bad bastard/on the trail of ninety-eight/and I found my nuggets waiting/when I searched for my fate . . .'

The clerks were all grinning when Thor turned back into the store – all but one. He was straightening out his hand painfully, and surveying his fingers, as though doubting they would work. Thor studied his chief clerk soberly.

'Oh, Horace, didn't I warn you not to shake his hand? His hand is pretty powerful.'

'Boss, I think you forgot to warn me,' Horace said, shaking his head.

The men burst out laughing, and Thor went back to the office, still grinning.

But he meant to seek out Mr. Sato and try to find out more about Leverett and Ewan, and their dealings. And he needed to find more . . . something final and thorough. Not some man's suspicions. Some hard evidence . . .

Chapter 28

Laurel had retreated again to her study, and occupied her mind and her hands with her painting. She had completed the painting of Brianna Koenig, and was starting on the portrait of Olaf Koenig at about the age of thirty.

By Sunday she was exhausted. She had been painting from morning to night, scarcely pausing to eat. On Sunday morning she and Jade went to church, and returned in the carriage driven by Mike Dugan.

Thor and Garth had gone out early on some mission of their own. Laurel thought bitterly that Thor was working so much he had no more time for God, much less his wife.

Jade was silent too. At home Laurel and Jade sat down in the parlor to talk before luncheon. The men had not returned yet, said Patsy Dugan.

'Should I set their places for lunch, Miss Laurel?'

Laurel shrugged; Patsy looked shocked and worried. 'If you wish, Mrs. Dugan,' she said. 'No telling when they will come. I'm sure Thor doesn't bother to tell me!'

'Now, Miss Laurel,' and Patsy shook her head, and retreated to the kitchen.

At twelve noon Laurel led the way to the dining room. She and Jade sat down at one end of the table and started their soup. They were halfway through the roast beef course when the men came in, talking and stamping in the hallway.

They washed up, and returned to sit down at the table. Thor had paused to kiss Laurel on the cheek, briefly. His face was cold, but not as cold as she felt.

Patsy brought in the soup, while Natasha was hastily setting their places and bringing water and hot coffee. Jade said nothing, neither did Laurel. The men were talking man-talk, seeming to ignore them, continuing their discussion.

Laurel thought, Thor doesn't do this deliberately; it's his natural way! He just doesn't think to include me in business talk! He must really think I'm stupid! And it made her all the angrier.

And Garth Fleming was doing the same thing to Jade.

'Mr. Sato seemed honest about it,' said Thor, looking troubled. He ducked his head to have another big spoonful of soup.

'I don't like what Mullenberg says,' said Garth. 'That's what sticks.'

It was all Greek to Laurel, as she had no idea what they were discussing, and they did not seem to think it worthwhile to inform their wives.

'Well, Mullenberg leaves for Wrangell on Monday morning. We may hear more when he returns. He promised to tell us whatever he might learn. That should be another two months. Let's see . . . this is early November; we should know by January. Then, when Leverett gets back about that time . . .'

Laurel was really listening now. And so was Jade, Laurel decided by the look on her friend's attractive face. The black eyes were alive with interest.

The men went on, sort of muttering to each other. Laurel strained to hear. When Natasha clattered the empty soup bowls, Laurel gave her a warning frown. The Indian-Russian girl nodded, and kept the dishes more quiet as she carried them out to the kitchen.

She returned with their plates of roast beef and baked potatoes. She set the bowl of gravy beside them. Laurel was toying with her coffee cup, waiting for them to catch up on the courses before ordering the dessert to be brought in.

'Nolans –' she heard. 'Mullenberg will hunt with Tom. Should get word – quietly – see the claim from a distance –' Thor carved a beef slice and took a big bite.

Garth added, 'I hope Tom doesn't get into trouble. He said they shot a warning shot at him.'

Jade gasped, and her hand went to her bosom. Laurel exchanged a quick look with her.

'Mullenberg is going on Monday morning. And several other

341

prospectors are going along, to go on into the mountains, looking for gold claims up the Stikine. If Hank hunts with Tom, that will give him the excuse to look around for us.'

Garth nodded seriously. 'Yes, I think that will be best. If you and I turned up at Wrangell, they might go to ground.'

Laurel could not repress the question. 'Thor, aren't we going to Wrangell? You said we would go in a couple weeks, and it's time –'

'No, I'm not going,' he said shortly. 'At least, not at this time. I have too much to do here, Laurel. And I've decided not to take you along. The weather is much too bad already.'

She glared at Thor. 'But you promised!'

He waved his big hand impatiently. 'Laurel, not now! We simply cannot go now. The rains have started, and there is snow in the mountains. You know how bad it can be on the mainland. We would need snowshoes to get through that stuff. I won't expose you to that.'

All Laurel could think was that Thor had betrayed her. He had made her wait, and now it was too late to go.

'I have lived in that area for years,' she said, fighting to keep her voice level and rational. 'I have no worries about the weather, Thor. I want to go – and go soon!'

'There is no need for you to go, Laurel! I have the situation in hand. And there are aspects you are not aware of. One claim doesn't make that much difference. I have other worries that are much bigger than one gold claim!'

'What?' she demanded, her fists clenching in her lap. 'What worries are bigger than some men taking my gold away?'

Thor stared at her. 'Your gold? It's my claim, and if I don't want to bother –'

'It is a claim my father discovered, and he would have left it to me.' Her voice shook. She was near to tears. 'My father died because of that gold, and now you say it doesn't even matter! Well, I want to know what's going on, and I mean to find out!'

'Laurel, you will not stir out of Sitka!' he blazed at her. 'That's an order! I don't want you in trouble over some silly bit of land –'

Natasha was just bringing the dessert tray of dishes from the kitchen through the swinging door. She stood, appalled, just inside the door, her soft brown eyes wide with horror as the master quarreled with the mistress in front of guests. Patsy Dugan, holding the door for her, bit her lips with anguish. All knew things were going wrong, and Laurel saw their faces.

With dignity Laurel rose and said 'Pardon me,' and left the room, her skirts swishing about her slim ankles. Her head in the chignon was high held, her face expressionless to keep back the anguish she felt. Thor, insulting her before them all!

'Laurel, come back!' he said sharply, half rising.

'Let her go,' advised Garth, worried.

Jade stood up and walked out too, without apology. She followed Laurel to the drawing room, on the other side of the house, and closed the door after her.

The girls looked at each other. Laurel expelled her hardheld breath in a sigh.

'That does it! That really – does – it!' Laurel said tightly. 'It doesn't matter to me, I don't understand, and I should stay out! And he orders me to remain in Sitka! And he lied to me! He said we were all going to Wrangell in a couple weeks!'

Jade nodded. 'And I looked forward to going to my parents. I am troubled,' she said simply. 'Garth does not tell me things anymore. What are they planning between them?'

Laurel began to pace back and forth, from the windows to the door to Thor's study, and back again. Her golden brown skirts swished on the carpets; she took no pleasure in her grand clothes – they were Thor's bribes to her.

This morning she had worn this fine dress to church, but Thor had not been at her side. And over it she had worn her new sable coat, of rich brown fur, and a matching hat of sable in the new, round, high Russian style. People had stared at her, but Thor had not been there.

And she had not been able to concentrate on the service, to understand the sermon, to enjoy the singing of hymns, because Thor had quarreled with her, and she was actively disliking him and distrusting him. What had happened to them?

'I cannot trust him,' she said aloud. 'He lied to me, and I know he's seeing Clarissa Leverett. He wants to pay a large sum of money to Addison Leverett, so the man will give him contracts. What does honor mean to Thor? How can I live with him, despising him so?'

Jade sat down on the sofa, on the edge of it, nervously, her black eyes grieved. 'And I – Garth does not trust me. I tried to ask about Ewan, and he bit my head off! He said I wanted to go to Wrangell to see Ewan! Why can he not understand that I am anxious for you, and for my parents?'

'I want to know what's going on at the claim,' Laurel said. 'I don't want to wait until spring! If Leverett is in on this, he'll strip my claim clean of nuggets before then! I don't care if it's in Thor's name, it's mine! It is my piece of Alaska! And the cabin too!'

Jade stared at Laurel in alarm. She had known her friend to be fierce, determined, stubborn. But she had never seen her like this – angry, wild, furious. She had always been in such control.

'But what can we do, Laurel?'

'Go,' said Laurel, 'Go by myself! If I have to, I'll take a boat on my own!'

Jade sat and thought; Laurel turned to look at her. 'Will you come with me?' she asked.

Jade nodded. 'Yes, Laurel,' she said. 'I cannot let you go alone. And besides, I want to see my parents. I am bewildered. I do not know what to think.'

'We will go, then. Now, how shall we go?' She strode the room again fiercely, striding from one window to another, pausing to gaze out at the beginning of the rain. The sky was gray, and the wind blew the raindrops and struck them against the glass panes like bullets.

'Hank Mullenberg,' said Jade, suddenly smiling, her black eyes sparkling. 'He is a good man, a strong man. He will protect us and ask few questions. Except – how do we get on his boat without our men seeing us go?'

Laurel came over and sank down on the sofa beside Jade. 'You have it! Yes, Hank Mullenberg. They said he was going to Wrangell on Monday morning. Tomorrow morning. Let me see. We have to pack our sleeping bags and a carpetbag of clothes. I'll take my Colt. Do you have a revolver?'

'Yes, and my rifle – and ammunition. I'll take some of Garth's. He can get more at the warehouse!'

'Let's go pack while the men are still talking!'

344

With a revengeful look at the dining room door, they crept past the hallway doors and up the stairs. Jade went to her bedroom, pulled out her sleeping bag and began to unroll it. Then she took out clothes for packing.

Laurel had a longer search for hers, and finally found it in the linen room storage closet, upstairs on the third floor. She hauled it downstairs to her study. Thor rarely came in there. He had not even bothered to see her portrait of his mother! She kept thinking up things to add against his score, she was so angry at him. She was boiling over!

Laurel found her sleeping bag in good condition, unrolled it, found some warm woolen blankets and laid them down in the bag. She added warm scarves, boots, a parka. Next she got out her carpetbag, which had done her good service in her early years. She put in blouses, sweaters, and undergarments of a practical sort, not the fancy lace concoctions made by Madame Bonheur.

Then she heard the men moving about downstairs, their boots thudding. She raced to shove all into the closet and shut the door. But nobody came upstairs. She tiptoed to Jade's bedroom to find Jade peering out the window, the lace curtains drawn back. Jade beckoned her to come, her eyes flashing.

Laurel went silently to the window, to peer out. The carriage below them on the gravel was driven by Thor, Garth sat beside him. They were headed downhill to Sitka, going out again.

'Garth did not even come upstairs to tell me goodbye, or say where he is going,' Jade said sadly.

'That does it; that really does it,' said Laurel, fiercely. 'Well, we'll take our luggage down to the boat, then. We can walk it, and walk back. I don't mind the rain.'

'I don't either,' Jade said forlornly, still gazing out at the back of her husband in the carriage.

They finished packing, then dropped the gear out of Jade's window. They put on coats and boots, and went out. To Patsy Dugan's curious look, Laurel said, 'We're going for a walk.'

'Not far,' Jade added hastily.

Mrs. Dugan went back to the kitchen. They waited until they could hear her thumping some dough, and humming, and then they went out. They retrieved their sleeping bags and carpetbags, and crept down the hill until they were out of sight of the house. The cold rain was blowing in their faces, but Laurel felt invigorated.

At last I'm doing something constructive, she thought. She was on her way.

In Sitka they bribed an Indian friend of Jade's to put their gear on Hank Mullenberg's boat. He giggled at them, thinking they were playing some trick on the big good-natured prospector. Then they returned, going more slowly up the hill as the rain poured down harder. They were getting soaked, but felt more cheerful and daring.

'I feel better,' announced Laurel. 'At last I'm going to find out what's going on with my claim and my cabin.'

'I wonder what Garth will say when he finds I have gone,' mused Jade. She gave a sniff. 'Well, maybe he will be glad I have gone!'

'Nonsense! He'll be sorry – and ashamed he treated you this way,' Laurel said vigorously, to hide her own small fears about the journey. If only Thor had been more reasonable, she argued to herself, I would not have been forced to take this drastic step. As for Thor, he won't notice for a week that I'm gone! He's too busy!

Both girls burst out laughing, partly in bravado, as they walked up the steps to the house. Thor flung open the door, scowling. 'And where have you been?' he asked ominously.

Laurel laughed again. 'Just out walking in the rain!' she cried, and the girls giggled and giggled.

'Have you been drinking?' Garth asked Jade, then leaned to smell her breath.

This struck the girls as hilarious, and they screamed with laughter, holding on to each other. They hung on each other helplessly, laughing and laughing, partly hysterical.

The men stared at each other and at the girls, then shrugged. The girls went upstairs to change to dry clothes, and to reassure themselves that the men would suspect nothing.

They ate dinner together, then excused themselves early. The walk had tired them, they said. The men stayed up late, talking in Thor's study, going on and on about something. When Thor came up, he went to another bedroom to sleep, to let Laurel rest.

Laurel wakened early in the morning, long before daylight, and

346

saw he had not been in their bed. Well, all the better, she said grimly, and got up to dress in the outfit she had planned. She put on her sturdy, blue wool skirt, a plaid blouse, warm woolen stockings, and house shoes. Later she would put on boots, and add her thickest parka.

The men were partly through breakfast when the girls came down, dressed in identical practical outfits, their hair in identical braids. The men frowned, identical frowns.

'You're not going out in this rain,' declared Thor.

'Just a short walk. I like the rain,' Laurel said cheerily. She told Natasha, 'Eggs and sausage, Natasha, and a stack of hotcakes, and coffee with cream.'

'I'm glad your appetite is better,' said Thor, smiling on her. 'Maybe the walk does do you good.'

'Of course it does. It is healthy,' she said demurely.

Jade began to giggle, and hid her face in her hands, giggling and giggling. Laurel started to laugh too.

'I'd swear you girls are up to mischief, but I don't know what,' Thor said in resignation.

At this Jade straightened up – so did Laurel – and they tried to compose themselves. The men left soon after, and she had one single impulse to tell Thor. But no, he would stop her, for sure.

She asked Patsy Dugan to fix them a picnic lunch. 'A picnic? In this weather, Miss Laurel?' she cried, scandalized.

Laurel was firm. 'Yes, Mrs. Dugan. Sandwiches, and hot coffee in thermoses, and some cans of peaches and cranberries. Oh, and some cups and silverware, just the cheap ones. I don't know where we will eat, maybe with some friends of Jade.'

'Oh well, that's all right,' said Patsy Dugan, her brow clearing. She went off to the kitchen, and returned presently with two large baskets of food, enough for a small army. Evidently she thought Laurel would be feeding some of the Indian friends.

The girls dressed in their thickest parkas, and best thick boots, and stuck their Colts inside the picnic baskets. The rifles they carried, to Mrs. Dugan's horror.

'Now where would you be going with them things?' she cried out.

'For safety,' Laurel said. 'You never know who you'll meet, and you know Thor wants me to be safe!'

She took a bitter pleasure in the words. They went off, with Mrs. Dugan staring dubiously after them and shaking her head.

The walk down to Sitka in the gray rain did not take them long. They struck out briskly and avoided the main roads, though not many noses were stuck out to see them pass. It was a cold, dreary November day.

By Laurel's gold watch on the chain, that had been her father's, it was about nine-thirty when they came to the wharf. To their relief the boat was still moored. Men were moving about the boat and a couple more on the dock. Hank Mullenberg was not in sight.

Laurel stepped boldly on board, leaping over the small water gap between the boat and the dock. One of the men said sharply, 'Hey, there, lady, what're you doing?'

She managed to look surprised. 'Isn't this Hank Mullenberg's boat?'

'Yes, ma'am, but we don't take ladies aboard!'

'But our gear in on board, in one of the cabins,' she said. He looked at her suspiciously, went below, and came back scratching his head.

'It sure is, but I don't know what happened to Hank. He didn't say anything to me about this.' He peered at her. 'Ain't you Mrs. Thor Koenig?'

'That's right. We're going to visit Jade's parents, Tom and Miriam Nolan,' and she indicated Jade. 'Hank is going hunting with Tom Nolan.'

His brow cleared, and the other man nodded silently. 'Sure enough, he said that. Well, come aboard; hope you don't get seasick! Should be all right when we get inside.'

He meant, when they got further into the Inside Passage, and she smiled. 'Oh, I don't get seasick, neither does Jade. Don't worry about us! We'll go below and get settled first, though. Want some hot coffee?' She took out the thermoses and cups.

They hid themselves in the cabin where the Indian had put their gear. They would face Hank Mullenberg when they were well along.

They heard voices, heavy boots, and then man-talk. No mention of their names. The men started the boat, got the sails up, and started out. Jade and Laurel looked at each other in silence. Last chance to turn back, but they would not.

They were undiscovered by Hank until evening. They ate in the cabin, kept quiet. At last he came below, and found them.

'Well, I'll be thoroughly and completely damned!' he yelled on seeing them inside the cabin, comfortably sitting on the bunks.

'Hello, Mr. Mullenberg,' said Laurel, brightly. 'Remember me, Laurel Winfield?'

'Yeah, and now Mrs. Thor Koenig! Does your husband know about this stunt?'

'Of course,' she said promptly. 'He didn't have time to take us over to Wrangell, and Jade wants to see her folks.'

'You're damn sure he knows about this?' he asked, very puzzled. 'He give me some stuff for Tom this very morning, and didn't say a word.'

'I am absolutely positive he knows about this,' Laurel said with a little laugh. She had written a note to Thor, and he should have it by now. The picture of him storming about gave her a fit of the giggles. 'I bet he was so busy he never thought to say a word! I swear, that man gets busier all the time; he scarcely gives *me* the time of day!'

'Now, little miss, you don't expect me to believe that,' Hank said with heavy gallantry. 'But here you be, and I got to believe my eyes. Well, come on up and meet the men. I got a good crew of fellows, none better. And Thor trusts me! Well, well, damn it all; he won't be sorry. You'll be safe here as on a lily pad, you girls.'

He took them up, introduced them to his crew, a group of five prospectors like himself, experienced, shy, tough. Most had come up in ninety-eight or nine, and had worked and drunk and fought together for years. Most had made their pile and were satisfied. Two were going back up the Klondike; others were going fishing on the Stikine, or staying the winter in Wrangell. The Stikine was frozen, and they liked ice fishing immensely, cold as it was; and they talked about the prospects with pleasure.

They treated the two young ladies with complete gallantry. The ladies were married to fine men, friends of Hank, and as such could have been covered with fine armor. They had the privileges of the boat. The men repressed their language as much as prospectors could. If the songs they sang in the evening were a bit bawdy, well, the girls were used to such talk and appreciated the rough harmonies. And their stories were fascinating, of the gold fields and the old times, the men they had known, the bandits and the good 'uns.

Laurel and Jade insisted on doing their share of the chores, and were assigned cook detail. 'With such ladies a-cooking for us, we're in heaven,' as one old codger said contentedly.

They fed the men baked fish, fried fish, broiled fish that the men caught. And besides that, they used the cans of beef to make beef stew, and beef upside-down pie, with Jade's best sourdough biscuits, and beef steaks. Jade made apple pie and cranberry cake and blueberry custards. Laurel made enticing dishes of fruit concoctions, using cans of peaches and cranberries, and salads of canned vegetables, inventing sauces from the vinegar and sugar and oil. They had never, ever, eaten so well, declared Hank.

The food reconciled the old-timers to the presence of ladies on their ship. They had to watch their language, but with the solace of pie and cake, they could stand it. And the ladies enjoyed their talk, and their songs, and stories, and paid flattering attention to their filled coffee cups and pots of tea.

The ladies never griped about the weather or the sailing conditions. They turned in early enough so the men could get their showers in naked comfort on deck, under pouring rain. And they never said a word about special privileges. They took everything as it came.

By the time they reached Wrangell ten days later, the prospectors were almost reconciled to the presence of ladies. But not completely – they were quietly relieved to be on their own when the ladies left the boat.

Hank and another man carried their gear for them to the Nolan cabin. Tom and Miriam were there, and greeted their child and Laurel with outstretched arms and beaming smiles.

They readily consented to have Tom hunt with them. 'Well, fine. I'll come over to your cabin in about a week, then,' said Hank. 'Give you time to clear up like you want, and get your ammunition and skinning stuff together. See you over there, Tom!' And after getting directions to the cabin, he and his friend departed.

'I am surprised you come without your husbands,' Miriam said soberly. 'Anything wrong?' And her keen black eyes surveyed them both.

'I want to see what's going on at my cabin and my claim,' declared Laurel. 'Thor is too busy to bother,' and her tone was bitter.

'Now, girl, you best stay away from there; men working it, bad men,' said Tom, shaking his graying head.

'I just want to look – from a distance. Is my cabin still in good shape?' she asked, wanting to check for herself the lie Leverett had told her, that the cabin was tumbledown.

'Sure, it is fine,' said Tom. 'But Ewan Koenig and his friends, I think they use it. You don't go near there, Laurel! Bad thing.'

'Well, let us go with you to your cabin, like the old days,' said Laurel. 'I want to live free for a time. I'm tired of dressing up for Sitka society,' and she made a face.

Miriam chuckled and chuckled, and Tom accepted this calmly. They could understand their girl Laurel being tired of city life. They didn't care much for it themselves.

Chapter 29

Laurel and Jade easily persuaded her parents to leave with them the next morning. Laurel said she was anxious to be at their cabin, and indeed she was.

She had a strong hunch that Thor would follow them, and Garth too, and she wanted to be away from Wrangell when the men arrived. In fact she meant to do her investigating and find out all she could before they arrived. The prospectors had made good time on their ship, sailing night and day, with few pauses to fish in the pouring rain.

Tom Nolan was pleased with Thor's gifts of Colts and rifles and ammunition, and could not be done praising him.

'What a fine good man you married, Laurel! What a man who remembers his friends! He sends me many men to go hunting, and we do well now.'

'I am glad of it,' she said with reserve. What was so great about remembering one's friends? Then she was ashamed of herself. Thor was a good man, and a generous one. Only he kept shutting her out! 'You should see my wardrobes of clothes, Father!' She gave him her affectionate address. Even since Jim Winfield had died, she had thought of Tom Nolan as her father. 'What silks, what velvets, what bonnets of lace and feathers! I spend half the day trying to think what to wear!'

Tom gave his gentle half smile. Miriam chuckled with pleasure and relief.

'There,' said Miriam. 'I said he would be a good husband to you! Think how kind he was when your good father died. Taking you back to Sitka, then to your mother's kin in Boston. And bringing you back to marry you! He did not forget little Laurel!'

* * *

They set out in the boat of a friend, who left them across from Wrangell on the mainland, well along the bay toward Tom Nolan's cabin. The snows were thick that week, and would probably become thicker.

They left the boat, strapped on their snowshoes, and set out. By the friend's generosity in taking them so far, they could get to the cabin by nightfall.

The snows were white and clean, marred only by little prints of the scurrying animals. Laurel recognized with pleasure the prints of rabbit, of squirrels, of ptarmigan, and the larger prints of deer, and an occasional moose. She watched for wolf prints, but was relieved to see none. Perhaps they were still up in the mountains. Bear tracks were there, though, and Tom Nolan pointed to them, and scanned the horizon.

'Maybe we get fat bear before he sleep for the winter,' he said in satisfaction, his dark face glowing.

'Hank Mullenberg would like that,' said Laurel. 'He talked about getting bear, and sending meat to the prospector camps. Make much money, he said.'

'Umm. Good. I help him, and Miriam skin good, and he send more men to us next summer.'

Tom Nolan was contemplating the prospect with pleasure. Laurel glanced down again at the marks of the bear and remembered that day more than four years ago when she and Jade had heard the crack of rifles and had gone to find Thor and Ewan injured and fighting the bear. She shivered a little, remembering Thor as the bear swiped his paw at him. What if Thor had died and she had never known him?

Her life would have been incomplete, she thought as she moved on smoothly, the feel of the snowshoes and the motion in the snow returning to her. Thor had become part of her life, a vital part, like the heartbeat of Alaska itself. She loved him. If only he did not dictate to her so!

They reached the small cabin past nightfall, and it was a marvelous sight. That small wood cabin, with the snug look to it, the brave chimney, the overhang where they rested while Tom went inside to light a candle. They went inside when the candlelight flared. Miriam bustled about the fireplace, while Tom set his rifle and ammunition down. The girls started their chores without a word, from long practice.

Soon the cabin was warm, and they could take off their thick parkas and spread out their blankets. The girls would sleep on the floor before the fire. Miriam had stew warming in the pot, and the coffee was bubbling and giving forth a rich odor.

They ate and drank, then lay down. Jade nudged Laurel. 'Tomorrow, early, we go out, yes?'

'Yes. I think maybe Thor will come soon. I want to find out first what's going on. And he'll be angry!'

'I wonder if Garth will be angry. Maybe he will shrug and not come,' and doubt saddened Jade's rich low voice.

'He loves you,' Laurel reassured.

'Maybe,' Jade sighed. 'He was cold to me for the week. He said I love Ewan, but I do not. Garth is my man.'

Jade rolled over in the blankets next to Laurel, and for warmth the girls lay close together. Laurel was unable to sleep for a little time. Doubt was closing in on her, now that the anger had had a chance to cool. Had she done right in coming, against Thor's wishes? A chill of fear raced through her, thinking of Leverett and his strange friend, Herman Ranke. It feathered along her spine, that fear, and made her shiver in the blankets and draw closer to sleeping Jade.

Laurel's plans to go out early were foiled. She overslept, from the unaccustomed exertion, and did not waken until dawn that came late.

She had trouble rising, she was so stiff and sleepy. She got up about ten o'clock. Jade rose too; they yawned, washed quickly in the cold air, and dressed in fresh clothes – thick skirts, plaid blouses. They did each other's hair, the way they used to, brushing it out, plaiting the long thick hair in a single thick braid.

'You look like twins,' grinned Tom, 'just like old days! Don't you two get into trouble, like old days!' and he frowned at them quickly.

'No, Papa,' said Jade.

They helped fix a large breakfast, chatted about the hunting, and told a little about Sitka and their life there. Jade said nothing about the house she and Garth might build. Laurel wondered about that.

Maybe Jade was truly unsure about herself and her husband.

Had they really quarreled so deeply? Laurel hoped not, and felt distressed now that she had brought Jade along with her on this dangerous trip. They had both been very angry and upset, and reckless. Yet, she felt much better for the presence of her close friend. Jade understood her, and she understood Jade – better than anyone else in the world.

Tom got out his ammunition and weapons, and laid them all out on the table that had been brought years before from Jim Winfield's cabin. Laurel touched the table, ran her fingers along it.

She was remembering the years when she and her father had sat at the table after the evening meal, and worked on their drawing and sketching, their painting. She remembered him sitting at the table, painstakingly making her gold nugget necklace of the biggest finest nuggets he had found. She remembered his shy half smile at her, his words.

Tom eyed her with compassion; he seemed to know what she thought. 'Your father was a good man,' he said. 'He would be glad to see you married to Thor Koenig, a good man. He liked Thor and father Olaf Koenig very much, he tell me. Good men.'

'Yes, very good men,' said Laurel. But . . . Thor had filed on her claim. And Olaf had been unable to keep his son from seducing Jade. She sighed deeply, and turned to Jade.

'Let's go out,' Jade said quickly. 'We could walk around, see if we can find rabbits, like the old days.'

'Maybe I have forgotten how to hunt,' said Laurel, taking her up quickly. She reached for her rifle and examined it carefully, then loaded it. Excitement was building up in her.

Today . . . today she must find out about the claim. She and Jade could go up there casually, and see who was there. If it was Ewan, he would scold them crossly and send them away. But then she would know! Know that probably Thor had sent him there. That Thor was secretly working her claim!

Laurel had to know for sure. She could never trust Thor again unless she found out, and if it was true, she must leave him. She could not live with a liar and a thief, no matter how generous he was to her!

Laurel set her mouth stubbornly. She had to push herself. She wasn't sure she wanted to find out the truth. She didn't want to leave Thor. But she had to know; she could not live with herself if she did not go ahead and know the truth.

The truth could hurt, but at least it was a clean knife.

The girls set out about noon; they wanted no more food – they had eaten breakfast late.

'Come back at dusk,' said Miriam. 'It grows dark early.'

'Yes, Mama,' they chorused, and went out into the cold and snow. The sky was blue today, and only a few white clouds drifted toward the mountains from the sea. They could see for miles across the plains toward the hills.

On their snowshoes the going was relatively easy. The snow was blinding white, and they had put on their wooden eyeshades, the narrow strips the Indian made and wore. The wood had two pieces joined with thongs, and they tied them over their eyes to keep the snow from blinding them.

The distance from cabin to cabin was not far, only a few miles. They came nearer to it, and Laurel strained to see it, the cabin she and her father and mother had made. Smoke came up through the little chimney she had helped build; she tensed.

What a pretty little cabin, so snug and warm it had been. Beautifully, sturdily made, the notches made so well by her artistic father. And her mother had insisted on putting the roof neatly, with every log just so. And the slender logs that made up the porch were carefully chosen and well set in place in the earth. Above them was the overhang, where one could shelter and knock off the snow, and take off snowshoes when returning from the hunt.

'Smoke,' said Jade, somberly. 'So, Ewan *is* there.'

Laurel shaded her gaze and looked to the hills. 'Look – two men up there!' She pointed. In the clear blue air of the winter, she could see two tiny dots bending over the area where the claim was on the cliff. The men bent and straightened, they were digging, tossing gravel into the rocker. She felt chilled with excitement; she would know soon who was there.

Laurel forgot the cabin; she must know about those men. They turned from the cabin, and set out, moving rapidly on their snowshoes to follow the snow trail to the hills.

* * *

'Halt right there!'

The harsh order shocked both girls. They stopped, frozen, then turned about slowly. They both saw Leverett as he came from the cabin, and held the rifle on them.

He motioned to them with the rifle. 'Come on back here!'

Laurel wanted to lift her rifle and shoot him; it was loaded. But the rifle was trained steadily on her, in steady hands, and the man's eyes were narrowed and sharp.

They returned slowly to him, moving across the marked snow. Now she could see there were snowshoe marks in the snow, and booted feet had come near the cabin. If only she had looked . . .

'Throw your rifles into the cabin,' he ordered.

Jade didn't want to, Laurel could feel it, but they had no choice. Silently they threw their weapons into the cabin; she could feel the warmth of it through the open door.

She saw the cabin was furnished with two bunks, blankets, a table. There was a lamp on the table, and papers, and a set of scales, with pokes of gold open and scattered about. She saw the glint of piles of golden nuggets. Leverett was working the claim, *her* claim. Fierce anger welled up inside her.

'Now your revolvers.' He motioned to their belts.

Teeth clenched, she took out the revolver, longing to try to shoot him. The rifle was at her head, and moved closer; Leverett gave her an evil, glinting grin. He would just as soon shoot me now, she thought. If I wait, I might have a chance.

Oh, God, she had really gotten herself and Jade into a tight corner! Why hadn't she listened to Thor? These men did not play for peanuts and fun! When a man stole a gold claim, he would not hesitate at murder to keep it. He knew the penalty if he went before the rough prospectors' courts in the open air of the camp.

He would be hanged for it – if he was caught.

She wondered how many times Leverett had done this. Maybe this was the way he had garnered his wealth. Wealth to send Clarissa to school in Boston. Wealth to build his mansion in Sitka. Wealth to start a base from which he would lever himself into the politics of Alaska and get more wealth – unending wealth.

Laurel tossed her revolver into the cabin; it landed with a thud on the wooden floor, across the door sill – where her father had lain in bloody violent death.

'Now, get going.' He motioned briefly with the rifle and the nod of his head. As they moved ahead of him, he was close behind with the rifle trained on Laurel's head. They started on the snow trail toward the hills.

They trudged along, not daring to speak, not daring to move closer together. Laurel was thinking, if they could separate and jump him from either side – but no, he would not let them get close enough for that. Yet she must try, something, anything . . .

She must stay alive, she must – and tell Thor she was sorry she had not obeyed him, that he was right, and she had been childish and impetuous, getting herself and Jade into bad trouble.

There must be some way . . . If Ewan was up there, he could help them.

She moved along evenly, her snowshoes sliding on the crisp snow, the new snow. How often she and her father had walked this way, through the snow, to the dark trees, and up in the hills and over to Jade's cabin.

Laurel lifted her head, and in the hills she saw the claim area more clearly. Two men moved about there, outlined against the white snow and the white-covered rocks – white snow and the dark forms of the men.

They came closer, moving up into the hills, around and avoiding the boulders, up the path, slippery now with ice. She lifted her head, as they neared the top, and the men were still working. And against the snow and the dark trees a dark form moved, heavily, awkwardly, his bulk against the white snow . . .

Oh God, Laurel could have screamed. It was the dark form that had haunted her nightmares, the dark form she had drawn again and again, the man who had murdered her father and slid away on his snowshoes through the snow toward the trees – the murderer!

There was no mistaking that ugly misshapen form, that awkward lunging of the body, the roll of the heavy head, the lunge of the legs against the snow. The murderer.

He lifted up, turned about, and she saw without surprise that it was Herman Ranke. His small dark eyes in the heavy face saw her face. He stared, and he knew that she knew. He started forward, toward her, his big hands lifted in menace. Big hands that had held her before, big hairy hands that had tried to crush the life out of her – the one who had attacked her in Sitka, the one who had killed Rex, had attacked Czar, had tried to kill her just as he had killed her father.

'You killed my father,' she said slowly. She felt calm, cool. Nothing real was happening, it was a nightmare. 'You – I saw you in the snow – going away – you killed my father!'

'I told you,' Leverett snarled at Ranke. 'You should have gone back and killed her too!'

'Arggg,' snarled Ranke. 'No worry, I'll kill her now, nosy girl.' He was moving toward her, lunging through the snow.

Laurel held her position – and looked at Ewan, who was standing there, shovel in hand, looking paralyzed. And he was drunk – swaying, red-faced, stupid of face, slow-moving, slow-thinking drunk.

'Well, Ewan Koenig,' she said sharply, to get his attention fixed on her. 'I'm surprised at you! Working Thor's claim! Stealing from your brother's claim!'

He blinked at her and wiped his wet face with one gloved hand. 'Huh? Thor's claim? Nah . . . it's your father's . . . said so,' and he motioned to Leverett.

'My father staked it, but he was murdered,' she said slowly and clearly. 'But then Thor came, and moved out my father's stakes; he put his own stakes there. He told me my father was dead and I was too young to work it. And I was going to Boston.'

'Nah . . . Belongs to anybody –'

So that was what they had told him.

'Didn't you think why they had moved my father's stakes? Did you not understand that someone else might've filed? Thor put his stakes there,' she repeated slowly, so it might penetrate his drink-blurred brain. Jade was standing rigidly near to Laurel, her fists clenched at her sides, saying nothing, a wary eye on Ranke. Leverett still stood behind them, the rifle trained on Laurel.

'No time. Thor ain't been over here,' insisted Ewan. 'He never come here.'

'Yes. He came back – after I told him about the gold on this claim,' Laurel said deliberately. 'He came back and removed father's stakes, because father was dead and could no longer file. He put his own stakes there, and went to Wrangell and filed on the claim. This is Thor's land, Ewan. You have been working Thor's claim.'

'No, no!' He shook his shaggy head. He was unwashed, filthy, and his good looks were blurred by dissipation. 'I would not steal from Thor. You're lying.'

Laurel turned slowly, cautiously. 'Leverett, is that not true? You know this is Thor's land; you moved the stakes. You're staying in my father's cabin, and you know it's not tumbledown. You lied to me, tried to keep me away.'

'If you had been smart,' he said in an even dull tone, his small blue eyes glittering with unholy light, 'you would've kept it to yourself, and stayed away. It's too late, miss. I'll have to kill you – and your friend.'

Ewan Koenig started violently. 'No, not that – You cannot kill *her!* She's married to my brother!'

Laurel realized, then, that her feelings about Ewan had been right. He had no respect or liking for women, but he loved his brother. He would not have stolen from Thor. And he would not allow any possession of Thor to be touched, including his wife.

Leverett snarled a mean little laugh. 'What does that matter? We cannot let them live; they've seen us. They know. The brat knows Herman killed her father. Do you think we can let them stay alive?'

'You have killed before,' said Laurel, softly. In the distance, in the valley, she had seen three dark forms move. And she knew that stride of swiftly moving snowshoes; it was Thor moving so quickly toward them, and Garth following and Tom Nolan on his smooth, gliding walk.

She kept their attention on her with an effort.

'I can see the pattern now, Mr. Leverett. You killed before for the gold claims; you never bothered to find your own gold! It was easier, wasn't it, to kill a man who had found gold, or have Herman Ranke to kill? Just as you killed my father –'

'No, I didn't . . . Herman did,' said Leverett, quickly. 'I told him he was a fool; I would have waited until the man was away, and taken it all from the cabin – but no, he had to rush in and kill! Damn fool!'

Herman gave him a dark foreboding look, snarling like an animal softly to himself. Leverett gave him a nasty grin, that wide grin he sometimes used to his political enemies. The two men were forced allies; they do not like each other, she thought. Allies, because of the knowledge between them, the dark past where both had killed and stolen and cheated, and killed again.

'Herman, get that girl,' Leverett said suddenly, moving closer to Laurel.

Herman moved faster than a snake, and Laurel shuddered. He grabbed hold of Jade from behind, jerking her about and holding a sharp knife to her throat.

'Do it now?' he asked greedily, his small eyes flaming with a maniacal eagerness.

'They're coming,' Laurel said swiftly, and pointed down below to distract them.

'Lying,' said Leverett, turning reluctantly. Then he started; the small dark forms had moved to the side of the hill and were now up the hillside path toward them. Thor was hidden from them for a moment, in the turn of the path.

Leverett hesitated, and his rifle wavered. Laurel started to move away, but he swung it back to her with a snarl. 'Stay there!' he yelped. She froze into stillness.

A face in the dark parka looked up at them; the man hesitated. It was Thor. Laurel opened her mouth to scream at him.

Leverett said sharply, 'You squeak, and your man is dead!'

Laurel gasped, shut her mouth.

Leverett cried out to them with false joviality, 'Come on up here!' And he waved his arm in a wide sweep.

Thor waved back. 'We're coming up!' he yelled.

Laurel had to watch helplessly as Thor and Garth and Tom Nolan toiled up the steep path, up to certain death.

She knew then that she loved Thor so deeply she would do anything so that he would live. When he came, she would fight, scratch, bite, use her cunning, use any weapon – her bare hands and fingernails, her teeth – just so that he would live.

Leverett should not defeat them! He would not! And Herman Ranke must die!

Infused with a deadly calm, Laurel stood there, balancing herself on the snowshoes, and waited while her husband and the other two men climbed the uncertain slippery path to the cliff where the gold claim lay.

In the sunshine the shovel lay glinting; the rocker was still in its streambed, half filled with gravel that glittered with golden nuggets. The half-frozen stream fell in little murmurings into the path of its bed, leaping over the cliff down the hill into the valley, ice on its sides, the blue waters shining in the sunlight.

And Laurel waited. She could make no plans; she must just depend on the quickness of them all, of Jade and herself, of Tom Nolan and his Indian swiftness, of Garth and his hunting instinct – and Thor.

They could not depend on Ewan to help them. He was not only drunk, he was uncertain in his loyalties. Yet surely he would not fight his brother, for he loved Thor.

So it would be two girls, three men – against two killers. It was good odds, and she would fight with them. It was all they could do.

Laurel forced herself to remain still, gathering her strength for the moment when the three men would round the last curve of the hill and come up to them in the open . . .

Chapter 30

Thor came around the bend first, and his rifle was quickly trained on Leverett. Laurel had her gaze fixed on Thor, but from the corner of her eye she was intensely aware of Leverett, with his rifle on her.

'Lay down your guns,' yelled Leverett. 'Or I'll kill the girl!'

Herman had his knife at Jade's throat. Garth saw her first, and kept his look on her. A deadly dark look, but he had to pause – the knife was pressed against Jade's throat.

In one move Thor flung down his rifle into the snow, but unexpectedly he lunged forward and gave a wild yell. Laurel's eyes opened wide behind the snow-shade of wood that shielded her eyes from the sun on the snow.

Thor leaped at Leverett, and wrenched the long rifle from him before he could fight or fire it. The look on his cold-reddened face was that of a Viking warrior, of fierce delight in the battle! His green eyes flared with fury, his mouth parted in a fierce grin of hate. Thor lifted the rifle high in his hands, gave a wild yell again, and flung the rifle over the cliff down into the valley below.

Leverett grabbed at Laurel, but Thor had her by the wrist, and he flung her bodily away from him, and away from the cliff. She lay panting, the breath knocked out of her. Then she rolled over out of the way of their heavy boots.

They fought above her head, her husband and Leverett. They had closed in on each other, and swayed back and forth, fists hitting where they could. Then Leverett pulled his knife.

The boots were closer. Laurel rolled over again, out of the way. She saw Tom Nolan, his rifle trained on Leverett, but unable to fire for fear of hitting Thor.

She heard Jade scream, and turned her head cautiously.

Herman Ranke was pulling his knife from Garth's arm and slashing at him again. Jade was hitting Herman's back, yanking at his short black hair, trying to distract him from her husband.

Ewan Koenig just stood there, blankly, staring from one to the other, his drink-sodden mind unable to take it all in.

Herman lifted his knife high in his hand and slashed again at Garth. Garth stepped backward, incautiously, reaching for his own knife, and slipped on a stone and fell, his head striking a rock. He lay still, and Herman bent over to finish him. But Jade slipped between the knife and her husband, her arm up, the thick parka sleeve protecting her. She lay over her husband, and yelled and kicked and hit out at Herman.

Boots kicked at Laurel, distracting her to Thor. He was yelling fiendishly at Leverett as their knives clashed and sang in the cold air. The men were right above her. Thor glanced down briefly, his green eyes brilliant, and moved to stand over Laurel, one leg on either side of her. She lay still, moved only her head and saw that she was on the edge of the cliff. Thor was trying to keep her from rolling over the side, and below her she saw a one thousand-foot drop!

Laurel shuddered in fear, and held herself tightly still as Thor's leg nudged her slowly back to safety. But Leverett was cunningly taking advantage of their dangerous position, and Thor's distraction with Laurel. He lunged out with his knife. Thor yelled at him.

'Bastard! Killer! You would try to kill my wife! Devil! I'll kill you – I'll kill you! Ewan, come on! Don't stand there – Come on!' And unexpectedly, shockingly, Thor laughed!

It was the laugh of an exultant Viking warrior, glorying in the battle. Laurel saw Ewan start, then pick up the shovel and advance on Herman Ranke as he tried again to knife Jade. Jade lay over Garth, her hands and feet thrusting out, pushing Herman off, trying with all her cunning to keep him from herself and Garth.

Herman flung about at the new threat from Ewan. He slashed out, and his knife thrust home into Ewan's shoulder. The young man did not seem to notice; his shovel hit Herman on the head. Maddened, Herman, yelled out, an animal cry without words.

They closed in on each other, and the shovel was wrested from Ewan's hands by Herman, and flung aside. Herman's knife glinted in the sun, red-stained by blood that dripped from it.

Thor yelled, wildly, and grabbed Leverett by the waist. With brute strength he lifted him high in the air. As Leverett screamed, Thor flung him over the cliff and down into the valley. Laurel saw him bump once, twice, then fall clear, sheer to the floor of the valley, onto the boulders covered by only a thin layer of snow. He moved, slid, then lay still. His parka had fallen back . . . the head lay at an odd angle.

Thor picked up Laurel, and for one mad moment she thought she would follow Leverett over the cliff! But he set her down roughly on her booted feet over near Tom Nolan and panted, 'Keep an eye on her!' Then he rushed toward Ewan where he fought Herman.

The knife in Thor's hand lifted high, and slashed down. It found a vital point; when he withdrew the blade to slash again, a great spout of red blood gushed from Herman's throat. He fell slowly, awkwardly, to his knees . . . then bowed down over his legs, to crouch in the snow, the blood gushing from him.

Slowly the grotesque body bowed further forward, until he lay in a twisted heap in the reddening snow.

Thor bent over him after a moment. He touched the hand, held the wrist, let it drop into the snow limply.

'Dead,' he said, and got up slowly, winded. His blazing face still burned with battle fever. His green eyes glared around at the scene, touched Laurel with fire, touched Tom Nolan, the rifle still held in his hands. Touched Jade and Garth, touched his brother, then finally calmed and cooled to green ice.

'How bad are you hurt, Ewan?' he asked.

'My shoulder –' Ewan said huskily. He shoved back the parka to show his brother. Thor pulled open the plaid shirt, examined the wound.

'Laurel . . . something for a bandage.' It was Thor ordering her about again, but she was glad to do as he commanded.

She lifted her dark blue skirt and tore off a length from her white petticoat. She came over to Thor and helped make a pad. Then Thor wound the rest of the material around the shoulder to keep it on.

'We'll put antiseptic on it later,' he said to Ewan. Then he turned to Garth. Jade was on her knees, tearing her white petticoat. Garth lay still, his eyes shut.

Laurel went over to her, and Thor followed. 'How bad is it?' Laurel asked.

Garth slowly opened his eyes. 'Hit my head –' he said weakly. Thor put his hand under Garth's head; it came back bloody. Jade gasped, hanging over Garth, her tongue licking her dry lips.

Garth was gazing up at her. 'You – saved me,' he said, his voice fading.

'Oh, Garth, oh, Garth,' was all she could say. Her hand went to his head and cupped it gently. Laurel bent over to help. Thor opened the parka, found the wound on the arm. He padded the wound and bound it loosely.

'We'll take care of the head injury later. I want Miriam to see it,' said Thor, after a quick examination. He got up and went to Tom, who was still standing there, legs apart, rifle loose in his hands. 'What are the chances of getting a sled to take the bodies to the ship?'

'I have a sled,' said Tom, rousing from the tension of the battle. 'I could not shoot; it might have hit one of you,' he said.

'You stood there, they could not leave,' said Thor, clasping his shoulder. 'Help us get them down to the cabin. Then go for Miriam, the sled and bandages. We'll all stay at the Winfield cabin tonight. Tomorrow we can go to my ship; it's about fifteen miles, on the bay. We must take the bodies to Wrangell, to the authorities, and tell them what happened.'

Thor had organized them briskly. Garth made his way down the steep slippery slope, with Jade's shoulder supporting him sturdily. They clung together more than the climb down warranted; they were very close, murmuring together.

Ewan, in spite of his shoulder injury, insisted on helping drag Herman Ranke's body down with them. He took one boot, Thor the other, and they dragged him callously down the slope. Laurel and Tom Nolan came last, carrying the knives and rifles and shovel.

She shuddered when she saw the body of Herman Ranke bumping grotesquely down the slope through the snow, the blood staining where it landed.

They all went to the cabin, leaving Herman Ranke's body in the snow. Ewan and Thor went back for Leverett's body, and Tom Nolan departed for his cabin.

It was late afternoon when he returned. They tied the two bodies onto the sled, covered them with a thick tarpaulin, and tied more ropes about that. They left the sled outdoors in the cold; the animals could not get at the bodies through the tarp.

While the men did that, Miriam tended to Garth's wounds. The head injury was not as bad as first thought. Thor decided they could travel tomorrow; he was anxious to be on their way.

While Miriam worked on Ewan's shoulder injury, Laurel ventured to ask Thor, 'How did you come so quickly? How did you know where we were?'

He gave her a dark green look. He had taken out his pipe and lit it. 'I read your note,' he said. 'Found out you had gone with Hank Mullenberg by asking about at the wharf. We left that night, Garth and I and two Indians. At Wrangell I found Hank and got out of him what you had done. When the Nolans weren't at their cabin, we figured you had come right over here. I found Tom, and we all came over at once. I knew for sure you were in trouble.'

He paused to drag on his pipe and look at Garth.

'Garth and I have been investigating Leverett, the checking wasn't finished. But we had learned enough to know that he had made his wealth at claim jumping – and he didn't draw the line at murder. That's why I wanted to wait, you impetuous girl! I didn't want us walking into a trap.'

Laurel said meekly, 'But I – I walked into the trap, and you had to follow. I'm truly sorry, Thor. I was wrong. I should have listened to you. And I got Jade into trouble too.'

Garth said, 'And we may not build our house next to you Laurel, if you do anything like that again!'

She stared at him, and he gave his slow half smile, his dark eyes shining. 'You . . . will build next door?' she gasped. 'Oh, Garth, thank you!'

'We talked about it on the way over. It'll be easier to keep our eyes on the both of you,' said Thor, drily. 'And after this, no more secrets,' he promised. 'I should have told you what we had discovered about Leverett; then you wouldn't have jumped into trouble with both feet. I thought I was protecting you.'

It was a generous apology; Laurel moved closer to him on the blanket spread before the fire, and tucked her hand into his arm. She liked to feel the hard muscular strength of him against her shoulder. 'Thank you, Thor,' she whispered, 'I'm so glad that you came – so fast!' She shivered, thinking they might be lying dead in the valley instead of Leverett and Herman Ranke.

Ewan spoke up finally. 'Laurel, you said Herman Ranke killed your father. How did you know?' He was sitting back in the shadows, his face dark in the corner.

'I saw him,' said Laurel. 'When father was killed, I had returned from the Nolans and saw a man going away into the trees, a grotesque form, twisted, moving awkwardly. When I saw Herman Ranke – up there, against the snow – moving the same way, I was sure at last. It was him. I had suspected him, and he did try to kill me in Sitka.'

When her choked voice ceased, Thor put his arm about her, holding her comfortingly. He squeezed her waist, as though to say he understood her feelings, he knew how she felt.

'He's dead now, Laurel,' said Thor. 'That's over. Ewan . . . tell me what you were doing here. I know you owed Leverett gambling money!'

Ewan started violently. 'You knew? Leverett said he would keep it quiet. I owed him an awful lot. He kept flattering me, said I should be running my own company and he would back me.'

'Cunning devil,' said Thor, dispassionately. 'He had no such intention. Ruin you, rather.'

'Yes . . . I see that now. But it made me feel . . . squeamish. I don't like Herman – didn't like him, didn't trust him – and when Leverett came . . .' He fell silent.

'Go on, Ewan,' said Thor, when he paused for a time.

Ewan finally roused, and continued in a husky, weary voice. 'Leverett moved into the cabin here and kicked out Herman, told him to sleep in the snow, that he smelled like a pig. Well, he did, but it was no reason to treat a man like that. Then he got out the pokes of gold nuggets. That's when I realized he was raping the claim, getting out all the good nuggets, leaving the small stuff. There's just one long streak here, I figure. He put us both to work, long hours. I didn't mind that, but it was his way – dictating, and laughing at us, and mocking us. He about drove Herman crazy; then he would laugh and send him outdoors into the cold. Herman was a killer, but so was Leverett. And both were afraid of each other.'

He shook his head painfully, then gazed broodingly at the fire. His voice sounded older, more mature.

'I was going to try to get away. He knew that, and he never slept hard. I'd get up in the night, and he'd be right at my back.' He shivered. 'Once, he had a knife on me. I figured I might not get out alive, so I drank all the more.'

'Learned your lesson?' Thor drawled bluntly.

Ewan nodded humbly. 'Yes, Thor. I never would have done it if I had known it was your claim.'

'Anybody else's claim, it's still stealing,' said Thor, patiently.

'Yeah, I know.' His voice was very low and ashamed.

After a silence, Laurel said, 'It's too bad about Clarissa Leverett. She was afraid of her father, and now – now she has no one.'

Thor pressed her hand. 'When men come up here,' he said, 'they often change their names, hide their past, and start anew. I don't see why Clarissa can't do the same. Whatever her name was in Boston, let the past be forgotten. She's not to be blamed for her father. We'll help her get a fresh start.'

'She is lovely and well mannered,' said Laurel, carefully. 'She will marry eventually, and change her name. Yes, let the past be forgotten for her. She can start again in Alaska, free of her father and his cruelty.'

Miriam and Jade fixed supper; they insisted on doing that. Thor and Laurel went outdoors to get out of the way, walking away from the cabin where the bodies lay on the sled, out into the cold pure night air. The sun had gone down, and the earth lay still and cold and snowy.

'I reckon everything is all right between Jade and Garth,' said Thor, his arm about her shoulders. She snuggled closer to him as the keen wind whipped about them.

Laurel said, 'She thought he didn't love her, or forgive her . . . about Ewan.'

'Not love her? He's only madly wild about her,' Thor said in amusement. 'He didn't sleep much on the way. He paced the ship, until I told him he was walking to Wrangell! He adores Jade, but I told him a few ways to keep her in line!'

'Thor!' Laurel stopped in her tracks and turned to him reproachfully. 'That's no way to talk about Jade! She's a fine woman, with a mind of her own, and she's very much in love with him. She'll make him a fine wife, but he must confide in her and make decisions about the house with her – not leave her out!'

'Yes, he will,' Thor said more gently. 'We both figured we made a mistake not telling you girls what was going on. But you're both so stubborn –'

'Thor!' Laurel could have wept at his cruel words. She had felt so close to him, and was so grateful to him for saving her life and that of Jade. 'How can you say this? I know I did wrong in coming, and in dragging Jade into trouble, but I am sorry, and I will not do that again.'

'But you did do it, honey, and you are stubborn! Only, I am too, and we have to find some compromise,' he said, his arm stealing about her once more. 'Look, let's make a bargain. We are to be honest with each other, tell each other the truth, not hide things. Trust each other. Okay? Will you make that bargain?'

'Yes . . . if you will!'

'I will, Laurel,' and it was like the wedding ceremony all over again. His rich coaxing voice had persuaded her. 'There will be trust between us, always, I promise. And no hiding things from you. Father bawled me out, said I didn't appreciate what a jewel I had!'

'Dear Father,' she said softly. 'He always was on my side!'

'No more sides, honey. We're both on the same side,' and he bent down and kissed her cold cheek. 'Now, do you promise – always the truth? No more hiding things from each other?'

She nodded. 'I promise, Thor. The truth. And speaking of the truth, why did you meet Clarissa Leverett for luncheon at the Red Mill?'

Thor groaned. 'So you saw us?'

'I was there with Madame Bonheur. Everybody was staring at you and at me, feeling sorry for me! A married man meeting a woman like her in public!'

'So that's why you've been so cold!'

'Yes. Why did you meet her?'

He closed his arm more tightly about her. 'I had a meeting with Leverett alone. Not Clarissa. She came first, said he was slightly delayed. I had to offer her luncheon, and Leverett was very late. We never did talk politics much on that day. I figured it was a putup job. He always did throw Clarissa at my head.'

'You weren't ducking!'

He flung back his head and laughed aloud, a rich rollicking boom of a laugh that echoed through the snow-covered valley. She finally gave in and laughed too, with relief and joy. The shadows over her head were finally giving way to bright skies.

'Honey,' said Thor, when he had calmed, 'I had an idea. I'm going to the land office in Wrangell – we are going to the land office – and I'll sign over a gold claim to you. We'll call it the "Forget-Me-Not" claim, all right with you?'

She gasped, unable to speak.

'Okay with you, honey?' he urged anxiously. 'I know you always wanted your piece of Alaska land, and that's yours, by right of finding.'

'Oh yes, oh yes,' she could finally say. 'Oh, Thor, thank you. Now I'll own my own piece of my beloved Alaska land. I will belong here, and the land will belong to me!'

Thor drew her even closer to his side, ducked down and kissed her forehead. 'I figured that's what you wanted. You know, let's file on the land here too, where the cabin is. In your name, of course,' he added hastily. 'We can keep up the cabin, use it for hunting, Tom Nolan will keep an eye on it. And summers or winters, we can come over and stay here, just by ourselves. Alone in the land we love, all right?'

She turned in his arms and flung her arms up about his burly neck. 'Oh, Thor . . . yes! Oh, that's just what I want! Oh, thank you, Thor!'

'At last I have given you something you really want,' he said drily. 'There's more enthusiasm here than over the pearls and the emeralds!'

Remorsefully, she said, 'Oh, Thor, I did appreciate all your generosity, but it seemed that you were giving me presents like

371

hanging things on a doll! This is for me, a woman, belonging to Alaska. This is land that lasts and endures. It makes me belong to Alaska, and I'm part of my country, and it will be part of me. Don't you see?'

'I see, and I understand now,' he said quietly, his face pressed to hers, their cold cheeks warming each other's. 'I didn't before, Laurel. You're such a lovely girl, so beautiful, so talented, so seemingly delicate. I didn't realize there is so much of your father and your mother in you – the pioneer, the outdoors girl, the woman who rejoices in the snow and the cold, the pines and the wind, the cruel animals as well as the lovely small ones. You are already part of Alaska, Laurel. It's there inside you, in your spirit, wild and untamed.'

Laurel leaned against him, speechlessly happy. He did understand her now! He did, and they would always be close now. Nothing could come between them.

He went on softly, his voice like the wind, like the sigh of the spruce and the hemlock. 'And I too am part of Alaska; I too belong to the wilderness, am one with the land, the waters, the mountains, and the skies. We shall be happy here, Laurel, and bring up our children here, to enjoy the freedom and the spaces.'

'Yes, yes! Oh, Thor . . . yes!' She was gazing up into his face, drinking in the words that she loved to hear. And then she saw beyond his bent head, and saw the sky. 'Look, Thor . . . look!'

Thor raised his head in time to see the white shooting star that blazed its way across the purple heavens. They gazed in wonder, in awe, held silent by the beauty.

Then it was gone, and after it came the northern lights. They began, rippled green and silky across the night sky. Wondrous, strange, silently displaying the marvelous scene of green changing to green-white and green-gray, then back again to pure green.

There was a low humming sound and a feel in Laurel's feet, the electric quality that came with the lights, when they glowed deeply. It was a strange marvelous feeling, of being one with the universe, part of the earth, the sky, the wind, the stars and the lights that glowed so strangely.

They watched, and were one, holding to each other, part of the world that was Alaska. She sensed that near them were the little animals of the earth – perhaps they too were watching – the rabbits, the otters, the ground squirrels and the wolves, the deer and the chipmunks. All the creatures of God's world, united for a few moments in time by the wonders of the universe.

And Laurel belonged too, forever to Thor, forever to Alaska, to the world, to the universe . . . belonged and felt at home there.

THE TREGALLIS INHERITANCE

Mary Williams

From the spellbinding author of TRENHAWK
comes a haunting West Country romance which
tells of the young gipsy girl Mara, who has the
power to bewitch and beguile any man who
crosses her path – even Justin Tregallis, the
handsome young heir to the wealthy Penraven
estate. But is Mara really what she seems?
Beneath her flashing eyes and fiery charm lies a
heart as wild and treacherous as the windswept
moors and dark woodland that were once her
home – and a reckless spirit that could lead a man
to his doom. . . .

WEST COUNTRY ROMANCE   0 7221 91227   £1.75

From the shadow of the dreaded guillotine
to the sparkling frivolity of England's
Regency heyday . . .

BURNING
SECRETS

DEBORAH
CHESTER

With her beloved uncle a captive of Napoleon's
terrifying secret police, lovely Catherine de Bleu knew
she had no choice but to comply with the Emperor's
wishes. But even so she quailed at the impossible task he
had set her. For her formidable mission was to voyage to
England, and there to assassinate no less a person than
the Prince Regent himself!

Catherine's charm and ravishing looks soon win her
access to 'Prinny's' dazzling set and she comes close to
carrying out her hateful orders. But she does not foresee
the machinations of the unscrupulous and arrogant Sir
Giles Thorne, a determined adversary who would test
her mettle to the last . . .

If you love the very best in Regency romance, you will
be enthralled by BURNING SECRETS, a breathtaking
new novel from the creator of A LOVE SO WILD and
SUMMER'S RAPTURE.

HISTORICAL ROMANCE   0 7221 2285 3   £1.95

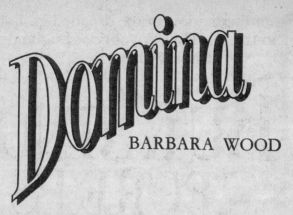

Domina

BARBARA WOOD

Samantha Hargrave grew up in the teeming squalor of
Victorian London, a motherless child of the cruel city
despised by her harsh father. It was in the crowded streets
where the poor lived and died like animals that she first dared
to dream her impossible dream: of becoming a woman doctor
– and it was there that she first fired a man's heart with
longing.

She knew that hers was a special destiny, that she would need
all her strength and will to fight against the prejudice which
had banished women from medicine. To train as a doctor she
would have to leave her friends, ignore her beauty, face the
contempt of women and the scorn of men. From the slums of
the city and the overcrowded wards of poverty-stricken
charity hospitals to the grandeur of society receptions and the
cloistered calm of medical school, Samantha fought to win the
title of a woman doctor – DOMINA.

GENERAL FICTION   0 7221 9200 2   £2.50

FLOODTIDE

Suzanne Goodwin

Stella grew to womanhood in a land torn apart by the Boer War, but the thunder and flash of guns on the distant horizon did not trouble her until her sixteenth year. To the battle-hardened British troops the fire at the farm was just another brutal act of war: to Stella it was a blazing beacon burning her past to ashes and lighting the way to a strange new life in distant lands.

Who would not pity a wounded soldier dying in the parched veldt far from his English home? How could Stella fail to nurse the pale, aristocratic Rupert Coryot back to health – to give him her frank young love? And how could she suspect that his summer passion for her, a Boer farmer's adopted daughter, would change in the colder climate of his ancestral home?

Viscountess, lover, actress and mother, Stella flees from the scorn and hatred of Edwardian high society to seek fame in the theatre. But as the Great War shatters the world she knows, she learns that her love will never die.

HISTORICAL ROMANCE   0 7221 3974 8   £1.95

A SELECTION OF BESTSELLERS FROM SPHERE

FICTION

CHANGES	Danielle Steel	£1.95 ☐
FEVRE DREAM	George R. R. Martin	£2.25 ☐
LADY OF FORTUNE	Graham Masterton	£2.75 ☐
FIREFOX DOWN	Craig Thomas	£2.25 ☐
MAN OF WAR	John Masters	£2.50 ☐

FILM & TV TIE-INS

THE DUNE STORYBOOK	Joan Vinge	£2.50 ☐
INDIANA JONES AND THE TEMPLE OF DOOM	James Kahn	£1.75 ☐
ONCE UPON A TIME IN AMERICA	Lee Hays	£1.75 ☐
SUPERGIRL	Norma Fox Mazer	£1.75 ☐
MINDER – BACK AGAIN	Anthony Masters	£1.50 ☐

NON-FICTION

THE YOUNG ONES' BOOK	Rik Mayall, Ben Elton & Lise Mayer	£2.95 ☐
WORST MOVIE POSTERS OF ALL TIME	Greg Edwards	£4.95 ☐
THE AGE OF DINOSAURS – A PHOTOGRAPHIC RECORD	Jane Burton & Dougal Dixon	£5.95 ☐
THE FINEST SWORDSMAN IN ALL FRANCE	Keith Miles	£1.95 ☐
POLITICAL QUOTES	Michael Rogers	£1.50 ☐

All Sphere books are available at your local bookshop or newsagent, or can be ordered direct from the publisher. Just tick the titles you want and fill in the form below.

Name_____

Address_____

_____

Write to Sphere Books, Cash Sales Department, P.O. Box 11, Falmouth, Cornwall TR10 9EN
Please enclose a cheque or postal order to the value of the cover price plus:
UK: 45p for the first book, 20p for the second book and 14p per copy for each additional book ordered to a maximum charge of £1.63.
OVERSEAS: 75p for the first book plus 21p per copy for each additional book.
BFPO & EIRE: 45p for the first book, 20p for the second book plus 14p per copy for the next 7 books, thereafter 8p per book.

Sphere Books reserve the right to show new retail prices on covers which may differ from those previously advertised in the text or elsewhere, and to increase postal rates in accordance with the PO.